THE OLD COOTS: TOM

D.L. Rogers

Copyright 2016 ©Diane L. Rogers
Similarity to any living person is strictly coincidental.
This is a work of fiction, based on historical fact, and may not be reprinted or duplicated in any manner without express consent by the author.
All Rights Reserved.

THE WHITE OAKS SERIES by D.L. Rogers (in the order they should be read)

Beginnings, a prequel, released June 2013
Tomorrow's Promise: Survival on the Plains, released 2008
Caleb, released 2010
Brothers by Blood, released 2008
Amy, released June 2011
Ghost Dancers, released 2007
Maggie, released June 2012

THE OLD COOTS: Sam, begins the **OLD COOTS TRILOGY** and continues the series, released June 2015

The Journey, released 2009 – A Romance
Echoes in the Dark, released 2009 – Vietnam Era Historical Fiction

Elizabeth's War: Missouri 1863, released 2014

Cover design by Glen Dixon
Edited by Claudia McHale

DLRogersBooks
www.dlrogersbooks.com

Cover Information:
All images are from the Public Domain

Front Cover: Tom's face is that of actor Henry B. Walthall from the 1930 silent picture "Abraham Lincoln."

The horses racing across the top are from Eadweard Muybridge's studies of motion (1872-1878). The lead horse and horse in second are both Man O'War.

The house is the Jumel Mansion, New York, photo taken between 1860 and 1920 (approx.)

Abby is stage actress Clara Morris, photographer of her picture is Napoleon Sarony (1866-1896 approx.)

The horse is Imp and the handler is Tom Tandy (1890 – 1900 approx.)

Back Cover: The Civil War scene is from the 1915 silent film "The Birth of a Nation." The Confederate soldier being shot is actor Henry B. Walthall.

The (old) Civil War veteran is from a 1939 promotional photo for the New York World's Fair and is labeled on the photo as from the Civil War.

Creation and Cover Design by Glen Dixon

DEDICATION

*To my husband, David,
the strongest, bravest man I know
in his fight against that devil—cancer.*

"America will never be destroyed from the outside. If we falter and lose our freedoms, it will be because we destroyed ourselves."

-Abraham Lincoln

Acknowledgements

Thomas Downes – Eighth Ohio Volunteers Re-Enactor and Historian
Thank you for taking the time to make sure the history contained herein is accurate, according to your research of the Eighth Ohio Volunteers

Patricia Decker – Beta Reader
Thanks for reviewing THE OLD COOTS: Tom for continuity, completeness, and, hopefully, your enjoyment

And as always to my Editor, Claudia McHale who makes sure my t's are crossed and my i's are dotted

**The Stone Wall at Cemetery Ridge
South of Gettysburg, Pennsylvania
July 3, 1863**

PROLOGUE

It was near to one o'clock as far as Tom could tell when the Confederate artillery began a fresh bombardment. Tom watched the guns pummel Cemetery Ridge and the Union forces mustered behind a low, stone wall there. For long minutes Tom recoiled with each belch of the enemy artillery—while he and the rest of the men waited for the Union guns to respond. After what seemed like forever, although it had only been fifteen minutes, the Federal guns finally answered from a grove nearby. What he knew to be eighty Union cannon exploded in unison, adding to the cacophony of noise in the usually quiet countryside. Dirt and rocks flew like projectiles thrown up from the bowels of the earth, mingling with the solid shot and detonating hollow cannon shells that sent flying musket balls and shrapnel through any unfortunate man in its path. Thankfully, B Company was still hunkered down in the ditch along the Emmitsburg Turnpike and out of the line of fire—for now.

Time stretched on and, as far as Tom could tell it was almost three o'clock when the artillery barrages on both sides quieted. He looked out over the field in front of him, littered with the dead and dying, took a deep breath, and knew what would come next—a full Rebel infantry charge.

"Get ready, boys," he told Collins, Baker, and the rest of his men, all gripping their rifles and ready.

The Rebs charged from the tree line at Seminary Ridge—their Rebel yell preceding them—and headed straight toward the Eighth and B Company.

Tom waited, his rifle at the ready, as the enemy advanced, screaming like wild Indians.

"Fire!" resounded down the line.

The sound of guns exploding in unison was deafening and line after line of Confederates fell, their screams of pain echoing the scream of rifles. Their lines broke. Men who didn't fall dropped their weapons, threw their hands up and surrendered—or ran from the battlefield.

Prisoners were taken and rushed away, rifles reloaded, and the enemy sighted again as another charge headed straight toward the Eighth.

Sweat beaded on Tom's brow and rolled down his face. He used his already wet sleeve to wipe it away, while keeping the next line of charging Confederates in sight. Beside him his two friends stared wild-eyed and ready.

"Fire!" came the order again.

Again their guns discharged, dropping more Rebels in their tracks. More men screamed, surrendered, ran, and died.

Tom's blood was up as men fell around him. He fired and reloaded, fired and reloaded, surviving this battle the only thing driving him.

Time felt as thick as the humid afternoon air blanketing the countryside as surge after surge of yelling Rebels raced up the hill, only to be shredded by rifle fire and bursting cannon.

Tom blinked, stopped firing, and shook his head in disbelief. A lone Confederate officer on horseback urged his men up the hill toward certain death. The men of the Eighth cheered and waved their own colors in response to the man's courage and fortitude.

The honorary flag waving didn't last long and quickly Tom and the Eighth continued their assault on the men running toward them. They fell by the dozens from the onslaught of guns and cannon. Rushing toward the threat of imminent death Tom watched cartridge boxes and haversacks thrown away as the Rebs turned and ran. Those that didn't run, or couldn't run, fell to their knees in surrender.

More Rebel yells reverberated through the air when another swell of Confederates ran into the wide open field to Tom's right and up the gentle slope—straight into more Federal fire.

Union artillery shredded the Confederates as they climbed a split-rail fence. Those who managed to breach the fence ran into the open field and up the hill toward the waiting Yankees. The Rebel yell became a shriek of pain as more men were hit with the solid shot and hollow shells from the cannon that sent hundreds of men to their deaths in a red cloud of smoke and left nothing of the man that had just stood there.

Tom swung toward the newest threat, moving as they moved. He fired and reloaded the black powder and mini-ball of his Enfield, now adept at the task and getting off two or three shots a minute, each minute like a mere second as the battle raged around him.

To his disbelief, and horror, the Confederates continued up the hill, regardless that hundreds had already been mowed down like a scythe cutting grass. He'd seen the Fourteenth Tennessee Volunteers' flag shot down and picked up so many times, he'd lost track. *Could any of the men from the Fourteenth still be alive? His brother-in-law, Henry? Other men from Clarksville? The place he'd called home most of his life.* A sick feeling washed over him as he sighted and fired at a man coming up the hill. *Could the man he'd just shot be someone he knew? Henry?*

Tom pushed the unwanted thoughts from his head. He was a soldier doing his duty and that duty was to hold this position. He reloaded and fired. Again and again until the wave of men running toward him became less and less. The battle was waning. The artillery had stopped and rifle fire was sporadic, but there was still intermittent fighting here and there.

The Rebel lines had been devastated, but a few still made their way toward the stone wall below Cemetery Ridge. Tom had moved with the fight and found himself alone and in the open between where the Eighth was taking prisoners and the wall giving the Union troops cover. He scanned the area. *Where were Collins and Baker?*

Afraid to get caught alone in the open, he ran toward the wall. His Yankee brothers cheered him on until he scrambled over the wall and plopped down behind it.

Breathing hard, glad to be alive, he poked his head up. A Rebel with long gray hair and long beard, a man who looked like any of the other hundreds of Rebs, was coming toward the wall and right into Tom's line of fire. But there was something familiar about this particular Reb, staying Tom's hand from loading and firing. Instead he watched the man whirl in a circle and dive to his right when he spotted a Union soldier aiming his rifle at his head. The bullet whizzed past. The Reb lifted his rifle and shot the Federal in the shoulder, who fell to the ground screaming.

Unable to fire, Tom watched the Confederate push to his feet and duck just in time to keep from being clubbed by the stock of a Yankee rifle. He turned and swung his own rifle by the barrel and caught the Federal in the side of the head. The man crumpled to the ground.

The Reb fought like a mad man. He whirled, went down on one knee, and reloaded. He stood up and was looking in front of him when a bayonet was thrust into his thigh from behind. He dropped to his knees, screaming, before he whirled and shoved his own bayonet into the belly of his attacker—a boy as young as Collins or Baker!

Tom couldn't watch any more. *Union men were dying at the hands of this crazed rebel! It didn't matter who he was, it was time to stop him!* Tom had been so intent on watching he hadn't reloaded. With an empty rifle he started toward the unknown, yet familiar, man his bayonet ready.

Tom worked his way through the dead and dying knowing the battle was nearly won, but this Reb was still killing and it was his turn to die. The moans of the men around him spurred him on to kill this Confederate still dealing death in this already lost battle.

He stood over the man, on his back on the ground, his eyes closed. *Was he already dead? Or playing possum like they said back in Clarksville?* Tom raised his bayonet, ready to drive it into the man's chest, but again something stayed his hand. *Something* tugged at him, told him not to do it.

The Reb's eyes opened—and Tom knew.

Chapter One

Tom Hansen watched a heavy hand land on the shoulder of his lifelong friend, Sam Whitmore. The two men stood side by side in the ballroom of *Marmoset*, the plantation owned by Sam's family. Today they celebrated the matriarch of *Marmoset's* birthday. Tom leaned forward for a better view as Walter, Sam's oldest brother, almost shouted, "Little brother, you and Tom both look like you swallowed a peach, pit and all. What in tarnation is wrong with you two? This is a party. Have fun! Or at least *pretend* you're having fun!" the tall, broad-shouldered man chastised with a squeeze to Sam's shoulder.

Tom turned to Sam. "I believe this is my signal to seek some refreshments." He half-smiled, cocked his head, and strolled away.

"Coward," Sam said to his retreating back.

Tom grinned. Yes, he was a coward when it came to Walter Whitmore, but he had no stomach for a confrontation with Sam's oldest brother, be it friendly or not. Since they were kids, Walt had lorded over them whenever possible, be it at the Whitmore plantation, in the classroom, or in town. Tom had an aversion to the oldest Whitmore son, heir to *Marmoset* when their mother passed. He was arrogant, self-centered, and just a plain bully.

Tom made his way to the long, white, lace-covered refreshment table against the wall and lifted the silver ladle from the punch bowl. He poured some of the pink liquid into a glass and stepped aside to allow the next person access. He walked to a corner, leaned against the wall and sipped his punch. Looking around he considered *Marmoset*, a plantation like most in the south with dozens of slaves running the household and farming the land's cotton, with a huge house where the owner's wealth was displayed for all to see. Several stories high with huge white columns out front and wide porches that reached from one side of the home to the other, they shouted "look how rich I am!" to all who visited. Large chandeliers hung in entryways into those huge homes with big libraries filled with shelves of books, expensive furniture and draperies, spiraling staircases, fancy carriages, and all the trappings of the "southern gentry."

Plantations Tom abhorred.

His family had settled in Clarksville, Tennessee, from Boston when he was a baby and, although settling in an area where slavery was accepted and mostly practiced, Tom had a great dislike for the institution. His family came to Clarksville with wealth of their own, inherited from descendants he could cite as far back as Boston's first settlement. *Real* gentry with "old" money, not earned off the backs of others and only within the last twenty or thirty years. But Tom didn't hold with his family's kind of gentry either. He was a plain man, by any standards, just like his friend Sam, who'd moved away from *Marmoset* after his father's passing a year and a half ago, purchased his own piece of property, freed the two slaves that went with it, and was farming the land beside them—not above them. Tom and Sam were as close as brothers, both having the same ideas about slavery and wealth as the other. If they obtained it, they wanted it to be from their own hard work.

"Are you holdin' up the wall, or is it holdin' up you?" The feminine voice drew Tom's attention from his musings.

"What? Excuse me?" he stammered, pushing away from the wall.

"I said," the woman drawled in a heavy, southern accent as though speaking to a child, "are you holdin' up the wall, or is it holdin' up you?"

Tom stared into the deep green eyes of the woman doing the asking and his heart started to pound, his mouth went dry, and his knees felt weak.

"You are a quiet one, aren't you?" she drawled, her smile revealing perfect, even teeth and a dimple in each cheek. "What does it take for a girl to gain an introduction, sir?"

Tom swallowed, blinked, and regained his composure. "My name is Tom Hansen, Miss…?"

She put out a green-gloved hand, the color matching that of the full, low-cut gown she wore—and her eyes. "My name is Abigail Conrad, Mr. Hansen, but—my friends—call me Abby."

Tom took her hand and nodded. "Pleased to make your acquaintance, Miss Conrad." He waved at the refreshments table. "May I get you a pastry or glass of punch?"

She smiled again, withdrew her hand, flipped an errant curl the color of light walnut wood away from her face, and met his eyes in a direct gaze.

Tom's heart flopped in his chest like a fish tossed on the bank of a river.

"Yes, thank you. I'd like a glass of punch, please."

"I'll, I'll be right back," Tom stammered before hurrying away, his mind spinning. He'd never had a reaction to a woman like he had Miss Conrad. She was lovely, with a smile that melted his heart, eyes the color of newly sprouting spring grass, an even, pert nose, and high, round cheeks that begged to be touched—by him.

He returned a minute later, glass of punch in hand. "Here, Miss Conrad. This is for you."

"Well, of course it's for me, silly," she trilled. Her voice sent shivers up and down Tom's spine.

"Of course." *What's* wrong *with you, Hansen! You're acting like some schoolboy instead of a twenty-one year old man. Get hold of yourself!* his mind screamed.

Miss Conrad cocked her head and smiled, as though able to hear his thoughts. She sipped the punch then slid her tongue seductively over her lips, watching Tom watch her. He thought his heart would explode it was beating so fast.

"There you are, Abby!" broke the moment.

Abigail whirled to face an older man. "Hello, Papa."

She sounded annoyed at the interruption and Tom was happy for it—both the interruption, so he could gather his wits—and the fact Abigail seemed annoyed by it.

The man stepped past Abby and in front of Tom. "Who have we here?"

"Papa, this is Mr. Tom Hansen. Mr. Hansen, this is Jeremiah Conrad, my father."

The tall, heavily-built, immaculately dressed man stepped forward and thrust out his hand. "I'm very pleased to meet you Mr. Tom Hansen."

Tom shook the man's proffered hand. "I'm pleased to meet you, as well, sir."

The big man drew back and laid his hand across his daughter's shoulders. "So what have you and Mr. Hansen been visitin' about, Abby?" There was a sparkle of mischief in his eyes.

Frustration crossed Abigail's face before she closed it off and answered her father. "We haven't conversed long enough to speak of anythin', Papa," she said tersely. "We've only just met."

Mr. Conrad threw his head back and laughed. Regaining himself he said, "I understand. I'll leave you two alone to get better acquainted."

Relief crossed Abby's face as the big man whirled and strolled away into the crowd of partygoers.

Sighing with relief, Abby turned back to Tom. "He can be...overbearin' at times. I believe he still thinks I'm a child, but I assure you, I am not," she said slowly and purposely.

Her eyes twinkled and, for a moment, Tom was jealous of the insinuation that, perhaps, she'd been kissed a few times.

"Do you dance?"

Her question pulled him from his musing. He nodded his head then quickly shook it no. "I do," he amended then explained, "but I don't enjoy it."

"Pish tosh, come along. Show me how you don't like to dance."

Without giving Tom a chance to refuse, she dragged him onto the floor where couple after couple floated around the room, dancing to the strains of *Home Sweet Home*. Tom was concentrating so hard on his steps, he barely heard what Miss Conrad said and just stared at her mouth as it worked forming words he didn't hear.

"Tom? Are you listenin'?" she pouted, causing him to stumble.

Regaining his steps he licked his lips and brought his lower teeth up over the thin, dark mustache that matched his dark hair. He chewed on his upper lip, a habit he seemed unable to break when he was nervous. And he was nervous.

"Miss Abby, I told you I don't like to dance. I have to concentrate on one thing or the other. Either I dance or I listen to you. I can't do both at the same time," he added with a nervous chuckle.

She stopped in mid-step and stood immobile in front of him.

Oh boy, he was in for a tongue-lashing now. She'd tell him how embarrassed she was to be seen dancing with a buffoon! The thought brought to mind many a dance lesson suffered with Sam, ridiculed for their ineptitude by both the young ladies *and* Walter Whitmore!

To his surprise she threw back her head and laughed, loudly, and most unladylike.

Tom's shoulders lifted in his attempt not to laugh with her, but he couldn't stop the rumble that rolled up from the pit of his belly until both of them stood in the middle of the dance floor, laughing, while being bumped and jostled and grumbled at by other dancers.

Abby grabbed his arm. "Let's get out of here."

Like a puppy, Tom followed her, uncaring where they went, as long as he was with her. Again his muddled mind screamed, *what is wrong with you? You're acting like some love-struck boy!*

They headed outside where Tom spotted Sam disappearing around the back of the house. *Hmm, where's he's going?* Tom wondered. *Walt must still be badgering him so he's getting as far away from his big brother as he can. Can't blame him. Not one bit.* Tom's mind flashed to his only brother, Ralph. Eight years older, Ralph had left Tennessee to pursue his own dreams when Tom was only ten years old, leaving Tom as the oldest and not having to endure the bossiness and harassment Sam had from his older brothers. Other than Ralph, whom Tom hadn't seen since attending his wedding to Miss Margaret Howard years ago, Tom's mind wandered to his younger sisters, Anne and Mary, still at home, and happy to spend the money they'd been *blessed* with. He almost snorted and frowned in his reflection.

"Hello? Tom? Are you there?" The annoyance in Abby's voice jerked him back to where he was—again.

"I'm sorry, Abby, I...I...."

She showed her displeasure at his lack of attention with a shake of her head. "If you find my company so unwelcomin' we *can* go back inside."

"No." Tom looked deep into her face, almost translucent in the moonlight. Her green eyes, now dark without the light inside the house to brighten them, sparked with ire, yet invited at the same time. Her mouth curled into a slight grin.

"Do you see anythin' you like?" she drawled, breaking his overlong perusal.

Tom cleared his throat and shook his head. At her horrified look, he nodded several times instead. "Yes, of course I like what I see. That's why I was staring. I like it very much."

Her irritated scowl changed to a huge smile, her white teeth almost glittering in the moonlight. "That's better, Mr. Hansen."

Tom heard the door to the parlor open and close, and watched a young girl step into the darkness and scurry in the same direction Sam had gone a few minutes before. He watched her disappear around the house before gentle fingers turned his face back to hers.

"You're givin' me pause to think you even care about bein' out here—with me—and not someone else," Abby said, her voice strained again.

Tom shook his head. "No, no. My friend Sam just went behind the house and was followed..."

"By that young lady?" she interrupted.

"Yes, the young lady who just came out of the house."

"Perhaps they have arranged to meet in the moonlight, without pryin' eyes all around them?" Her eyebrows rose in question.

Tom shrugged. "That's not like Sam. Likely he went out to get away from his brother and she, well, perhaps she's trying to get away from an older sister and just went out for a breath of air and happened to go in the same direction."

Cool fingers caressed his cheek. "Perhaps, but enough talk about them, Tom. Do you want to stroll in the moonlight with me or worry about your friend?"

Tom cleared his throat. *How brazen and forward this girl was! So different from other girls who flitted around like butterflies, batting their eyelids, acting coy, and barely speaking to someone they might be interested in getting to know better. But Tom liked it. Liked her!* He bowed at the waist and flung his arm across his body. "Miss Conrad, if I'm not being too forward, will you accompany me for a walk in the moonlight?" He snapped upright as a broad smile lit her face.

"Yes, Tom Hansen, I would like to walk with you in the moonlight." She slid her arm into Tom's offered elbow and they walked into the darkness, Abby talking non-stop and Tom straining to hear every word.

Chapter Two

Tom and Abby strolled arm-in-arm toward the stables. Abby talked and Tom listened as they entered a huge barn, the horses shifting and nickering at their entry.

"I love horses. Do you love horses, Tom?"

"I do. I even have a few…"

"How many is a few, Tom?" she asked before he could answer her first question.

"Two thoroughbreds," Tom said then added, "I race them."

She pulled away and clapped her hands. "Oh, I love to watch the races. Do you race at the track here in Clarksville? Do you win?" she asked in a rush.

Tom didn't want to brag, but he did win, regularly, which was how he was attaining his own money.

"I have two horses I race at the tracks in Clarksville and Nashville," he began. "One of my horses is a pure black thoroughbred stallion named Satan's Pride, a gift from my father for my fifteenth birthday. The other is a steel-dust I call Gray Ghost. He was a gift from my mother for my seventeenth birthday. Both are from Belle Meade, one of the premiere producers of thoroughbreds. They both carry the Epsilon bloodline and run like the wind. They're nearly unbeaten on the big tracks, as well as the *friendly* races in the county," he finished with a proud smile.

"Oh, tell me more." Her eyes sparkled in the moonlight.

"Men offer to buy them all the time, but I firmly decline. When their racing days are over, I'll put them to stud. Their colts will be sought after from one end of Tennessee to the other and beyond. They'll be the beginning of my becoming a well-respected breeder of fine thoroughbreds."

"It sounds exciting. Perhaps I'll be able to watch you race sometime?"

"That could be arranged." He tilted his head.

Abby grabbed Tom's arm again, squeezed it tight, and led him deeper into the stable, oohing and aahing over the beautiful horses housed there.

They came to an empty stall and Abby pulled him into it. She leaned against him, pressed her cheek next to his, and whispered in his ear in a husky voice, "Would you like to kiss me?"

Tom swallowed, certain now she'd been kissed many times and wondering why he was so drawn to her knowing it. *She was toying with him. How many other men had she toyed with in her young life?*

He stepped back. Their eyes locked and he couldn't keep himself from moving toward her again. She melted into his body, sighed when their lips met—and Tom was lost.

***

Tom leaned back, his head spinning. "Stop."

Abby's eyes went wide. "Stop?" Her voice was incredulous. "Well, that's a first," she said with an unladylike snort.

Tom felt a rush of something so foreign he didn't know how to handle it. *Was he jealous?* He pushed away from Abby and stared into her wide, green eyes.

"Listen, Miss Conrad…"

"I think we're beyond Miss Conrad. My name is Abby."

Tom shook his head to gain his wits. "Abby, we should go back inside."

Abby continued to stare at him before she suddenly began to laugh. "You *are* old-fashioned, aren't you?"

"Old-fashioned or respectful, call it whatever you like, but this isn't right *or* proper."

"Proper?" She laughed again. "My dear Tom, I have never been proper a day in my life. And I've never been told to stop, either." She ran a finger down his cheek and glared at him a moment before she added, "But I seem to like it from you. Your respect for me, that is."

"You're not angry?" Tom's mouth was dry.

"How can I be angry when you're worryin' about my honor? No, Tom Hansen, I'm not angry. In fact, I'm more intrigued than ever."

Tom felt unsure of everything that was happening. He had feelings he'd never felt before for anyone. He wanted more than anything to kiss her, but knew it was wrong. He didn't want to do anything to damage her reputation, although, it seemed, many others had already done so, which made him angry and jealous. How many others *had* kissed her?

"Oh Tom?" she trilled, drawing his attention back to her. "Listen to me. We've done nothin' to be ashamed of. We'll go back inside and, if you're of a mind, which I certainly hope you are, you may court me. Of course, you'll have to ask my father properly, but he won't deny you."

Tom's eyebrows drew together and he recoiled from her statement, said so matter-of-factly. "How do you know that?"

She giggled. "My father and I have been doin' this dance a long time, Tom Hansen. I've been a rather…difficult daughter," she said with a grimace. "He'll be very happy when the day comes he sees me wed."

"Wed!" Tom stumbled backward he was so shaken by the word. "By God, Abby, we've only just met. Why would you say such a thing?"

Abby giggled. "I'm just sayin' he'll be happy to see me courted with the possibility of bein' wed—someday. I am nineteen, you know.…"

The words hung between them, Tom knew that nineteen was almost a spinster when it came to being marriageable. *Was there a reason she wasn't wed yet? Perhaps because she was so free with her kisses?*

"Oh Tom, stop worryin'. I'll be a good little girl," she said in a pout, her head cocked in a condescending way.

Tom knew even thinking about courting her was crazy. He just knew it. The thought of marriage was far from his mind. He didn't *want* to marry anytime soon, yet he was drawn to her like a pesky no-see-um to the light.

"Toooom," she drew out, pulling him from his thoughts. "If you're afraid, we can say our goodbye's right now."

"I'm not afraid, Abby," he snapped. "I'm just, well, surprised at how this conversation has gone. I never thought this evening would turn out this way."

"And what way is that?" she chided.

"Talking about things that never crossed my mind before."

"Are you sorry I was so brazen to ask for an introduction?" Her eyes pierced him to his soul and he felt a shiver go up his spine. *Was it a shiver of anticipation—or warning?*

He shook off the feeling and smiled down at her. "No, Abby, I'm not sorry to have met you. I just want to do things proper so we don't regret anything later." He swallowed.

Her smile nearly blinded him. "Thank you, Tom Hansen. Now take me back inside before someone comes lookin' for me and my reputation is sullied—or you have to marry me tomorrow for our indiscretions." There was a gleam in her sparkling green eyes.

Chapter Three

The months flew by in a whirlwind of parties, parties Tom hated but attended to keep Abby happy. There was courting, and racing, too. Abby was always among the crowd, watching from the stands at the track in Clarksville and sometimes even Nashville, or along the pre-determined route of a "friendly" race between Tom and a challenger convinced he could best Satan's Pride or Gray Ghost.

Abby was always easy to spot, her big hats matching the brightly-colored dresses she wore, waving and cheering wildly as he rode to the starting post. His winnings in the friendly races were minimal, but the purses at the established tracks became larger as his horses continued to win, their reputations growing at the same time.

His nest egg grew, too. The bigger it became the more his mind went toward how to use it, and it always went to Abby. Despite the fact she was oftentimes self-centered and obstinate, she was beautiful with her soft brown hair, green eyes, and pinchable cheeks—and Tom was completely in love with her. Abby had his heart wrapped so tightly he could barely breathe sometimes. The thought of losing her made his chest constrict, his mouth go dry, and his heart race. It'd been a three month whirl of courtship, wooing, and keeping her happy, the task sometimes daunting. Regardless she was difficult—at the least— he loved her and no matter how hard he tried, it was a fact he couldn't deny to himself or his heart.

***

The parlor of the Conrad home was flooded with warm June sunlight and Tom was sweating under his collar to prove it.

"Stop worryin', Tom. You look like you just swallowed a peach," Abby chastised, waving a young slave girl away like she was swatting a gnat. The girl snatched up a tray of tea and cups from the table beside where Abby stood and hurried from the room, the cups rattling in her haste.

Tom's skin pricked. He and Abby hadn't talked yet about the issue of slavery and how it would affect their future together. It was going to be a difficult conversation, one Tom did not look forward to, but one they *would* have. He didn't hold with slavery and wouldn't allow it in his home. Abby would just have to accept it.

Pushing the foreboding conversation from his mind, Tom couldn't help but grin. Abby's words threw him back to the night of the party at *Marmoset* where they'd met. Where Sam met Ellie, the woman who had followed him outside and whom he quickly married, Tom and Abby attending their wedding only last month.

"There, you see? A smile is so much better." Abby brushed imaginary dust from his shoulder, whirled, and sat down beside him, her beige day dress swirling around her ankles just as her father entered the room.

Tom jumped up and offered his hand to Jeremiah Conrad. Jeremiah shook it firmly before he sat down in a black, winged-back chair across from the settee where his daughter sat, Tom now standing rigid in front of her, hopeful looks on both their faces.

The older man had a gleam in his eyes, even though Tom had been there almost daily since meeting Abby three months earlier.

"To what do I owe this visit, Tom?" Jeremiah asked.

Tom stood there, his hands flat against his thighs. "Sir, I've..." he turned and raised his hand for Abby to take it and stand beside him. She stood up and went to him, a wide smile on her face, giving Tom the courage he needed to finish his task. He turned back to her father. "Sir, I've come to ask for Abby's hand in marriage." His voice was strong and confident.

"Hot damn! It's about time. I was beginning to think you'd never ask!" Jeremiah's voice boomed throughout the parlor as he jumped to his feet again.

"Papa..." Abby drawled.

The older man strode to Tom, his hand extended. The two men shook before he pulled Tom into his chest and slapped his back. "Welcome to the family, son."

Tom swallowed. "Thank you, sir."

Jeremiah stepped back and waved his hand. "Call me Jeremiah, Tom. No need for formalities any longer, is there?"

"No sir."

"Jeremiah."

"Jeremiah," Tom repeated, not all together comfortable with the request, but doing as asked.

"Wonderful!" Abby's father boomed again. "When will this wedding take place? And where? Here, I hope?" Abby's father asked in a rush. He stilled then, his voice gentle when he said, "I wish your mother were alive to see you married, Abigail Jane Conrad."

Abby swallowed hard beside Tom and nodded gently. "I do, too, Papa. I wish I'd known her, even a little."

She turned to Tom and he smiled sadly, his having learned in their earliest conversations that her mother died giving birth to Abby.

"But this is a day to be happy." Abby wiped her eyes and put a wide smile back on her face.

"You're absolutely right, Abby girl. Let's have a drink to celebrate. I believe we have some rather good port for the occasion." Jeremiah turned and shouted out the doorway. "Martha, come back here this minute!"

The same slave girl hurried into the room and skidded to a halt before Jeremiah, her eyes darting around as though awaiting punishment for a wrong deed.

"The port, in the cabinet, get it and serve us."

Again Tom recoiled from the way the girl was treated and resolved he would never treat another human being like such.

The girl nodded and mumbled understanding. She scurried to the cabinet, pulled out three delicate wine glasses and began to pour. In her haste, some slopped over the side and dripped onto the floor.

"You stupid girl!" Jeremiah thundered. He started toward her, his hand raised, but checked himself when he saw Tom's face. Instead he stopped in the middle of the room. "Clean it up." He bellowed, his voice hard and condescending, as though he spoke to an idiot child.

"Yessir, masser Conrad. Yessir."

The fear in her voice made Tom want to vomit and when he turned to Abby she was grinning with a gleam in her eyes. He swallowed. Their conversation about slavery would have to take place soon. Very soon.

***

A week later, Abby sat in the same spot on the settee in the parlor where Tom asked Jeremiah Conrad for her hand. She stared at the ring Tom held between his fingers, a forced smile on her face. Her hand, frozen in mid-air, reached for the ring, unable to take it.

Tom seethed with anger. "What's wrong? Don't you like it?"

"Well...." She cocked her head and lowered her eyes in what Tom had learned signaled her displeasure. "Do you want me to be honest, Tom?"

"Of course, Abby. You *don't* like it, do you?"

"Well, no, I don't. It's too...simple," she said of the ruby, surrounded by small diamonds. Tom had especially liked and bought it because it *was* simple—like him.

"I want lots of diamonds that sparkle and shine and shows how much my affianced loves me," she trilled.

Ripples of anger tore up Tom's spine. Abby was difficult, at best, but he hadn't expected this. He'd been assured by the jeweler any woman would love this ring. *Any woman except Abby, apparently.*

"Do you want another one? One you pick?" he asked between clenched teeth.

"Oh yes, that's what I'd truly like. May we go, right now, and return this one for one I truly like?"

Tom tried to understand her. Tried to understand how important an engagement ring was to a woman—the symbol of her acceptance of the man who gave it to her—and one she would gladly wear for the rest of her life. *Of course she should like what she wore as a symbol of their love*, he told himself, swallowing his anger.

He smiled and put the ring back in his vest pocket. "Of course, Abby, we can go right now and find exactly what you want."

The trip to the jewelers was quiet on Tom's part, while Abby chattered on about exactly what she wanted for the engagement ring *she* picked, pointing out repeatedly it wasn't Tom's fault.

"Silly men just *don't know* what a woman wants!" she said numerous times before adding, "I don't know *why* you didn't take me with you in the first place, Tom. We wouldn't be doin' this if you had," she chastised.

Tom sighed, wondering if he ever did anything right where Abby was concerned. It seemed the only thing he *did* do right was win at the track. Abby enjoyed his celebrity more than he did. She couldn't wait to hob knob with the track owners, horse owners and all the gentry at the clubhouse parties after the races. She spoke to everyone, giggling like a schoolgirl, sometimes causing Tom to doubt her sincerity in her profession of love for him, before she wrapped her arm around his and kissed his cheek, removing his doubt, filling him with love for her. She was as high-spirited as one of his stallions, and loved people, he assured himself, and if he wanted her he had to take what came with her.

"Are you listenin' to me, Tom?" broke his musing. He turned to see her pouting face.

"Yes, Abby, I was just thinking about, well, about what kind of ring you *might* like."

"I *told* you. See you weren't listenin' to me." She sighed. "I want one with lots of diamonds, lots of diamonds," she reiterated. "Diamonds that sparkle like the sun and will make every girl that sees it jealous beyond control!"

Tom stared at her face, full of expectation, and greed.

"Is that all you're concerned about? Making your friends jealous?"

She fell backward against the carriage seat and laid her gloved hands in her lap. "Of course not, Tom," she said after a few moments thought. She turned back to him. "I care that it represents our love."

"Seems like you want it to represent something a lot more than that, Abby," Tom said, his back up.

"Oh, Tom, don't be like that. An engagement ring is special to a girl. I'll wear it every day for the rest of my life and I want it to be somethin' I like, no love, and I want everyone else to love it, too." Her eyelids fluttered and Tom doubted her sincerity, but understood what she was saying.

"Fine, we'll get whatever you want—within reason," he amended, refusing to spend more than he intended. He had plans for the money he was accumulating and Abby would have to live within those bounds.

She grabbed his arm and snuggled close. "Thank you, Tom." She looked up, her green eyes melting his anger. "I do love you, you know that, right?"

Tom kissed her forehead as doubt washed over him. *Did she love him, or did she love the idea of the money and prestige he was gaining in the racing world?* He couldn't shake the thoughts and opened his mouth to tell her yes, he knew she loved him, but couldn't.

Hours later Abby danced around the parlor like a little girl, her right hand in front of her, admiring the ring one minute, holding it close to her chest the next.

"Ooooh, I love it, Tom. Love it, love it, love it! Thank you so much!" She whirled in a circle, her hand, and the ring, clenched against her heart.

"I'm glad you do, Abby." He grimaced. He'd spent much more than he intended, but she'd beguiled him until he couldn't refuse her.

Extending her right hand in front of her again she admired the oval shaped, one-carat diamond, ringed by smaller diamonds with more along the length of each side of the golden band. The ring shouted *money!*—and Tom hated it.

Chapter Four

"What are you trying to say, Tom?" Abby shook her head as though Tom spoke in a foreign language.

"I'm telling you, Abby, that when we marry there will be no slaves in our home." There, he'd said it, plain and simple. There…would…be…no…slaves in their home.

Her face contorted in silent rage. Her eyes turned an icy green, like leaves withering on a tree right in front of him. She swallowed hard, like *she* was trying to swallow the peach pit he'd been accused of swallowing more than once so recently. Her mouth puckered in a sneer that made her look like the mythological old hag. Her nose flared and she stomped toward him, stopping only when her face was so close he could see every freckle he'd never seen before, always hidden by heavy powders.

"That's ludicrous, Tom!" she shouted, then checked herself, just as her father had the day Tom asked for her hand. *Was her entire persona a lie?* he wondered. *Was everything he saw what* she *wanted him to see, what she thought* he *wanted to see?*

"No, Abby, it's not ludicrous." Anger of his own crept up his neck. Slavery was accepted here, but it would not be accepted in *his* home! "When we marry, we will own no slaves. Period." He stood his ground. If he backed down, he would lose all credibility for their future. She was as strong-willed a woman as he'd ever met and he'd given in to her too many times. He likened her to one of his spirited stallions, one he had to take plenty of time to break into a willing, subservient creature, one that did as it was told, when it was told to do it. He had to prove to her—and himself—that he was the alpha in this relationship, and she would do as she was told. *He could not waver!*

She stood in front of him in the same parlor he'd asked for her hand, her green eyes snapping with so much anger his heart clenched. *Was this the real Abby? Was* this *the Abby he would have to live with forever once married?* His heart clenched and he stopped breathing. His mind flashed back to all the times she'd worked her magic to get her way. At the tracks, mingling and flirting with the rich and powerful of the county, the way she treated Martha and the other slaves in her home, her ring—and her kisses. A chill ran up his spine. She was a master manipulator—and he was the puppet.

Her face suddenly softened and she kissed his cheek. "Oh, Tom! You're such a silly man!" She wrapped her hands around his arm and led him from the room. "It's gettin' stuffy in here. Let's go outside and discuss this in the fresh air," she cooed, as though they'd been talking about the color of a room or what dress she should wear to a party.

Tom wet his lips and nodded, unable to speak, allowing her to lead him from the house. *This was the Abby he was used to seeing. But was* this *Abby a complete and total lie?*

They went out of the huge, white-washed plantation house and down the front stairs before Abby turned on him. "We're goin' to finish this discussion now, Tom Hansen. Right now."

He stared into her icy green eyes, snapping again with anger and venom, as though she'd become a serpent and he was her prey.

"Now...." She pasted one of her false smiles on her face, but Tom knew them now. She suddenly looked like a doll someone had painted that face onto and if those lips moved her entire façade would crack and he would see her for who she truly was.

"I don't want to hear any more of this foolish talk about not havin' slaves in *our* home, Tom Hansen."

"But we won't, Abby. I forbid it."

She sucked in a deep breath. Her chest puffed up like a bullfrog before it croaked, and her mouth pinched. "Tom, be reasonable. I...I don't know how to run a household without my people," she began, her tone pleading.

"You'll learn."

She swallowed. "But I don't *want* to learn," she forced out between gritted teeth. "I'm quite happy directin' my slaves to do what I want in *my* home."

"But you see, Abby, it will be *our* home, purchased by *me*, and in *our* home there will be no slaves for you to tell what to do..." He stopped before saying, *or treat like inconsequential pieces of chattel and property!*

Abby swallowed hard and took several huge breaths. Tom watched anger race from her eyes to her nose to her mouth and back again, but he would stand strong on this and prove to her he would not be thwarted.

She stood in front of him, unmoving, and, watching her, his heart swelled with love—despite her overbearing, selfish character. It would be a great sacrifice for her to do as he wanted, but she loved him, he told himself, and because she loved him she would do as he asked. He hadn't ruled out the possibility of hiring freed-men or locals to work as house servants, stable hands, and trainers, but that was long in the future. Right now his mind was set and he could not waver.

Finally, her chin came up and she cupped her hands together in front of her. "Is there no way I can change your mind?"

"No, Abby, you cannot. I stand firm on this."

Her nose flared with the silent breath she took. "Very well, Tom. There's no changin' your mind?" she asked one last time.

"No." His answer was quick. "That is my final decision. We might consider hired men later, but for now, my answer is final," he said, hoping to temporarily assuage her anger.

She raised her chin even higher and said, "Very well, Tom. If there's no changin' your mind, I can no longer marry you."

He almost dropped to his knees. He couldn't move, couldn't speak, couldn't form another coherent thought or say a single word, not one word. Someone might as well have been standing at the bottom of the wide stairs with a double-barreled shotgun pressed against his chest, threatening to pull the trigger and blow his heart into a thousand pieces. His mouth was suddenly dry in the hot, August sun. He heard her voice in his head say again and again, "I can no longer marry you," before she pressed the engagement ring he had given her only a few weeks ago into the palm of his hand and rolled his fingers closed around it.

Tom had expected her to argue against his decision, but he never expected this! She'd professed her undying love for him for months. *How could this be what would destroy that love?*

She sensed his wavering and leaned toward him. "I will, of course, change my mind if you change yours." Her eyes sparkled with the challenge.

Tom's back came up and he pursed his lips with determination. "No," he managed. "I will not." He was seeing the real Abby and it sickened him. She'd played him for a fool, leading him around by his love, and he hated himself for it—and her. She was a user and he was damned glad he found out soon enough who she really was to keep from being saddled with her manipulations for the rest of his life!

She stared at him, waiting for him to buckle, but he would not. He finally knew who the real Abby Conrad was and why, at nineteen, she was unmarried.

Her eyes pinched and her back grew rigid. She turned on her heel, her yellow dress swirling around her ankles like a low-lying fog, and she stomped up the porch steps without a backward glance.

He stared after her, his heart slamming around inside his chest as though trying to break out. Tom forced himself to breathe—sad, angry, and relieved all at the same time. He sucked in huge, gulping breaths as his hands rolled in and out of fists at his side. He could go after her, tell her he'd changed his mind, but he wouldn't be able to live with himself if he did—for more reasons than just one. If she won this battle, he would lose the war forever. *She'd become the stallion that could never be broken because he'd given in to her and he'd be the puppet who did her bidding for the rest of their lives.*

He stood at the bottom of the wide steps, the strong scent of the roses lining both sides of the porch filling his senses. *Someone might as well press the muzzle of a shotgun against my heart and pull the trigger!* he thought, sure that it would shatter from his resentment and grief.

In silent anger and despair, he watched the huge oak doors slam behind her, shutting out his dreams of their life together—forever.

Chapter Five

Tom stood on the front porch of the modest, two storied, brick and white-washed clapboard home he'd purchased a week ago, one thumb tucked into the pocket of his vest and smoking a locally grown cigar. He scanned the property. Seven hundred acres—for now—of cross-fenced, cleared pastureland full of green grass that would, in time, hold scores of horses, more barns, even a training track. With numerous streams cutting through the lush pastures, fields of corn, oats and hay for the animals, and crops for his own needs, there was plenty of room to spread out when he needed to expand.

His mind wandered to the what ifs of his past, but he shut them down as quickly as they began. There were no ifs in his life anymore. Especially when it began with "what if Abby…."

Everything these past years revolved around his horses. He'd retired Satin's Pride and Gray Ghost a long time ago, replaced them with two studs from the same line that ran as well as their predecessors and he continued to win. And when they retired, he replaced them with two more. He studded them out after their racing days were over, and now they would enjoy their retirement while his dreams of a breeding farm came to fruition.

Unwanted, Tom's mind wandered back to Abby again. He shook his head, trying to dispel the thoughts, but as always, she persisted. Although he stood on the porch of his new home, he was suddenly thrown back in time to the day of her betrayal and she was standing in front of him telling him goodbye. He saw her face as clearly as if she stood here today.

He sighed, recalling the years that followed her dismissal. He'd poured himself into his horses, did nothing but work his stock and race, and didn't socialize anywhere in Clarksville. He didn't want to accidentally run into Abby. He didn't want the anger, hurt, and embarrassment he'd suppressed to rise again—ever. He only wanted to do what he loved and forget everything about her.

He hung his silks at the Jockey Clubs in Clarksville and Nashville, and spent time with William Giles at Belle Meade at his personal invitations. He felt comfortable only in the company of other men who understood his passion for racing. He ran every race he could enter. At his lowest point in October of 1843, he traveled from Clarksville to the Burns Island track in Nashville where Satan's Pride barely lost to Peytona in what was the biggest race ever run in the world with a purse of $35,000. From Nashville he went to Winchester and every other of the ten tracks in Tennessee where he could race. He won, again and again, adding to his nest egg until in 1855, at the ripe old age of 33, he'd garnered enough wealth to buy the horse farm of his dreams and the home he would occupy—alone.

***

"Nathaniel, I like the settee better over there." Tom pointed and said to his freed house man. "Let's move it." Tom grabbed one end of the settee. Nathaniel did the same and, both men grunting with the effort, moved it in front of the window where warm, early spring light filtered through. All the people who worked at *Champion Farms*, renamed in honor of Tom's champion racers, were slaves Tom purchased with the property, or purchased separately, and immediately freed. Former slaves he now paid wages, with instructions to carry their freedom papers with them at all times.

Nathaniel, tall and slight, had been the house man here for at least twenty years. He knew his way around and kept the house and its staff running like a well-oiled piece of machinery.

"I likes it better there, too, Mista Tom."

Tom nodded and smiled. His home was coming along. His horses would arrive today from his mother's stables and he would start building his stock immediately. Although Satan's Pride and Gray Ghost had been bringing in money from stud fees for years, Tom never kept any of the foals. Now he intended to purchase quality brood mares to build a fine stock with his studs and raise more quality racers and mares. Everything he had was tied up in Champion Farms. His money, his time—and his emotions. It was all he thought about. He pushed any potential relationship with a woman from his mind. Abby had destroyed him emotionally and he had no intention of letting another woman into his inner sanctum to do it again.

The horses began to arrive around noon and it took until early evening to get everyone settled into their new surroundings.

"Hold him!" Tom shouted to Bull, the huge, coal black foreman who handled the stallions. With arms and legs the size of tree branches, he was well-suited for controlling the animals as they arrived. He was fearless and kept the horses from losing their heads in their new, unfamiliar surroundings.

"He's a strong one, sah," Bull said, breathless.

Tom reached up to calm the stomping horse. "My Dreamer," he cooed, laying his hands on the sides of the animal's face and blowing into the animal's nose. "Shhhh, My Dreamer. Shhhhh."

The animal immediately calmed, snorted and warily eyed his owner.

"That's my boy, Dreamer. Shhhh."

"You sure do gots a way wid them horses, Masta Tom."

Tom sucked in a long breath. "Just Mister Tom or sir, Bull. Or even Tom. I'm not your master. I'm your employer, or even boss if you prefer that, but I'm not your master."

"Yessir, Mista Tom. I forgets. Bein' a slave fo' all them years, an' now not bein' one, it's hard fo' a man ta reckon sometimes."

"I hope it's a good reckoning?" Tom grinned.

"Oh, yes sah!" Bull thundered, making My Dreamer dance again.

"Shhhh shhhh shhhh," Tom cooed, calming the horse. "Leave a stall between him and Satan's Pride. We'll put one of the younger studs between them. Those young ones will learn from the older boys." Tom chuckled. "They'll teach 'em the ropes and keep 'em in line. Show them who's the alpha in the herd."

"Yes sah, they sure will." Bull nodded and smiled, his white teeth gleaming against his dark face.

Tom handed his most recently winning stallion to his foreman, who walked the animal toward his new home, a long barn with sixteen stalls that opened on one side into long individual paddocks and on the other into a huge, open work area. Each stall had a floor to ceiling, two-inch thick, rough-wood dividing wall separating the stallions—to keep them from doing injury to each other—and each paddock had a high fence between them. Although some of the animals had been raised together, stallions were stallions and had to be kept apart, especially if they caught the scent of a mare in heat.

Tom snorted, his thoughts running from mares in heat to Abby. *Damn! Why couldn't he get her out of his head? It'd been twelve years since she left him. She should be nothing but a slight blip in his memory—but she wasn't. She was always there in the back of his mind, taunting, calling him every kind of fool for giving her up. For what? His ideals about slavery? No, it was more than that,* he justified to himself. *Much more. It was about Abby being who she really was, and him finding out just in time. He was better off caring for nothing but his horses.*

One by one the animals arrived until six stallions were tucked away in the barn, getting used to their new homes by kicking, stomping, and running up and down the fence lines of their new paddocks, stopping for a few bites of grass before they did it again. There were whinnies of dominance and those of acquiescence as Satan's Pride and Gray Ghost established themselves as the alphas—despite their ages.

The geldings and mares that pulled Tom's wagons and coach were housed in another barn that opened into one huge paddock where they raced and played like children, stopping for a few bites of grass like the stallions, before racing around the pasture again, learning the breadth and depth of their new home.

Tom had a few matches in mind and had talked already to William Giles out at Belle Meade about the purchase of several brood mares to start his stock. The next few years were going to be exciting and full of hard work—and it beckoned him like the next chapter in a book.

Chapter Six

"Damn!" Tom's hand came down with a resounding slap on the wide arm of the leather chair in his study. Surrounded floor to ceiling with shelves of books containing the histories of the world he wondered how things in the country could be so out of control. *Hadn't man learned by his mistakes? From the history contained in the books around him?* He shook his head in bewilderment.

"I tell you it's true, Tom. Montgomery County voted overwhelmingly to secede in the June 8th referendum, along with the rest of the state." Harold Gardner, Tom's attorney, leaned back in the chair across the room, crossed his legs, laid his arms in his lap, and sighed.

Tom pursed his lips and shook his head again. He'd worked so hard these past six years and now everything he'd accomplished and acquired would be lost in the wake of a war. And Clarksville was right in the thick of it! He took a pull on his cigar. "What happens next?"

Harold shook his head and worried at his lower lip. "Regiments are mustering. Three are forming right here in Clarksville. There's talk of nothing but the war everywhere you go. You must have heard it, even out here in your own little world."

Tom frowned and waved his hand absently. "Of course I've heard it, that's all anyone talks about when I'm in town. And when it does come to Tennessee's involvement in the war, everything I've worked for will be lost. Every...single...thing."

"You can't be sure of that. Your horses will be requisitioned for the most esteemed officers in the Confed..." Harold came to an abrupt halt, realizing Tom would never willingly condone his stock being taken for the Confederacy. "Oh."

Tom snorted. "You see my point. How could everything not be lost, Harold? My horses will be stolen for the Confederacy."

"Requisitioned," Harold rebutted quickly. "You will be paid for them."

Tom scoffed loudly. "No, Harold, I will not. Those loyal to the Cause may be reimbursed for them, perhaps, but not me. I was born a Yankee and even if I held slaves instead of freed, hired men, I'd still lose my prized studs and mares. And to what end? A war the South cannot possibly win."

It was Harold's turn to scoff. "You seem rather sure the South cannot win. On what do you base that assessment, Tom?"

"I base it on the sheer numbers of men and availability of materiel to fight a long war, Harold. The North has more of both."

"Why, this war won't last more than a few months," Harold corrected. "The South will whip those Yankees..."

Tom's head was shaking when he interrupted. "This war—when it comes—will not be as short as everyone believes. Although I've tried to ignore it, I do know what's going on around me. The South believes they'll beat down the Yankees in a few glorious months, perhaps even one huge battle, but that isn't going to happen. Neither side is going to back down, and it's going to be long and bloody."

"You are quite full of gloom and doom." Harold drew on his cigar, exhaled, and watched the smoke rise into the high rafters before he turned his attention back to Tom. "And what do you suggest to stop it? Let the Yankees take more and more control of what is ours? Let them continue to overburden us with taxes on *our* cotton and tobacco that lines their pockets instead of ours? Allow the federal government to tell our states what to do from hundreds of miles away? Let them stop slavery, when it was northern ships that brought the first slaves here in the first place, without a thought to how it will devastate our economy?"

"We shouldn't fight a war over it; I can damn well tell you that."

"And if it does come to war, Tom? Will you fight?"

"I'm thirty-nine years old, Harold, an old man by most standards, but if it comes to it, I'll fight."

"On which side?" the attorney challenged. "I know your blood, Tom. I know your family is from Boston, that your people are freed men, and that you've always been against slavery. But this war isn't just about slavery. You and I both know that. It's about everything I just spoke of—our rights as states to make our own decisions. Bein' overtaxed, the northern states benefiting from our profits and their realizing if they—allow—the South to secede, that windfall will disappear. And, of course, the North's pompous decision that the institution of slavery should be stopped *immediately*, without a care for how it will affect our people. What do they know? Our people know only us and what they do *right now*. They have no education and no idea how to take care of themselves. If slavery is done away with, they need *time* to be *taught* how to care for themselves and their families. And there's been no regard for the South economically. We need time to find a way to discontinue slavery—slowly—to replace it so the economic balance of our states isn't destroyed. So I ask you again, Tom, if war comes, what side will you fight for?"

Tom stared at his attorney and friend of five years—and could not answer.

***

To Arms! To Arms!

The Leaf Chronicle, Clarksville's paper, screamed daily. The men of Montgomery County flocked in huge numbers to one of three volunteer regiments they had to choose from, the 14th, the 49th or 50th.

Tom, in the library where he'd discussed what was happening with Harold only days before, slapped the newspaper and sighed. It was only a matter of time before they would be on his doorstep, taking what wasn't theirs, leaving him with his own choices to make. He'd told his friend Harold he'd fight, but hoped against hope he wouldn't have to, hoped *someone* was smart enough to figure it out *without* starting a war. But in a few short months there would be no choice left. Even amongst Tom's freed men there were rumblings of running away. Leaving all they knew to run for freedom up north. *But would that freedom be what they were looking for? Would the people there who railed against slavery receive them as easily as they shouted for their freedom when they were right on their doorsteps to take their jobs or live next to them?* Tom thought, no, but who was he? One man in a sea of millions who couldn't predict the future, but had a pretty good idea where it was going. Full blown war and not he nor anyone else could stop it now.

Rubbing his temple against the oncoming headache he heard horses coming up the drive. Tom swallowed and knew the time had come. He took a deep breath, stood up and went to greet the men coming to take everything he'd worked for. He met Nathaniel at the front door.

"I'll receive them, Nathaniel. I know why they're here and I might as well face it."

Nathaniel swallowed and frowned. "Yessir. I knows why they's comin', too. It's a sad day at Champion Farms, to be sure." He shook his head and walked away, his back a little more bent than it had been earlier this morning.

Feet stomped up the porch and Tom opened the door before the Confederate officer could knock.

"Good morning, gentlemen." Tom pasted a smile on his face, knowing it would, most likely, be the last one he'd have for a long time. "What may I do for you today?"

The officer pulled out a sheet of paper from his waist belt. "I'm Captain Walker. We're here to requisition horses for the Confederacy."

The man hadn't even formally addressed him as "sir" after the request, and Tom knew they intended to take everything—without compensation.

"I've been expecting you." Tom's insides churned like butter, *but what could he do?* He'd known this was coming; it was just a matter of when. Now he faced it as sure as he faced the new day.

He waved his hand toward the barns. "May I accompany you?"

The officer snapped his heels. "As you wish," he said, his tone condescending.

Tom stepped onto the porch and looked down on the twenty or so men waiting below, many of whom he recognized. He nodded and smiled, but they quickly looked away. He was a Union sympathizer, everyone in the county knew it and for them to acknowledge him with a smile or nod was *not* in their best interest, no matter whether they'd been friends, or not, in the past. They were headed toward war and in war you choose sides—and he'd chosen the wrong one.

Tom snorted, looked away, and followed Captain Walker toward the barns. They were met by Bull, whose face said everything Tom couldn't say. They would take his precious animals and leave him with nothing except a piece of worthless paper in their stead—*if* he even got that.

Captain Walker oversaw the *requisitioning* of Tom's horses. One by one his prized stallions, mares and geldings were handed off to waiting soldiers, the animals straining against their lead ropes, nickering their confusion at being led away by unfamiliar men. Satan's Pride, no longer the alpha, but still full of the pride he was named for, reared. The rope ripped through his handlers hands. The man screamed and dropped the line as the horse raced off across the open pasture into the woods. Tom grinned. *At least they wouldn't get Pride.*

Walker stomped up to Tom, scratched off something on a piece of paper and handed it to him. "Your receipt, minus the horse that just ran away. Submit it to the proper authorities for reimbursement." The man was as stiff as his well-recited words.

"Certainly," Tom responded, knowing everything he'd worked for these past ten years was being walked away without recompense. He swallowed hard, trying to keep his emotions in check. The last thing he wanted was for a disturbance to break out. His horses could be injured and that was something he would not abide. They were civilized men, gentlemen, for now, and, although war was about to come a-calling in a brutal way, there was no need for brutality right here and right now. Besides, *who would be the loser?* There was no question it would be him, and on a larger scale than just losing his precious animals. Much larger.

***

A sea of black faces stared up at Tom from below the porch where he stood, legs braced, arms clasped behind his back. "I imagine you're all wondering why I brought you together. The time has come to let you know exactly what's happening, where you stand in the midst of it, and what I plan to do."

Nathaniel and Bull, in front of the others, looked at each other, knowing on their faces.

"As you all know, our horses have been taken by the Confederacy. Only Satan's Pride escaped and is now hidden in the woods until such time as I retrieve him, thanks to Bull." He looked directly at his foreman. "The horse is as stubborn as any I've seen, but, thankfully, he's loyal to a fault—like my people," he said with as much of a grin as he could muster while he scanned their anxious faces. "Pride went to Bull as soon Bull found him in the woods."

Tom looked up at the sky and took a deep breath, trying to keep a rein on his racing emotions. Rolling his lips and exhaling, he looked back at the men and women who had been in his employ, some as many as six years. They were good people, loyal people, who would now be forced to make decisions on their own as to how to survive the coming war. Many, although freed by Tom, knew nothing more than Champion Farms. Many had been there their entire lives, and for them, freedom was both exciting—and frightening.

"Y'all know a war is coming. Regiments are mustering in Clarksville and across the country. And we're caught right in the middle. Although you've been given your freedom, you're in an area where that freedom won't be recognized once you leave these premises. I've made my decision as to where I'm going. Now you must make yours."

"Sah?" Nathaniel's voice cracked.

"You must run. If you stay here you'll be forced back into slavery. You've known freedom and to keep that freedom you must go north." He looked directly at Bull. "You must lead them."

Bull nodded.

Tom's eyes left his foreman and he addressed them all again. "You must go, right now, and gather whatever you can carry." Nervous voices twittered throughout those gathered before they quieted to hear the rest of what Tom had to say. "You should leave tonight when the moon is full and head north into Kentucky. From there you can go wherever you want, as long as it's north. You must go where you can remain free with your families—and that's north."

"Where you goin', sah?" Nathaniel asked.

Tom pursed his lips, his emotions threatening to embarrass him. His sisters, now married with families of their own, had moved in with their mother when their husbands joined up with the Fourteenth Tennessee Volunteers. The sisters were considered staunch confederates, and would be safe, even looked after, among the remaining population of Clarksville. Tom had considered moving in with them, but decided his presence would be detrimental because of his known sympathies.

He looked out over the sea of anxious faces, still waiting for an answer to where he would go. His shoulders slumped and with a deep sigh said, "North, as well."

As simple as that, the life he'd worked to create for over these last years was done. He turned, went into the house, closed the door behind him, and went to his room to pack. He had a long ride ahead of him and planned to leave long before the sun rose.

Chapter Seven

Tom didn't intend to go near Clarksville, the town openly mustering for the southern cause. He'd gone into town last week to see his family, and had wound up saying his final goodbyes after he'd been openly chastised for "bein' a Yankee," the townspeople more than hostile.

After days of pondering the safest thing to do for himself, his sisters and his mother, he'd decided to make his way to Cleveland, Ohio, and his older brother, Ralph. He'd catch the Memphis-Clarksville-Louisville train in Kentucky—while he still could—and head for Cleveland.

He'd spent hours after Captain Walker and his men departed trying to decide whether or not to enlist in Cleveland. Once he decided *to* enlist, he chose the Eighth Ohio Volunteers because of a wire he'd received only days prior from his twenty-four year old nephew, Gerald. The Eighth Ohio Volunteer Infantry was mustering in Cleveland and Gerald wanted Tom to join up with him. Tom had balked. *Why would he enlist anywhere but with a cavalry unit? Pride would be as good a cavalry horse as there could be, despite his age.* But young Gerald had explained in the wire the cavalry ranks were already full. *He'd waited too long to decide.*

Younger by almost fifteen years, Gerald had enough enthusiasm for both of them for what lie ahead, and Tom decided if he was going to join up, even if it *was* with an infantry unit, he preferred it to be with kin in a state that was wholly committed to saving the Union.

He had to get to State Line first, thirty miles over the Kentucky border, to board the MCL and head north. And in State Line he would do one of the most painful things he would ever do—leave Satan's Pride behind to join an infantry unit and fight a war he didn't want to fight.

***

Tom stood next to Satan's Pride, his hand resting on the horse's back. The animal munched hungrily on grain from a trough in front of a boarding stable in State Line where Tom had the horse tied following their trip through the back woods.

"How much do you want for him, Mister?" the stable owner asked with a gleam of appreciation in his eyes.

Tom could barely speak, let alone think of how much money to take for his best friend of the last twenty four years. All Tom could think of was Judas taking thirty pieces of silver for his betrayal of Jesus.

"Mister? How much? He's a fine animal, but he *is* old."

Tom didn't want much. All he wanted was for Satan's Pride to be happy in his remaining years.

"I can tell he's old by his teeth," the man said to prove he knew his business, before adding, "but he's in fine shape otherwise. He'd be good to pull a wagon or a rental."

Tom's mind was spinning. *This horse had won thousands of dollars in hundreds of races, and fathered dozens of valuable foals, and he would be reduced to pulling a wagon or becoming a rental horse?* Tom wanted to jerk Pride's head up, jump on his back and ride away—anywhere—to make a new life with his best friend away from the insanity engulfing the country.

But he couldn't. He'd made a commitment to Gerald and he couldn't just ride away and live off the land somewhere. He was too old to start over with nothing but a horse. He was, at least, a realist, no matter how much it pained him.

Tom swallowed and looked into the expectant eyes of the stable owner. "What can you give me?"

The owner took a deep breath and raised his forefinger. "Just a minute." He hurried into his office, returning a few minutes later.

"I kin give you thirty dollars."

"Thirty dollars!" Tom shouted. "Do you have any idea how valuable this animal is? I could get ten times that...."

Tom stopped, unwilling to disclose exactly how valuable Pride was. He wanted the horse to be happy in his new life without the strings of his former life attached.

The owner cocked his head and raised his eyebrows. "No, I do not know his value. What I do know is that I kin give you thirty dollars for him."

Tom saw something pass in the face of the man and knew he was holding back. "Fifty, no less."

"Fifty dollars! Why, that's highway robbery."

"Take it or leave it. I can go down the street to the next stable and see what he's willing to pay."

"Aw, old man Granger won't give you any more than I can."

But Tom saw the gleam in the man's eyes and knew he wanted Pride. Badly. "Fifty dollars and no less."

The man stomped around a minute, rubbed his chin, and mumbled to himself. He finally stepped beside Tom, his back straight, his lips pinched as though the words would suck every breath out of him, and said, "All right, mister, you got a deal. Fifty dollars. But you gotta include the saddle and bridle."

The saddle alone was worth a hundred dollars, one of the finest made in Montgomery County. He reminded himself again he didn't care about anything but making sure Pride was well taken care of. And, for now, he didn't need money. Regardless he'd given Bull, Nathaniel and all his people a good sum of cash to start their journey, Tom had plenty left to reach Cleveland, but he still intended to be frugal with it.

Thinking of Bull and Nathaniel, Tom remembered the night he'd said goodbye to the people who had been trusted employees and friends. They'd gotten their belongings as Tom had instructed, gathered at the bottom of the stairs that same night, and said their goodbyes. Tom's heart broke a little each time he shook one of their hands or hugged them for the last time before he sent them on their way. Bull and Nathaniel had been as hard to say goodbye to as any family member might have been, their friendship and loyalty etched into his heart and soul. Nathaniel had stood straight and tall while he shook Tom's hand, but Tom saw the man's inner turmoil and wished he could just shout out that it wasn't true. But it was true. Tom recalled how the frail man's tears rolled down over his cheeks as he and Tom said their last goodbyes.

The farewells said, Tom had stood on the top step, unable to move, and watched them disappear into the dark line of the trees and out of his life forever.

"Mister? You listening to me?" The stable owner's voice pulled Tom back to the present.

He took a deep breath. "I agree to fifty dollars on one condition."

The man lifted his brow. "I'm listenin'."

"This horse has known no hard labor and I want your solemn promise it won't start now. He's one of the finest stud horses in Montgomery County, Tennessee, and, even though he's older, he throws exceptional foals. So, pulling a wagon or buggy is fine, even renting him to the occasional traveler, but he is *not* to become a work horse. If you agree and break our deal, I'll find out, come back and take it out of your hide." Tom leaned in to let the man know he meant business.

The owner rubbed his chin again. He thought a moment before he thrust out his hand. "Deal."

Tom shook the man's hand, his sorrow threatening to overwhelm him. "Give me a minute, will you."

"Sure, mister. Take as much as you like. I'll get your money."

Tom thought his heart would shatter. There'd been only one other time he felt so bereft and he'd hoped never to feel that much pain ever again; but there was no hope for it. He couldn't take Pride where he was going.

He pulled Pride's head from the trough and rubbed his hand over the horse's dark head, now spotted with white dots that belied his age. "I'm so sorry, Pride. If there were anything else I could do, I would do it, but I have no choice. So many things are happening that you can't understand—hell *I* can't understand them. You can't go on the train and you're, well, there's no delicate way to say it, but you're too old to make the journey overland. I've made a deal with Mr. Jones and he's promised to take good care of you. I have to believe him because, again, there's no choice." He closed his eyes, laid his cheek against the length of Pride's face and rubbed the horse's neck. "I'm so sorry, boy."

"Here's your money." Tom opened his eyes. The stable owner stood with his hand out and a wad of money in his fist. *Thirty pieces of silver....*

Tom swallowed one last time and stepped away from his beloved horse. "Goodbye, Pride."

Tom took the money as Satan's Pride dropped his nose back into the trough, unconcerned and not realizing his life would be completely different after today.

"I mean it, you be good to this horse or I'll find out and take it out of your hide." His finger wagged at the stable owner.

"I believe you, mister. I believe you. I'll pamper him like a fine racer."

Tom's chin came up. "Why did you say that?"

"No cause, just that I plan to use him for stud, like you said, and see if I can't make my money back on fees and the foals he throws."

Tom nodded and relaxed. "You'll do that—and more. Just tell them who he really is."

"And who might that be, Mister?" The owner's head cocked with anticipation.

"One of the best damned horses that ever ran a Tennessee race track, that's who."

***

Tom stared out the train window at the changing scenery. Open land and rolling hills had become farms and now the train was chugging into a city. It wouldn't be long until he disembarked and everything would change—yet again. Throughout the trip he'd reflected on his life, wondering if he could have done anything differently, and he always came back to the same thing. Abby. If only she'd given in to him and they'd married, he would have gained everything he ever wanted. The woman he loved, his horses, status, and a family of his own, which he would never have now.

Being realistic, though, Tom knew he would still have lost everything because of the war, like everyone else in Clarksville, despite where their sympathies rested, but he would have had a reason *not* to go off and fight—a family. He envied other men their children, the boys they molded after themselves and girls who became women like their mothers. Instead, the one person who could have given him all that had turned him away and left him bitter, always searching for whatever filled the void she'd left.

He let his head fall back against the seat and forced Abby from his mind. Instead, the day he said goodbye to Pride and boarded the train for his new destiny flashed into his mind. The lump in his throat almost made him gag. He'd left his best friend behind—a friend who had been with him since he was fifteen years old, loyal and more faithful and giving than any person, and constant in his affection—until the day Tom said goodbye.

The train screeched to a halt and Tom's pulse raced like it used to from atop his horses' backs as they neared the finish line. But here, in truth, was just the beginning—the beginning of the war for him. He'd lost everything precious to him, his horses, his property, his status in a town he'd grown up in, but now he would begin this new journey as a soldier, fighting a war he knew would tear the country apart and last much longer than the few months everyone predicted.

Stiff from the long train ride, he stood up, grabbed his bag, started down the aisle, and out the door. He wasn't sure if he'd even recognize Gerald. It had been over ten years since Ralph and his family visited Clarksville. Gerald had been a lanky, cocksure youth, his only intent during their two-month visit to woo the girls in Clarksville whenever they went into town.

Tom scanned the platform, searching for a tall, skinny, dark-haired boy. Instead, a tall, dark-haired, muscled man with a well-groomed beard and mustache approached him.

"Uncle Tom! Uncle Tom!" The man yelled and waved.

Tom's face scrunched with the realization that this handsome, powerful looking *man* was his nephew. "Gerald?"

"It's me all right, Uncle Tom." He stepped back and swept his hands up and down the length of his body. "I grew up." He was grinning and Tom hoped the boy's cocksure attitude hadn't grown up with him.

Gerald wrapped himself around his uncle and hugged him so tight Tom coughed.

"I'm glad to see you, too, Gerald, but you don't have to crush me."

Gerald stepped back, reddening at his overzealous greeting. He shoved his hands into his pockets and once again looked like the boy Tom remembered. Tom slapped his nephew's shoulder. "I'm glad to see you Gerald. More than you know."

A fresh grin covered the young man's face and he stepped back. "Mother and Father are anxious to see you, too."

Tom looked around. "So anxious they couldn't even meet me?" Tom was annoyed his older brother and his wife couldn't force his arrival into their busy schedule.

Gerald frowned. "Mother had a committee meeting she couldn't miss and insisted Father accompany her. She said I could represent all of us." He paused, thought a moment then added. "Mother is a bit..." he searched for the word then said, "strong-willed for, well, for a woman. Don't get me wrong, I love Mother, but she dominates Father and he lets her." He paused again before his back straightened and he added, "A woman will never dominate me like that. Never. I'll stay a bachelor all my life before I let that happen, just like you."

Tom looked at Gerald and realized he likely had more in common with his young nephew than his brother. From what Tom remembered of his sister-in-law and Gerald's description of his parents, this trip could well give Tom a glimpse of how life might have been with Abby. A life that wouldn't have been much to Tom's liking.

Chapter Eight

Tom walked across the elaborate entry hall toward the parlor, hand extended, his brother standing just outside the ornate double doors. "Ralph." In his quick assessment of the house, Tom took in the large glass chandelier, sparkling in the afternoon sunlight, numerous paintings of sweeping landscapes and fields of flowers that hung on heavily papered walls, and two flawless, white marble statues of women in various stages of dress, one on each side of the doors. It was excessive extravagance as far as Tom was concerned.

"Tom!" Ralph met Tom with open arms and a hug. "I'm so glad you're here!" He slapped Tom's back, his voice echoing through the entry hall. "How was your trip? And tell me, how are mother and the girls?" he asked when he drew back.

"They're fine and will be fine. They send their love."

Ralph's face grew hard. "And why, may I dare ask, did you leave them, Tom? I should think they would need a man's protection since Anne and Mary's husbands are fighting with the Rebs."

Tom felt the stab of the insinuation and kept his temper. It was too soon for bad feelings to flare. "The girls' are staunch Confederates, Ralph. Regardless mother is not, she's the mother-in-law of two men fighting for the Confederacy and is still well-respected in Clarksville. I am not. It's as simple as that. They'll be safer without me than if I'm there to draw unwanted attention to them."

Ralph thought a moment. His back eased and he smiled again. "Well then, we're glad you're here!" he boomed again.

"I'm glad to be here. I just wish it were under different circumstances."

"Ah, yes, me too, but we're in a tough situation with the southern states and their insurrection. It must have been difficult for you, living in a state that has seceded from this great nation, listening to all their drivel about *why* they were seceding."

Tom swallowed. The last thing he wanted upon his arrival was to get into a political debate. He knew well what the basis of the southern states' *insurrection* was. He recalled his conversation with his attorney only weeks ago, but he was in no mood to enlighten his brother. Regardless he didn't stand with the South's opposition, he completely understood their discontent.

"Come, Tom, Margaret is waiting." Ralph ushered his brother into the parlor like a conquering king into his castle. Waiting across the carpeted room stood Ralph's wife. She was a stunning beauty when he first met her when Tom, his parents, and his sisters went to Ohio for a two month visit to attend hers and Ralph's wedding when Tom was a youth, and Tom recalled her effect on him even then. From across the room it looked like Margaret had changed little. Blond hair, slightly streaked with gray, was drawn up in the typical fashion, exposing creamy, slender shoulders. Her rose-colored lips, turned up in what appeared to be a forced smile, were in perfect symmetry to her tiny ears, high, powdered, cheekbones, and small nose. However, as Tom drew closer, lines from her eyes to her hairline came into view, with more creases around her chin and upper lip. There were dark circles under her still blue eyes, unsuccessfully hidden with powder, all of which belied her forty years.

"Margaret." He strode across the room to where she waited in front of a long, white couch. Her back stiffened and her lips grew tight, but she smiled. She watched him like a lioness watching her prey, more anxious than welcoming, and in her demeanor and physical attributes, the face of another woman flashed into Tom's mind before he willed it away.

"Tom." Her voice was cold, controlled and reminded him of the statues outside the door, stiff and unyielding.

Margaret raised her hand for Tom to take and he did so with great formality. "Hello, Margaret. It's good to see you again."

She curtsied ever so slightly, a slight smile on her face.

"It's good to see you, too, Tom." She withdrew her hand after Tom kissed the back of it in welcome, and she waved it around the room. "Welcome to our home." Her eyes sparkled, inviting him to take in all the wealth they had acquired.

"I see you've gotten reacquainted!" Gerald's voice echoed through the room. "The carriage has been put up, I saw to it myself."

"Excellent." Ralph turned to Tom. "It's difficult to find good help these days," he lamented.

An arrow of regret pierced Tom's heart when thoughts of Bull and Nathaniel popped into his mind.

"You must watch them constantly," Ralph continued, "or you'll find them stealing you blind or out in the stables gambling when they should be working," his brother finished in a harsh tone.

Tom furrowed a brow and Ralph continued with a wave of his hand. "I was forced to fire two of my men last week. I caught them in the stables playing cards when they were supposed to be tending to my needs. They were so involved in their game they didn't even hear me approach. I'd been calling for a carriage for thirty minutes—thirty minutes—before I ventured out to find my groom and stable boy so deeply enmeshed in their card game they completely disregarded their duties. Margaret and I were already late for an appointment and, well…"

"I drove the carriage since father had just fired the driver," Gerald finished with a flourish.

Margaret nodded, her back stiff as a nail, her hands clasped tight in front of her. "It was most humiliating on our arrival explaining why our *son* was driving the carriage!"

Tom stood transfixed, watching her face and expressions until a slight, red-haired girl of perhaps twenty entered the room carrying a tray laden with tea and sweet treats.

Margaret waved her hand at a table beside the couch. "Put it over there, Glynis, and pour us each a cup."

The girl walked toward the table with the heavy tray. Her foot caught on the carpet and she mis-stepped. The cups and plates clattered loudly before she gained her balance and set the tray down. The ceramic teapot clattered as the girl poured three cups of tea then, with a shaking hand, set them on a long table between the couch and two matching, oversized chairs. Bending at the waist, she looked up at Margaret, who waved her away with an angry frown.

Tom felt as though he'd stepped back in time. The girl backed away and hurried from the room.

"As Ralph said," Margaret's shrill voice drew Tom back to the present. She waved her hand back and forth, encompassing where the maid had just vacated the room. "It is impossible to find good help these days. That girl is as clumsy as a new foal, but we can't seem to find any better. Believe me, if we could, I would remove her from this house immediately." Margaret waved a second time, again throwing Tom back to the day he'd asked for Abby's hand, recalling how Abby and her father had chastised their slave girl, Martha, for slopping wine.

Dinner that night was a test of Tom's will not to run out the door screaming. After being informed they "dressed" for dinner, he'd gone to his room and pulled out one of the few shirts he had with him that could pass for dress attire.

Stepping into the dining room, which could have been any one of the opulent plantation homes in Tennessee, he felt their immediate disdain as though it were a living thing.

Tom slid into a chair in the middle of the over-sized table, his sister-in-law on his right.

"Did you hear about the Reed's?" Margaret asked her husband as he assisted her into her seat following a dismissive look toward Tom and his not so dress attire.

"I did." Ralph slid her chair in and strode to the one at the opposite end of the ten person table. "It seems Charles has been stepping out on Gloria."

Gerald strode into the room, clapped his hands together then rubbed them in anticipation. "What is tonight's gossip?" Tom was unable to decide if his nephew *really* wanted to know or mocked his parents.

"Oh, Gerald, why must you be such a boor?" Margaret batted her eyes coyly at Tom, seemingly appalled her true nature might be revealed by, all of people, her son. "I just asked if your father knew what was going on with the Reeds."

"Mother, it is *how* you ask, with that gleam in your eyes like a lioness ready to pounce on her prey."

Tom almost spit out the water he was sipping at the comparison Gerald had made of his mother—the same he'd made only a few hours earlier. *Perhaps he wasn't so far off.*

"How unkind of you, Gerald!" His mother had the decency to blush and Tom knew he'd met a kindred spirit in his young nephew.

Gerald pulled out his chair across from Tom, plopped into it, and said, "Please tell us, mother. We await your news with baited breath." His eyes gleamed and Tom raised his napkin above his lips to hide his grin.

Margaret lifted her chin, straightened her shoulders, and shifted uneasily in her chair. She continued to blush and her lips rolled in and out in her indecision. "I don't believe I shall."

"Gerald, be kind to your mother."

Gerald's face contorted, his eyes pinched, and his head went back and forth. "As kind as mother is to everyone else?" he challenged.

Margaret grabbed the napkin from her lap and held it to her face. "Gerald, why do you attack me tonight? We have a guest and you're being extremely boorish!" She sniffed and wiped at her eyes and nose.

Tom sat, unable to say a word. He wanted to shake his head at his brother and his wife, and applaud his nephew, but he did neither and remained mute.

After several moments of strained silence, and Margaret staring at her son with venom in her eyes, Ralph finally asked, "Tom, how long will you stay?"

Tom swallowed. He *wanted* to say as short a time as possible, but didn't want to be rude, although rude didn't seem to matter at this table. "I haven't really thought about it, but not overlong. We should join up as soon as possible."

"Why? There's no need," Ralph said. "You may stay with us as long as you like."

Tom glanced at Margaret who pasted a smile on her face. "Of course, Tom, stay as long as you like."

"Oh, I'm sure Uncle Tom wants to enlist as soon as possible." Gerald stared, wide-eyed at Tom. "Don't you?"

Saved by a most perceptive nephew! "It depends upon how quickly Gerald plans to enlist. I certainly don't intend to enlist without him."

"I've only been waiting for your arrival. Tomorrow or the next day at the very latest," Gerald said. "We're running out of time to join the Eighth here at Camp Taylor. Word is they're planning to move out in a few days for Camp Dennison in Cincinnati and their ranks are filling up fast, so we don't have much time. Actually, Uncle, the sooner we enlist, the better," Tom's nephew said with a knowing grin.

Tom almost sighed in relief. Only one or two days and he would be free of his brother and his wife. Tom's heart started to pound. He wanted to be away from here, away from Margaret as soon as possible, because in her he saw much more than he wanted to see, a woman who reminded him of too many things he wanted to forget. As he'd surmised would happen, he was glimpsing what his life *might* have been like with Abby—and he didn't like what he saw, at all.

He wouldn't tarry overlong. Tomorrow or the next day he and Gerald would join the Eighth Ohio Volunteer Infantry.

Not soon enough as far as he was concerned!

Chapter Nine

Tom was restless. He had been since his head hit the pillow. His mind rolled with thoughts of Abby and he shuddered more than once at how his life *might* have turned out if they'd married. As much as he'd loved her and for so long mourned her departure, over the years he had, at least, recognized it was a blessing she *had* walked away. All he saw when he looked at Ralph was a sad image of who he might have become, and the image sickened him.

In his restlessness Tom thought about his friend, Sam, and the life he'd built with Ellie and the children that had come from their marriage. Of course, their lives hadn't been conflict free. Ellie was a fine, strong woman, but she and Sam had their differences. When Sam's tobacco plantation failed a few years after their marriage, Ellie insisted they leave Clarksville and return to her home state of Missouri. Over the years they'd made a new life for themselves—but they did it *together*. In his unsettled mind, Tom wondered how his friend was doing now that the war had come. Tom hadn't received a letter from Sam in well over a year now, and that unsettled him more than his thoughts of Abby. Sam and Ellie were right on the border between Missouri and Kansas where hostilities had run hot with thievery and murder for years, and he feared something had happened.

Tired of not getting any relief from his unanswerable questions, Tom got out of bed and pulled on one of Ralph's robes, it and a pair of slippers left for him at the bottom of the bed for his use. He tightened the belt, slid on the slippers, and headed down the dark hall. Maybe a good, long talk with the horses would clear his mind of Abby and Sam and all his unanswered questions.

In the quiet darkness Tom went down stairs that creaked so loudly he was sure everyone in the house would waken. He stepped out the back door into the cool, clean air. He took a deep breath and thrust his hands into the robe's pockets. Walking in the moonlight toward the stables he admired the stars and constellations illuminating the black, cloudless sky.

Tom stopped at the double barn doors and slid one open just enough to step inside. He sucked in a deep breath of the interior. The smell of hay and horse, manure and leather, swept through him and, for the first time since leaving Champion Farms, he felt at home. *How he missed the life he had carved out for himself! How he missed his horses and his people, all gone because of this damnable war!* he wanted to scream. Instead he took another deep breath and stepped deeper into the long barn. Unable to see much in the murky darkness, he searched for, and finally found, a lantern on a peg beside the door. Fumbling for matches, he found them in a cup nailed to the wall beside the lantern, lit one, and the room sparked to life.

It looked to Tom like there were at least twenty stalls from where horses' heads protruded in curiosity on opposite sides of the aisle.

He raised the lantern to see better. "Hello, boys and girls. How is everyone tonight?" He went to the first stall where a tall bay with a white star on its head eyed him.

"And who are you?" In answer the animal thrust its head out for a nose rub. Tom noticed a small plaque to the right of the stall that said "Star of the North."

"Hmmm, nice to meet you, Star." He gave the horse several pats and strolled to the next stall where a dapple gray that reminded him of Gray Ghost moved anxiously inside. He glanced at the plaque to the right and said, "Nice to meet you, Lord Buckingham."

He headed down the aisle of stalls and horses, stopping to check names and rub noses, but stopped in his tracks when he realized someone was behind him.

"You haven't met our pride and joy yet, Tom. I must introduce you."

Margaret's robe billowed out around her as she breezed past him to the rear of the stable. She lit another lantern, hung it on a peg on the back wall then turned and rubbed the solid white nose that stuck out of the farthest stall. She beckoned Tom to join her.

"This is Beauty, our most prolific brood mare. She's thrown more prize-winning foals than all our other mares combined," Margaret announced with a wide, genuine, smile.

Tom couldn't help sliding up to the snow white mare and laying his left hand on her nose. He eyed her critically, noting the pink eyes. Pink eyes always unsettled him and caused him to believe she was an albino. Whatever she was she was tall, with fine lines. There wasn't a mark on her to detract from her whiteness. Her mane and tail were long, and white, and carefully tended, without a burr or knot in them. Her coat glistened in the lamplight and Tom had to admit she *was* a beauty. And high spirited, he realized when he stopped rubbing her nose and she thrust her head at him for more.

"She doesn't like it when you withdraw," Margaret cooed. "Once she gets what she wants—she wants more."

Margaret's tone and insinuation unsettled Tom. He drew farther away, but Margaret grabbed his hand and laid it back on the horse's nose. The mare quieted instantly as Margaret slid his hand up and down. Tom swallowed and wondered at his sister-in-law's game.

"There you go. See how calm she is, now that's she's gotten what she wants?" Margaret's voice cut through Tom and he backed away.

"Thank you for introducing me to Beauty, but I should go back inside now. Good night, Margaret." He turned and started from the barn, but stopped abruptly when she laughed.

"Oh you poor man!" she purred, her voice deep. "You've been bitten, haven't you?" She paused before adding, "And I *don't* mean by a horse!"

He whirled on her, his heart hammering, but it wasn't Margaret standing there. It was Abby, laughing at him because, after all these years she still held him emotionally captive and could so easily injure him.

He strode toward her, no idea what he intended to do once he reached her. His heart beat like an Indian kettle drum, louder and louder in his ears the closer he got until he stood only inches in front of her. His chest rose and fell in his anger. He stared at her face, Abby's face, until he couldn't look anymore. He put his large hands on her slender shoulders and shook her—hard.

"Why can't you go away and leave me alone? Why must you continue to torment me?"

The woman threw her head back and laughed again—harder—until his arms slipped around her back and his lips crashed down on hers.

She mewled like a cat as his kiss deepened and he pulled her closer. Her arms snaked around his shoulders and she melted into him. He forgot where he was, who he was, and who *she* was. All he felt was the kiss, and what he'd felt so long ago with the woman who'd betrayed him. Abby.

They stood in the middle of the stables for long minutes, entwined like lovers, until clarity hit Tom like a lightning bolt striking in the middle of a desert. He shoved Margaret away like a flaming torch.

"Oh my God! Forgive me, Margaret. I'm so sorry! I didn't…I don't know what happened…."

"I do," she cooed with a knowing smile as she laid her palm on his cheek.

He shoved her hand away.

She laughed again, deep and throaty. "You've been in love and lost her." It wasn't a question. She stepped closer. "I *was* her." She tilted her head ever so slightly and smiled invitingly. "I'll *be* her—any time you want me to."

Tom swallowed and grabbed her by the shoulders for a second time. He looked deep into her eyes and saw the same kind of blankness he'd seen behind Abby's eyes the day she said goodbye. His mind and heart warred. He wanted to taste the sweetness of this woman's lips again, but knew the consequences his actions might bring.

She smiled knowingly, her eyes sparkling with continued invitation. In that moment of clarity he shoved her away, shook his head to clear his mind, and backed two steps away to *keep* that clarity.

"Her name was Abby and she shattered my heart when she left me. Apparently, as hard as I've tried and like to think I've succeeded, I've never gotten over it—or her. I'm so sorry, Margaret."

Margaret shrugged. Her lips turned up again and she became even bolder. She lifted a delicate brow. "I can help you forget her," she whispered.

Tom stepped farther away. "No! I would never.... Not intentionally...."

"You just did," she interrupted, her eyes still sparkling with invitation.

Fear streaked up Tom's back. *If she told her brother what he'd already done...."*

Margaret smiled knowingly. She was gaining the upper hand and she knew it.

"Margaret," Tom began. He wiped his lips, trying to wipe away the taste of her and regain control. "I have no intention of doing any more than I've already done. I was not myself a few minutes ago—and for that you have my sincerest apology."

"I don't want your damned apology!" she exploded. "I want you to *do just what you did* a few minutes ago, again and again."

"I would never..."

"Save your excuses!" she interrupted. She squared her shoulders, raised her chin, and stepped toward him. "You wanted me. I don't care who you *thought* I was. *You wanted me*! Well, here I am, for the taking. Just reach out, touch me, and I'm yours."

She lifted her arms to display all of her through the clinging robe.

Tom couldn't stop himself from staring at the curves beckoning him.

She grabbed his hand for the second time that night, slid it inside her robe, and over the swell of her breast.

Tom thought he would come undone. It had been so long since he'd sated himself with a woman, none of whom had meant a damn to him after Abby. Warmth surged through him in a way he hadn't felt in too many years to remember. Every nerve ending in his body tingled with anticipation, and for a moment, he almost gave in to his baser needs.

His emotions obvious, Margaret continued her assault. "Your brother and I have been married a very long time, Tom. Things change and, with him being so much older than me, let's just say he's not the man he used to be."

"I don't want to hear about you and my brother!" he snarled. "Or your marriage. What you want isn't right and I'll have no part of it."

During his defense against her invitation, he'd completely forgotten where his hand rested until her hand slid over his, wrapped his fingers around her breast, and kneaded its softness. He sucked in a deep breath. His blood thickened and he felt himself harden.

Her knowing smile deepened. "No one will know, Tom."

Again, he almost gave into his baser needs before he reined himself in. He closed his eyes and shook his head, fast and hard. *This was another man's wife. His brother's wife! He wouldn't dream of cuckolding his brother with his wife!*

He jumped away from her. "Absolutely not! I made a huge mistake a few minutes ago and I'll not knowingly do so again. I pray you don't tell Ralph what happened here and cause pain for all of us. It was a mistake. One I've apologized for and never intend to make a second time. I'll be gone first thing in the morning. Good night, Margaret."

He spun on his heel and almost ran for the doors. Margaret's angry taunts followed him all the way out.

Chapter Ten

Before the sun rose, Tom was up and ready to leave. What little he had was packed and sitting beside the door waiting for Gerald to awaken so they could take their leave and be on their way.

It was barely nine o'clock when the door to his nephew's room finally opened and Gerald met him in the hallway.

"Gerald! Good morning," he said.

Gerald took a startled step backward before he flashed a surprised smile at Tom. "Good morning back, Uncle!" He raised his brows. "You're up early? I'd have thought you'd languish in bed until noon after your long trip."

Tom wished he *could* have stayed abed, but the events of last night changed that. All he wanted was to be away from here, but most especially, he wanted to be away from Margaret. "I couldn't sleep. Just anxious to get going, I guess."

Gerald slapped him on the shoulder. "Then I say we break our fast and get on our way. What do you say?"

"I say that sounds like a great idea." Now all he had to do was make it through breakfast without Margaret bringing the house down on him.

***

"You're leaving already? But you just got here." Ralph's tone was like fingernails scratching up and down a blackboard.

"Well," Tom began, "the more I thought on what Gerald said last night about how quickly the ranks of the Eighth are filling, I thought it prudent not to waste a minute before enlisting. If we wait too long, there may not be room for us."

Ralph's laughter thundered throughout the dining room. "There's a war on, Tom. They'll take men who want to enlist as long as they want to enlist."

"I don't want to take any chances." Tom chanced a look at Margaret, sitting at the far end of the table, her chest rising and falling with restrained anger. Although he didn't know her well, he knew her kind well enough, and knew she was ready to explode like a geyser from the depths of the earth.

Gerald came to his rescue—again. "Father, I've told you how full the ranks are already. The regiment probably has a set number and once they reach that number they'll stop recruiting and head to Cincinnati for training. Tom is just being cautious about getting in, and I agree."

"I think you're both rushing into it. If you wait long enough the war will already be over."

Gerald jumped to his feet. "I don't want the war to be over!" he shouted. "And I don't want to wait for other men to fight whatever war there is while I do nothing, in the hope it will *be* over! I'm sure Uncle Tom feels the same way."

Gerald looked at Tom, whose heart was thundering in his chest, as much from his being put on the spot as wanting nothing more than to finish this discussion and be on his way. He nodded his head. "I'm afraid I agree with Gerald, Ralph. The sooner we enlist, the better off we'll be. Nor will the war already be over if we wait as you suggest."

With a loud slap of her palms on the table Margaret jumped to her feet.

Tom's heart stopped beating and he thought he'd swallow it as he waited for her to speak. Everyone waited in silence for whatever Margaret was going to say.

She eyed the three men like the cat Tom and Gerald had likened her to, deciding which prey to pounce upon first.

Tom's heart beat wildly as he waited. He swallowed several times to keep from screaming out an explanation of what had happened before she could.

Her eyes went from her husband to Gerald and finally to Tom, where they stopped and held.

Tom wished he was invisible so he could run away before she exposed him in front of his brother and nephew.

She stared at Tom then Gerald again before she sucked in a deep breath, held it and released it. "I think you're both foolish, running off to war," she finally said.

Tom breathed again. *A reprieve.*

"This…war…" she raised her hand and waved it in the air as though speaking of something inconsequential or batting at a gnat. "This war should be fought by *young* men." She looked directly at Tom.

"Well, *I'm* certainly not too old," Gerald announced. "And Uncle Tom isn't too old, either!"

Tom blessed his nephew again for the continued distraction.

"He's not even forty and men older than him are flocking to enlist." Gerald's head snapped up then down like he'd made the most profound statement ever.

Margaret stood like one of the statues outside the parlor door, but beneath he saw the bubbling liquid about to explode from its cauldron.

"Let me put this another way, Gerald. I've indulged you in your whim to enlist, but now it's time to stop this war playing."

"Indulged me! War playing!" Gerald's palms slapped the table like his mother's had moments ago. "I'm a grown man mother, not a snot-nosed child and I don't need to be *indulged* by anyone—least of all, not my mother! And this is not war *playing*! This is a real war where real men will be killed!" His eyes flashed with anger.

Margaret cleared her throat, raised her chin and shook her head before she straightened her shoulders and took in another deep breath. She licked her lips. "I want to clarify something…."

Tom steeled himself for the hammer that was about to come down.

"I don't hold with this war. I think you're both being foolish rushing off to fight for a cause that doesn't affect you…"

"Doesn't affect us!" Gerald interrupted again with a snort. "This nation is being torn in half, Mother. How can it not affect us? This is our home and whatever happens to the nation will affect us *and* our future."

He looked at Tom, waiting for his confirmation as to why they should fight.

Tom frowned and sighed. "I know why this war is being fought better than most, having lived in a state in 'insurrection.' I have no real desire to fight, but I won't let other men go off to do what must be done, either. I also don't believe, as Ralph believes, that if we wait the war will be over quickly. I've seen the boot heel the North has put on the South and I believe this war will not be short like everyone *wants* to believe. Once we are engaged, it will be long—and bloody."

Silence hung like a shroud in the room. Tom knew those in the North believed southerners to be pompous, overdressed, Beau Brummels who didn't know how to fight except in prearranged, gentlemanly duels. On the contrary, Tom knew them to be tough fighters, who could ride for hours and would fight for what they believed until their last breath. And that was exactly what Tom expected them *to* do. The South was fighting for their way of life, which would drag this war out for years until they ran out of men to fight it with.

Ralph stood up and cleared his throat. He opened his mouth to speak, but closed it and exhaled heavily, instead. He stood in silence a moment before he finally said, "If this family is any indication of what is happening throughout the nation, I fear Tom may be right. What if he'd chosen to fight for the South?" Ralph asked. He looked at Gerald. "You could well meet him on the field of battle." He swallowed. "Oh my Lord," he whispered. "Our brothers-in-laws are fighting for the South. Either of you could well come up against them in battle." Ralph scrubbed his face and sighed. "I hope and pray you're not right, Tom, but given you may be, I wish you would both reconsider, knowing this war could be long and, as you said Tom, bloody." He looked directly at Gerald then at Tom. "I don't want my son's blood, or my brother's, to soak the earth before it's over."

For the first time in too many years, Tom saw his brother as *a big brother,* who cared about what happened to his little brother, and for a split second Tom considered abandoning his quest to enlist—wondering, in truth, why he felt so compelled to do so? *Was he, in reality, still running from Abby? Or was it because the South had taken everything he had—Champion Farms, his horses, the life he'd worked so long and hard to build? Or did it come down to blood? Was it* because *of his northern blood he had to fight for the preservation of the Union, even though he'd lived in the south most of his life? Or was it just plain duty?* His mind whirled for several moments, trying to decide *why* he must enlist. *Yes, at thirty-nine he was an old man by current standards. Lincoln had called for 75,000 volunteers. He* could *sit the war out if he wanted to, like Ralph suggested, but he didn't want to...*

"Of course we don't want either of your blood to be spilled," Margaret interrupted his thoughts, drawing Tom's attention. When he looked up she was staring at him. "And, because you may feel somewhat, displaced, without a place to live, please consider this your home for as long as you like, as Ralph suggested last night," she was quick to add.

There it was; the invitation to stay, to be at her beck and call. Tom swallowed, but knew what he must do.

"Thank you for the kind invitation, Margaret, but I must decline. I've made up my mind." There, he'd said it. Now he had to wait for the storm—if it came—and, in her anger, she would reveal his indiscretion to all.

They remained silent and still for several moments, their breathing the only sound in the room, until Gerald finally said, "Father, Mother, it's our duty to enlist to protect the sovereignty of this nation and if it means giving my life to do so, then so be it. What if every man, young or old, decided it wasn't his duty, and let someone else fight? Who would save this nation from being split in two and remaining that way?" His shoulders straightened a bit and his chin lifted.

Tom watched his brother's head fall slightly as though accepting his son's words before it lifted again. "Very well, son, you fight your war—and make me proud, but can you do so without getting killed?" he added with a trembling grin.

Gerald grinned back and snapped his head up and down. "I'll do my best, Father."

"You, too, Tom," Ralph added with another shaky smile.

"I'll do my best, too."

Tom glanced at Margaret. She was seething, but he couldn't tell if it was because she was angry, scared, or deciding if she had more to say. And what more she might have to say was what scared Tom more than anything right now.

The arrival of the servants to set out the meal broke the tension in the room. Gerald and Margaret regained their seats and Tom breathed again, but still wasn't sure he'd won this race.

Breakfast progressed with little talk and when the meal was finished Gerald stood. "It's time we take our leave."

Tom stood and nodded agreement. He looked at Margaret, whose lips were rolled tight, her eyes pinched, and he realized what had caused the tiny lines around her mouth and eyes.

His heart pounding, Tom waited as she decided whether to try one last time to get her son and brother-in-law to change their minds about enlisting—or reveal his indiscretion.

Chapter Eleven

Margaret stood up and threw her napkin down on her plate. "Is there nothing I can say to either of you foolish men to change your minds?" She looked directly at Tom. "I will remind you, again, you may stay with us for as long as you like if you stop this foolishness. I want you to understand that—fully—Tom."

Tom did fully understand what her invitation meant, and he was not in any way inclined to accept it. In fact, it pushed him out the door quicker. He just prayed she wouldn't incriminate him before he got there.

"I completely agree, Tom. You're welcome here as long as you want to stay. We're family. Please, reconsider."

Tom shook his head. *Yes, they were family, and Margaret, his brother's wife, was offering an invitation to be much more if he stayed.* He looked at Gerald, standing rigid, afraid his uncle might be swayed by his parents' offer.

"Again, I thank you both for the kind invitation to stay and make this my home for however long I might need it to be, but again I must decline. And," he glanced at his nephew and grinned, "*if* I changed my mind, Gerald would never forgive me!" He hoped his boast would lighten the tension in the air.

"I would not!" Gerald boomed. "That said, it's time we get on our way." He turned, strode purposely to his father, shook his hand then gave him a hug before he went to his mother, embraced her, and kissed her cheek.

For the first time, Tom saw real emotion on Margaret's face as she said goodbye to her son. His goodbye's said, Gerald waited for Tom beside the door of the dining room, his hands folded in front of him.

Tom went to his brother and the two hugged warmly before he walked to his sister-in-law. She met him with a raised jaw and open arms. He went to her and she embraced him. She leaned into him, allowing him to feel all he was turning away, before she whispered in his ear, "Someday you'll wish you'd stayed. Be safe, Tom, and take care of my son."

She pulled back and he watched a tear slide down her cheek before she fled past Gerald and out of the room.

***

Relieved Margaret hadn't exposed last night's *mistake*, Tom was breathing normally again, but he was now more than anxious about what the day, and following months, would bring. As the carriage he and Gerald shared approached the recruitment building, that anxiety and excitement grew. The carriage rolled to a halt in front of a building where several men lounged, chatted, smoked, and leaned against the wall.

Tom glanced at Gerald and for the first time he saw uncertainty in his young nephew's face. "Second thoughts?"

Gerald remained silent a moment before he set his shoulders and said, "No...and yes. I was thinking about what you said earlier. That the war was going to be much longer than anyone anticipates. You obviously believe that, or you wouldn't have said it, right?"

Tom now *heard* the uncertainty in Gerald's voice, but he nodded, unwilling to lie. "I do believe that. Regardless, Lincoln has called for only ninety day enlistments, I'm certain this war is going to go on for much longer than that." He shook his head, remembering the men he'd known throughout his life in Tennessee, many of whom had rushed off to join the Confederacy long before he was forced to leave his home and all he'd created over the years. "The men I knew in Clarksville and the surrounding areas were tough men, determined men, strong men, who would ride until they fell out of their saddle from exhaustion, who would fight until they couldn't raise their hands, and who would not surrender, no matter the cost. These are the men you and I, and the Union army will face in this war."

Gerald remained silent, and Tom wondered if his nephew had enough doubts to change his mind. *And if Gerald did change his mind, what would that mean for Tom? Would he enlist alone? If he didn't enlist, where would he go? He certainly couldn't go back and live happily with his brother and Margaret. That would be a living hell!*

"You want me to come back or wait for you?" the newly promoted driver yelled down from his perch atop the coach.

Gerald looked out the window and at Tom before he called back, "Take the carriage home." He took a deep breath. "Let's get this done before I *do* change my mind." He threw open the door and jumped out.

Tom stepped out behind Gerald and sucked in a deep breath for courage. Once it was done, there was no turning back until their ninety days were up—at the very least.

***

The physical examination and swearing in over, Tom and Gerald were turned around and pointed back outside to wait—in the same clothing they'd enlisted in! They were told they'd spend the night at Camp Taylor and ship off to Camp Dennison near Cincinnati tomorrow.

And that was it.

Disappointment rode their backs. They'd hoped to somehow enlist in a cavalry regiment, but nothing had changed. The cavalry units were still full. The Eighth was infantry, and now so were Tom and Gerald, and that was all there was to it.

"Well, that's it, Uncle Tom. We're part of the Eighth Ohio Infantry. And we haven't a thing to show for it other than they *say* we've joined up. This is pathetic."

Gerald's statement pulled Tom from his musing at how little was involved. A cursory physical exam that most anyone could pass, the raising of your hand and swearing to abide by the rules, and you were in. "Yes we are. I hope we don't regret it."

Gerald raised his brows. "Do you?"

Tom shook his head. He had no regrets, so far, other than the war itself. This was something he had to do. This was his fight as much as anybody's. He just hoped there was a little more to it than what they had right now. Nothing.

Tom turned to his nephew. "Gerald, from now on call me Tom. Tom will work just fine."

Gerald grinned and nodded. "As you wish...Tom."

A man stepped out from the building in front of them.

"Ten hut!"

Tom and Gerald came to attention. The other men who had been standing around in front of the building when Tom and Gerald arrived scrambled to do the same beside them. The sergeant walked down the line of eight men then back again. "I'm Sergeant Mills. Now that you have mustered in it's time to get you to Camp Taylor." He waved his hand down the road. "You boys got here just in time. We board a train for Camp Dennison tomorrow."

With no further introductions or by your leaves, he shouted, "Right face!" Three of the men turned left. When they saw Tom and Gerald facing the other way, they awkwardly swung around.

The sergeant groaned. "We'll work on *that* when we get to Dennison!" he snarled. "For'ard march!"

The first man in line stepped forward. The second man followed, and so on, until Tom and Gerald, the last two in line, marched down Kinsman Street like the undisciplined soldiers they were.

Tom heard shouting in the distance, what sounded like drilling, and he surmised Camp Taylor wasn't far.

A few minutes later they entered camp, a sea of white tents with men drilling or waiting to drill, officers shouting orders, and men scrambling to follow those orders.

Tom swallowed. Gerald slid up beside him, staring as he was. "Well, I guess this is it," Gerald whispered.

"No talking!" Mills shouted, ushering the men into camp.

After being assigned a two-man tent for the night, Tom and Gerald got in line with hundreds of other men for the evening meal of undercooked potatoes and stringy beef, slopped onto a metal plate they were handed when they got in line. A ladle full of gritty water was poured into metal cups. Both men gaped at what they knew was a precursor to what their lives would be like for, at the very least, the next ninety days.

Shoved by the men behind them, they gathered their wits and shuffled back to their tent.

"How can this be? We're supposed to be in the great Union Army and *this slop* is what we get for food? A starving soldier cannot fight," Gerald complained.

Tom listened as Gerald grumbled until they reached the tent and plopped onto the thin mat inside the tent where they stared down at what was their supper. With much trepidation, Gerald scooped up a spoonful and put it into his mouth— and just as quickly spit it out. "This is the worst thing I've ever tasted." He threw his plate on the ground at his feet and wiped at his mouth as if his mother had washed it out with soap.

"It can't be that bad." Tom eyed his plate.

"You put some of that into *your* mouth then tell me it isn't that bad."

Tom shook his head, filled the spoon with what was supposed to be a potato and put the food in his mouth. If he were a child he would have gagged and spit it all out with an exaggerated shout. It tasted like a mouthful of flour—weevily flour at that! He forced it down with a grimace.

"See, I told you." Gerald's look was smug.

Tom threw the plate aside and wiped his mouth as Gerald had. He grabbed the cup and drank down the gritty water, trying to get rid of the horrible lingering taste.

"Well, I guess we'll be hungry when we get to Dennison." Gerald said. "At least we'll only have to starve for one day. In a big camp like Dennison they've *got* to have plenty of food— good food—for their soldiers." Gerald grabbed both their plates and shoved them outside the tent.

Little did they know this might be their finest meal in the days to come.

***

Tom slept little, if any, that night. Gerald tossed and turned, mumbled and grumbled about the terrible accommodations, the food, and the snoring of the other men. When Gerald didn't keep him awake, Tom's anxiety did.

When morning finally came, Tom felt like he'd been dragged through a rocky mud field tied behind Satan's Pride. *Maybe he could catch some sleep on the train,* he hoped while gathering his few belongings to depart.

With a silent, bleary-eyed Gerald beside him and the sun just rising, they boarded the Little Miami Railroad train bound for Fort Dennison. They found seats and plopped into them. For the first time since their arrival at Camp Taylor, Gerald was quiet, as were most of the men who boarded with them, lost in their own thoughts of where they were headed and what the future would bring.

Tom laid his head back against the hard seat and closed his eyes as the reality of what he'd done sank in. He was one soldier in the Union army and nothing he could do would change that—except getting killed, of course.

Chapter Twelve

Tom stared through the window at the passing landscape. The tall ridge on his right decreased in height as the train pulled into Camp Dennison. American flags flapped in the breeze from tall poles and atop numerous buildings.

He shook Gerald. "We're here."

Gerald groaned and repositioned. "Leave me be, mother. I'll get up when I'm ready."

Tom grinned and nudged his nephew harder. "I'm not your mother and it's time to wake up."

Gerald's eyes popped open and he groaned deeper with the realization of where he was. "Oh," was all he could manage, other than the grimace on his face.

Sergeant Mills went up and down the aisle, rousting men still asleep. "Get up, men! Up and at 'em!"

Tom took a moment to look out the window as Gerald gathered his wits and his few belongings. Camp Dennison looked like a city unto itself with acres and acres of flat land, lines of buildings, and lots of open area for drilling.

Gerald shoved Tom's shoulder. "Let's go."

Tom grabbed what little he had and followed his nephew down the aisle and off the train. Stepping onto solid ground, he, Gerald and the other men were hurried into line outside what, he presumed, was the headquarters building. As he waited for whoever would present himself, he looked around, assessing the camp further. Hundreds of men drilled in the center of the camp. Sergeants bellowed orders and men scurried to follow those orders. Much like he'd seen yesterday at Camp Taylor, but on a larger scale.

A few buildings stood out. What he believed was the headquarters building was in front of where he and the other men waited. The two-storied, brick building had five windows on the second floor, four on the lower floor, two on either side of the door in the center. There were two chimneys, one on each end of the structure, a hitching rail out front, and two men standing guard.

To the south, on his right, were rows and rows of buildings, what he presumed were the barracks, stretching from one end of camp to the other. Between those buildings and where he stood was the open parade ground where the men drilled. Behind the barracks were tall hills with trees at the top that ran halfway down the slope toward camp. Further away Tom was barely able to make out the Little Miami River he understood flowed nearby.

His assessment was cut short when the door of the headquarters building opened and an officer stepped out. Tom held his breath.

The tall, impeccably dressed officer strode purposely toward the men, stopped ten feet away, and surveyed those in front of him.

"Ten hut!" Sergeant Mills shouted.

The men came to what they believed was attention. The officer shook his head and frowned for all to see. He stood rigid with his legs spread and his hands clasped behind him.

"Welcome to Camp Dennison." The general's tone was even as he waved his left arm to encompass the parade ground and compound beyond. "I am Brigadier General Melancthon Wade, commanding officer here. You are volunteers in the United States Army, Department of the Ohio. Tomorrow your journey to becoming soldiers begins. There," he pointed at the parade grounds where men drilled, "is where you will learn to become that soldier, *how* to take orders, and *how* to survive.

"The men who teach you are qualified to do so. Learn from them. Obey them. It may save your life.

"There is a chain-of-command here. That chain begins with the sergeants within the company to which you are assigned. You *will* obey—at your own peril if you do not. You volunteered for service to your country and are no longer civilians. You are soldiers in the United States Army and will act accordingly. Sergeant."

Mills stepped forward and snapped to attention with a crisp salute before the general. "Yes, sir!"

"That gentlemen, is a proper salute and response when greeting an officer. Take heed. For now, Sergeant Mills will get you settled in. Take the rest of the day, for tomorrow your training will begin. Dismissed." General Wade turned on his heel and walked back into headquarters.

Tom chanced a glance at Gerald. The boy looked as uncertain as he was.

***

Tom's uncertainty turned to a stomach ache when they reached what passed for the men's barracks. Each twenty-five man company was represented by eight dirt-floored shacks, four on each side of a street about 25 feet wide running east and west from the foot of the hills. At the foot of the hill the street was closed off by the officers' hut with the other end opening onto the parade ground to the east. They looked like they'd been thrown together with whatever materials were available to shelter the huge influx of men from the weather—most of which couldn't keep a soft rain out, let alone a downpour. Many of the original frame structures had been added on to and looked like a mix of shanties and weekend cottages. Tom snorted when he noted the numerous rough-hewn plaques hanging above doors announcing Astor House, Burnett House, and Eagle's Nest.

"Well, I guess this is home sweet home for the next few weeks," Gerald said with a grimace.

Tom shook his head. *The North had plenty of men, money and materiel, why was this place such a dump? Where was the grand camp? Certainly, it's early in the war, but this? These are nothing more than shacks, thrown together for hundreds of men....*

"Come on...Tom." Gerald grinned. "I guess we'd better claim a spot and get settled in."

Gerald led the way into the barrack they'd been assigned and Tom felt the weight of the whole war crash down on him. *If they had such horrible housing, how were the men fed? Men can't drill all day without decent food. They were already hungry from not eating last night at Camp Taylor. If the food was as bad as the housing, they were in big trouble. And the uniforms—or lack thereof! He was still in his street clothes for God's sake!*

Tom gaped at the straw pallets lining the outer walls of the so-called barrack.

Gerald stood rooted to the floor beside him as other men shuffled in around them, stopping to stare once they got inside. In his entire life Tom surmised his nephew had never seen such raw accommodations. *Come to think of it,* he'd *never seen such rough accommodations either.*

"We'll get used to it." Tom hoped to help his nephew through the adjustment with his comment. He hoped to help *himself.*

Gerald swallowed hard and shook his head. His hand encompassed the room. "I'll never survive—this. I don't think I can do it."

Tom stepped in front of his nephew. "You can and you will. You have no choice. *We* have no choice. Do you think you can just change your mind and walk away? We're at war, Gerald. We're not *playing* war like your mother suggested. You volunteered for three month's service—at the least. Changing your mind is not an option. This is our life for at least the next three months, so you'd better get used to it."

Gerald took a deep breath and nodded before he dropped onto the pallet next to where Tom stood.

"We've got the rest of the day. I suggest you rest as much as you can. It's going to be a rough couple of weeks," Tom said.

Tom lay down on the lumpy straw pallet beside his nephew, threw his arm across his face, and groaned. *I* am *too old, and too soft, for this. What in hell have I done?*

***

"These are your rations for the week, men." Sergeant Mills strode in front of the men assembled later that day. "Each man has provisions of rice, potatoes, bacon and coffee."

The men looked at the sacks they held and Tom heard the silent questions each and every man asked. *"Where's the rest of it? And how do we cook it?"*

Mills raised his hand, as though to quiet those silent questions. "Find out who can cook and they will cook. If none of you cook, learn. And if you can't learn." He stopped and thought a moment before he said, "Well, raw potatoes aren't so bad, but bacon and rice...."

Tom tried to make sense of what Sergeant Mills was saying. *Find someone in your company who can cook or eat your provisions raw. What kind of army was this?* he wanted to shout as, it appeared, the men around him wanted to shout, too. They shuffled in their spots and groaned.

"Enough!" Mills ordered. "This is the way of it. Accept it and make the best of it. There is nothing to be done unless you do it yourselves."

Tom stood in stunned silence with the others. *A man could starve in this army—or get ptomaine poisoning from eating bad food!* But according to Mills, that was the way of it, so they needed to do the best they could with what they had.

"Dismissed!" Mills stalked away, the men gaping after him.

"Dismissed? That's it?" Gerald said. "Just figure it out or starve?"

"That's the whole of it. So let's figure it out, shall we?" Tom stepped in front of the men. "Does anyone know how to cook?"

A thick-set man in the back raised his hand. "I'm a hunter and have cooked over a fire since I was a boy. I can show you. All you need is a fire."

"Well, you might as well start that lesson right now soldier." Tom waved him forward.

The remainder of the day and evening was spent with those few men who knew how to start a fire, teaching those who didn't, and how to cook over it. It was a lesson most of the men eventually grasped. The men who grasped it became the company cooks and the rest ate whatever was put in front of them. There was a lot of burnt food that night, but as the days passed, the food became more palatable. At least it wasn't raw.

The next weeks were a blur of drilling and more drilling, learning how to cook and survive, and falling into what was supposed to pass as a bed so exhausted they were asleep before their heads hit the pallet.

The second week of July they were issued guns and swords—wooden ones—for drilling, and corn stalks to mount guard![1] They learned tactics and drilled with their wooden equipment, and marched at sentry with their corn stalks. They drilled in the sun, in the rain, and in the heat. And they learned.

Now all they had to do was use it.

---

[1] Pg. 2 *The Valiant Hours* by Thomas Francis Galwey, Eighth Ohio Volunteer Infantry, The Stackpole Company, Harrisburg, Pennsylvania 1961.

Chapter Thirteen

"I don't know if I can do it, Tom." Gerald shook his head and closed his eyes. "If we re-enlist, it'll be for three years this time. Three years!" He opened his eyes and stared at his uncle from the pallet beside him.

Gerald fidgeted then added. "We've got sixty days before *our* ninety-day enlistment is up. We can wait and see what happens before we do anything—unreasonable. Enlisting for ninety days is one thing, Tom—but three years? That's different."

It was Tom's turn to shake his head. "For the past month these men, the Eighth Ohio Volunteers, are the men we've trained with, starved with," he said with a grimace, "and become soldiers with. I can't 'wait to see what happens' to decide if I should stay. I can't, Gerald. Can you? It's our duty," he added.

Gerald frowned. "I guess not." He sucked in a deep breath. "As long as we muster in together, I suppose I can do it." Gerald's face puckered and he snapped his fingers. "Wait a minute. Why don't we try to get into a cavalry unit this time? That's where we should have been in the first place. We'd do the most good there," he said in a rush. "Maybe now...."

"This is an infantry unit, Gerald. There *is no* cavalry. At least not yet."

"Damn. With the way we both ride, we could do some real damage to those Rebs from the back of a horse."

"That we could," Tom agreed. "But we can't, at least not right now, so we have to make the best with where we are—and that's in the infantry."

Gerald thought a moment, sighed, and jumped to his feet. "Well then, we'd best get at it before I change my mind. The others are already assembled outside."

Gerald was contemplative as they walked toward the men waiting to be sworn in again. "I guess someone higher up decided this war is going to take a lot longer than they thought," he finally said.

"I guess they have," Tom replied. "Lincoln's call for 42,000 more volunteers for three years says it all. He apparently no longer believes this war will be as short-lived as everyone thought."

"Hell, the war hasn't even really started and most of the men of the Eighth *should* be mustering out already. They're a hearty lot to re-enlist like this." Gerald grinned. "And so are we." He paused. "Or crazy."

Tom sighed. "Three years. It's a long time and I'm afraid this war is going to take every bit of it—and more."

Gerald nodded agreement. The two stepped into line with the other men waiting to muster back into service of the Eighth Ohio Volunteer Infantry. Only this time it would be for three years—not a mere three months.

***

Jacob Butler, Arnold Watson, and Lawrence Haynes, men Tom and Gerald had become friends with since coming to Dennison, danced around like they'd been given a reprieve from the hangman's noose. Tom almost joined them, but sat nearby laughing instead.

"Where you boys gonna go?" Gerald asked the three men when they finally stopped dancing around like fools.

"Home, where else?" the tall, dark haired, heavily whiskered, Jacob answered.

"Home for a week of rest, relaxation, and, hopefully, some well-earned pampering from the family," the slight, blonde, Lawrence said with a grin.

"We'll go home as heroes and the women will swarm to us like flies." Arnold's stocky body shook with laughter, his red, curly hair bouncing on his head.

Gerald nodded and slapped Arnold on the back. "Now *that* I agree with! A swarm of women!"

"What about you, Tom? Where you headed?" Lawrence asked.

"Home with me, of course," Gerald answered before Tom could.

Where else could *he* go? He no longer had a place of his own, other than Camp Dennison, and when they moved out he'd be damned glad to leave it behind.

"Just a quick train ride and we'll be back in Cleveland where my parents will take good care of us." Gerald slapped his uncle on the back.

"Yep, just a short train ride and we'll be back," Tom managed with a swallow. Gerald's parents would take care of them, but the question on Tom's mind was just how much would *one* parent offer?

A lot could happen in a week.

***

"Gerald!" Margaret hurried to her son and threw her arms around him.

Ralph strode across the train platform toward Tom, his hand extended. "Tom, it's good to see you! You look...well," his brother forced out after his assessment of Tom.

"I look tired and thin, but I'll survive."

Margaret released her son and turned to her brother-in-law. "Tom," she almost purred. "Welcome home." She seemingly floated toward him. Her back to her husband, she wrapped her arms around Tom, letting him feel every inch of her with her embrace. Her cheek then lips brushed against his face.

Heat rushed through Tom like warm water poured over his head. His heart pounded and his breathing grew quick.

"I'm so glad you've come home." Margaret stepped back and stared into his face.

Her eyes locked with his and in them he saw the same passion she'd shown him a month ago. Nothing had cooled since his departure.

"I'm glad to be here," he managed.

Margaret stepped back and took a good look at Tom and then her son. "You're both so...so un-kempt," she tried to be kind. "And thin!" she almost shouted. "What have they done to you? What have you been eating—or not eating I should ask?"

Tom looked at Gerald and Gerald at Tom and they busted out laughing.

"Not much, that's what. And we have to cook it ourselves," Gerald lamented with a groan.

"How barbaric! Are there no cooks in that army of yours?" she hissed. "Well, we'll do something about that. Cook will make you the finest meals in Cuyahoga County while you're home." She sniffed suddenly and tears gathered in her eyes.

"What's wrong, Mother?" Gerald asked, alarmed.

She dabbed her nose with a handkerchief Ralph handed her.

"A week. That's all I'll have you for is a week. Both of you! Why, it's hardly enough to get reacquainted." Her eyes fell on Tom for a long moment before they slid back to her son.

"And we'll make the most of that week, won't we, Tom?" Gerald waited for a response from his uncle.

"Of course we will," he managed, his heart thrumming again.

Margaret's eyes sparkled the way Tom knew they did when she got her way—or was about to. She would *try* to get her way, Tom had no doubt. For *whatever* reason she wanted him, she intended to get her way and didn't plan to quit until she succeeded. A chill ran up Tom's spine, cooling the heat that had rushed through him only moments ago.

"Shall we?" Ralph raised his hand toward the exit.

"We shall." Gerald stepped up beside his father.

The two men headed for the exit. "I say we shall, also," Margaret cooed, locking her elbow in Tom's, her eyes sparkling. "We've got a lot to look forward to in the coming week."

Margaret dragged Tom forward. It was going to be a long week, to be sure.

Chapter Fourteen

"You simply *must* attend," Margaret pouted hours later. "The ball is in your honor." She stood in the parlor in the same place she had the day Tom came to Cleveland, the sun illuminating her form in the long windows behind her. It was as though he had stepped through time and was arriving all over again.

"What is in Tom's honor, Mother?" Gerald strode into the room, freshly groomed in a clean suit, polished shoes, and a smile on his face.

"Why, a ball, of course! In yours and your uncle's honor." She whirled toward her son. "But your uncle is trying to beg off. I began planning it the moment I learned you two were coming home. But *he* doesn't want to attend," she pouted.

Gerald faced his uncle. "Mother is right. You must go. Just think of all the eligible ladies who will be clamoring for your attentions. I won't be able to handle *all* of them you know." He grinned, one that, with a chill, reminded Tom of Margaret when she was attempting to get her way.

Margaret stepped toward Tom. "Yes, just think of all the ladies that will be clamoring for your attention. You wouldn't want to disappoint them."

Tom couldn't believe her boldness. The last thing he wanted was women clamoring for his attentions—especially not one particular woman. "I don't feel it's proper to have a ball right now. There's a war on..."

"But it's not here," Gerald interrupted. "And according to Mother, there have been as many balls, perhaps even more than there have always been, since the war started. I for one will be happy to dance the night away in the arms of many a sympathetic young lady who thinks I'm a hero for going off to fight for our country." Gerald waited a moment then rushed on. "What harm will it do? Let yourself be pampered for a few hours. Lord knows once we go back it'll be a long time before *that* happens again."

Tom wasn't worried about what would happen once they returned to Dennison, he was worried about what might happen right here.

Margaret took Tom's hand. "Please, Tom, you mustn't disappoint me. I've been planning for days to make sure this ball is perfect." Her eyes sparkled with invitation only Tom could see from where he stood.

Gerald stepped beside Tom and Margaret looked away. "Don't disappoint Mother, Tom. She's an artist when it comes to planning. Let her give you a night you'll never forget."

That was what Tom was afraid of.

***

Tom was enjoying himself, despite his worries. He'd spent the night dancing with one lady after another. Most too young for his interest, others whose husbands were enlisted men who only wanted to talk about the war and Tom's thoughts on what might happen, and more too old to worry about other than dancing slow enough not to step on their toes.

Enjoying the music Tom spun the dark-haired woman around the loud, crowded ballroom.

Back in his arms, Camille pouted, "I can't wait till this war is over. I'm so tired of it already. The parties are becoming very dull without our men here. It's time they get this silly war over and come home so things can get back to normal."

Tom stopped and stared at her, his mouth open. He wanted to shove her away. To yell at her that those men might well be killed in the months to come and things would *not* get back to normal anytime soon. How insensitive to speak of them only because of their absence at parties! He pushed her to arm's length. "Madame, this war is only just beginning. It will be a long war and the men who are missing from your *parties* will be in the thick of it and may not return—ever." He took a deep breath, wanting to say more, wanting to shock her into understanding what was to come, but said instead, "You should plan accordingly." He removed his hands from her shoulders, bowed and stalked away leaving her gape-mouthed and alone in the middle of the dance floor.

"What happened with Miss Camille?" Gerald stepped up beside Tom at the refreshment table and threw a look over his shoulder at the woman stomping off the dance floor alone.

"That woman...she...."

"Take a breath, it can't be that bad."

Tom shook his head and took that breath. "Are all women empty-headed with no idea of what real life is about?" he railed. "And this war?" he continued. "Do they have no idea what it will cost in destruction, devastation, and lives?" He gulped down a mouthful of punch.

"I believe the answer to that is yes. The fairer sex *is* empty-headed about the war and just plain doesn't want to know, Tom. They don't want to understand what it's about or how it will affect them, most women, anyway. Some understand, but the majority of them want to go on as though nothing is happening."

"Until the war affects them directly," Tom said. "And it will. This war will get worse before it gets better." He sighed. "No matter who wins, this nation will never be the same again."

Gerald laid his hand on Tom's shoulder. "That's one way to dampen a party, Tom. Why don't you go outside, get some air, and calm down?" Gerald suggested.

"I think I will. I'm finding it difficult to breathe in here."

Tom stalked to the side doors, stepped outside, and headed for the stables. The only place he felt truly at ease, anywhere, was with the horses. *God how he missed Pride and Ghost and the joy and excitement he'd had with them!* The weight of all he'd lost crashed down on him and he grew angrier and angrier as he stalked toward the stables. He kicked the ground, picked up stones and threw them, and punched the air.

He shoved his way through the doors, lit the lamp hanging on the peg with the matches he knew were beside it, and went inside.

"Hello, Star." He ran his hand along the forehead of the bay whose nose stuck out over the first stall.

"And you," he peeked at the next plaque to remember, "Lord Buckingham. How are you tonight?"

The horse threw its head up and down and Tom rubbed his nose to calm the gelding. "That's a boy. A good nose rub is good for any horse."

He made his way down the aisle, rubbing noses and necks until he reached the albino white in the last stall, her rump turned toward him.

"Not in a visiting mood tonight, Miss Beauty? That's all right. I'm not in much of a talking mood myself. If I do start talking, I'll probably explode. How can people be so foolish?"

The mare turned her long neck and pink eyes stared at him. He stepped toward the stall door and reached out to rub her backside.

In a split second she was completely turned around and lunged at Tom with teeth bared. He jumped back just in time to keep from having a chunk taken out of his hand.

"Whoa, girl! You really don't want to talk, do you? And when you want, or don't want something...."

The confrontation he'd had with Margaret in this very place jumped into his head.

Had he lost his mind? Why was he here? Deep down was he hoping she'd follow him like she had before? He had to get out of here before something did *happen.* He turned and almost ran for the doors.

He blew out the lantern, hung it back on the peg, stepped through the door, and closed it behind him. His heart beating wildly, he started back toward the house, happy he'd made it out of the stables without meeting Margaret.

He was halfway there when he spotted her on the trail ahead of him in the moonlight. Unable to avoid her he stepped up to her.

"Were you hoping I'd follow you? Or be waiting for you?" she asked in her too-familiar throaty whisper.

"No."

She laughed. "Don't lie to yourself, Tom, or me. You hoped I would follow you just like I did before." She stepped toward him and ran her finger down his cheek. "You've missed me, haven't you? Thought of me when you were alone and needing—comfort."

"No. No, I haven't," he stammered like a child. *Get a grip Hansen!*

"Why won't you admit it? You went to the stables in the hope I would be waiting—or come to you there."

He shook his head in denial, *but why* had *he gone there?* "I went to see the horses. I needed some air. It was getting stuffy inside. I had to get out of that ballroom. The stables are the only place I can relax," he defended.

"And where you and I had our—indiscretion."

"Stop, stop it right now!" Tom took a deep breath to calm down. "It was a mistake then and I have no intention of repeating it. I went to calm down where I feel most at home, with the horses. The same reason I went there the first time. That's it, that's all there is to it. I was not looking for you, or anyone else for that matter. I was trying to get away from those silly females inside."

"Away from all those lovely ladies clamoring for your attentions?" she asked, her brows rising?

Was that jealousy in her voice? "All those women wanted was to dance or a shoulder to cry on about their missing husband or brother or son. They didn't want me or even Gerald. We're just surrogates for the men who have gone off to fight that are missing from your precious party—who might never come home. They don't give a whit about us, and neither do you."

She stepped closer. "Oh, but you're wrong about that, Tom. I care a great deal about you."

"You don't *care* a thing about me, aside from getting what you want. And for some strange reason you've decided on me. Why is that, Margaret? Is it to hurt Ralph? Has he had an indiscretion of his own and you want revenge?"

Her face hardened and Tom wondered if he'd hit on the reason for her determination.

"Or are you bored, Margaret? Is it that all the men in town are gone and there's no one left to flirt with and make you feel special? Or is this your usual behavior behind my brother's back?"

Her spine stiffened, her eyes pinched, and she inhaled deeply, but said nothing.

"It doesn't matter why you've decided to pursue me. It's not going to happen, Margaret. I'm not interested."

She regained herself and smiled the smile that gave Tom chills. "You certainly seemed interested that night in the stables." She reached out to touch his face again and Tom stepped backward to avoid it.

She smiled wider and Tom knew she wasn't going to give up easily. "That night was a mistake. I've told you that a dozen times. A mistake that won't happen again."

"We'll see about that, Tom. You want me. I know you do."

"I don't want you! I wanted Abby—*that's* who I wanted that night in the barn—not you!"

Margaret jumped backward as though slapped, but recovered quickly. "I know that. I knew it that night you were holding someone else and not me. I even told you so. But what do I care? Me, Abby, I'll be whomever you want me to be. I told you that then and I'll tell you the same again and again." She stepped forward and Tom took another step back. "I'll be whoever you want me to be, Tom. All you have to do is reach out and take me, just like you did before."

She reached for his hand as she'd done in the stable a month ago, but Tom wasn't having it. He walked around behind her, keeping his back to her.

"Stay away from me, Margaret," he said over his shoulder. "Just stay away. I don't want any part of what you offer. You're my brother's wife and I will not do anything to hurt him—or my nephew. If you really care anything about me then leave me alone. I'm not interested in what you offer—as Margaret, and especially not as Abby. Accept it."

Tom hurried to the house. Her taunts didn't follow him this time, but he felt her seething anger as though she walked right beside him railing at him.

She remained where she stood silently raging, and Tom made his way back inside.

Neither saw the shadowy figure that hid off the trail watching.

Chapter Fifteen

He pushed deeper into the shadows of the big oak tree as Tom strode by. Peeking out from his hiding place after Tom passed, he watched Margaret stomp her feet and talk to herself in the middle of the trail, the moonlight illuminating every motion of her slim figure. It was several minutes before she drew up her back, smoothed her dress and hair, pasted on a smile, and started for the house as though nothing were amiss.

Gerald's blood slogged through his veins like molasses through a pipe, gumming up his thoughts. *Who was this woman? Was this really his mother, so casually trying to cuckold his uncle into—what? He couldn't even think about it. This was his mother for God's sake! What about his father? Did he know? Suspect? Should he tell him what he'd seen and heard—or keep his tongue? And what, exactly, had their 'indiscretion' been? Had his uncle been a willing participant before his conscience got the better of him?*

His eyes closed and he leaned against the tree trunk as his mother passed in a flurry of swirling gown and petticoats. His breathing was shallow and anger billowed up inside him like a churning dust storm as he recalled conversations cut short when he joined a crowd in town; his friends and townsfolk refusing to meet his eye, as though they knew something he didn't. *Well, perhaps they did know something and he was the poor, unsuspecting fellow they pitied.* He'd heard words like *free* and *easy* and *unladylike* whispered before mouths snapped shut on his arrival into the conversation, but he'd always put it off as gossip about someone he didn't know or care about. He'd never asked who they spoke of—perhaps because deep down he already knew.

But now he did care! And the fact it made him a laughing stock. In front of the whole town! What did it make his mother? A harlot? A free and easy woman like they insinuated? He felt like he was going to lose the punch and cakes he'd eaten earlier. He leaned away from the tree, put his hands on his knees, took deep breaths and, eventually, was able to breathe again.

Gerald's heart was pounding so hard he thought it would launch itself right out of his chest. He was angry, confused then angrier. *How dare she? How dare he! He'd come into their home and cuckolded his own brother with his wife!*

He kept his hands on his knees, breathing deep to keep the bile from coming up until, eventually, he was able to stand up without feeling sick. Leaning back he let his head rest against the tree. *Why? Why would she do such a thing? His father was a good man. He'd done nothing but give her everything she wanted. Everything. And that was the problem,* Gerald realized. *The woman got everything she wanted, and if that was pleasure somewhere else, apparently she had no qualms about getting that, too.*

He whirled and slammed his fist into the tree. Pain exploded through his hand, but he ignored it and hit it again and again, hoping to draw the pain from his heart. He felt deceived and the fool and in those moments he vowed he would never give himself over to a woman the way his father had to be betrayed as his mother betrayed him.

"Gerald!"

His father's voice cut through the darkness and Gerald jerked upright.

"Are you out here son?"

Gerald froze then gathered himself, stepped away from the tree, and onto the trail. He spotted his father standing outside the ballroom doors. He forced himself to calm down before going back into the house. *He had to think this all the way through. Get all the facts. This was his family! Right now the only facts he had were the* assumption *that his mother was an adulterer—but what about his uncle? Even though he'd rebuffed her advances tonight, what had happened before? That was what he had to find out. And once he did, what the hell would he do about it?*

***

Tom's heart wouldn't stop pounding. Back inside he paced, he sat down, he got up and walked some more, he drank punch, and still his heart beat as though he'd just run a mile race through sand. *He had to get away from this place, from Margaret. But how? What kind of an excuse could he give to go back to Dennison days earlier than he had to? I'm sorry, Ralph, I have to go. Your wife decided she wants me and if I stay any longer I might give in.* He closed his eyes to quell the desire to slam his fist into something.

"You look like a bull cornered for branding."

Tom's eyes lifted to his brother, standing in front of him. *That's exactly what I feel like!* he wanted to scream.

Ralph slapped him on the shoulder and sat down beside him. "Come on, Tom, this is a party. I know you didn't want to attend, don't feel it's proper right now, but you're here and you should enjoy yourself. I saw you dancing with Camille earlier. She may be a little young, but she's available."

Tom held up his hand, palm out, in front of his brother's face. "Stop right there. I'm not interested in Camille or anyone else here tonight." *Especially not your wife!* He frowned and rolled his lips. "I'm sorry, Ralph, I just want to sit here quietly and alone. I don't want to dance and I'm not interested in getting better acquainted with any of the ladies. If I can't be left alone I'll simply go up to my room where no one can bother me."

Ralph pulled away, clearly injured. "Well then, I'm sorry I was worried about your welfare. Rest assured, I won't bother you further. Do as you will, Tom." Ralph stood up and walked away.

Tom watched his brother walk away, sorry for his abruptness but sorrier for the secret he held. *Damn! Why had he come here? He'd feared this would happen. Hoped he'd been firm enough with Margaret when he left. Apparently he hadn't. Or had he known, deep down that he hadn't, and came back anyway? What the hell was wrong with him? With her!*

Tom looked up just as Margaret floated back into the ballroom, her smile as vibrant as the sun. She scanned the room, searching. When her eyes fell upon Tom her lips hardened and her eyes sparked with rage. It was only seconds before she regained herself, pasted her smile back on, hurried to her husband, grabbed his arm, and pulled him onto the dance floor for the waltz the band began to play.

Good, keep her occupied Ralph, so I don't have to deal with her again tonight, Tom thought.

Tom watched the well-dressed couples twirl in front of him. A few more minutes and he would excuse himself and go to the solitude of his room to decide what to do next.

He lifted a glass of punch, but stopped before it reached his lips when Gerald pushed through the doors and stepped inside, his face a mask of controlled anger. He searched the room as his mother had done only moments before. He spotted Margaret and his father and Tom saw the anger flow through him. Gerald turned, searching again. His eyes locked with Tom's—and Tom knew. Knew his nephew had heard his and Margaret's exchange.

But how much had the boy heard—and how much did he *think* he knew?

Chapter Sixteen

Gerald's eyes held Tom's and Tom felt like the proverbial child caught with his hand in the cookie jar. *But he was innocent! Well, mostly innocent. She was the pursuer. She was the one that wouldn't take no for an answer. She was the one that wouldn't leave him alone!*

Gerald stared only a moment longer before he stalked from the room. Tom wanted to go after him, to explain, but couldn't amidst all these people.

Tom swallowed, repositioned on the settee where he'd spread out to discourage anyone else from joining him, and heaved a sigh. Everything was going wrong. And it was all because of this damned war. If only....

He stopped himself in mid-pity and mentally slapped himself. *So what! It didn't matter what the cause was or how he'd gotten here. He was here!* He could spend all night moaning and groaning about why this was happening, why Margaret was pursuing him, or why this war had started in the first place, but it wouldn't do any good toward solving the problem—Margaret.

How could he get back to Dennison without raising suspicion as to why he wanted to leave long before his furlough was over? And what about Gerald? His nephew knew something was going on. Tom knew he knew and that meant they'd have to talk about it or they'd never make it to camp without a confrontation, possibly at a very bad time. Tomorrow was soon enough. Tomorrow he'd talk to his nephew and the cards would fall where they may. Either he'd believe him—or not.

***

Tom woke the next morning bleary-eyed and irritable. He wanted nothing more than to be gone from here, to wherever that was when the Eighth was assigned, regardless of the danger. *Anywhere would be better than here!* He hadn't slept a bit and his mood was black. *He had to talk to Gerald, explain what* happened, and make him understand it wasn't his fault. But in doing so, he could well destroy a son's vision of his mother. Could he do that? Expose what she truly was? Or should he take the blame to keep from tearing a family, his brother's family, apart?

And what of his and Gerald's relationship? How could they serve in the same army with this between them without explanation? Tom's mind was spinning with unanswerable questions when there was a knock.

His heart hammering he slid off the bed and opened the door. Gerald stood in the hallway, his face a mask of that same controlled anger Tom saw last night.

"Come in." Tom swung the door open wide and his nephew stepped past him without a word, rubbing what looked like heavily bruised knuckles.

Gerald whirled when the door closed behind him. "I want to know the truth, Tom. I know something happened between you and Mother and I want to know what it was. I don't want lies, regardless who they protect, you *or* her. I want the truth."

Tom had spent all night trying to decide how to tell his nephew—what to tell his nephew—and now was the time. Gerald wanted the truth, *but could Tom give it to him and destroy a son's relationship with his mother?*

"Sit down, Gerald." Tom's hand hovered over a chair at the foot of the bed.

Gerald sat down, his back stiff.

Tom ran his fingers through his hair and over his face. This was a conversation he did not want to have.

"Well?" Gerald was impatient. "I want the truth. I deserve the truth. At least from you." Gerald looked out the window and sighed. "I won't get it from her."

He turned back to Tom his eyes sparkling with unshed tears and Tom felt his nephew's pain.

Tom took a breath and stepped closer. "It's not what you think."

"Then tell me, what should I think? I heard you two on the trail last night. You and Mother. She was waiting for you when you came from the stables. I followed her when she left the house."

"Why did you follow her?" Tom asked.

Gerald shook his head. "I, I don't know. I just felt like I had to. I followed her and hid when you two met on the trail." He fell silent.

"Go on. What did you hear?"

"She asked if you hoped she'd be waiting for you in the stables, or that you hoped she'd follow you there where...where...."

"Where we had our indiscretion?" Tom finished.

"Yes!" Gerald jumped to his feet, uncertainty and pain in his eyes. "What the hell was she talking about?"

Tom swallowed and put his hands on his nephew's shoulders, who shrugged them off. "Gerald, calm down and I'll tell you everything, but you have to calm down or you'll wake the entire house, and neither you nor I want that."

Gerald's lips compressed and his nose flared with his anger, but he sat down again. "Tell me."

"When I first arrived, before we enlisted, I was drawn toward your mother immediately upon seeing her again. She's a very beautiful woman and reminds me of, of someone I used to know. I couldn't help myself. I was drawn to her and couldn't stop it."

Tom paused to think, to keep the lie in place. He would play the bad guy in the hope of keeping his brother's family from being torn apart. It was all he could do.

"Go on." Gerald's face was intent, his voice hard.

"That first night I was plagued by thoughts of Abby, the woman your mother reminded me of, and other questions I couldn't answer about my friend, Sam, and his family, and this war. So I went to the stables to try and gain some sense of what I was doing. The stables are the only place I feel at peace, with the horses, you know that." He paused again, thinking carefully about his words.

"I'd been inside visiting the animals for a few minutes when someone came in. It was your mother. She knew something was wrong. She tried to talk me through my anger with Abby. She tried to help me, but the longer we talked I no longer saw her—I saw only Abby. How she'd hurt me, how much I'd loved her and how easily she'd thrown what we had away. It was as though she stood there in the flesh, right in front of me, instead of your mother." He stopped again, remembering how it really happened.

"Go on."

"I don't know what happened to me. I couldn't help myself. I wanted her more than the air I breathed. I kissed her. She struggled against me and I kissed her harder until she was finally able to push me away and run from the barn. I'm so sorry. I never meant for it to happen, but it did—and it'll never happen again."

Gerald glared at him in silent rage. He finally stood up, face to face with his uncle. "You're a liar."

Tom swallowed and shook his head in denial. "I'm not lying. That's what happened."

"You're lying and I know it. I *heard* you and mother on the trail last night. I *saw* you try to get away from her. *Saw* how she tried to goad you, *kept* goading you, into a tryst with her. Offering herself as anyone you wanted her to be. And I *saw and heard* you rebuff her, Tom. Watched you walk away and saw the rage in her face when you did. Don't try and shield me. I'm not a child. I've lived in this town all my life and certain things have occurred that have made me suspect of my mother's virtue for a long time. Perhaps that's why I followed her last night, because deep down I know her and wanted to catch her in one of her indiscretions. Wanted to justify or discount my suspicions. I never dreamed it was you she was tormenting, trying to seduce. Tell me what really happened, Tom. Tell me everything."

Tom tried to beg off, but Gerald wouldn't hear of it. He wanted the truth and Tom had to give it to him. Tom told his nephew *most* of what had happened. How she'd followed him to the stables; played on his sense of loss of Abby, and offered to *be* Abby. He told him everything except his hand on her. Tom didn't think her son needed to hear that. But he told him about the lingering kiss and her rage at his dismissal.

Gerald plopped back into the chair and sat in silence, rubbing his bruised hands, his head drooping as he absorbed what he'd been told. Tom wanted to reach out and console him, but his nephew had to work through it himself.

Slowly, Gerald's head rose and Tom saw the pain there. "I'm so sorry for what Mother has done."

"Gerald, I..." Tom began, but was stayed by Gerald's raised hand.

"Let me finish. "I wish I could change things, but, obviously, I can't. I've known, deep down for a long time, mother wasn't as dedicated to my father as she professes to be, but I chose to ignore it." He paused, searching for words. "Now I've been hit full in the face with the realization of what my mother really is and I have no choice but to accept it." He turned simmering eyes to Tom. "And you were willing to take the blame to spare my feelings and keep our family from being torn apart by my *mother's* indiscretions and, for that, I'll be forever grateful to you, *Uncle* Tom."

"So what do we do now?" Gerald asked after a few moments of lingering silence.

"I need to make up some kind of story as to why I have to leave. Now. Today. I can't stay another day."

"You're right. We have to leave."

"We? You'd go with me?" Tom asked. "Give up what's left of your time home?"

"I can't stay, either, knowing what my mother's done, what she is, what I'd know and see every time I look at her. Eventually, I'd explode and it wouldn't be pretty. It's better for all of us if we both go."

Tom put his hands on his nephew's shoulders again, and this time Gerald allowed them to stay. "No matter what has passed between me and her, she's still your mother."

"Who's made her husband, *my* father, and I laughing stocks in town!" Gerald interrupted with a raised hand. "I've known something was wrong when conversations, many conversations, halted abruptly when I joined them. Or people turned away looking guilty. I never understood why. I do now and I'm ashamed and angry and...."

"And you can't let her know you know. You'll never be able to repair the damage it'll do. We must leave it behind us by going back to Dennison early."

Gerald pursed his lips and nodded. "I agree, but what excuse can we use to leave without causing suspicion? At least without father suspecting something, too? I don't care if mother *thinks* I know or not. Let her worry and stew. Maybe she'll change her ways. But I don't want father to find out and get hurt in the bargain. He doesn't deserve it."

"The only excuse I can come up with is that our leave has been cancelled. But unless we get some kind of 'official' word, it won't ring true," Tom said. "We can't just walk into breakfast and announce our furlough has been suspended."

"Leave that to me." Gerald stepped toward the door then turned back to Tom, his face pinched with pain and sorrow. "I'm so sorry for all she's done, Tom. So sorry." He hurried out and closed the door gently behind him.

Breakfast was a quiet affair. Gerald and Tom both ate in silence; Margaret looked between the two of them, *wondering* what was going on between them. Ralph, still nursing his hurt pride from Tom's rebuff last night, ate in silence, as well. No one spoke and, when they did, it was merely to address one another to pass the jam or bread—until one of the servants hurried into the room with an envelope addressed to Tom and Gerald, care of Ralph Hansen.

"What is it?" Margaret asked, alarmed.

"It looks official." Tom ran his hand over the paper envelope when he took it from the servant.

"Well, open it and find out." There was a slight gleam in Gerald's eyes that only Tom would notice.

Tom ripped open the letter and read it aloud.

"Effective Immediately all leave has been suspended. Return to Camp Dennison post haste."

"That's it?" Margaret's voice was shrill. "Leave post haste? What about your furlough? Why is it being cancelled? How dare they! You still have five days left!" she shouted.

Gerald shook his head, as did Tom. "Don't have a clue," Tom answered. "But it's an order so..."

"It looks like we must leave," Gerald finished before Tom could.

Tom stood up. "I'll gather my things."

Gerald shoved out his chair, threw his napkin down on his plate, and stood up, too. "Damn!" He shouted for effect. "Only a few days and we can't even be allowed that!"

Tom hid his grin.

"This is so unfair. We have five days left! I'm not ready to go back!" Gerald shouted dramatically.

"Orders are orders, Gerald."

Gerald shook his head and grumbled aloud as he and Tom headed for the door, Tom's only thought that it was only a matter of minutes before he could quit this place and head to calmer waters.

The two men stormed out the door, unaware that the comparative calm waters of their visit would soon erupt into raging seas—the two of them caught right in the middle.

Chapter Seventeen

After the side glances, hidden smiles, and solemn train ride back to Cincinnati, reality hit. Tom and Gerald were back at Camp Dennison and the war was real again.

Upon return from their furloughs, Tom and Gerald, Lawrence, Arnold, and Jacob, were assigned to Company B as skirmishers for the regiment.

On July 8th they boarded a box car headed for Columbus where they received new field equipment—real weapons and real ammunition.

Tom turned his new Enfield rifle over in his hands, inspecting every bit of it. He and the others had turned in the undependable muskets that had replaced the silly wooden rifles, swords, and cornstalks they'd been given on their arrival at Dennison and happily taken the Enfield's.

"Hallelujah, our days of drilling are over," Gerald almost shouted when he and Tom returned to their temporary tent while waiting to move out again.

It was obvious to Tom that Gerald's passion for the war was returning, now that their training was finally over and they were ready to move.

"The drilling and training may be done, but now the real fighting begins," Tom reminded his nephew.

"I know that. I'm not a child, Tom, regardless you still treat me like one." He blinked his eyes at his uncle and Tom felt heat rush to his face.

He thrust his forefinger up in the air. "I plead guilty! But it's because I don't want anything to happen to you ne-phew."

"I know un-cle, but I'm a grown man and you don't have to protect me."

Tom grinned and nodded. "We'll see about that when the shooting starts."

Gerald reddened just as Tom had only moments ago. "I'm just happy to be away from Dennison. I was so tired of the drilling, of eating the same thing day after day, and not getting enough *of* it. I'm ready to be a part of this war."

"No more wanting to wait and see what happens?" Tom asked.

"No more wanting to wait and see what happens. We're in it now, Tom, and I want to make a difference. We can do that with this reassignment."

Tom shrugged. "What makes you so sure?"

"We'll be at the forefront, charging into the Confederate lines, forcing them to tuck tail and run." Gerald's tone brooked no argument.

Tom laid his hand on his young nephew's shoulder. From all Tom knew of his southern counterparts it would take a long time for that to happen.

"I hope you're right, Gerald. I *sure* hope you're right."

***

The following days blended one into another. There was no excitement of battle, only the motion and boredom of the train they were on as it chugged from place to place, following Rebs that didn't seem to exist. They got off the train then got back on the train, crouched on their knees in the box car, fingers on the trigger at the ready, peering through the slats, hoping for a glimpse of their prey, Garnett's Confederates.

A hand landing on his shoulder woke Tom with a jerk from a shallow sleep.

"We're stopping," Gerald said.

Tom swiped at his eyes and yawned. "Where are we?"

"Oakland."

"Where's Oakland?" Tom asked, groggy from his continuous broken sleep.

"How do I know?" Gerald grumped, his eyes bleary and blood-shot from his own lack of sleep. "The sign in the station says Oakland, that's all I know."

"I guess it doesn't really matter. We are where we are. We'll find out where it is soon enough. Here comes Sergeant Galwey." Tom couldn't help but shake his head when the short, dark-haired sergeant stepped up into the box car. The little man, if he even *was* a man, wiry and personable at the same time, had been promoted to sergeant upon his return from furlough. Tom suspected the sergeant was barely old enough to shave, if he did, but had somehow gotten himself promoted. Tom shook his head at the wonder of it. He was almost forty years old taking orders from a snot-nosed boy! It rankled him, but Galwey was his sergeant and he would take whatever orders he gave.

"Where are we, Sarge?' Arnold grimaced, his knees popping when he stood up beside Tom and Gerald.

"Oakland, Maryland."

"What's in Oakland, Maryland?" Arnold asked.

"It's where we get off."

"And do what?" Arnold pressed.

"Walk."

"Walk where?"

"Wherever they tell us to walk," Galwey said before continuing into the car, rousting men and answering more questions.

"Well, that's a fine howdy do," Arnold grumbled. "Where do you think we're going?" he asked the others, standing around him, shaking themselves to waken feet, arms, and muscles that had fallen asleep.

"I just heard Galwey tell Tommy Gordon we're headed south to West Union. So, I guess we're headed to West Union, wherever that is," Lawrence said.

"What's in West Union?" Gerald wondered aloud.

"Rebs would be my bet," Lawrence said. "Guess we'll find out when we get there."

They disembarked and stepped into the gloomy night.

"Line up men!" Galwey shouted when he jumped off the train behind them.

The men scrambled and within minutes were in line at attention.

A few moments later Galwey, now standing in front of the men, pointed toward the road he wanted them to follow. "For'ard march!" Two by two they turned and marched south into the hazy darkness behind him.

"This is a fine pickle. We've been marching all night. My feet have blisters on their blisters and now it's starting to rain."

"Stop your complaining, Arnold," Lawrence snapped. "Are you going to melt? All our feet hurt, and our backs, too. All we've wanted these last weeks was to get away from Dennison. Well, we're away and here we are."

"But I didn't want to walk my feet off and get drenched in the doing!" Arnold countered.

"Buck up. You're in the infantry and this is what we do. We walk! We eat food you wouldn't otherwise give a dog, sleep under the stars, and march through mud and heat and rain. Yes, rain, Arnold." Lawrence slapped his friend on the back and the two continued side by side down the road, Arnold grumbling, Lawrence laughing.

"Do I sound that bad?" Gerald asked with a groan.

Tom nodded. "You do."

Gerald thought a moment and said, "Then I give you leave to punch me in the arm every time I do."

Tom's left eyebrow rose. He looked his nephew in the eyes, careful not to trip. "I have permission to punch you in the arm every time you complain?"

Gerald thought again. "Well, on second thought, it seems it may give you *too* much pleasure to do so. Maybe not *every* time," he recanted.

Tom laughed under his breath and slapped his nephew on the shoulder. "As you wish. I won't punch you *every* time, but often enough to keep your complaints to a minimum." Tom chuckled again and hastened his step to catch up with Arnold and Lawrence ahead of him. Gerald hurried to keep up, the rain relentless on their backs.

***

"Get up!" Galwey shouted at the men, bivouacked out of the rain under the tents they were issued with the new equipment at Columbus. In the early morning hours of their march they'd been allowed to stop and catch some sleep.

The men's grumbling turned to an anxious buzz when they learned why they were being rousted at four in the morning from the little sleep they'd been allowed.

"Word around camp is that Garnett's Cavalry has been found. Supposedly, they weren't far away last night. If we'd kept going, we might have intercepted them," Gerald told his uncle after he'd questioned some of the other men about what they'd heard.

"Wherever we're going, we're doing it on sore feet." Tom wondered how he, or any of these men, would make any distance with their bleeding and blistered feet.

Gerald frowned and nodded.

"What's going on?" Arnold asked when he, Lawrence, and Jacob slid in beside Gerald and Tom.

"We're going after Garnett," Gerald said.

"Where?" Lawrence asked.

Gerald shrugged. "No idea. All I heard was that we're going after them. Where that takes us, I have no clue."

Their orders came quickly. They fell into line and marched. For miles they picked up Confederate stragglers dressed in beautiful militia uniforms, scared of what would become of them, yet happy to give themselves up for a meal.

"Look at them." Gerald said to Tom as they passed the frightened men, cowering on the side of the road, shoving bread into their mouths as fast as they could tear it apart. "They're scared, but appear hungrier than scared."

"And I thought we had lousy food. I guess they have lousy food, too, but even less of it." Tom stared at the men as he and the others marched past and wondered *who was running this war when men who fought starved? It wasn't like they'd been fighting for years—it'd only been a few months. What did that bode for the future for them—or us?*

They'd walked for hours, probably five miles. They stopped at a ruined house and the officers disappeared inside.

Happy for the respite, Tom, Gerald, Jacob, Arnold, and Lawrence found the least soggy spots they could around some trees in the yard, sat down, and nursed their sore feet and bodies as well as they could.

Snapping off a bite of the hard tack they'd been given before leaving Columbus, Arnold asked anyone who would answer, "What're they doing in there?"

"Looks to me like some kind of pow wow," Tom answered. "I wonder if they have an idea where we are or where we're going."

Gerald shook his head. "Seems to me we've walked for miles with nothing to show for it but a few hungry prisoners. Speaking of hungry, I'm starved. When do we get some grub? Some real food? Not this hard tack that breaks your teeth…"

Tom punched him in the arm.

"Ouch!"

"You told me to." Tom grinned.

"I told you not to hit me every time." Gerald rubbed his arm.

"Well, this wasn't every time, it was the first time," Tom laughed.

Gerald pouted a minute, rubbed his offended appendage, and laughed, too.

The five men were cackling over Gerald's discomfort when the officers emerged from the ruined house. A few minutes later Sergeant Galwey came with news.

"Prepare to march. We're turning back for West Union."

"What?" Gerald shouted. "But the Rebs are that way!" Gerald slung his arm in the opposite direction."

"Word is we're heavily outnumbered so we're heading back to get reinforcements. That's all I know."

Galwey turned and started to walk away, but stopped when Gerald grumbled, "That's it? We've been marching for days and now we're going back before we've even engaged the Rebs? Instead of waiting here for reinforcements, we'll *all* walk back to West Union then *all* walk back again. And will the Rebs wait for us? Hell no! Who's leading this army anyway?" he asked no one in particular.

Galwey turned back to the men and stepped in front of Gerald, who stood at least six inches taller. "Someone you don't want to hear you is leading this army." Galwey leaned into Gerald and eyed him hotly. "Don't question orders again, because if one of those officers hears you instead of me, he'll slap you with the reality of keeping your mouth shut! Is that understood?"

Gerald glared down at the younger, shorter sergeant and swallowed hard. "Understood."

Tom stepped up beside Gerald. "That was better than a punch in the arm."

Gerald had the decency to turn red before Tom slapped him on the back and they gathered their gear to start back to West Union.

Chapter Eighteen

"Does anyone running this army know what they're doing?" Arnold grumbled to anyone who would listen. "We've only marched a short way toward West Union and we're setting up camp again already." He shook his head and scratched it. "I'm just a soldier doing what I'm told, but it sure doesn't seem like our officers know what they're doing."

Tom looked at Gerald and Gerald said not a word. Tom grinned and leaned into setting up his tent. All around men dropped their heavy knapsacks on the ground, grumbling at the weight and having to lug them around day after day, and seemingly going nowhere.

Tom, although tired of dragging it around and his back aching because of it, was glad to have it. Also issued with the equipment in Columbus, they now had a gum blanket, the tent, eating implements, canned meats and a pan to cook it in, a canteen, a belt with cartridge boxes and multiple rounds of ammunition, percussion caps, and a scabbard covering a bayonet that affixed to their new Enfield rifles. They were also given thick, blue, woolen uniforms. The gray shirt that went with it was also woolen and Tom was more than thankful the few shirts he'd brought with him from Champion Farms were white linen and could be worn in place of the heavy, scratchy one they were issued. There was also a kit with a comb, a razor, and other grooming products.

Happy for the respite, Tom finished setting up his small camp. He broke out a can of meat, sat back and ate while the others grumbled about all their aches and pains, the heat, the food, and poor direction. Tired of watching grown men complain, he laid his head back, wondering what the next days and months would bring.

"It's eight o'clock—at night!" Gerald complained through gritted teeth later and without a punch in the arm from his uncle. Tom was just as angry and uncertain as his nephew. *They'd only been bivouacked since this afternoon and now they were being*

ordered to move again? Why? Had the Rebs been spotted? Were they close? Would they give chase? Where were they going now?
"What are they thinking? It's night and we're setting off now? In the dark! Again!" Gerald shoved his things into his knapsack, continuing his tirade as he went.

"I guess they're thinking it's time to go." Tom pushed his own gear into his knapsack. "No sense yapping about it. We're moving out and that's that."

Gerald stopped and stared at his uncle before he shook his head and finished packing.

Minutes later the men set out, on foot, grumbling under their breaths, headed where, no one knew.

***

They marched through the night in the direction they'd just come from, crossing a covered bridge rumored to be where the Rebs had been yesterday when the Eighth turned around. On the other side of the bridge they continued seven more miles to Stony Creek and camped for the night.

The next day, the 16th of July, they marched again, and again the next day, and the next. They set up breastworks around camp at night to keep out the unseen Rebs, then left it all behind and marched the next day. It was a seemingly useless march that went nowhere.

"So far, what have we done?" Arnold asked Tom, Gerald, Lawrence, and Jacob, gathered around the fire inside the ring of tents that afternoon where they'd been camped for days. "We've marched on sore, bleeding feet, broken our backs setting up breastworks when the Rebs were nowhere around, waited, and marched some more. We don't have a thing to show for it," he complained.

"We haven't faced the Rebs in a fight and still have our lives. I'd say that's something," Tom said.

Arnold jumped up, fists balled. "But I *want* to fight the Rebs! That's why I joined up in the first place. Why I re-enlisted after my ninety days were up. I *want* to fight and we have yet to even see a Reb *to* fight!"

"And I've told *you* those southern boys aren't going to run away like you all think they will."

"Scuttlebutt around camp is that our boys tucked tail and ran when they met those Johnny Rebs at Bull Run Creek near Manassas a couple days ago," Jacob said with contempt.

Tom cocked his head. "I told you those boys shouldn't be discounted. They're a tough lot and won't give up easily."

"That's the truth," Lawrence said with a snort. "That general of theirs, Jackson, I think his name was; yes, that's it, Jackson. They're calling him Stonewall because he didn't budge when McDowell's boys attacked. They say he stood like a stone wall."

"Sounds like you admire him, like he's some kind of hero," Arnold snarled.

"Well, I sure think he did a better job than our boys, who ran back to town like a bunch of scared rabbits!" Lawrence defended.

"Stop!" Tom shouted. "We shouldn't be arguing between ourselves. That doesn't help our cause one bit. Yes, McDowell's boys ran. It was the first battle in what is going to be a long war, despite what everyone thinks. We'll do better next time, and the next, and the next."

Arnold threw a twig into the fire making it spark and pop. "You're right, Tom," he grumbled. "No cause to fight between ourselves. We've got bigger things to worry about—namely *finding* some Johnny Rebs *to* fight in the first place."

There was general agreement and Tom knew the others must be realizing, perhaps for the first time, that this war might last for much longer than the few months everyone on both sides had presumed. The North was beaten back in the first real battle of the war, but they would learn from their rout and regroup. The South didn't have the men or materiel the North had for a long engagement and would, eventually, become lacking. It was only a matter of time. At least that's what Tom told himself to keep doubt from settling in his mind that the South *might* actually win this war with the determination and grit he'd seen most of his life.

***

Gerald leaned toward the fire and poked at the bacon sizzling in the pan with a long stick. "I'm tired of bacon, and canned meat, and hardtack," he groaned.

"It's better than what we had at Dennison and there's plenty of it. At least for now," Tom reminded his nephew.

Gerald nodded. "Yes, there's more. And plenty of boredom to go with it, too," he grumbled, moving aside with a grin to avoid Tom's punch at his arm.

Arnold took up the complaining. "Hell, it's been months since we've done anything of merit. We built Fort Pendleton."

The men snickered at the reference to the breastworks they'd helped build around the house of Major Pendleton.

"We've guarded the railroad," Arnold continued when the laughter ceased. "Big deal. We've done little to nothing so far in this war. It's the end of September and we've fought nothing but boredom and lice!"

"Stop your bellyaching," Jacob said. "You've got a full belly and I'll take boredom over getting shot at any day."

"So why did you enlist?" Gerald asked. "That's part of fighting a war, Jacob, getting shot at."

"Seemed like the thing to do at the time. Everybody I knew enlisted after Sumter. Ohio's ranks filled faster than, well, faster than most of the other states in the north. Men flooded the enlistment stations and I didn't want to be left behind like some coward afraid to go off and fight," Jacob defended. "Hell, that's why we all volunteered." He waved his hand to encompass himself, Arnold and Lawrence. "We've been friends since we were kids and one of us wasn't going to go off and fight without the others."

Arnold and Lawrence nodded agreement.

"Well, I don't feel like we're contributing, either," Gerald complained.

"There'll be plenty of time for that, boys. Trust me." Tom laid his hand on his nephew's shoulder.

"And that time will be sooner than you think."

The men gathered around as Sergeant Galwey stepped into their circle.

"What do you mean, Sarge?" Tom asked.

"We've been ordered to march. Gather your gear, boys, we head for Romney tonight."

Chapter Nineteen

Their force of eleven hundred men, including the Fourth Ohio Infantry with Colonel Cantwell in charge of all the troops, their own company of the Eighth Ohio, a company of cavalry, and one piece of artillery, started toward Romney at eleven the night of September 20th. Although it was another night march, their hopes were high that *this* march might bear more than just boredom and moving from one place to another. They hoped to find some Rebs.

"I'm walking in my sleep," Gerald grumbled beside Tom. "That's it. This is a dream and I'm spending another night walking in my sleep."

Tom looked at his nephew and shook his head.

"Am I walking in my sleep, Tom? I'm just dreaming and we're *all* walking in our sleep, right?"

When his uncle gave him a scowl instead, Gerald looked up at the sky. "What time is it?"

"It's still too dark to tell, but my guess would be five or six in the morning."

"How far do you think we've gone? We had eighteen miles to go. Do you think we're close?"

He was as anxious as a child standing at a counter, picking out a penny candy. "I can tell you we're closer than we were when we left." Tom's eyes sparkled with laughter.

"Very funny. Of course we are. Unless we've gone in circles, which I wouldn't discount," Gerald added with a groan. "I just want to know how close we are after walking all night."

Tom lifted his hand. "Wait, we're stopping. Here comes Galwey. Maybe he knows something."

Galwey stopped just up the line and the men gathered around. "What's going on, Sarge?" Tom asked.

"We're close to our destination. We're sending in a cavalry unit to reconnoiter what's ahead. So right now, we wait."

There was some grumbling in the ranks, but most of the men happily dropped their knapsacks and welcomed the time to rest sore bodies and even more sore feet.

Minutes later there was a volley of shots from up ahead before the cavalry company raced back to where the anxious men waited.

"Form ranks on both sides of the road!"

The Eighth, including B Company, formed on one side, the Fourth on the other and waited until Captain Kenney called them out.

"We've been ordered to draw out the enemy at Mechanicsburg, just west of the gap that leads to the bridge over the South Branch of the Potomac and into Romney. Let's march."

Gerald looked at Tom and Tom looked at Gerald. Their three friends looked at each other as they grabbed their gear and headed up the road behind Kenney and Galwey toward Mechanicsburg and the unseen enemy.

No one spoke, but Tom thought hard about where they were headed. *How many men were waiting for them? What kind of cover would they have? Would they be able to draw the Rebs into the ambush Colonel Cantwell planned for them along the road?* His mind whirled as he walked, the others silent around him and lost in their own thoughts of what was ahead.

The company stopped and Kenney signaled them into the road that led into the little, mostly deserted town.

"Mind yourself," Tom said to Gerald.

"You, too."

They walked onto the main street staying close to the buildings, careful of what was ahead of, and behind them. Tom hadn't gone far when shots ricocheted overhead off the building he was crouched next to.

"Find cover!" he shouted to Gerald as the shooting intensified. Together they ran behind another building and fired down the street where the shots had come from.

The rest of B Company scattered throughout the seemingly empty town, firing at the unseen enemy as they worked their way toward the end of the street.

Tom's heart beat wildly, but he was in control, even though he had no control. Gerald was wide-eyed and flushed beside him, but kept his wits. Arnold, Jacob, and Lawrence, on the opposite side of the street, were bunched together, moving from building to building, covering each other as they went.

The firing was sporadic, at best, and only a few minutes passed before Kenney shouted, "Cease firing, men! Cease firing!"

They stopped and listened. Silence. Slowly, they finished working their way to the end of the street. Tom checked inside buildings, behind carts, wagons, and barrels as he went. He checked anything a man could hide inside or behind, but found nothing and no one. They reached the end of the street a few minutes later with no further resistance.

What Rebs had been there were gone.

Near the blacksmith's shop at the end of town a scout on horseback raced to Captain Kenney. Within earshot, Tom heard him say, "You and your men have been ordered to return to command."

Kenney nodded. The scout turned his mount around, raced back up the street, and out of sight.

"Men!" Kenney shouted. "We've been ordered back to command."

Buoyant from their first encounter with the Rebs, even though they hadn't *seen* any Rebs, with much back slapping and congratulations, Tom, Gerald, their three companions and the rest of B Company turned and went back into Mechanicsburg riding a wave of victory.

***

They marched ten miles to the ford where they would cross the South Branch of the Potomac and into Romney. The men slogged along like floppy puppets, half asleep on their feet as they walked. It was four in the morning when they arrived, a heavy mountain mist hanging over the ground like white down. The low fog was so fluffy Tom wished he could gather it up, fall into it, and sleep for a week. The silence surrounding them was comforting, like the mist, lulling them into dreamlike states—until they heard voices in the distance.

"Shhh, shhh, shhh!" Tom waved his hand at Gerald and the three friends. "Listen. That's Jack Sheppard's voice up ahead," he whispered, his nephew so close Tom was sure he could hear Gerald's heart beating if he tried.

"I told you, cain't nobody cross here," the unfamiliar voice said.

"We're crossing, whether you've a notion to let us or not," Sheppard said.

"Well, come on then, an' see what ye git," the voice challenged."

Moments later Captain Kenney shouted, "At the double-quick, men, across the river!"

Without hesitation and despite being bone-tired, the men charged into the water, splashing and cursing, falling and laughing.

Soaking wet but safely across Tom turned to Gerald, "That sentry must have high-tailed it out of here when he realized a whole regiment was crossing and not just one man. Where are the rest of their men? Not a single shot was fired to stop us."

"That's agreeable to me!" Lawrence almost shouted, dumping water from his boots and wringing the tail of his shirt. "I'm soaked clean through. This uniform must weigh an extra twenty pounds!"

"And no time to dry out." Galwey stepped up beside the five men, wringing out what he could of his own clothing. "We're to keep going." He pointed to the right, back along the riverbank and under a cliff whose summit rose above the low hanging mist.

Gerald groaned. "Well, boys, you all know the drill," he growled. "There's no rest for the weary. Although I do feel better since our bath," he joked.

"Then get at it. For'ard march!" Galwey shouted.

The men trudged the short distance alongside the river then under the outcropping of rock toward Romney. They'd been marching only a short time when the men in front of the five came to a sudden halt.

"What's going on?" Gerald asked Tom.

"Well, how would I know?" Tom snapped, as anxious as Gerald as to why they'd stopped so suddenly.

"I'll find out." Arnold stepped out of line and looked ahead. Stepping back into formation he said, "Something's not right. A tree's been dragged into the middle of the road."

"So, we'll go over it." Galwey walked to the tree and stepped over.

Arnold scrunched his shoulders and followed Galwey. The others flashed wary glances at one another then did the same. They scarcely made it over the log when an explosion and wall of flames from the top of the cliff knocked them off their feet.

Staggering from the explosion, feeling as though someone had boxed his ears, Tom barely heard Lawrence's exclamation of "Mother Mary, Jesus, and Joseph!" as everyone scrambled back to cover under the ledge.

"What was that?" Tom barely heard Arnold's shout through the ringing in his ears.

Trying to keep his wits, Tom took a deep breath to fill lungs that felt like they had a hundred pound weight on them from the concussion. "Keep your heads, boys. Keep your heads. They can't get to us under this ledge. As long as we're below them we're safe."

"Will you look at that?" Arnold stood with his back to Tom and the others, his finger pointed in the direction they'd just come from. "The rest of the regiment is high-tailing it out of here!"

"Not everybody," Lawrence corrected sliding along the cliff wall to stand beside his friend. "G Company is still here. I see some of the Fremont boys there in the shadows."

Arnold swung around to face Lawrence. "I don't care about a few Fremont boys! The damned regiment left us! Retreated like rabbits!" Arnold ducked when shooting erupted from above, but did little damage under their protective ledge.

"How long are we going to sit here and wait, Galwey? There's no sense in it," Jacob growled. "I say we head back to the ford with the rest of the regiment—that's probably already back across the river!"

Tom tried to keep his senses amidst the shots being lobbed at them from above. Jacob was right. "No need to make targets of ourselves—or wait for them to find a way to reach us from above, Sarge. I say we retreat with the rest of the regiment."

"I say that's right!" Arnold agreed.

Men grumbled agreement all around. Galwey shushed the men to silence. "I can't give that order, boys, you know that." He looked down the line and raised his hand. "Wait, here comes Captain Kenney."

"What about it, Captain?" Arnold asked. "Are we going to sit here and let them take pot shots at us or go back with the rest of the regiment?"

"We go back, follow me." Kenney scooted past the men clustered along the wall, headed for the ford they'd just crossed and, under the protection of the ledge, led the men back to the river. It wasn't long before they were splashing through the water to the applause of the men on the other side. *For what? Staying to do their duty when they had run?* Tom wanted to shout.

Reaching solid ground, the five friends found a spot away from the rest of the men, plopped down, and wrung out their clothes again, all of them wondering what the next few hours would bring.

***

Tom slept like the dead. His limbs felt heavy yet he seemed to float at the same time. It was peaceful, such a peace that he reached for it, clawed at it, when that sleep was being dragged away.

"Get up, Tom!"

Tom's eyes popped open. Gerald stood over him, a severe look on his face, and Tom's easy sleep drained away like water through a sieve as reality struck.

He jerked upright. They were still on the bank of the river, awaiting orders. He hadn't meant to sleep, but his tired, old body didn't do what he'd wanted. He'd merely closed his eyes for a second and fell helplessly asleep.

"Come on, we're moving again." Gerald helped his uncle to his feet, the older man's joints snapping and popping like corn exploding on the stalk in the blazing August sun.

"Where we going? Tom asked, his mind still fuzzy.

"Word is we've been ordered back to Romney. We're to take it at any cost."

"Well, isn't that a fine howdy do," Arnold grumbled, stepping next to Tom and Gerald. "We were halfway there just hours ago and left behind at the first sign of resistance, and now we're to do it all again? If our officers had any grit, we'd have forged ahead earlier instead of retreating. We'd have taken the town and be celebrating right now with whiskeys all around!"

"Button it, Watson!" Galwey shouted when he came up behind them. "We're moving out—now!"

"Yes, Sarge," Arnold had the sense to sound contrite as he fell in with the rest of the men wading back into the water.

Across the river again, they marched under the protection of the overhanging ledge and beyond without incident, until they reached the hills just north of Romney.

Leaving the road they headed toward town. It wasn't long before the march was called to a halt.

"Why are we stopping?" Gerald asked Tom, again, as though he were the knower of all things.

"Don't know."

"Let's find out." Gerald headed toward Galwey before Tom could stop him and returned a few minutes later.

"So? What did you find out?" Tom asked in a whisper.

"There are Rebs over there." Gerald pointed toward town. "They don't know we're here. We can take 'em easy as you please, but Colonel Park is wavering."

"What do you mean, wavering?" Tom asked.

"Sarge said we've got surprise on our side, but the charge should have been sounded by now if we were going to attack.

"What's the colonel waiting for?" Tom asked.

Gerald shook his head. "Don't know and neither does Galwey. He's waiting for orders just like the rest of us. We'll know as soon as he does."

A few minutes later Galwey gathered the anxious men around him with those orders.

"What?" Tom hissed. "We're to retreat? Again? But why?" he asked a just as befuddled Galwey.

Galwey pursed his lips. "I don't know why, but those are the orders and I do as I'm told, so turn it around, boys."

"But Colonel Cantwell and his men are behind us, waiting for our attack so they can follow." Tom argued. He knew it was fruitless to argue with a sergeant who had no more control over where they went and what they did than he did, but he couldn't help himself. *They were retreating! When the enemy was in their sights with more troops behind their own waiting to join the fight! What was Colonel Park thinking? Or* not *thinking by retreating?*

Gerald slapped Tom on the back. "There's no help for it. Come on, let's go."

Tom shook his head with disbelief. Although he didn't want to run headlong into a fight, they would have the advantage in this one and were running instead! He just couldn't fathom the reasoning behind it, other than pure, simple fear. Unwilling to dwell on it, he followed the others back under the ledge and through the river. They made it back to camp by nine that night, met by the rest of the regiment that was just as confused as they were.

Chapter Twenty

Tom slept hard that night, until roused early the next morning. He wasn't refreshed as he should have been. Instead, he was more sluggish than the day before, in desperate need of *many* days of rest to regain strength in his tired, old body.

"The rest of the regiment is going through the gap and over the bridge into Romney," Galwey reported to the men gathered around the morning fire.

"The *rest* of the regiment? What about us?" Tom asked.

"We've been ordered to stay behind and cover a retreat if one should occur."

Tom stared at the sergeant. "We're not to attack with the rest of the regiment?"

Galwey shook his head. "Not this time. We're to act as a rear guard to cover a retreat," Galwey said for a second time. "Those are our orders."

There was major grumbling amongst the men. Arnold threw things, Jacob kicked at the dirt, and Lawrence walked back and forth with his hands in his pockets, talking to himself.

"Why are we being left behind?" Gerald asked Tom. "Did we do something wrong?"

Tom grimaced. "I don't think we did something wrong. We went first yesterday and stayed when everyone else high-tailed it back across the river, so they're letting someone else go in first instead of us is my guess."

"But I don't want to stay behind." Gerald stalked back and forth.

"I don't want to stay behind either, but those are our orders, Gerald. Orders are orders and we're to cover a retreat should there be one. Period."

"It's not fair. It's just not fair," Gerald whined like a little boy.

"Who said the army was fair my dear nephew? Life isn't fair so why would we expect the army to be?" He smacked Gerald on the back. "Buck up, there'll be plenty of fighting in this war and

I, for one, am happy to miss as much as I can. I've no death wish."

Gerald frowned and nodded. "I guess you're right. There'll be plenty of fighting if this war lasts as long as you say it will."

"Oh, it will. I've no doubt."

It was eleven that morning when the men of B Company watched the cavalry race toward them out of Romney, charge across the bridge, and back into the Mechanicsburg Gap.

"Prepare to move, boys," Galwey told the men as the cavalry rode past them.

"Are we retreating then?" Gerald asked.

Galwey sucked in a deep breath. "It appears so. Be ready to offer cover."

"*Why* are we retreating? Do you know?" Tom asked.

Galwey shook his head. "All I've heard is that the fighting was heavy in Romney. The Rebs must have been reinforced overnight." Galwey spit and kicked his foot. "If we'd attacked yesterday we would have had surprise in our favor. We might have routed them and taken the town and saved another retreat!"

Tom sensed the anger in the young sergeant's attitude, but it was the tone of the entire company. Men were raging in anger all around, stomping, spitting, grumbling, and throwing things, but there was no help for it. A retreat was coming and B Company was to cover it.

The cavalry past, the men of B Company waited for the rest of the regiment's return from Romney. At noon the first of the men appeared on the bridge and, as the last of them straggled by, B Company fell in behind them, ready to do their best to ensure an orderly retreat.

A short way from the gap Tom looked over his shoulder and almost tripped. A cloud of dust was rising behind them.

"Sarge. Look!" Tom pointed at the dust cloud.

"At the double quick, men. At the double quick!" Galwey shouted.

Blistered, bleeding feet and aching bodies forgotten, Tom and the others stepped lively, unwilling to let the Rebel cavalry catch them in their present position—out in the open and very vulnerable.

***

"Form a skirmish line over there men!" Captain Kenney shouted and pointed as the rest of the regiment continued on ahead of them.

Tom, Gerald, Arnold, Lawrence, and Jacob scurried to the top of the designated hill and flopped on their bellies with weapons ready.

They hadn't waited but a few minutes when Tom jabbed Gerald with his elbow and whispered, "I hear horses."

"Horses? Where?" Gerald craned his neck to see down the hill.

Tom listened only a moment more before he flipped on his back. "Behind us!" he shouted. He leveled his Enfield and fired at the cavalry unit approaching from the rear. The others flipped around, their guns discharging at the attacking riders.

Men shouted, "Save yourselves!" as they jumped up and scrambled away.

Tom grabbed Gerald's arm and yanked. They ran down the hill that was to have been their protection against the riders, Arnold, Lawrence, and Jacob right behind them.

Tom had to concentrate on keeping his balance as he charged downward. Between the heavy knapsack he'd hefted back over his shoulder and the angle at which they ran, one missed step would mean his rolling down the hill instead of reaching the bottom on his feet.

Gerald had forged ahead of him, as had Arnold, Lawrence, and Jacob, the younger men passing him as though he were skipping. Gerald turned and waved for him to hurry, but he was already running as fast and hard as he could.

Reaching a fence the men scurried over. They threw their haversacks to the other side ahead of them or tried to squeeze through the slats with the sacks still on their backs and looked like turtles trying to push through a too small hole in their shells. *If this weren't such a dire situation, it would be funny.*

Tom threw his own sack over the fence and climbed as fast as he could, snatching it back up when he hit the ground, his knees almost buckling under him.

Gerald was waiting for him on the other side. He grabbed Tom by the arm and dragged him along behind him like a father dragging an errant son. Only Tom didn't resist, he let his nephew help him along as quickly as they could go away from the pursuing Rebs.

Gunfire popped and whizzed overhead as men charged into the ford of a creek that allowed only one man's crossing at a time. There was cursing and shoving as each man jockeyed to cross first.

"Go!" Gerald shouted, shoving Tom ahead of him. Tom surged into the water, splashing and churning his way through, Gerald pushing him from behind, the three friends somewhere ahead.

"Can't you go any faster?" Gerald yelled, shoving Tom out of the way.

"I'm going as fast as I can!" Tom screamed back, annoyed that he *couldn't* go faster. In all his life he'd never *had* to run anywhere. Instead he'd sat *astride* his horses and chased the wind without expending his own energy. He could barely breathe. His lungs were ready to explode. His legs burned like fire and felt like they were mired in molasses at the same time.

Gerald slogged past him. "Grab my pack and hang on," he shouted.

Tom grabbed his nephew's pack and held on. He half ran and was half dragged the rest of the way until they reached the other side. Tom crawled up the bank and dropped to his knees, his chest heaving as he tried to refill his lungs and stop the trembling in his wobbly legs and body.

"Come on, Tom, we can't stop." Gerald hauled his uncle up and off they went again.

Minutes later Tom chanced a glance over his shoulder. No one was chasing them. Barely able to talk, he slapped at Gerald's arm, the younger man still dragging him along beside him. "Stop! They're not coming." He pulled away, bent over, and put his hands on his knees to catch his breath. He had a stitch in his side and his legs burned like fire again. Lifting his arm back toward the creek he managed, "They're not coming."

"We don't know that, Tom. We've got to keep going."

Tom swallowed, sucked in some air, and nodded. "All right then, let's go."

He stood up, every muscle in his body screaming, sure his heart would explode before they got wherever they were going. Gerald grabbed his arm again and the two hurried forward. Moments later Arnold, Jacob, and Lawrence appeared beside them. Arnold grabbed his other arm and between Gerald and Arnold, Tom was running again.

"Come on, old man, we'll getcha where we need to go!" Arnold shouted as the three charged on like drunkards.

"To be sure, old man!" Jacob shouted. "If those two can't get you where you're going me and Lawrence will!"

"Don't worry, Uncle Tom, we've got you," Gerald added.

Far from the creek they finally slowed down. No one was following and they were allowed time to regroup and catch their wind. Tom let his sopping wet, heavy knapsack fall to the ground. He dropped to his knees then onto his back. He threw his arms out from his body. Not usually a praying man, he looked up into the sky. "Thank you, God, thank you for sparing me, for sparing all of us, in our run from Johnnie Reb."

First there were chuckles and then laughter as Gerald, Arnold, Jacob, and Lawrence dropped down beside him like fish flopping on a bank, each man shouting, "Thank you God for our deliverance! Thank you!"

Chapter Twenty-One

"Drill, drill, drill. Pull guard duty. Then drill some more. I feel like I'm back at Dennison." Gerald dropped to the ground near the small fire in front of their tents where the company had been bivouacked for days. He turned his head to see how close his uncle was and whether he would get a punch in the arm for his grumbling. Tom just shook his head and slid down beside Gerald.

"Would you rather make another run with Rebs on our tails?" Tom asked. "I surely would not!"

"I suppose you wouldn't, old man." Gerald grinned with affection, using the new nickname Tom had acquired since their flight from what had turned out to be Ashby's Cavalry. "I wouldn't either, to be honest."

Tom punched his nephew in the arm.

"Hey!"

"That's for your complaint."

"I'd hoped you'd forgotten your threat." Gerald rubbed the offended spot.

Tom lifted his hand to slap his nephew on the back, but Gerald jumped away. Chuckling, Tom said, "I may be an *old man* who can't run and whose bones snap and pop, but I *will not* forget my promise to punch you when you complain. So mind yourself, Gerald."

Gerald stared at his uncle with pinched eyes before he laughed out loud and shouted. "Drilling is wonderful. I love to drill! I could drill every day for the rest of the war!"

"Don't overdo it, Gerald, or I'll punch you again," Tom warned with a gleam in his eyes. Turning from his nephew he shook his head, grabbed the pot from the fire, and poured himself a cup of coffee.

Lawrence, Arnold, and Jacob joined them around the fire.

"The end of another glorious day, boys." Arnold lamented.

Gerald shook his head. "Better keep your tongue or the old man will pop you sure."

"Ah, Tom won't hit me. I'm not related."

"No, I wouldn't. I'm only obliged to punch kin." Tom's tone was solemn.

Arnold laughed out loud. "See, I'm safe!"

Gerald frowned and shook his head. "I should be so lucky!"

Lawrence snorted. "We're doing what we're told to do and I'm happy with that. I prefer not to become cannon fodder. I'll take drilling and boredom any day." Lawrence stood up and raised his arm to encompass camp. "Besides, you've got a multitude of games of chance to choose from to keep you lively."

"And if I don't choose to play cards or bet on lice or beetle races?" Gerald asked.

"Well...there's always a good book," Lawrence chuckled. "Or a letter home."

Tom watched the interaction between the four men and realized he was more comfortable with these men than most others throughout his entire life—except his people at Champion Farms and, of course, Sam. They'd risked their lives for him. Made sure he made it safely away from the Rebs. They came back for him when he fell behind. They were a brotherhood, family.

He punched Arnold.

"Hey, what was that for?" Arnold asked, rubbing his arm like Gerald had done only moments ago.

"You boys *are* family, so mind your complaints. We're *all* family now and you boys will get the same punch in the arm Gerald gets." He pointed his finger in the air. "The old man has spoken!"

The four younger men looked from one to the other. Gerald busted out laughing and the others joined him. "The old man has spoken!" he shouted.

Arnold turned to Tom. "I like the sound of it. Family watches over one another and that's our solemn vow from now on."

They each poured a cup of coffee and lifted it high. "To family!"

Tom hoisted his cup, completing the circle above the fire.

"Welcome to the family, boys!" Gerald shouted. "And enjoy the punch that goes with it!"

***

"*Another* night march? What do they have against marching during the day like normal troops?" Gerald asked.

Tom ignored his nephew's grumblings, because he felt like grumbling right now, too.

"Why do we always march at night?" Gerald complained as he and Tom rolled up their tents and packed their equipment. "We've been bivouacked for days and now, at ten o'clock at night on this, what day is it, I've lost track?"

"The twenty-fifth of October, I think," Tom supplied.

"Thank you. At ten o'clock on this twenty-fifth night of October, eighteen hundred and sixty-one, we are rousted from our beds, yet again, for another night march. What do they have against sleep?"

Tom wondered the same thing.

They marched until two o'clock that morning before the order was issued to stop and set up camp again.

After little sleep, while eating their morning rations, the five friends considered where they were going.

"We're headed back to Romney," Arnold said, snapping off a piece of hardtack.

"I think you're right," Jacob agreed. "I just hope we get a chance to fight this time."

Tom shook his head. "Always anxious for a fight, aren't you boys?"

"That's why we're here, isn't it?" Arnold asked.

"I'd be happy to miss a few fights," Lawrence sided with Tom. "I want to stay alive, not get my fool head blown off."

Jacob frowned. "I want to fight, but when the odds are in our favor, like they were the day before we retreated from Romney the first time."

There was agreement around the circle.

"Well, let's hope the odds are in our favor today, boys. It looks like we're moving out." Tom stood up, threw away the last of his coffee, stowed his cup, and prepared for yet another march.

Gerald slid up beside his uncle. "Hey, we've got one thing in our favor."

"What's that?"

"It's morning. We'll get a whole day of marching in before it turns into another night march." Gerald slapped his uncle on the shoulder and stepped out.

Two hours later the company halted again.

"Take a snort, men! A few swallows for courage." Captain Kenney wandered through the lines, pouring whiskey to any man who wanted it.

Tom, Gerald, Arnold, Jacob, and Lawrence dropped to the ground where they'd stood, each holding a cup of whiskey. Arnold sniffed it several times before he took a sip. He smacked his lips and finished the rest in two gulps.

"That alone, gentlemen, was worth this march." His voice was gruff from the strong drink.

Tom took a sip of his, as did the others. Each man closed his eyes, savoring the taste of it as it went down.

"I've had worse." Jacob's voice was rough.

Tom thought back to what seemed like another life and compared it to the fine whiskey's he'd savored in many a winner's circle. His heart did a flip flop. *Would he ever have that kind of life again? No matter who won this war, everything would be different, on both sides of the line. At least in what remained of this lifetime.*

"I've had worse, but this'll do in a pinch." Tom finished his cup with a sigh, happy to have it, as the warmth of it spread through his body and calmed his nerves, doing what it was intended to do.

"What time do you reckon it is?" Gerald asked Tom when they stopped again.

Tom looked up, gauged the sun a moment and answered, "I'd say noon."

"No wonder my stomach is growling."

"Well tell it to stop, here comes Galwey, and he's not smiling."

"We've been ordered to act as skirmishers."

"Why sarge?" Arnold was the first to ask.

Galwey pointed. "That piece of artillery might have something to do with it."

The men gaped only a moment at the single Reb cannon blocking the road that led into Mechanicsburg before Galwey shouted, "At a run!"

***

Tom and the others took off at a dead run, racing toward the threatening cannon, screaming as they ran. Tom's heart raced as fast as his feet, barely keeping up with Gerald and the others.

The ground erupted and spewed around them, debris falling like rain on the ground. Onward they charged, rifles at the ready, until they realized the shells were exploding *behind* them.

"We made it!" Gerald shouted. "We made it to the mouth of the gap where the gun can't reach us!"

Tom stopped beside his nephew, put his hands on his knees to catch his breath, and waited for orders whether to chase or retreat, like they'd done so often recently.

They stood catching their breath only moments before the Rebs turned the cannon and *they* retreated.

"After them, men!" Captain Kenney led the company in pursuit of the fleeing Rebels, guns popping from both directions.

The rest of the regiment joined the pursuit and within minutes had reached the bridge over the South Branch of the Potomac, again.

"Halt!" Kenney called, assessing the situation. He pulled out his glass and surveyed the hills ahead of them. Snapping it shut he spoke to Galwey, before Galwey turned and went among the men.

"They're ready for us. They've got two twelve-pounders in the hills overlooking the bridge. Get ready, boys, we're going over," Galwey said.

Tom looked at Gerald then at the other three men he now considered family. They straightened their backs, gripped their rifles tighter, and prepared to run for their lives.

"Charge!" Captain Kenney shouted, leading the way onto the bridge at a run. The men followed, yelling and cheering for courage as the howitzers opened fire.

Tom ducked and ran crouched over when water poured down on them like a drenching summer thunderstorm as the balls hit the river instead of the bridge. Cheering wildly that the bridge had been missed, the men hurried the rest of the way across the bridge.

Before Tom realized, they were on the other side and on the road into Romney, the rest of the regiment right behind them.

They charged into town. As they'd done in Mechanicsburg, they checked behind wagons, barrels and horse troughs, and inside buildings. Anywhere a man could hide.

"Check the back, I'll check the front," Tom said to Gerald when they came upon a wagon sitting in the middle of the road.

Gerald ran to the rear. "We're coming in. If anyone's in there, you best come out now. We prefer not to shoot you, but be assured, we will if you think to fire upon us," Gerald shouted.

Movement inside made the wagon shake. Crouching low, Tom worked his way to the front. "Don't make us shoot you. Come on out now," he shouted.

"Don't...don't shoot. We're coming out," came from where Gerald waited.

Tom raised his Enfield to make sure no one tried to run out from his end.

"I got 'em," Gerald called from the rear. "I've got 'em! Come on outta there you mangy Rebs!"

Tom waited a few more moments to make sure no one tried to sneak out the front before he hoisted himself onto the seat and peered inside. It was empty and he breathed a sigh of relief before he jumped down and went to join his nephew.

"Look what we got here, Tom." Gerald's rifle was pointed at the bellies of three men as Tom stepped next to him. "Three Johnny Rebs a hidin' in a wagon," Gerald said in a sing-song voice.

The men's hands were high above their heads and fear was plain on their faces.

"What do we do with them?" Arnold asked when he, Jacob, and Lawrence joined Tom and Gerald with two more prisoners.

"We take them to the Captain. He'll know what to do with them." Gerald nudged the three men forward with the barrel of his Enfield. Arnold and Jacob shoved their prisoners next to the other three. Lawrence and Tom looked at each other, both sensing the other's uncertainty, before following.

They marched the prisoners through town, greeted by cheers as they walked up the street.

Later that day, the town taken and everything inventoried, Gerald plopped down beside Tom and the others outside their tents where they were bivouacked for the night. "It was a good day. We all survived, we *finally* took Romney, B Company led the way, and we took lots of prisoners and supplies," he finished with a flourish.

"Word is six cannon were captured." Arnold was grinning.

"And wagons, lots of wagons for transport," Jacob said. "Maybe we'll get to ride instead of walk for a while and give our poor, aching feet a break," he added, hopeful.

"I wouldn't count on it," Arnold snarled.

"It's a good ending to the day when the five of us can sit together around a fire all breathing and in one piece. We did our jobs today, boys. We did it well," Tom said.

Everyone nodded in agreement. Until Gerald asked, "So, where do we go from here?"

Tom rolled his lips. "That, my young nephew, is the question of the day. For now, pull up some dirt and get some rest. There's no telling what tomorrow will bring."

Chapter Twenty-Two

"This insipid boredom is driving me crazy." Gerald threw a log on the morning fire around which he, Tom, Arnold, Jacob, and Lawrence were huddled outside their hut, a comfortable structure constructed with boards gathered during their stay in Romney.

Tom rolled his hand to punch his nephew then unrolled it. His threat had gone far enough. If Gerald wanted to complain, or any of the others for that fact, who was he to stop them? Besides, he'd taken to grumbling quite a bit himself since they took Romney. It was mid-December and they'd done nothing but sit around town and wait. They even had a new commanding officer, Colonel Samuel Sprigg Carroll, a West Pointer, who took command after Colonel DePuy's and Lieutenant Colonel Parks's resignations following the early retreats from Romney.

"It's been weeks, Tom. Weeks and we've done nothing. We don't even drill anymore. Not that I miss it, mind you, but not doing *anything*, even drilling, just adds to the boredom."

"I agree, but the men find things to do," Tom said.

Gerald snorted. "Oh yes, I've forgotten the lice and beetle races. And getting liquored up like those boys that passed through town and caused all that trouble back in November?"

"Well, liquor does bring out the worst in men." Tom shook his head.

"It brought murder might I remind you uncle."

"I know the story, Gerald. How the boys got all liquored up and someone put a bayonet through poor, Stephen Carr's throat."

"*Our* Stephen Carr." Arnold's face was hard.

Tom sighed. "I know who he was, Arnold. And a drunk Walter Griffis was arrested for the murder, sent to Cumberland jail, and that was the end of it. And just one more reason I don't get drunk, not with friends, family, or soldiers I don't know one bit about who might get mean and murder someone. Besides, I'm too old for it—and the splitting head that goes with it the next morning."

Gerald leaned toward his uncle. "You're one of the few in this army who feel such. I've been known to imbibe myself. It makes the time pass more pleasurably while we're stuck here."

"So you have. And as long as you don't bother me, and we're not marching off to fight, have as much pleasure as you like!"

Gerald thought a moment then said, "And what about the ladies who ease our boredom? We mustn't forget those who have taken up residence in their wagons at the end of town."

"At a high price, I tell you, in greenbacks *and* the clap!" Jacob said, joining the conversation.

Tom shook his head. "I hear a lot of men in camp have the clap from those camp followers. It's like being back at Dennison when so many got it from the *ladies* outside camp there."

"Aw Tom, stop being such an old man. Haven't you ever, you know, taken a woman just for the sake of taking her? Especially one that's willing with no encumbrances to propriety?" Arnold asked with a rude gesture.

Tom frowned as Abby's face exploded into his mind. Then Margaret's. Had he wanted a tryst, Margaret would have happily obliged. Yes, after Abby tore his heart out he'd taken a few women just for pleasure and to ease himself, but he didn't intend to do it with women known to be diseased! "I don't and won't."

"Well I do and I will old man!" Arnold shouted. "All this talk about a man's pleasures has made me randy. Any of you boys game for a toss?"

Lawrence and Jacob jumped up. Tom and Gerald stayed seated.

"Aw come on you two. Come with us and have some fun!" Jacob said. "It's better than spending the whole day sitting around here."

"You boys have your fun," Tom said. "And insult me all you want, but it won't change my mind."

"You won't change mine, either. When you're scratching and itching and complaining, I'll remind you all of this conversation." Gerald poked at the bacon popping in the pan. "I managed to keep from catching the clap before. I'm of no mind to hedge my bets and catch it now." He shivered.

The three friends laughed and turned their backs. "Have it your way! We're gonna have some fun! Save some of that bacon for us. We plan to work up a powerful appetite!" Jacob shouted over his shoulder as they headed toward the far end of camp where the soiled doves waited.

***

In early January of 1862 the regiment marched away from Romney. Word got around that Stonewall Jackson was at Winchester only forty miles away, and was planning a movement that could impact them. Marching night and day through the cold and rain, they reached Patterson Creek hungry, tired, and ill-humored.

Camp was set up and the men returned to their days of gambling, drinking, and waiting. For what, they didn't know, but when it came, they would surely wish they were back in camp, grumbling about the boredom.

Chapter Twenty-Three

In March the Eighth was ordered to Winchester, Virginia, recently vacated by the Confederates, and joined by the Fourth Ohio, Fourteenth Indiana, and Seventh Virginia.

Tom, Gerald, Arnold, Lawrence, and Jacob stood in line with the rest of the Eighth at the edge of camp, awaiting orders. Tom turned his face to the sun, shining bright after several days of snow had blanketed the area. In the surrounding countryside where no humans had touched, the ground glistened like crystal, and where men's feet had trod it sloshed and slopped in a cold, gray slush.

The explosion of artillery in the distance alerted the men it was only a matter of time before it would be their turn to fight. Many crossed themselves, others, their faces turned to the sky, prayed to God for deliverance, while others stomped their feet, shoved their hands into their pockets, or blew on them to keep warm.

Gerald leaned toward his uncle and whispered, "Scuttlebutt is Stonewall Jackson and his Confederates are attacking from the south, trying to retake Winchester."

"And he's running straight into our artillery." Tom jutted his chin toward the sound of the pounding guns. "I imagine it won't be long before it's our turn." He turned to his nephew. "Gerald, if things go bad today, I want you to know…"

"Nothing will go bad," Gerald said before Tom could finish. "Word is we've got a bigger force and will hand General Jackson a defeat. We'll have them scurrying away faster than hell can scorch a feather."

"How long before we move out?" Arnold leaned forward from the other side of Gerald to join the conversation, his dark eyes wide and his face expectant.

Tom shook his head. "Don't know, but we'll find out soon enough." He pointed at the man coming toward them who was replacing Galwey while the young sergeant was temporarily reassigned to a recruiting station in Columbus, Ohio.

"Get ready, boys," the older, bewhiskered Sergeant Steadman said to the men in line. "Jackson and his Rebs are spread out west of Kernstown and advancing toward Winchester. We're to stop their advance and keep them from retaking the town."

A regular occurrence, Tom almost snorted. Possession of Winchester had changed hands so many times it was hard to keep count.

The men eyed one another and Tom steeled himself for battle. He recalled the run from Ashby's Cavalry and hoped his old body could withstand what was ahead. While encamped these past months, realizing how much he needed to strengthen himself beyond his training at Dennison, Tom had exercised every day and was in better physical shape than he'd been during that run. *But was it enough? To keep from winding up on the rolls of the dead because he couldn't get out of his own way fast enough?*

The sergeant waved his hand and charged forward. "At the double-quick, men, follow me!"

The men fell in and started toward the sound of the pounding artillery. They hurried toward what Tom had learned while encamped was Sandy Ridge—where they would meet Jackson's stone wall—up close and personal.

***

Was time a curtain? Did one have to pass through layer after layer to reach their destination? To succeed in their quest? Tom shook his head and followed the men in front of him toward possible death, but he walked on, as ordered, feeling as though his mind *and* body were wading through molasses.

Once they stopped they could see a long, stone wall giving cover to the Rebs in the distance.

"Charge!"

The men in front of Tom, Gerald, and their three friends surged forward in waves toward the protected enemy—and fell. They screamed and died as smoke poured into the air from the hidden Confederate muskets that slammed lead balls into them.

Tom ran toward the unseen enemy, the others beside him. Men fell in front of him before he went to a knee and fired. He reloaded and fired again, the others doing the same around him. He was in a sea of men, yet alone in that any moment one of those Confederate mini-balls might find him. Still the wave ebbed and flowed forward.

His legs and lungs burned like fires from hell and his heart pounded the same beat the drummer boy struck, yet Tom kept up with those around him.

Men dropped to the ground like discarded dolls, a bullet in their heart or head. They shrieked in pain, rolled and bucked before they stilled in death, or fell without a sound. Still they charged forward.

"Stay close!" Gerald shouted beside Tom.

Tom nodded. The men of B Company slowed as they drew closer to the long wall that protected the enemy with seemingly never ending return fire. Tom crouched, his knees screaming, but hoping to make himself a smaller target as the enemy guns popped in front of him.

Still they charged onward.

Hours had passed since they left Winchester. Guns continued to explode and men continued to die. Tom felt every minute of his forty years, the only thing on his mind living through the day.

By mid-afternoon, by Tom's calculation, it seemed the return fire was slowing. *Perhaps they're running out of ammunition? Perhaps it was only a matter of time, and men, before the Rebs would be forced to retreat—or all of us will be dead.*

Gerald remained as close to Tom as a second skin and Tom wondered if it was to protect his uncle or himself. It didn't matter, they were together and that was most important. Arnold, Jacob, and Lawrence, however, had spread out in search of cover, away from Tom and Gerald and were no longer visible.

Lying on his back, breathing heavily, Tom was so exhausted he could barely lift his arms. Only then did he realize how little ammunition he had.

"How much ammo you got left?" he asked Gerald, huffing to catch his breath on his belly beside him.

Gerald rolled to his side and lifted the cover of his pouch. He shook his head. "Not much. If we don't quit this battle soon, I'll be out."

Tom looked around. "No you won't. We've an endless supply right there." He waved his hand at the sea of fallen men. "There are extra cartridges, powder, even another rifle, or a pistol, if you can find one," he added.

Gerald shivered and nodded. "I guess there is plenty to be found, although I'm reluctant to search for it."

Tom laid his hand on his nephew's arm. "We'll do whatever it takes to survive this battle, and any others we face. Understood?"

"Understood."

A bullet whizzed overhead and both went flat to the ground, their conversation forgotten. Reloaded, Tom rolled to his belly and turned to face the wall. He waited for a target and when a head popped up, he fired. The man screamed and grabbed his face, blood spurting between his fingers, before he fell away out of sight.

Tom took no time to celebrate his success. He immediately reloaded for the next shot.

He was lying on his belly in a puddle of cold, wet, slush. The sun heated his backside while his chest and legs were freezing. His breath came in quick, white puffs. His hands were near to frozen and he blew on them, trying to keep them warm.

"Will this battle never end?" Gerald asked from beside Tom. "I'm so tired I can hardly lift my rifle."

Tom looked at him and gave him a *"how do you think I feel?"* look, and Gerald frowned.

Past mid-afternoon Tom noticed the return fire had waned considerably more and it wasn't long before there was none.

Cheers erupted through the Union lines, Tom and Gerald cheering just as loud as the others. "We did it!" Gerald shouted, dancing like a drunkard. "We drove them back. Ole Stonewall didn't stand like a stone wall this time!"

Tom grinned and nodded, but understood that greater Union numbers had played a significant role in their victory. Had

Jackson had more men, which meant more ammunition, they could have staved off a Union attack much longer.

And how many more men might have died? Tom wondered. He scanned the battlefield littered with hundreds of dead and dying men, wondering at the fates of Arnold, Jacob, and Lawrence.

Had his friends survived the day?

Chapter Twenty-Four

Tom and Gerald searched the battlefield until they found Arnold, Jacob, and Lawrence. Arnold and Jacob were on their knees beside Lawrence, stretched out on the ground between them. Tears streamed down the two friends' faces as Tom and Gerald dropped to their knees beside them.

"He took a ball to the shoulder early this morning, right after we all got separated." Arnold's voice caught. "He laid here for hours, just waiting to die. We tried to stop the bleeding, but the firing was so hot.... We had to watch out for ourselves, or wind up catching a ball, too," Arnold finished in a tearful rush.

Tom reached down and touched Lawrence's face, cold with death. His eyes were open, staring into the sunny sky, and Tom forced them closed.

Jacob rocked back and forth on his knees, tears flowing. "He didn't want to come. Didn't want to fight, but he came because we came."

"It's nobody's fault, boys," Tom said. "We all had one reason or another to be here. No matter what it was, we're here, and every one of us is at risk of getting killed. The best we can do is look out for each other as best we can, but that doesn't mean we can stop a ball from finding a friend. We do the best we can to stay alive and that's all we can do."

Arnold swallowed, nodded, and stood up. "You're right. We're grown men and we knew what we were doing when we enlisted. What it could mean. But so many of us thought we'd march off to glorious war, whistling a tune, and we'd whip those damned Rebs in a month with one great battle and victory for the Union. But that's not how it happened and we're in it for the long stretch, whether we want to be or not." He sucked in a sobbing breath and scrubbed at his face. "I know I shouldn't feel like this is my fault, but I do." He looked down at Tom with haunting, tear-filled eyes. "He was my friend, he came because we came, and now he's dead."

"As did all these other men, Arnold," Tom said. "These men are sons, brothers, husbands to a great many people. They fought today for what they believed, whether it was the preservation of the Union, for family, friends, or glory. Like I said, each man has his own reasons for fighting and each man has the same chance of catching lead before the war is over. It's no one's fault, it's just how it is."

Tom stood and laid his hand on Arnold's shoulder as Gerald stood and helped Jacob to his feet. "We've still the four of us. We'll stay together and watch each other's backs as much as we can. And if one of us falls, we'll say a prayer over him and do our best to stay alive. Agreed?"

The three men nodded, a smaller, tighter circle of friendship formed around the fallen Lawrence, a vow made.

***

June, 1862

My Dearest Ralph,

"*Most of the men's feet are bare, or might as well have been, for the shoes that flopped on their feet, mine included, when we joined McDowell's corps at Falmouth in mid-May. Since our victory at Kernstown we've followed General Jackson through the Shenandoah Valley, harassing when we could. At least the weather is warm,*" Tom wrote in his first letter to his brother. He wrote to let Ralph know he and Gerald were both alive, but also to put into words his feelings on all they had experienced these past months in their pursuit of the elusive General Jackson.

"*You will be pleased to learn Gerald and I have survived the marches through the Shenandoah Valley from New Market Gap to the Luray Valley to Front Royal in our army's effort to catch General Jackson and his Confederates. By the time we joined McDowell's forces in May, we looked more like beggars than soldiers. What a birthday present for me when some of the men (happily I was one of them) were refitted with new uniforms and shoes before we were hastily ordered back to the Shenandoah*

Valley. Unfortunately many were not as lucky as Gerald and I and marched off with bleeding, exposed feet.

"At Front Royal we surprised the Rebs and took some three hundred prisoners. While on the Winchester Turnpike, we watched an exchange between our boys and Ashby's Cavalry, the latter still causing mischief, and Gerald and I with personal experience retreating from them, before they withdrew from the Turnpike.

"It has been a whirlwind of marching and fighting, the Eighth engaged in the seemingly constant pursuit of Stonewall himself, although he continues to elude us."

Gerald flopped down beside his uncle and raised one foot in the air and then the other. "Thank God for the shoes I got at Falmouth. I feel for the poor fellows who still haven't been refitted. How will they cross the mountains tomorrow?"

Tom glanced at Gerald, his letter forgotten for the moment. "Word is General Shields will allow those that haven't been refitted to stay behind. If they can't walk across mountain roads full of sharp rocks, how can they fight?"

Gerald nodded. "I've heard the same. Guess that means we'll march since we've been blessed with shoes." He paused and thought a moment before he said, "Do you think we'll ever catch him? It seems like we've been following ole Stonewall since this war began and only see the backside of his horse—if that."

Tom's eyebrows shot up. "It seems we have, doesn't it?"

"Do you know where we're headed tomorrow?" Gerald asked.

"From the scuttlebutt, all I can figure is that we're headed for a place called Port Republic where a bridge connects the valley with Gordonsville and Richmond. Supposedly Jackson's there. So we follow."

Gerald ran a sleeve across his lips. "I guess we'll find out tomorrow. For now, I'm catching whatever rest I can. I suggest you do the same." He flopped onto his side and was snoring before Tom finished his letter.

***

The next morning, a Sunday in mid-June, the Fourth Brigade under Colonel Carroll led the way to the bridge in pursuit of General Jackson's troops. The First Brigade, including B Company, fell in behind them.

"Do you hear that?" Gerald asked Tom as the First Brigade followed Carroll's Fourth.

"Sounds like Jackson met our boys on the other side of the river. Maybe General Fremont will end this cat and mouse game we've been playing with General Jackson all these months."

"I hope they leave some Rebs for us!" Arnold stepped up beside Tom and Gerald, the man more anxious than ever to pay back any Rebel soldier he could for Lawrence's death. "I say bring 'em on!"

"There'll be plenty left for us, Arnold," Tom said to his friend whose eyes gleamed with the need for revenge.

"I hope so. I'm tired of those slippery Johnny Rebs getting away from us. All we see are the ass-ends of south-bound horses!" Arnold snarled.

There was a sudden exchange of gunfire up ahead. "What's going on?" Gerald asked no one.

"Sounds like whatever it is, it's headed our way," Arnold said happily. "We're gonna have a fight, boys!"

Tom looked at Gerald and Gerald at Tom. "Are you ready?" Tom asked.

"As I ever will be."

Tom and Gerald waited with the rest of the First Brigade at a bend in the river near the base of the mountain, rifles ready and waiting for orders to join the fight.

They watched and waited with the Second Brigade as the Third Brigade rushed forward to help Colonel Carroll's men. But the Fourth was already retreating to a position near an ironworks along the river.

The fighting was furious between the Rebs and the Third and Fourth Brigades, while the First and Second waited for orders in relative safety.

"When are we gonna fight?" Arnold almost whined, his lips pinched, his eyes wide, his breathing labored.

"When they tell us to," Tom growled.

Jacob laid a hand on his friend's shoulder. "We all want to fight, Arnie, but we can't until they tell us."

Arnold shrugged his friend's hand off him. "You act like you don't even want to fight. To make them pay for what they did to Lawrence."

Jacob's face turned hard. "And you're acting like a jackass! What good does it do Lawrence, or any of the men who have died, for us to rush off and get our own selves killed, in their names? Tell me, Arnie, what damn good does it do?"

Jacob stared his friend down before Arnold raised his hands in front of him. "You're right. I'm acting like a jack-leg. We're all angry Lawrence was killed." He took a deep breath, as though ready to say something he didn't want to say. He swallowed, hard. "It *is* my fault. My fault Lawrence is dead. He didn't want to join up, but I goaded him into it. I bullied him into it. Told him he was acting like a little girl because he didn't want to fight. So he came, because of me. Lawrence is dead because of me!"

"I know what happened, Arnie," Jacob stepped close to his lifelong friend. "He told me."

Arnold's head snapped back and his eyes pinched in confusion. "You knew?"

Jacob nodded. "He came to me afterwards, unsure and afraid. We talked for a long time and he told me all about how you were pressing him about joining. He wanted to, Arnie, he really did, but he was afraid, for himself *and* about leaving his ailing mother. But he did it, and not because of you or your badgering, but because he knew it was the right thing to do, like so many boys who joined after Sumter. It was the right thing to do, Arnie, and Lawrence did it. And that's that."

"And there's not a thing we can do about what's happened. And our getting killed won't change a thing," Arnold said, his voice low in acceptance of the truth. He laid his hand on Jacob's shoulder as his friend had done to him only moments ago. "Thanks for watching over me, keeping me from running off to get my head blown off."

Jacob smiled and put his hand on top of Arnold's. "We're friends, all of us." He waved at Gerald and Tom with his other hand. "And our vow was to watch over each other—as much as we can. And keeping you from running off and getting killed is as much part of that vow as anything."

"Agreed." Arnold craned his neck to see what was going on ahead of them. "We wait."

They didn't wait long before the Third and Fourth Brigades retreated amidst shelling from the Confederates on the other side of the river. In disarray, the two brigades hurried past the First and Second, still waiting in reserve.

Falling back, Tom wondered at yet another retreat and in the settling dust, determined General Stonewall Jackson and his army would, again, slip away to fight another day.

Chapter Twenty-Five

August 23, 1862

My Dear Brother,

"I write from Newport News, Virginia. Word spreads amongst the men we are to make our way by water to Alexandria, across from Washington City, in the next day or two.

"At the end of June our company was assigned to General George McClellan and so we marched out from Front Royal, again, on our way to join his Army of the Potomac. After going by rail to Alexandria (yes Alexandria, stay with me and I will explain), we steamed our way up river, past the wreckage of the Cumberland, sunk by the Confederate vessel Merrimac. Seven days the battle raged both on water and on land between their General Lee and our General McClellan, affectionately called "Little Mac" by his men.

"We disembarked at Harrison's Landing where everything was in a flurry. McClellan's army had been in a great battle at Malvern Hill the day before and the town was full of stragglers with terrible stories of the previous day's battle.

"The following morning we stepped out again, passing hundreds of troops that had withdrawn from the field, demoralized and soaked in the torrential rains that fell upon us.

"When we reached our destination, our brigade was ordered right away to the front to stop the advancing Rebels. We ran headlong into enemy skirmishers but suffered no losses amongst our company when their battery opened fire.

"The Fourth of July passed with minor skirmishes throughout the day and a visit by General McClellan himself, available to the men with handshakes and smiles all around. It lifted our morale considerably, I must say.

"When next we stopped it was within a pine tree forest, our company called upon to help clear it to set up camp for all the men. For several days we felled those giants until they were cleared and camp was established.

"We got very excited when we learned President Lincoln was here reviewing the troops, and we waited expectantly for his arrival. Alas, he didn't come to see us and we were greatly disappointed.

"Since then we have been reassigned again to General W.F. Smith's division, of the Second Corps, commanded by General Edwin Sumner.

"In early August we were aboard a supply transport with forty of our company gathering ammunition when we were ordered to pull for shore post haste. I spotted our gunboats, the Monitor and Galena, steaming toward us on one side of the river and within moments a Confederate gunboat came into view on the other and opened fire with such an explosion of noise I thought I'd ever hear again!

"On August 5th General Hooker met the Rebs again at Malvern Hill where he was injured and his ambulance sped right past our camp. A few nights later we marched again, our mission to capture some rebels, but it was just another night of lost sleep with no results other than more exhaustion and grumbling.

"Because we lack clean water, the men are afflicted with diarrhea. Quinine is passed among us like child's candy, along with great quantities of onions to help keep away the scurvy because we have such bad food. So now we not only have disagreeable bowels, but sour breath, and cannot speak directly to one another without turning away in disgust. Are we soldiers in this army allowing for such bad provisions—or prisoners!

"So many men became ill they were sent by transport to Yorktown, along with our knapsacks and any extra baggage we carried with us. Those of us still able trudged away in retreat, yet again.

"On our departure we were ordered to act as the rear guard to the division as it marched for Newport News where we have been in camp now for several days.

"Sergeant Galwey, returned from his assignment in Columbus, told the men earlier tonight we will leave for Alexandria again by steamer tomorrow. From there we don't know where this war will take us.

"*Despite all I write and all Gerald and I have endured, we both remain hale and hearty. Until I am able to write again, I remain, your loving brother,*"

Tom

Tom put down the paper and pencil, worn to a short nub, and slid onto his back in his bedroll. He threw his arm across his face and tried to relax into sleep. They'd been fighting for over a year now, with disastrous results for the Federals. Even though he'd known the war would last much longer than anyone originally thought, knowing it was one thing—living it was quite something different. *How much longer could it last* was his last thought before he drifted into the fitful darkness of sleep.

***

They were so close to Washington City Tom could see the glow of the gaslights across the river and the people there racing around with excitement! Tom hefted his weapon from one shoulder to the other, turned on his heel and paced in the opposite direction where he was on guard duty against possible attack. Walking from one end of his duty post to the other Tom wished that if ole Stonewall was coming, like everyone believed he was, he would hurry up and get it over with. Tom was so tired of chasing, and being chased by that ghost. He fretted over never even catching *sight* of the man, let alone catching him!

His picket duty done Tom fell onto his pallet beside a snoring Gerald. When they woke the next morning, it was with orders to march.

"We've been marching for days," Gerald complained to his uncle, trudging mindlessly beside him several days later.

"And we'll walk for twenty more if that's what they tell us, Gerald. When will you stop your incessant complaining and just do what they tell us to do?" Tom groused. *Yes, they were all tired—tired of marching, tired of eating poor food, and tired of following an army that couldn't be found.* "We're not in as bad a shape as the men straggling past us from the battlefield. Look at them." Tom raised a hand to encompass the dozens of stragglers coming toward them from the new fight going on at Manassas Junction. "They look worse than we ever have. Every man that's spoken tells horrible stories of slaughter at the front. Would you rather be there, Gerald? Fighting with what's left of General Pope's army?"

Gerald's shoulders slumped and he shook his head. "Of course not. The men who pass us and what's left of Pope's army, tell stories of being cut to pieces. No, uncle, I wouldn't prefer to be at the front. I'll walk and be happy to do it." He looked up and groaned as a fat raindrop hit his face. "Even in the rain."

Onward they marched.

"What time do you think it is?" Gerald asked Tom in his usual assumption that his uncle knew the answers to all his questions.

"Somewhere around midnight, I'd guess." He pulled up short. "Look over there." He pointed at twenty or more what looked like ammunition wagons lying in a ditch on the side of the road.

Jacob jogged up beside his friends. "Looks like we missed whatever happened here."

"I wonder what did happen?" Gerald asked no one.

"There's no telling, but it doesn't look good. Those are our wagons. Those boys who've been straggling past us all day probably retreated from here." Tom sighed. *Things weren't going well for the Union in this second battle being fought at Manassas, the first at the start of the war having been a complete rout of the northern boys. What did that bode for them, walking right toward it now?*

Arnold ran up beside them, puffing from his run. "I've got news."

"Well, tell us." Tom had no patience. He wanted to know any news from the front.

"General Phil Kearny is dead!"

"What? Where? When?" Tom asked in a rush.

"Yesterday in a fight at some plantation. The damned gray backs have whipped us again, boys. Pope's retreated and General

Kearney's dead. General Stevens is dead, too. They're making minced meat of us." Arnold punched at the air.

"And we've got Rebs behind us," Jacob added, looking over his shoulder. "They're not close, but they're there, just following."

"Well, the best we can do then is keep going. Come on boys, let's go." Tom charged ahead to catch up with the rest of the company.

They walked through the night and into the next day before they reached a peach orchard at mid-day. Allowed time to enjoy their dinner, they pulled fruit from the trees, ate their fill, and relaxed.

Tom was dozing when he was yanked from his sleep by shouting.

"Fall in, men! Fall in!"

The men fell in and minutes later were racing from the orchard.

They hadn't gone far before Tom spotted the light battery unit in the woods to their left— a cavalry unit beside them ready and waiting. He'd no sooner noticed the guns when they opened fire.

"Step fast, boys! Get out of range!" Sergeant Galwey ran amongst the men, shouting.

Tom and the others needed no prodding. Their sore feet were forgotten as they raced to get away from the guns, throwing up clods of grass all around them.

They ran fast and hard to get out of range, but the pursuing cavalry was another story. Instead of swooping down on them, they dogged them and kept them going for hours with no rest.

"I don't think I can take another step," Gerald grumbled.

"It's getting dark. They'll drop off once it gets dark," Tom said.

"I hope so, because I can't go much farther. My feet hurt in places I didn't know existed."

Tom stopped and listened. Quiet. "I think they've stopped following us."

"For now. They're still behind us and I imagine they'll pick right up again tomorrow."

Tom turned on his nephew. "That's tomorrow. Right now it looks like we're stopping. I'm going to pull up a patch of dirt, lay my old bones down, and get whatever sleep I can."

Gerald ran a sleeve under his nose. "And I'll be doing the same."

"We're right beside you." Jacob and Arnold plopped down beside Tom and Gerald and were asleep within minutes, the rest of the company snoring around them, save the unlucky pickets.

At daylight they started out again. They hadn't gone far before they met up with several hundred Federals in the woods, exhausted, hungry, and dug in.

"There's Reb cavalry behind us, boys," Tom and the others told them. "They've been dogging us since yesterday. You should come with us or move along or they'll find you for sure."

"We're not goin' anywhere, boys. We've done our fighting and we're staying right here," the man speaking for everyone said, the others grumbling quick agreement. "You see? We're not goin' anywhere."

"But they're behind us." Arnold waved his hand wildly down the road. "And they're coming this way."

"Then let them come. We'll face 'em when, or if, they get here."

"Have it your way, but I'm heading that way." Arnold got back in step as the company continued away from the pursing Rebs toward the Leesburg Pike up ahead.

Crossing the road Tom felt some relief that they were getting closer to Washington City and safety with each step—until shouting erupted behind them.

"What's that?" Gerald swung around, his rifle ready.

Tom turned and listened. Fear streaked up his spine. "It's the Reb cavalry, and they're headed this way at a gallop!"

The men scattered into the woods on both sides of the road, ready to take on the charging Rebs. Suddenly, guns exploded from the trees south of the turnpike where they'd encountered the stragglers.

"They're covering our retreat!" Jacob yelled, laughing with relief.

"And they're doing a fine job of it!" Arnold shouted.

Tom watched as the men who, only minutes ago had refused to move, fired round after round at the threatening cavalry, dropping the riders like a Sunday afternoon turkey shoot.

Arnold jumped out from behind the tree he was using as cover and waved his arms wildly. "They're running. Those Rebs are scattering like leaves in the fall!"

Cheering erupted throughout B Company when the skirmish was over. "Thanks, boys!" was shouted to their rescuers more than once.

The men smiled and tipped their hats, saluted, and melted back into the woods like they'd never been there.

Chapter Twenty-Six

September 6, 1862

My Dear Brother,

"*We are camped at a place called Tenallytown[2] on the Washington City side of the Potomac. We were again given new shoes and fresh ammunition, the shoes replacing those issued not long ago that were already falling apart from all the marching we've done. We are horribly dirty and lousy and without our knapsacks, still stored somewhere in Washington City or Alexandria, we have no clean clothes in which to change.*

"*Jack Sheppard, one of our fellows, goes from man to man gathering lice from the cuffs of their pants then strings them around his neck. His collection of the vermin does not help in lessening their numbers, or our discomfort. They infest us all, officers and enlisted man alike, biting and causing us to scratch and itch until our skin is raw. Oh what I would give for a long, hot bath and a clean uniform!*

"*We are told to get some good rest tonight, as we will pull out tomorrow, September 7th. We are now in pursuit of General Lee, instead of the illusive General Jackson. I pray we fare better in catching him than we did Ole Stonewall!*

"*I apologize for the shortness of this letter, but I must retire and get whatever sleep I can. Tomorrow will bring more marching and, although we have new shoes, I fear my feet will never recover from this war—if I survive. Gerald fares well and I appreciate his companionship more than he knows and much more than I thought I would.*

"*As always, I remain,*"
Tom

***

---

[2] Tenallytown is now a part of Washington where River Road joins Wisconsin Avenue.

"It's so quiet." Gerald lay on his blanket in his tent in camp, facing his uncle. "After hearing the cannon and gunfire all day, it's unnerving."

"It is unnerving, and an omen, too."

"What kind of omen?" Gerald sounded leery.

"That tomorrow there will be a huge battle. This is the quiet before the storm, so to speak. So get some sleep so you can face it with all your wits."

Gerald blinked and frowned. "I will, Tom. I will." He curled his arms together in front of him, closed his eyes, and spoke no more.

Tom tried to do the same, but his mind wouldn't rest. They'd left Tenallytown and marched for ten days to get here, to a place called Antietam Creek. They'd had the good luck to bivouac in many an orchard along the way, stuffing themselves with as much fruit as they could eat. When they'd entered the city of Rockville, only recently vacated by the Rebs, they were greeted warmly by the residents and treated to lemonade, smiles, and long, sympathetic conversations with many a lonely lady, desperately hoping for news of a loved one.

He recalled the men's excitement when their baggage finally caught up with them near Clarksburg, Maryland. *How happy he'd been for a change of clothing!*

Tom smiled at the memory of their gallant entry into Frederick, where the Stars and Stripes waved high above the rooftops of the city. Women waved handkerchiefs from windows and cheered their arrival. Overwhelmed by the welcoming hospitality someone from the ranks shouted "We're in God's country again!" causing the men to cheer wildly.

They'd crossed the Catoctin Mountains, the men's feet still smarting from the rocks and rough road they'd traveled, not much better than an old goat path.

Tom's mind rolled. He tossed and turned, recalling their march toward Boonsboro, Confederate guns issuing from both sides of the gap around Middletown, before they marched through more orchards full of fruit where they gorged themselves again.

Sadness washed over him at the thought of General Reno, now dead in one of today's battles. He repositioned, trying to force his mind to rest, but it kept rolling. Faces of the dead haunted him, called to him. As though right in front of him, the images of two dead Rebs lying face to face under an outcropping of rock flashed into his mind's eye. *Had they crawled there together, wounded and dying, their last words spoken to each other? Had they known each other? Been friends? Relations as he and Gerald were? Or were they strangers who became brothers in death? Had they died in agony, one watching the other give up his fight for life before giving up his? What had they spoken of in their last minutes, knowing they wouldn't live to see another glorious sunrise?*

A shudder went through him and he wondered what tomorrow would bring. *Would he be among the dead? Or Gerald? Or both of them?*

He sucked in a deep breath. Slowly he let it out and closed his eyes until a restless sleep finally claimed him.

***

"It's too pretty to fight," Gerald announced the next morning. He stretched and popped then grabbed the coffee pot from the fire. "It looks like it's going to be a beautiful day, boys. Not too hot or too cold. A day that would be best served doing something other than fighting."

"It *is* a glorious morning, and barely six o'clock!" Jacob grabbed the pot from Gerald and poured a cup.

"Well I, for one, think it's too early for man or beast to be up and about, whether preparing for battle or readying to plow crops. I do *not* appreciate rising with the cock's crow. Never have and never will," Arnold griped, snatching the pot from Jacob to pour the last of the coffee.

"It isn't raining, so hot you can't breathe, or so cold you can't feel your toes—so be happy." Tom threw his arms wide. "Like me!"

"Always the optimist!" Arnold slapped Tom on the back and took a gulp of coffee.

"Step lively, boys. We're moving out!" Galwey made his way through their camp passing the order to march as they finished the last of their cold breakfast.

The day was spent trudging through woods and over rocky terrain, Tom begging God to make his feet stop hurting. Emerging from the trees, he studied a lone farm in the distance with a cornfield, house and barn. Down the road on the right about 400 yards was what appeared to be a meeting house and between where they stood and the meeting house was a sunken road to the left that looked like it had been hollowed out by years of water rushing over it.

Tom was surveying the immediate area when gunfire popped up ahead. It was a quick volley and lasted only a short time before the brigade that had just marched ahead of them came running back in their direction.

"What the?" Gerald asked from beside his uncle.

Tom shook his head and waited.

Another volley of fire exploded up the road, and within moments, more of their own men ran past them, racing for the woods they'd just exited.

At the sound of approaching horses Tom pulled Gerald around in time to see General Kimball ride in amongst the ranks. "Now boys, we are going, and we'll stay with them all day if they want us to!" he shouted, urging the First Brigade, which included the Eighth, forward.

"What're we waiting for?" Arnold charged toward the enemy, Jacob on his heels, both still looking for payback for Lawrence's death.

Gerald looked at Tom and the two took off after their friends. They climbed fences and ran through another orchard, each step taking them closer to the enemy hidden in the sunken road.

With their heads down as though running through driving rain, they ran closer and closer to the Rebs in the protected trench.

The day turned as ugly as any could get. Men fell by the hundreds as they charged onward into a hail of bullets.

"Stay close!" Tom shouted to Gerald, regardless it didn't matter how close his nephew stayed. If a mini-ball was in his or Gerald's path, it would strike, no matter how close they were.

They ran for the regimental flags, somehow still flying above the diminishing troops. First Sergeant Fairchild, up ahead, shouted encouragement to the men, his face covered with blood.

Young sergeant Galwey charged forward, Jacob and Arnold behind him, Jack Sheppard on Galwey's right. Jack suddenly dropped to the ground without a sound, like a puppet whose strings had been cut, blood spewing from what appeared to be a dozen hits.

Gerald stopped to stare at the unmoving Sheppard.

"Don't stop!" Tom shouted, dragging Gerald along beside him. "You're less of a target if you keep moving."

"Tell that to Jack!" Gerald looked back at his fallen friend as they ran past.

Tom threw himself to the ground, dragging Gerald with him, as a volley of shots whizzed over their heads.

Ahead Tom heard a scream he recognized as Jacob's. Frozen where they lay, unable to do anything to help their friend, Tom and Gerald watched Jacob grab his neck, and drop to his knees, his eyes wide with surprise. Blood spewed through his fingers before he fell face down on the ground.

Arnold dropped to his knees beside Jacob, tears streaming from his eyes. His face hardened and he turned toward the Rebs. "I'll kill you, you dirty Reb bastards!" He regained his feet and ran toward the sunken road screaming, "I'll kill you! I'll kill you!"

Tom and Gerald watched in helpless horror as Arnold was hit with a flurry of bullets that sent him spinning, his eyes wild and searching, perhaps for them, before he landed face first atop another fallen soldier.

Tom swallowed and his head dropped to the grass where he lay. Gerald groaned beside him, the sound like a wounded animal.

Tom heard someone behind him and he turned to see General Kimball, staggering among the men, muttering, "God save my poor boys."

God save his poor boys, indeed! Tom wanted to shout. The Confederate battery pounded at them from the meeting house up the street, while the rest of the Rebel army hammered at them from the safety of the sunken road.

Tom looked up and spotted Sergeant Galwey and Lieutenant Lantry not far ahead. In an instant the top of Lantry's head was gone, severed by an incoming shell.

Gerald lay bug-eyed beside Tom.

"Dear God, we're being decimated. If we stay here we'll surly die." Gerald rose as if to flee.

Tom grabbed his nephew's arm and hauled him back down. The look in Gerald's eyes made him weak, but they had to stay. They were soldiers. It was their duty. They couldn't run.

"So we just stay here and wait for a ball with our name on it to find us?" Gerald snarled.

"We hold our position until we're told otherwise."

"There's nothing to hold, but everything to save—our lives, Tom. Are you so ready to give yours up? And for what? A patch of dirt!" Gerald tried to scurry away again, but Tom wouldn't let him go.

"Gerald, don't. We've got to hold until we're ordered otherwise."

Sergeant Galwey slithered up beside them. "We're to charge, boys."

"What? Charge? Who gave such a stupid order? Are they crazy?" Gerald shouted, barely heard above the cacophony of noise around them. "Don't they see what's happening? We're being slaughtered like sheep!" he shouted to Galwey's back, the sergeant having already moved along to pass the order.

Tom shook his head, as confused as Gerald. "We have no choice, Gerald. That's the order. Affix your bayonet and get ready to run."

Gerald's chest heaved and he stared at Tom like he'd lost his mind. He sucked in a couple deep breaths and calmed down enough to do what his uncle told him to do. They affixed bayonets and prepared to charge.

With a wild cheer, the men got to their feet and raced forward. But their cheers were strangled in their throats when the next wave of gunfire struck, stopping them in mid-stride, throwing them to the ground like discarded rag dolls.

"We can't reach them!" Tom shouted.

"Do we go back *now*? *Before* we're hit?" Gerald shouted, his eyes wild again.

"Yes, go back." Tom started backward, removing his bayonet as he did. Stepping carefully he worked his way over fallen men, tripping and falling more than once, and saving his life as a mini-ball sailed overhead.

Gerald did the same until they were back where they'd started.

Hunkered down again out of rifle range they checked their cartridge boxes. "I'm almost out of ammo," Gerald called to his uncle above the noise.

Tom checked his pouch. "Me, too." Tom looked around recalling another battle when they'd run short. "There's plenty here." Tom scooted back, picking up cartridge boxes from the men who didn't need them anymore.

Gerald did the same until both had plenty, aware all they had to do was pick up more whenever they needed it.

"We *must* charge!" someone shouted down the line.

Tom could barely breathe. Whether from fear or sheer exhaustion, he didn't know. They'd been fighting for hours and were no closer than they were when they started. *They'd done nothing more than watch men die! Damn, they needed to siege that trench! But how?*

"We're to charge again." Galwey had slipped up beside Tom and Gerald again, his face bloodied and haggard—and looking much older than the tender sixteen years Tom knew him to be.

Affixing bayonets again, they screamed like savages and charged forward, through the cornfield and up a ridge. Cresting the ridge, Tom's flesh crawled and he stood gape-mouthed when he spotted two lines of Confederates marching right toward them.

"We've got to get out of here." Gerald's head was shaking and fear etched his face. "We've lost too many. There're hardly any of us left. The brigade has been decimated. We've got to get out of here before we die, too!"

Tom grabbed his nephew and shook him—just as a bullet slammed into Gerald's right arm a few inches above his elbow. Gerald screamed and dropped to the ground like a rock, holding his arm, rolling back and forth.

Tom kneeled beside him. Blood gushed from his nephew's wound and Tom knew he had to stop it quick or Gerald would die in a matter of minutes. He pulled off his scarf and wrapped it as a tourniquet around Gerald's arm. "We have to go. I've bound it as tight as I can, but we have to go. They're coming."

Tom tried to sound calm, but his heart was slamming around in his chest like a bullet ricocheting inside a tin can.

Gerald had stopped whimpering. His eyes were glazed and Tom knew if he didn't get him help soon, his nephew would die. They might both die if they were caught by the advancing rebels, and he wasn't ready. Not yet.

He mostly dragged Gerald off the battlefield and back to the barn they'd passed earlier in the day. Once there, Tom was happy to find it being used as a hospital.

Gerald was gathered up and taken inside and Tom slid down the wall onto the floor near the door to wait. Exhausted beyond anything he'd ever experienced, Tom dozed where he sat until roused by a doctor, his apron bloody from his chest to his knees.

"I'm told you're Gerald Hansen's uncle." The doctor's voice was gruff with exhaustion.

Tom jumped to his feet. "I am. Is he, alive?"

"He's alive, but we had to take his arm to keep him that way."

Tom felt like he'd been hit in the gut by a tree limb, like his stomach had fallen out, his knees too weak to support him and he slid back down against the wall.

"Come, sit down." The doctor guided him to an overturned feed bucket and Tom sat down.

"The bone in his arm was shattered. He'd lost a great deal of blood, despite the tourniquet you applied," he added when Tom's eyes widened. "If you hadn't done so, he would have died long before you got him here."

Tom grimaced and nodded, thankful he'd been able to do *something*.

"If we'd tried to save the arm, gangrene would most likely have set in and eventually killed him. I'm sorry, but it was all I could do." He waved at the men pouring in through the doors. "And with so many others to tend…." He let the words hang only a moment before he hurried wearily away to take care of his next patient.

Tom didn't try to stop the sob that came from his mouth. His head fell to his chest as he cried like a babe.

Gerald's arm was gone. But he was alive! And *that* was all that mattered.

Chapter Twenty-Seven

October 13, 1862

Dear Ralph,

"I write today with good news—and bad. I'll start with the good to help prepare you for the bad. Gerald and I are coming home! We have been granted leave and should arrive soon by rail. Gerald will remain. I, on the other hand, will stay for only a short time before I will return to the front.

"Now for the bad news. Gerald was injured during the battle at Antietam. He is doing well, so do not fret. He took a mini-ball in his upper arm. It shattered the bone and, well, there is no easy way to say it, the arm was removed to save Gerald's life.

"Physically, his body recovers, although he is in pain always, as though his arm is still there. He says he can feel it, feel the pain in it, but when he reaches to soothe it, he grabs only air and I see the confusion in his face.

"He cannot accept that he now has only one arm. He broods, cries in his sleep, and speaks to no one, not even me. His eyes are haunted and ringed from his restless sleep, if he gets any. When he returns home you must accept him as he is, and HELP him to accept it. He is your son, no matter what his disability. You, and Margaret, must accept that and him.

"We leave in two days and will hire a hack upon our arrival in Cleveland, so be ready for us shortly after this letter arrives. Be prepared and have faith that all will be well. It may take some time, but Gerald is strong and will recover, and thrive, I'm sure of it. He is alive and physically well, and we must take strength in that. For him, the war is over, so you may be assured of his safety.

"Until then, I remain,"

Tom

***

The train rolled to a stop at the station in Cleveland and, for the first time in weeks, Tom saw a spark of excitement in his nephew. *Or was it relief that he would never have to return to the front?*

Tom tried to help his nephew when Gerald almost fell down trying to stand up as the train chugged to a stop, but Gerald shrugged him away.

"Leave me be. I can do it without your help."

Tom stepped back and raised his hands. "As you wish." He was tired of the brooding, the anger, and the silence, but given the circumstances, Tom swallowed his own anger and did what he could to help. At some point, however, Gerald had to accept his impediment and start living his life accordingly, and without his uncle's help.

Tom waited as Gerald walked unsteadily toward the exit. Gerald grabbed the rail with his left hand and took the steps slowly, but without fault.

On the landing Tom walked up beside his nephew, who stood silent, looking around, as though seeing it for the first time.

"More than once I never thought I'd see home again." Gerald's voice scratched with emotion. "I never thought I'd see *anything* again."

Tom smiled, hopeful being home would help in his nephew's recovery. "I had my doubts that *either* of us would ever see this again, but here we are." Tom stepped in front of Gerald. "Wait here, I'll hire a hack and we'll be on our way."

Gerald grabbed Tom's arm before he could walk away. "I..." he swallowed and took a deep breath, "I need to say this while we're still alone, to you and no one else." He took another steadying breath. "I'm sorry for the way I've been since, well, since, this." He waved his left hand over where his right arm should be. "I've been less than kind and you've done nothing but try and help me in any way you could." Tears shimmered in his eyes. "You saved my life, *Uncle* Tom. I never would have made it from the battlefield if you hadn't dragged me off."

"What else could I have done? You're my nephew, my blood, and my best friend."

Gerald swallowed the emotion he was obviously feeling. "Well, you saved my life and, even though I haven't seemed grateful for it, I am. Thank you, Uncle Tom. Thank you."

Tom laid his hand on Gerald's left shoulder and squeezed. "And I thank God every day you're a fighter, you survived, and you *will* make the best of it. Now let's go home."

Gerald blinked and nodded. "Let's go home."

***

The hack rumbled to a halt in front of the big, whitewashed house and within moments Gerald was enfolded in his sobbing mother's arms.

"Oh, thank God, Gerald. Thank God you've come home to me!" Margaret cried.

His son and wife otherwise engaged, Ralph walked to Tom with his hand stretched out in front of him. When Tom took it, Ralph pulled him into a hug that nearly took the wind out of him.

"Thank you, Tom," Ralph whispered in his ear, his voice gruff with unconcealed emotion. "Thank you for bringing my son home to me."

When Margaret finally relinquished her hold on him, Ralph took his turn and hugged Gerald fiercely, yet careful of his healing shoulder.

"Welcome home, Son."

Gerald pulled back, his eyes wet, his nose running before he swiped it with the back of his hand. "I'm lucky to *be* home. If it hadn't been for Tom…"

"I didn't do anything anyone else wouldn't have done," Tom interrupted.

"You could have easily been killed in the doing, so no, not everyone would have done it. I'm alive because of you and I want everyone to know. And I am grateful."

There was a sparkle in Gerald's eyes. He *really* smiled for the first time since he'd been injured and Tom was glad for it.

Margaret stepped forward and gave Tom a perfunctory hug and peck on the cheek before she stepped away as though Tom were nothing more than a second thought. Tom wondered at it and hoped it was a sign she'd given up her foolish notion of enticing him into something he wanted no part of. She wrapped her arms around Gerald's left arm, snuggled close, and led him into the house.

It appeared to Tom her main concern was her son now—and that suited him just fine.

Tom went to his room, dropped his dirty knapsack on the floor and walked, stiff legged, to the bed. He leaned over, spread his fingers, and poked the mattress to feel its softness, as though he'd never seen or felt one before. He stripped off every filthy piece of clothing he had on, used the wash water in the basin on the dresser to scrub the worst of the grime off before he slid, naked, between the clean, soft sheets with a groan. *He'd forgotten how good a real bed felt!*

How long had he slept? A long time. He felt it in his body and in the room itself. The sun was shining, despite the closed curtains, and he felt somewhat refreshed for the first time in too long to remember. A fresh basin of water was on the dresser beside the door and he took full advantage of it. He re-washed every part of his body he could reach, then his hair, a difficult task at best, leaving the water murky and thick. His dirty uniform was gone and clean clothing lay on the bench at the foot of the bed. When he slipped into it, he felt like a human being again, the war far behind him. He wished he could freeze time at least long enough to enjoy everything around him then shook his head. It wouldn't be long before he'd have to re-board another train and head back to the war.

Stepping in front of the mirror, he stroked his long, scraggly beard and mustache. Grooming scissors and a straight razor were on the dresser and he took advantage of them, too. When he emerged from the room, it was clean shaven, in clean clothes, and feeling like a new man.

"Tom!" Ralph jumped up from his seat at the head of the dining room table and met Tom at the door. "Come in, come in! Sit down and eat. You must be starved. You, and Gerald, have been abed since your arrival and it's noon of the next day! His brother slapped him on the back. "One of the maids said she heard Gerald stirring in his room so he should be down soon, as well."

Tom nodded and wondered at his nephew's progress. He'd seen Gerald's anger flash too many times at his inability to do the simple things he'd done before without thought, like dressing and washing, and Tom had always been the one to assuage that anger and help him do whatever needed to be done. *Who was helping him now?*

Tom got settled at the table and noticed the side bar laden with ham, potatoes and gravy. His mouth watered and he realized just how hungry he was, not having had a good meal in too many months to count, and having slept through last night's supper and this morning's breakfast.

A few minutes later Gerald came through the door, clean shaven in a suit with the arm pinned up. Margaret stood beside him and the slender house maid Margaret had chastised upon Tom's arrival stood just behind them, a slight sparkle in her young eyes as she watched Gerald enter the room.

Margaret turned to the girl and waved an impatient hand. "That's enough, Glynis. You're dismissed."

"Yes, ma'am." The maid curtsied with a last longing look at Gerald, turned and disappeared down the hall.

Margaret heaved a heavy sigh and strode purposely to her chair. Ralph jumped to his feet and pulled it out for her before he hurried to another and slid it out for Gerald.

"Here son. Sit where you always have."

Gerald slipped awkwardly into a chair to the left of his father, his face red. Before he could say a word, Margaret announced, "I'll fix you a plate, dear." She made a great show of selecting the perfect piece of meat and heaping potatoes and gravy onto the plate. She then sliced the meat into small, bite-sized pieces and, with a flourish, set the plate in front of her son as though he were a five-year old child.

Tom watched the familiar color creep up his nephew's neck. But Gerald held himself in check, at least for now, by taking a deep breath before he thanked his mother for her kindness.

"Oh my darling, you're so welcome! I'm so thankful you've come home to us!" she trilled before kissing him on the top of the head and flouncing away to make her own plate.

Tom felt Gerald's anger hovering in the air above him. He silently congratulated his nephew on keeping his tongue, and his anger, from ruining their first meal together, although certain it would come out later.

Ralph pushed his chair back. "Shall we?" He flung his hand toward the side-bar and walked up beside Margaret, almost done filling her plate. When Tom joined them he noticed Margaret lingered, tears brimming in her eyes, and he realized how difficult this transition must be for her, as well as Gerald.

And, for a split second, Tom felt sorry for her.

Chapter Twenty-Eight

Tom was in the library when a carriage pulled up in front of the house. He was unconcerned, *after all who would be looking for him?* He returned to reading the *Cleveland Morning Leader*, anxious to keep up with reports of the war. Although the news was days, sometimes weeks old, he followed it closely. Since his arrival in Cleveland there had been little to no activity on the war front and for that, he was thankful. There were still accountings of Antietam on a regular basis because of the Eighth's involvement, and day after day names were added to the rolls of the dead, names like Jacob Butler and Arnold Watson.

Regardless the battle at Antietam was over, it haunted Tom and Gerald in their sleep and while awake.

Tom felt sorry for his nephew. Not because of the loss of his arm, but because the moment he stepped out of his room of a day he was accosted by his mother. She tried to anticipate Gerald's every need before he did. She doted on him, made up his plate, helped him dress, and, in essence, became his right arm. And in doing so was also doing Gerald a huge disservice in his healing, both mentally and physically.

A knock drew Tom's attention and he listened as Charles, Ralph's butler, answered the front door. There were high pitched squeals and giggles and Tom's brows knit with confusion.

"Is Mr. Gerald available for visitors?" the squeaky voice of what sounded like a young girl or very young woman asked.

His interest piqued, Tom laid the paper on the settee and quietly walked to the library door where he spotted four women huddled together on the front porch.

"Yes, the young master is in residence. Whom should I say is calling?" Charles asked.

"Tell him Jane, Susan, Harriet, and Lydia. We've come to offer our assistance in his…his time of…."

The woman doing the talking turned and whispered, the others responding with more whispers until she turned back to Charles and completed the sentence with, "restoration," with a tilt of her head and a snap of her chin.

"Won't you please come in?" Charles opened the door more fully to allow them entry.

The women ogled the front hall with its large chandelier, paintings, and statues, before following Charles into the parlor, opposite the library from where Tom stood.

Tom stepped into the foyer. "I'll fetch him."

Charles nodded. "Very well, sir."

Tom shook his head at the man's stiffness, but if that was what Ralph demanded, he was getting what he paid for. He went up the stairs to Gerald's room. When there was no response to his knock Tom went in and found his nephew napping.

He shook Gerald's shoulder. Gerald jerked upright and rolled awkwardly onto his right side, drawing a whimper before he shouted, "What! No sir! I'm ready sir!" He tried to balance himself but kept rolling back to his right side.

"Gerald, wake up. It's Tom."

"Uncle Tom?" His eyes blinked open. "Where are we?"

"You're home and there is a gaggle of ladies downstairs who want to see you."

Gerald rolled to his back, closed his eyes again, and shook his head to clear his mind of, what Tom perceived, had been another nightmare in a string of many that didn't stop—for either of them. "What?" He tried to rub the sleep from his face. "Who's here?"

"Four young ladies are here to help you in your time of...restoration," Tom chuckled.

Gerald frowned and shook his head again. "My what?"

"I believe they mean your rehabilitation."

Gerald frowned again and he sighed. "They want to get a look at the one-armed man is what they want." He waved his hand. "Tell them I'm indisposed. Tell them I don't want to see them. Tell them I'm not some oddity to be pitied or become their next *restoration* project. Tell them whatever you like that means I don't want to see them."

Tom saw the familiar anger rising. "Gerald, do them, and yourself, a favor. See them. Be polite and let them know you need no help. You can't stay in this room, and angry, for the rest of your life. You have to meet people, see people, even if it makes you, and them, uncomfortable. You lost your arm in a horrible battle. Yet you survived when so many didn't. You're alive and that's the whole of it."

Tom grabbed Gerald's hand and helped him up, Gerald wobbling unsteadily on the bed. "Come along. Comb that dark mop of hair you've been blessed with, put on some of that smelly tonic you've used since you were thirteen and discovered girls, and come downstairs." He walked to the door, put his hand on the knob, and stopped. "Who knows, Gerald, the next Mrs. Hansen could be just a few steps away."

Gerald eyed his uncle angrily a moment before he grinned. "Very well, *Uncle*, I'll do as you ask. I'll keep my tongue and let them dote over me, if that's what you'd like. And I'll be polite. It may be rather humorous." He slapped his leg and stood, rocking on his feet before he gained his balance.

Tom ran to help him and Gerald's anger flashed again, but to his credit, he controlled it quickly.

"Come down when you're presentable." Tom waited until Gerald walked to the table and grabbed the comb before he quit the room and headed downstairs.

Tom entered the parlor to find Margaret had joined the ladies, circled around her like a queen imparting the secrets of the ages. Five pairs of eyes popped up when Tom entered the room.

"Tom!" Margaret jumped to her feet and hurried to her brother-in-law. She wrapped her hands around his right arm and guided him into the parlor. "Have you spoken to Gerald? Is he coming down? These young ladies are very anxious to see him."

Tom kept the frown from crossing his face. "He'll be down shortly. He's freshening up a bit."

There was twittering amongst the four girls and Margaret's eyes flashed with delight. "Wonderful!" She whirled to face the visitors and swept back to the settee where the ladies awaited Gerald's entrance, dragging Tom with her. Thankfully, there was no room so Tom opted for a chair beside the couch.

Gerald came down the stairs ten minutes later, a jacket on, no tie, his hair combed, and smelling fresh and gentlemanly.

Tom jumped up and met him in the entry. "They're in the parlor. Remember to be polite." Tom lifted an eyebrow and cocked his head.

Gerald sighed and didn't move for long seconds before he finally nodded. "I won't make promises I can't guarantee I'll keep, but I'll try."

Tom stayed in the foyer after Gerald entered the parlor, as nervous as a mother hen. He'd been the one to look after his nephew before coming home. He'd been the one to quell his anger or help him when Gerald allowed him to get close enough. This was merely the next phase in his healing, so why was he so nervous? *Because he expected the worst.*

"Gerald, I'm pleased to present Miss Jane, Miss Sue, Miss Lydia, and Miss Harriet," Margaret introduced her son.

Tom had to contain his chuckle. Margaret was announcing to her son that these ladies were single and available, should he want to take advantage.

"I'm pleased to meet you, ladies. To what do I owe the pleasure of this visit?" he asked.

"Well," the one named Jane, seemingly the spokesperson for their little group, said, "We heard of your terrible mishap in the war. We can't begin to imagine how horrible it must have been and with, well, with so many of our boys not coming home…" She stammered to a stop. "I mean, well, you're a hero and we wanted to tell you so."

Silence filled the room.

Tom imagined Gerald's face as red as a ripe tomato, until Gerald responded.

"Ladies." Tom heard the tightness in Gerald's voice. "I am no hero. I fought like all the men fought. Thankfully, my uncle and I survived. My uncle is the hero. He's the one who dragged me off the field to safety where I was tended by the surgeon."

There was more twittering about the room and Tom's heart stuck in his throat. He did *not* want to be called upon to meet these silly females with stars in their eyes and full of hero-worship so he actually stepped behind the wall where he couldn't be seen. Thankfully, the conversation moved on without a request for him to join them.

"That horrible battle at Antietam? Is that where you were injured? Where you lost your arm?" one of the women asked.

Tom closed his eyes and shook his head.

"Harriet is it?"

There was silence again and Tom imagined the silly girl smiling wide at Gerald's remembrance of her name.

"To answer your question, Miss Harriet, yes. It was Antietam where I was injured. My bone was shattered and the doctors knew if my arm wasn't removed I'd die."

There was a unified intake of breath.

Did they want to know all the gruesome details? Tom wondered. *Weren't women supposed to be averse to questions and details like that? Maybe the war had changed the women, too and, through Gerald, they could understand better what their brothers or fathers had faced or would face?*

Charles entered the foyer with a tray of tea and cakes. He looked at Tom, obviously eavesdropping now, and grinned, before he went into the parlor.

"Ah, here's Charles with some refreshments," Margaret trilled.

"Here, let me pour a cup for you, Gerald," one of the ladies said.

"I'll make a plate for you," said another.

"I'll do it," said another.

Tom held his breath, waiting for Gerald's explosion of temper. He didn't wait long.

"Stop! Stop right now!" Gerald shouted.

There was immediate silence until Margaret said, "Now Gerald, these ladies are only trying to help."

"Do *not* patronize me, mother!"

Tom heard Gerald's deep intake of breath before he said, "Why are you women here? Really? Is it because your men, *men I served with*, were killed at Antietam and you're assessing who is still whole enough to be marriageable? Is *that* why you're *really* here?" There was silence for two beats before Gerald asked, "Do I pass your inspection?"

There was stammering and stuttering around the room and suddenly a crash of what sounded like a chair being overturned.

"This is who I am. I'm angry and I don't want empty-headed females asking me stupid questions about how I was injured or how it feels! It pains me! How do you think it feels? Can you take that pain away? Make it stop?" he challenged, and Tom felt it was time to step in before Gerald said something he couldn't take back.

Tom hurried into the room. "Ladies, Gerald and I will take our leave now."

Gerald pulled away from Tom's grip on his arm.

"Maybe I'm not ready to leave. Maybe I have a few more things to say to these, ladies, who have come to see the man with one arm."

Tom waved his hand toward the exit. "We should leave, Gerald. Now," Tom said through gritted teeth, staring his nephew down. "Let's go."

Gerald stood rooted to the floor, the overturned chair behind him, his nose flaring and eyes flashing. Finally, he swallowed and grinned.

"My dear uncle to the rescue yet again." He whirled on the women, including his mother, cowering together in front of the settee. He swept low in an awkward bow then straightened quickly, wobbling a little before he regained his balance. "Good day, ladies. I hope I haven't ruined it over much."

He swung around and stormed from the room, Tom behind him.

Tom followed Gerald up the stairs, the door slamming in his face before he got into the room behind his nephew. Undeterred, Tom shoved it open and stomped inside.

"What is wrong with you? I thought you were going to be polite? The least you could have done was to excuse yourself to have your tantrum!" Tom shouted.

Gerald whirled on his uncle, his eyes ablaze. "They wanted to see the one-armed man! Size me up! See if I was still a viable candidate for marriage. Don't you see? They wanted to see how badly I was maimed to decide if I was still good enough to *allow* me to court *them*! One of the few eligible young men left in this town after Antietam!"

"That's not what I saw at all." Tom tried to deny Gerald's words, regardless that was exactly what he saw in their tones and stupid questions.

"Then you're blind," Gerald snarled. "I want nothing to do with those empty-headed females. Not a damned thing!"

"Suit yourself. It's no skin off my back if you want to spend the rest of your life hiding in this room. I'm leaving in less than a week and you'll be here on your own to fend for yourself." Tom lifted a finger and raised his eyebrow. "On second thought, you won't be on your own. Mommy will be here to dress you, wash you, and wipe your nose!" Tom glared at his red-faced nephew, seething with rage.

Gerald stood silent but his eyes still blazed. Tom knew now was the time to give his nephew the full tongue-lashing he'd been itching to give him for weeks.

Tom stepped closer. "You've pushed me, cursed me, belittled me, and screamed at me," Tom began. "And I let you, because you're going through a very tough time, but no more, Gerald. You're a grown man and it's time for you to accept what's happened and take control of your life."

Gerald flapped the empty sleeve of his suit coat. "Minus my arm," he snarled.

"Yes, minus your arm, which makes you no less a man than you were when you left for this damnable war. You survived. Would you rather have wound up like Jacob or Arnold or Lawrence, buried with hundreds of others on the field of battle? Would you?"

Gerald started to answer, but Tom interrupted before he could.

"We lost twenty-eight men from our thirty-two man company at Antietam, Gerald! Twenty-eight! Would you prefer to switch places with any one of them? Maybe with Lieutenant Delany, shot in the belly to die a painful death. Or what about our friend Jack Sheppard, shot so many times he didn't even have time to cry out before he hit the ground? Or would you rather have lost a leg instead of an arm, left to hobble around on a cane for the rest of your life or carried about on someone's back like excess baggage? Would you?" Tom shouted, uncaring who heard him.

Gerald had the good sense to look contrite. He blinked his eyes and tried to answer but again, Tom gave him no chance.

"I can't know what you feel. All I know is that you have to figure this out or you're going to be miserable for the rest of your life," Tom said more calmly. He placed his hands on Gerald's shoulders. "You have to accept it, Gerald, or you might as well have died with our friends. And what kind of legacy is that to them, those who *did* die? Are you going to walk around the rest of your life whining because you're *alive*, but only have one arm?" Tom challenged.

Gerald's anger deflated and he plopped down on the bed. He shook his head back and forth and a sob exploded from his throat.

"I'm so angry, Tom. Years ago I would have played up to those women. Would have made one after the other wait on me to see how far they would go to please me. But now all I see in their eyes is pity—and them deciding whether I'm *good enough* to marry. It's insulting and humiliating."

Tom sat down beside his nephew. He didn't look at him. He just spoke for Gerald to listen. He lifted his arms to encompass the room around them, the fine chest of drawers and everything on it, the fancy lighting fixtures on the walls, the thick woolen drapes that kept out the heat in summer and cold in winter, and soft, inviting bed they sat on, piled high with warm blankets. "Gerald, this is where you come from, who you are. This is no backwoods cottage. You've been privileged since you were born, have always had servants and maids to look after you and take care of you. When have you ever had to worry about doing anything for yourself? Why would having one arm impede anything you do—other than the pride of not having it? Tom asked. "You have plenty of money, Gerald, and that alone will take care of many of the problems other men would have trouble solving in your situation."

Tom got up then turned and dropped to his knees beside the bed. He looked up into his nephew's face. "Stop feeling sorry for yourself. You're alive, Gerald. Your body is whole, except for one arm, and healing. You'll learn how to live without it. Certainly, it'll be awkward and frightening and maddening, but it's better than the alternative. To be like Jacob or Arnold or Lawrence or any one of the other of our company that was left behind. And be thankful it wasn't your leg taken off by a ball, or your eyes, blinded by an exploding shell. You're no different now than you were a year ago. And if those silly women, and you, don't realize that, there's nothing left to say."

Gerald swallowed and snorted. He swiped his nose.

"Here." Tom pulled a handkerchief from the pocket of his brother's fancy borrowed coat.

Gerald grinned. "Uncle Tom, to the rescue again."

"As long as you need rescuing, I'll be there."

Gerald smiled. Tom stood up and embraced his nephew.

A battle won.

Chapter Twenty-Nine

Tom noticed a subtle change in Gerald since his tongue-lashing. Gerald was still angry, but he was trying harder to keep that anger under control.

Walking past his nephew's room two mornings later, Tom couldn't help but hear the heated exchange between Gerald and a female who sounded very much like Glynis, the Hansen's maid.

"Yer're an ungrateful sot." Glynis' singsong voice rolled out from under the door along with what sounded like a pile of clothes and boots hitting the floor.

"Ungrateful?" Gerald sounded incredulous.

"Indeed ye are. Ye whine about not bein' able tae do what ye could before and expect me tae walk about behind ye, pickin' up yer discarded clothes and changin' yer dirty water while ye go about makin' more just as easy as ye please." Tom imagined the tiny girl with her hands splayed on her hips and her blue eyes snapping, her cheeks on fire to match her hair. "Yer're no different than ye were before ye left here *Mister* Gerald. I thought this might humble ye. Ye were a snob and a slob then and yer're a snob and a slob now."

Tom almost laughed out loud. He smiled and leaned against the wall to continue eavesdropping. If Gerald wouldn't listen to him trying to impress upon him he was the same man he'd been before he lost his arm, maybe this slip of a girl could make him realize how little he'd changed—both good and bad.

"Live in a pigsty if ye will," she continued, taking a big breath. "But if ye plan tae do anythin' on yer own again, like dressin' or feedin' yerself without someone doin' it fer ye, ye'll need tae take the time tae learn how. Ye whine, but ye won't even try tae do the things ye used to. Ye jest wait fer someone tae do it fer ye."

She paused again and Tom swiped away a tear of laughter. *How he was enjoying this!*

"From now on, I'll help ye when I must—after ye've tried and failed. Maybe after ye've tried two or three times. Yer're a grown man…"

"With only one arm!" Gerald interrupted.

"Oh, me poor man, with only one arm. Who lives and breathes pity and will be perfectly capable of takin' care of himself, with a little practice, I'll give ye that."

Tom imagined Gerald's face, lips puckered, eyes flashing, his one fist rolling in and out, and Tom could barely hold his laughter. *Glynis was getting the best of his arrogant nephew!*

"I'll remind you who I am, Glynis," Gerald ground out.

"By the saints, I think I bloody-well know who ye are. I've been in your employ for four years, and have ye said one word tae me in those four years other than Glynis get this or Glynis do that? No, ye have not! Not until yer mother made me responsible fer helpin' ye, because she gave up on ye, have ye said more than one word!"

There was a lapse in the conversation and Tom imagined Glynis waving her hand in the air to encompass Gerald and his missing arm.

"And what a chore it is!" she exploded, shattering the momentary silence. "Tryin' tae teach a man full grown how tae dress an' cut his meat who can bloody-well learn tae do it himself, if he tried!"

Tom covered his mouth to keep from laughing out loud and cocked his head to hear every word said behind the door, embarrassed to be eavesdropping, but enjoying every minute of it.

"I don't pity myself." Gerald sounded like a petulant little boy trying to defend being caught with his hand in the cookie jar.

Glynis snorted loud enough for Tom to hear. "And I'm the Queen of England. Ye do pity yerself, but when someone else pities ye, ye throw a tantrum, like ye did with them ladies that come to visit ye. Ye can't have it both ways, *Mister* Gerald. Either you want tae learn how tae take care of yerself again or ye want people tae pity ye an' do it fer ye."

The room went quiet again and Tom imagined Gerald's eyes flashing and his lips rolling, trying to decide what to say next.

Glynis finally continued. "I'll help ye where and when ye need help, but ye'll damned well, excuse me foulness, make an effort tae do it yerself first. If ye don't like what I'm about then run tae your mother and have me released, but if ye want tae get better, learn tae do it yer own self!"

In the next instant the door flew open. A surprised Glynis almost ran into Tom when he jumped out of the way and in front of her to avoid being hit by the door. She dodged around him with an unsure smile, lifted her skirts, and hurried down the hall.

Gerald wasn't far behind her, ready to offer chase, when he ran right into Tom, watching the retreating Glynis.

Tom whirled, his lips locked to keep from laughing at his nephew's confused look.

Red-faced Gerald asked, "Did you hear everything?"

"I heard enough." Tom said through clenched teeth.

Gerald blinked his eyes, scratched his head, and stared down the hall Glynis had just vacated. He looked over at Tom, trying to control his laughter.

Gerald's eyes knit. His lips pinched, his face went hard, and Tom steeled himself for his nephew's temper to unleash itself.

Instead he laughed, in short bursts, as though he'd forgotten how, and once he started he didn't stop.

Tom bent over, put his hands on his knees, and laughed like he hadn't in months, perhaps years, the hallway echoing with both their laughter.

Gerald slapped Tom on the back and looked at his uncle with confusion before he smiled wide again.

"You know what? I like her Uncle Tom. I like her a lot!"

***

Eligible women, the very young and not so very young, paraded through the house every day that week for tea with Margaret with the understanding, of course, they would meet Gerald before they left. More like his old self though, Gerald enjoyed the women. He baited them and pitted them against one another to see who would scurry the fastest to do his bidding, just like he used to. It was an old game he'd loved to play and he enjoyed playing it again, but now it left Margaret fuming until the ladies came no more.

It wasn't a game when Glynis was around, though. Tom watched her push Gerald like he'd never been pushed, not even when he was a soldier. She treated him like she was his equal and as the days passed Gerald began treating her the same.

"Try it again." Glynis's command was quiet, yet full of authority.

How Tom wished he could *see* what was going on in the dining room where she was helping Gerald relearn his skills at the table.

"I don't *want* to try again. I can't do it!" A fork landed heavily on a plate, moments before the plate shattered against the wall.

Tom started into the dining room to see if he could be of assistance, but stopped inside the doorway when the little Irish sprite said, "Is that how it is, *Mister* Gerald?" the word *mister* heavily drawn as it usually was these days. "Ye can't do it the first time, so ye'll get rid of whatever it is that's vexin' ye like a spoilt little boy?"

She stood her ground and Tom decided the better part of Gerald's rehabilitation, and his own valor, was to let this slip of a girl have her way, pushing his nephew to anger then pushing him to do whatever it was that needed to be done.

"Do *not* call me that!" Gerald shouted.

"Then quit actin' like one. Ye'll be better served tae jest sit down and try again."

Margaret flounced past Tom into the dining room. "What is going on in here?"

"Nothing to be concerned with, Mother. I had an accident and a plate was broken."

Margaret's eyebrows knitted and she waved a hand at where the plate lay in pieces against the wall. "Across the room? I'll have you know that is very expensive china, Gerald. I won't have you destroying it in a fit of temper."

Gerald rolled his shoulders and neck in an effort to control his temper, but it exploded anyway, as it so often did with his mother and father. "Get out, Mother! Get out! We're busy and don't need, or appreciate, your interference!"

Margaret's eyes bulged. Her lips worked in unspoken words before her hand fluttered to her chest and she hurried past Tom, her face ashen. Tom smiled. Margaret had been bested, again, as she had been many times in the last couple days. And not only by Gerald, but by Glynis, who challenged Margaret when she questioned how Glynis took care of her son. It was when Gerald stepped up to defend Glynis that Tom realized there was more between the two than just Glynis's tutelage being in question. Feelings were growing. All Tom had to do was look at them when they were together, challenging each other, fighting, or nose to nose in discussion. There was a spark between them and Tom cheered every time it flared.

***

All too quickly it was time for Tom to return to the front. Tom stood in what had been his room for the last week and sighed. He looked around, putting to memory everything that had happened in that week. Coming to this house he'd brought a confused, angry young man who now accepted his situation, who he was, and what he wanted to do with his life. Remembering their conversation just last night, in the quiet of Gerald's room, Tom couldn't help but smile.

"I was so angry after this." Gerald circled his hand around his empty sleeve. "I was mad at everybody, even you, the man who saved my life." He stopped Tom from interrupting. "Let me finish. I need to say this. I was angry with you because you somehow managed to come away from Antietam unscathed, when so many didn't. You're an old man," he said with a snort, eyes sparkling, "and you survived when so many others are buried there. I was jealous it was me that lost my arm and not you or someone else, and I sorely apologize for that. Glynis was right. I *did* pity myself more than anyone. Well, perhaps not more than mother or father," he added with another snort. "I came home angry that I wasn't like I was before, yet expected everyone to treat me differently *because* I wasn't, while complaining that I didn't want to *be* treated differently. You, and Glynis, pointed out I couldn't have it both ways."

Tom nodded. "I can't tell you I understand what you've gone through, Gerald. I can only imagine. But in the time I've been in the war I've learned one thing. Every situation could be worse—unless we die on the battlefield. We were only two of a very few men from our company that survived Antietam. I saw young Sergeant Galwey before we left, so I know he was also one of the few, but so many others didn't, Gerald. So many of the men we fought beside, who became our friends like Arnold and Jacob, stayed at Antietam, are buried at Antietam, and will never see their families again. So many in our regiment were injured and lost legs and arms, and if it were me, I'd be thankful it was an arm and not a leg. You're still mobile. You won't need someone to carry you around on their back when you're an old man and you won't be forced to walk with a crutch that'll give you painful sores under your arms for the rest of your life. You can smell and hear and see everything around you." He leaned in and punched Gerald's good arm like he used to. "Like Glynis."

Gerald smiled and nodded. "All right, if we want to list the good things that came from this, Glynis is definitely one of them."

"You admit it then?"

Gerald nodded again. "I will. She's, well, she's like no woman I've ever met. She speaks her mind and," his eyes went to Tom's, "she's as tough as most men I've met, regardless she's the size of a pea. She, and you, made me realize just how lucky I am to be alive, to be home, and to have the ability to do everything I could before, with a little extra effort, of course. I can dress myself now. Perhaps it takes me longer and it's a bit awkward, but I can do it, thanks to Glynis. I eat like a grown man again, thanks to Glynis. And I have a plan for what I want to do with my life, other than sit around and entertain people who don't give a damn about me, only my money."

Tom's eyebrows lifted. "And what is that?"

"I want to help others who have experienced what I've experienced. I want to seek out other soldiers who have lost a leg or an arm and help them learn what it takes to get on with living. To make the best of it and be happy they're alive."

"Like you are?" Tom's eyes sparkled with pride.

"Like I am. I don't want to be that man who carries his injury with him in everything he does and says for the rest of his life. I want to prove that I'm the same as I was before. Prove I'm as good as I was before, maybe better, and that one arm or one leg doesn't change who I am."

Tom couldn't help the tears that welled in his eyes. He blinked trying to expel them, but not before Gerald saw them and cocked his head in question.

"You're so much more to me than just a nephew, Gerald. Of course, you're family, but you're also my best friend. A friend I've trusted with my life."

Gerald swallowed and threw himself into his uncle's chest. He wrapped his arm around Tom's shoulders. Tom did the same and they held on, both knowing it could be the last time they might see each other for a very long time—or ever.

Gerald pulled back. "You leave in the morning?"

Tom nodded.

"I wish I were going with you."

Tom shook his head. "No, you don't and I'm glad you're not. I'll miss having you to punch and push around, but you'll be safe, and that's what's most important." Tom paused. He had more to say and had to say it the right way. Tom laid his hands on Gerald's shoulders.

"Gerald, I want you to know how proud I am of the man you've become. You started this adventure a curious, somewhat romantic, young man, but you've survived horrible circumstances and grown from them. And you're going to use those experiences to help others. I couldn't be more proud if you were my own son."

The smile that blazed from Gerald's lips could have lit the room if it were dark. He grabbed Tom's left hand and pulled his uncle into another embrace. "Thank you, Uncle Tom. Thank you. That means more to me than, well, most everything," he managed.

"It's well deserved. I'm proud to call you nephew—and friend."

They remained together for several moments before Tom pulled away. "I'd better say goodnight, it's going to be an early morning." Tom stepped back and headed for the door.

"Good night, Uncle Tom. And thank you, for everything."

***

It was time to say goodbye. Tom stepped to Margaret, standing stiff beside Ralph on the front porch, and gave her a quick hug. "Thank you for your hospitality, Margaret. I'm thankful to have a place to come to when I can."

"You're welcome anytime, Tom." She pulled away. "Be careful and come back to us." She sniffed and stepped back into the house and as Tom watched her, he was thankful she'd allowed him to enjoy this visit without any unwanted attentions.

Ralph stepped up and laid his hands on Tom's shoulders. "Do as Margaret says, Tom. Come back to us. Don't do anything foolish or heroic, just come back." His brother pulled Tom into a hug and held on tight, Tom savoring the feel of it.

"I will, Ralph. I'll be careful and I *will* come back."

Ralph stepped away, but remained on the porch. Tom stepped to Gerald. The two men faced each other. Most of what needed to be said had been said last night.

"You do as they say, Uncle Tom. Don't do anything foolish."

"Like drag someone off the field after he's been shot?" Tom asked with a grin.

"Touche. You're allowed that, but nothing else that might keep you from coming home."

Tom nodded and pulled his nephew into a hug. He felt bereft, yet relieved he wasn't coming with him to be in harm's way again. Gerald was a good man and would become even better now that he'd accepted his impediment and planned to help others because of it. And the boy was happy. Tom glanced over Gerald's shoulder at Glynis, standing behind him like the dutiful servant girl, but knowing there was more to that relationship than his parents knew. *Oh, to be a fly on the wall to see their reaction when Gerald told them!*

"Be happy, Gerald. Take what life has to offer and be happy," Tom whispered in his nephew's ear. "And let her help." Tom leaned his head toward Glynis.

"I will. You can bet on it." Gerald pulled him in for one last hug before he stepped away.

Glynis stepped forward and curtsied. "I'm proud to know ye, sir. Be safe an' come back tae us." She looked around at Gerald, entering the house. "Fer him." She smiled, fully aware Tom knew hers and Gerald's secret, before she curtsied one last time and followed Gerald inside.

Charles, as stiff as ever, cocked his head. "Be safe, Master Tom."

"I will, Charles. Thank you."

Tom was in a hurry now to get away. Lingering did no good. It was time to go.

"The hack will take you to the station, Tom. Be safe, brother!" Ralph called as Tom descended the steps to the waiting wagon and his return to the war.

Chapter Thirty

Tom rejoined his division, bivouacked at Harper's Ferry, and tried to get back into what had been a normal routine before he left. He'd been back for two days, but it seemed more like two months as he listened to the horror stories of the gruesome task of burying the dead after Antietam. The stench of men and horses had been almost unbearable in the aftermath and Tom was more than thankful he'd been granted leave to take Gerald home.

Without cause for leave, the men in Tom's division had gone into bivouac to rest, relax, refit, and wait for new orders.

On the 29th of October, after new recruits had joined the ranks, the men were refitted with new clothes and shoes. Food was prepared for a long trip and the Eighth Ohio Volunteers left Harper's Ferry.

"Where we headed Sarge?" Tom asked young Galwey, not looking as young as he had at the beginning of the war, the boy still gimping on a leg injury he'd sustained at Antietam.

"East. We're to act as wagon guard behind the Second Corps."

"How many wagons?"

"I've been told about three hundred."

Tom whistled. "Three hundred? That's a lotta wagons."

"It is, but those are our orders. We move out in an hour."

With the creak and rumble of wagons they departed Harper's Ferry into the darkness, headed east toward where, or what, Tom didn't know. He only did what he was told, and right now that was to act as wagon guard heading east.

Trekking through the dark, Tom couldn't count the number of times he turned to listen for Gerald's complaints about the rough road or the rocks or the darkness. But they didn't come and he missed his nephew more than he realized he would. Other men grumbled ahead of and behind him, but it wasn't the same.

Throughout the night the wagons rumbled along then suddenly jerked to a stop in a hole or rut. They bumped into each other in the darkness, ran over rocks causing them to veer out of control and crush feet and men caught in their path.

It grew cold as the night progressed and a heavy rain began to fall. Tom slid deeper into his coat, wishing he were back in Cleveland easing under the covers of his bed instead of slipping and sliding in the ever thickening mud.

"Bet you're missing that soft bed you slept in when you were on leave, eh, Tom?"

Tom turned to Jim Benton, who stepped up beside him. Tom snorted. "That I do."

"Why'd you come back?" the balding, heavyset Benton asked.

Tom's brows knit and his head cocked in confusion. "What do you mean, why did I come back? I had to come back. My leave was up and it was my duty."

Benton snorted in return. "Duty. If it'd been me I'd a gone and never come back."

Tom halted and stared at the man. He didn't stand long, the wagon behind him rumbling toward him, threatening to run over him. He caught up with Benton in a few slippery strides. "You really wouldn't have come back?"

"No, I would not." Benton shook his head. "If I had the chance right now, I'd be long gone."

Tom looked down at the ground, watching for rocks in the darkness that might trip him and send him sprawling, to be crushed by the wagon behind him as had already happened numerous times to others tonight. He didn't want to listen to Benton's kind of talk and made him uncomfortable.

Benton chuckled, apparently sensing Tom's discomfort. He dropped back and spoke no more.

It was almost daylight when they went into bivouac, Tom more than ready for the rest. His feet hurt and he was exhausted. He was soaked to the bone and lonely for his nephew. He hadn't realized just how much Gerald's company had meant to him until tonight. He'd even take the unending complaints, but was still relieved his young relation was safe and far from here. His last thought before he dropped off to sleep was to write his nephew a letter and tell him just that.

The next morning Galwey charged up to Tom, a piece of paper clutched in his hand, his face awash with excitement.

"What is it, Sarge?"

Galwey's chest puffed up like a rooster. "I'm not your sergeant any more."

Tom's brow's knit in confusion. "So, what are you then?"

He looked at Tom with eyes full of pride and excitement. "The Adjutant just informed me that effective September 17th, at Antietam, I was promoted to Second Lieutenant."

"Well, hot damn, Sar...I mean Lieutenant!"

Galwey stared hard at Tom then grinned. "Looks like my old job is open, Tom. You want to apply?"

Tom shook his head rapidly. "I don't think so, lieutenant. I'm an old man..."

"Which makes you perfect for the job," Galwey interrupted. "You're responsible, and reasonable, and you think things through. You're," he sighed. "What's a delicate way to say this? You're mature."

Tom hooted with laughter. "I am that!" Tom thought a moment and cocked his head. "Are you sure about this, lieutenant? About me?"

Galwey nodded. "I am."

Tom snapped to attention and saluted his new lieutenant. "Who am I to argue?"

***

November 10, 1862

My Dearest Gerald,

"It was an arduous trip from Harper's Ferry where we went into camp for only a few short days before moving east as wagon guards behind the Second Corps. While in camp we received the devastating news that Little Mac had been replaced by General Burnside. The men were angry. Even those who usually complained loudest about General McClellan stomped about, shouting at the injustice of it, charging that the civilian buffoons in Washington brought it about, possibly at Burnside's urging.

"In parade the morning of November 7th we said goodbye to our beloved general. He rode straight and proud in all his glory past the ranks, many of the men stifling sobs or shouting loud exclamations of reverence as the man passed. Many a red eye was seen before the men were excused back to camp. It was a sad day for the troops as we waved farewell to our beloved commander.

"Since my return to the front I've also realized, my dear nephew, how much I miss your companionship and even your complaints. I find myself waiting for your grumbling beside me when the food is bad or it rains too long or exhaustion claims me. But then I remind myself that you are safe and I'm happy for you.

"Our young sergeant Galwey has been promoted. He is now a Second Lieutenant! Imagine that young colt a lieutenant. And in his vacating of the sergeant's position, he has awarded it to me! Yes, me. So, thank your lucky stars you're not here for me to badger you as your sergeant!

"In seriousness, I miss you sorely, nephew, and hope all is well with you—and Glynis. How does it go with her? Is she keeping you in line?

"How are your parents? Have they adjusted to your situation yet? I fear they, well, your mother, will have more difficulty than anyone accepting it, even more than you, as her son is no longer perfect. Have you pursued your idea of helping other soldiers returning from battle dealing with the same type of loss as you? I do hope so as it is a noble calling and may save more than one life.

"We hear rumors that after we rest a few more days we'll march toward Falmouth, Virginia, directly across the river from Fredericksburg. With the approach of winter I wish I were marching nowhere and was somewhere inside, enjoying a big, warm fire, but alas, this is my lot and I must carry on.

"I fare well, as well as anyone sleeping on the ground in the cold and rain and enduring the indignities of being a soldier can. I could go on and on, but you know it all as well as I. Ah! I'm beginning to sound like you! Other than our hardships, the countryside we traverse is a paradise.

"*I miss you and hope all is well. Until we meet again, I remain,*"

Tom

Chapter Thirty-One

The Union camp lined the Rappahannock for miles, Fredericksburg visible across the river. Trees were felled to make room for the burgeoning camp and Tom's back felt ready to snap after chopping for days to clear the area now populated by a sea of dirty tents.

At picket duty along the river Tom tried to stay warm. They'd been in camp for weeks now and he wondered how much longer it would be before they saw action again. Not that he wanted to fight. He was just tired of the insipid boredom and picket duty, as he always was between battles. He was either scared out of his wits or bored out of his mind. He sighed. *Christmas was only two weeks away. Where would they be on Christmas Day? Would he be here to enjoy it?*

Tom shook his head to clear his mind of the unwanted thoughts, turned on his heel, and continued his picket duty. Hearing activity in the distance, he stopped, cocked his head, and watched cannon being positioned on their side of the river. Swallowing, he realized he may just get the battle he'd been wondering about. He marched back and forth watching big gun after big gun positioned along the river until it looked like every cannon the army had was aimed at Fredericksburg.

He fell into his cot that night missing Gerald, even missing Cleveland and all it offered as a substitute home, worrying tomorrow could well be his last.

***

Galwey pointed to the ravines that ran along the plateau opposite Fredericksburg on their side of the river. "Position the men over there. And do it at the double-quick. The batteries are scheduled to commence firing at ten."

Tom hustled the men at a run to the spot Galwey had indicated. With a few minutes to spare, B Company hunkered down and waited.

At ten o'clock the big guns Tom had seen positioned along the river the night before exploded with such a roar he had to cover his ears to keep them from bursting. One after another the guns launched their destruction on Fredericksburg, and the men's ear drums.

For hours Tom and the men watched and waited. The noise was deafening as the cannon pounded the city while hundreds of pontoon boats waited at the ready to be dispensed across the river.

Once the Rebs were finally driven from the city by the Union cannon, the boats would cross the Rappahannock carrying troops into Fredericksburg.

By afternoon the cannonade stopped and the pontoons pushed away from shore toward the opposite bank. Tom popped upright when unexpected fire exploded from behind a low wall on the opposite bank as the boats approached.

The boats retreated under the barrage of fire. Reaching friendly shore again the men jumped from the boats and ran splashing through the water for cover. Tom's eyes were glued to the unfolding battle, thankful he was watching it from the bluffs, instead of engaged below.

But his time would come, he had no doubt.

The flags of the 17th Michigan and 19th Massachusetts suddenly appeared on shore, waving proudly ahead of the men that climbed into the boats to attempt their own crossing. The smaller 7th Michigan poled their way toward the other side in another of the pontoon boats.

More guns exploded from behind the stone wall as the boats came into range and were met with return fire from the advancing 17th, 19th, and 7th.

More boats were launched and the engineers rushed to connect them as a bridge across the river for an infantry charge.

Tom stared at the battle below, the men around him as fascinated by the unfolding scene as he, and probably as thankful they were still being held back. For how long that would last, he couldn't know, but the longer the better as far as he was concerned. He had no death wish.

Guns popped from both sides of the river throughout the day, while the engineers and pontooniers worked feverishly to get the bridge erected. By late afternoon the bridge was complete and the infantry swarmed across it like ants on chicken at a summer picnic.

Still in reserve, Tom and the men of B Company watched, transfixed, as other regiments charged across the bridge, flooding the streets of Fredericksburg.

Darkness came, the battle continued, and still they waited.

Fires raged throughout the city, the houses burning so brightly night became day. Men fought in the street, illuminated in the firelight. Watching from above, Tom and his men were as wide awake as if they fought, too.

Throughout the night fighting continued in the streets of Fredericksburg and still B Company was held. Not until morning did they finally get orders to move out.

Almost numb from the lack of sleep, his adrenaline pumping all night with the anticipation of battle, Tom led the men down the bank, across the pontoon bridge, and into the now mostly abandoned city where large tobacco warehouses were the first buildings they came upon.

The men charged inside before Tom could stop them and grabbed what they could.

"Look, Sarge! There's enough tobacco here to last the rest of the war, if we can just carry it!" a new recruit whose name Tom didn't know shouted while displaying hands full of dried tobacco leaves.

Tom was uncertain. *Should he make them stop or let them take what they wanted? He had no orders to allow the men to confiscate anything from within the city, but he had no orders to stop them, either.*

Their need to plunder sated for the moment, their pockets and haversacks bulging, the men continued up the main street only to find more empty buildings. Stepping inside one of the vacant homes, Tom realized just how quickly the residents had fled, their clothing strewn across the floors, whatever they couldn't carry left behind.

Tom stood on the walkway and watched homes being stripped of anything that could be carried out. Breathing heavily Galwey stepped up beside Tom, his eyes aglow in the firelight. "It's a sad sight, isn't it?"

"Has an order been given to allow the men to loot these homes or to keep them from it?"

Galwey shook his head. "No order has been given either way, so the men are free to do as they please."

Tom sighed and shook his head. "Is this what the war has come to?"

Galwey frowned. "The men have fought long and hard and this is their reward." He pointed to a building on the corner. "We're to bivouac there."

Tom nodded. "I'll gather the men."

The men from B Company, mostly strangers to Tom, gathered inside the specified house. Each man found a spot to call his before venturing back into the streets of Fredericksburg. Unable to join in the pillaging of the city, Tom found a bed upstairs, fell into it, and slept for several hours before awakened by boisterous voices below.

"What's going on here?" he asked Collins, a tall, lanky, towheaded youth, whose name he had to think hard to recall.

"Scotch, Sarge! We found it in the cellar of the bakery next door!" he slurred. "And sweet treats!" He raised a pastry in front of Tom's face before he shoved it into his mouth with a groan of delight.

Although not usually a drinker, Tom had imbibed in a scotch here and there in his former life in many a winner's circle. "I'll take some of that if you can spare it," he said to Collins.

"Sure, Sarge! Have as much as you like. There's plenty for everybody!" Collins handed Tom a stone bottle that sloshed half full of the liquid.

Tom sniffed what was in the bottle then lifted it to his lips and swallowed. He expected rot gut but was surprised by its smoothness. It spread through his body like a soothing balm. He smiled at its calming effect then took another pull.

Unwilling to get drunk, he took one more swig and handed it back to Collins.

"There's plenny more, Sarge!" Collins drawled before taking another long pull.

"Thanks, but no. I've had enough." Feeling only slightly refreshed from his nap, but calmer from the scotch, Tom found a spot against the wall, sat down, and watched the men. Absently he wondered what Gerald, Arnold, Lawrence, and Jacob would have done if they were here. *Getting drunk, just like the rest of 'em*, Tom almost snorted. *Oh, how he missed his friends and nephew!* Amidst all these young, raw recruits he felt alone and ancient. They called him *Sergeant Pops* behind his back. He wasn't *that* old. Although he was the oldest man in the company, the words stung because they weren't said with affection like they'd been said by his friends earlier in the war. These were disparaging instead. So he kept to himself and let the men, boys as far as he was concerned, do as they would.

The men drank and slept then drank some more until later that afternoon when the city erupted with cannon fire. The Confederate guns opened fire and buildings exploded, including the one they were in.

"Drag the bed ticking downstairs to use for cover!" Tom ducked and covered his head when window fragments exploded behind him.

Their drunkenness forgotten the men raced upstairs and returned minutes later dragging all the bedding they could find behind them. The mattresses and blankets were strewn across the floor then used as cover against the chimney bricks, windowpanes, shingles, and every manner of building parts that flew into the room as the shelling continued.

In the corner, his back against the wall and covered with blankets to protect against the flying debris, Tom stayed as small as he could until the barrage finally stopped.

The cannonading over, men came out from under the bedding and bottles were pulled out again.

"What happens now?" Collins, on the floor next to Tom, asked.

Tom shook his head and listened at the silence. Slowly, the faint sound of churning wheels became a rumble throughout the city. "It sounds like the artillery is being positioned for tomorrow."

Collins sighed. "I was hoping the Johnny Rebs would skedaddle and there'd be no battle. Guess I was wrong."

Collins was solemn and Tom stared at a face that *might* be eighteen years old. *When did they start sending babies to the front!* he wanted to scream before he remembered Galwey, distinguishing himself every day despite his youth.

"Guess there's no help for what's coming tomorrow. We might as well enjoy what's left of the night." Collins hefted a bottle and took a generous drink. He offered it to Tom who waved him off then thought otherwise.

"What the hell? I'll take a pull or two." He grinned at the young soldier in front of him. *Why not? If he was going to die tomorrow he might as well enjoy tonight.*

Chapter Thirty-Two

Fog lay over the city like a soft, cottony blanket. Where the Rebs were easily seen last night on the hill in the distance, nothing was visible this morning, the billowing white stuff hanging like a shroud.

"You men take it easy on the drink. We may not be ordered to the front right this minute, but when we are you don't want to go drunk."

"Aw, come on Sarge. What's to do except wait and drink?" Collins implored, the others grumbling agreement.

"You're grown men and I'm not your father, although a lot of you boys seem to think that." Tom looked out over the sea of young, anxious faces. "Do as you will, but have a care not to get so drunk you're left behind when the fighting starts—or wind up getting your heads blown off because of it."

"We won't, Sarge. We promise." Collins, who had become the spokesman for the men, had a silly smile on his face.

It was near noon when the order came to move out and most of the men weaved and bobbed as they got to their feet. Within minutes, with the reality of battle looming, they overcame their drunkenness and stepped to.

"Take the men west on Hanover Street and outside the city toward the Heights," Galwey told Tom. "The other regiments are going up the adjacent streets and will join us when we reach open ground."

"Yes, sir." Tom saluted.

"I'm still not used to that," Galwey said with a shake of his head and a grin.

"Neither am I," Tom agreed with an equal smile.

"Then move 'em out."

B Company headed west on Hanover Street and met the other regiments on the outskirts of town a few minutes later.

Tom pointed, opened his mouth to tell the men where to position, and wound up flat on his belly as a bullet whizzed by his head. "Take cover! Take cover!" he shouted as guns exploded all around.

Tom was still on his belly when Galwey slithered up beside him. "General Couch has ordered a charge."

Tom blinked at the boy. "A charge? We're already under heavy fire and we're to charge?"

Galwey nodded. "Those are the orders, Sergeant. Pass them on and make sure the men are ready when word is given."

Tom shook his head and wondered how many lives would be wasted today. *And would his be one of them?*

When the order came Tom pushed up on wobbly legs, waved the men forward, and ran as hard as he could toward the Rebs dug in at the base of the hill. The men cheered and yelled as they charged forward, the color bearer's flag waving them on in advance of the surge.

Bullets slammed into men and earth as they ran past several small buildings on their right. Once past the buildings, they were out in the open again and the fire became even heavier.

"Up there!" Tom pointed to several structures up ahead. "Take cover there!" he shouted.

The younger men charged around Tom in their race against the hail of bullets dropping men like felled trees along the road. Running as fast as his forty year old legs would carry him, he splashed through a small creek right behind the others and straight for cover.

"Over here, over here!" a heavy-set soldier named Baker yelled from behind what Tom saw was a grocery store. Moments later he slammed against the wall out of the hot fire.

Tom peeked out. He jerked his head back when a bullet slammed overhead, but in that short time Tom saw where the firing came from. Several stone walls lined the base of the hill and numerous rifle pits were dug out at the top. Every wall and pit held rebel guns trained on their positions behind the grocery store and blacksmith shop across the road where some of the men had taken cover.

Leaning against the protective wall, Tom's heart pummeled his chest, his Enfield tight in his hands. They had nowhere to go that wasn't teeming with gray backs except backward.

Explosions rocked the hillside as Union artillery opened fire above the troops' heads with thunderous noise. *If they did make it up the hill, would they be shredded by their own guns?* Tom wondered.

The few troops that had charged ahead of the Eighth were mowed down by the heavy fire. Tom slammed his back against the wall again, breathing heavily, praying for courage.

Gunfire rained down on them, keeping them pinned where they were. Shouting drew Tom's attention as more troops ran past, only to be cut down in a hail of bullets, while the Union's big guns exploded from behind them, exploding on the hill in front of them.

Regardless of the pounding of the Union artillery, the enemy fire continued, relentless, driving back wave after wave of Federal troops that ran past where B Company was pinned.

"What the hell is that?" Collins asked Tom.

Tom squinted at the next wave of men coming out of Fredericksburg at the double-quick.

"It's the Irish Brigade." Tom looked up at the taller Collins then pointed at the charging Irish. "See their green hats?"

Collins nodded, his mouth agape, as they watched the Irish pass, their caps waving, a sprig of greenery fastened to show who they were, a look of gaiety, and murder, in their eyes.

Tom swallowed. These were men of the toughest sort who had been bloodied heavily in many a battle so far, and would be bloodied again now as they cheered and waved their way into glory.

Replacing their hats they ran screaming toward the stone walls and were cut down like hay in a field.

Tom held his breath as the Irish fell, bellies to the ground, unable to advance, unable to retreat, while musket fire rained down upon them.

For an hour Tom watched and waited for something to happen to give the Irish a chance to gain their feet and retreat, but they lay there, unable to move.

A flurry of new fire exploded to the south where General Franklin's troops had been positioned, drawing Tom's musing from the fate of the Irish and back to his own.

Baker slid up beside Tom. "Where are General Franklin's troops?" he asked.

Tom shook his head. "Seems they've retired and left us to defend ourselves."

Baker ran a grimy hand over his pudgy, lightly bearded face. "We're running low on ammunition, Sarge. How long do they expect us to hold out here? And without Franklin's troops protecting our flank?"

Tom swallowed, the boy voicing his own fears. "We've got to do the best we can and hold out as long as we can until they send replacements."

Baker shivered, although the weather was tolerable for December.

Tom and the men of B Company stayed hunkered down, firing sporadically at an enemy they rarely saw, while wave after wave of Union men charged toward the hill only to be sliced to pieces like pats of butter.

"We've got to conserve our ammo," Tom said to the men gathered along the wall. "Shoot only when you can actually see what you're shooting at. Understood?"

The men nodded, happy to stay behind what cover they had as long as possible.

Across the road at the blacksmith's shop, Tom wondered how they fared with their ammunition situation. He watched Corporal Brown fire repeatedly out the door of the shop, until it was shredded in an instant by a cannon ball. Tom held his breath, wondering at the corporal's fate, when the man shoved his musket out of what remained of the door and shouted, "Bully for you, by God!" and started firing again.

Tom wondered at the tenacity of some men and timidity of others. *Where did their courage come from?* He certainly understood the fear. It was the brazen courage that puzzled him.

The Union guns continued to fire from behind their position, but at irregular intervals now, aware, Tom hoped, of the men on their bellies in the open field below the hill swarming with Confederates.

"How much longer do they expect us to hold on, Sarge? We've been here for hours," Collins asked.

Collins had no sooner finished his query when Galwey slid up alongside. "We're ordered to retreat. Hooker's Division will relieve us."

"Thank God!" Baker groaned, sliding down the wall onto his chubby rump.

Collins' long frame relaxed. His eyes closed and his head fell back against the wall.

Men groaned with relief and Tom shouted across the road to the blacksmith shop, "We're to be relieved!" His announcement was met with resounding cheers.

Tom looked out over the field of battle as they began to pull back. There was hollering between them and their replacements, while muskets and cannon continued to spew death and destruction behind them.

Tom took a last look at the men strewn about the field and wished there were something he could do to help them. But there was nothing to be done except pray. Turning away Tom followed the others in their retreat back into Fredericksburg, a feeling riding his shoulders that today he'd seen a *brief* glimpse of Hell.

***

Tom and the rest of B Company trudged their way back through town where every church, barn, schoolhouse, and large residence was being used as a hospital. The wounded rolled through the city in the backs of wagons, loaded like cordwood, blood staining the streets as they passed.

A shiver raced up Tom's spine, thankful he had, again, survived battle. Fresh troops passed on their way into the fray and Tom wondered how many of those men wouldn't return from the withering fire that would meet them?

"Sergeant Pops?" Collins stood wide-eyed beside Tom, a grin on his face.

Tom frowned at the use of the name, but took it as a sign of acceptance among the younger men. "What is it Collins?"

"You mind if me and Baker stick close to you?"

"Of course not. I'll welcome the company." Despite his exhaustion, Tom walked briskly to the house where they'd recently bivouacked, Baker and Collins on either side of him. He had one thought on his mind. "The first thing we do when we get back to camp is put on a big pot of coffee."

"I second that!" Baker shouted and hurried to keep up with Tom.

Throughout the night the rumbling of wagons carrying ammunition, returning batteries from the front, taking supplies to the front, and bringing in the dead and wounded, kept Tom from any real sleep. All afternoon he and the men had fought to stay alive under deadly fire, and now others, having taken their places, fought through the night to save theirs.

He slept little, while Collins, Baker, and the rest snored loudly around him.

At first light Tom bolted upright at the sound of exploding cannon and rifles outside the city. It wasn't long before everyone was awake, listening, and cognizant that within hours they could be back in the thick of it. Coffee was put on to boil, mouths were rinsed of last night's sleep, and the day began with the threat of battle looming over them like a pendulum waiting to fall.

"Will they send us back out?" Baker was anxious. "Didn't we fight enough yesterday?" he almost whined.

"I don't know. We certainly saw our share yesterday, but how many more troops can they send up there to be slaughtered?" Tom stopped in thought then added, "I wonder how many of those Irish boys survived the night?"

"They're a hearty lot, to be sure," Collins drawled in an Irish accent, causing Tom to recall Glynis' heavy Irish lilt.

"That they arrr," Tom replied in kind.

"Maybe those Johnny Rebs are as wore out as we are and won't bother us today," Baker said, hopeful.

Collins snorted. "I'd rather spend the day drinking more of that Scotch we found and telling stories."

Tom grabbed the pot of coffee and poured a cup. "We can hope."

That hope was realized as the day passed waiting and watching ambulances cross the river on the pontoon bridges while preparations were made for, what looked like, another retreat.

Chapter Thirty-Three

February 20, 1863

My Dear Gerald,

"We are back at Falmouth in winter camp again after our retreat from Fredericksburg. You must be aware of the great battle that was fought there from accountings in the Cleveland newspaper.

"For hours B Company held what is being regarded as the "high-water mark," the farthest our troops were able to penetrate without incurring huge losses. Thousands upon thousands of men were killed and wounded, Gerald, but we held valiantly until ordered to give up our position. You should stand proud when you tell someone you were a soldier of B Company, a Hibernian, in the Eighth Ohio Volunteer Infantry!

"Our days here are as usual when in camp. The men drink, fight, gamble, and whore. Such will never change as long as men are men and drink, cards, and women are available to them. I choose, instead, to write my favorite nephew to tell him what goes on in my army life, and to learn what goes on in his.

"It's been four months since I left you and my curiosity gets the better of me as to how things are progressing with Glynis. She is a willful sprite, and good for the likes of you! Have you acknowledged your affection for her yet? Has she told you of hers for you? Yes, she has them if she hasn't told you so already. And the biggest question which gets the biggest grin from me is whether you have told your parents? If so, how did they react? You, the heir to their dynasty, in love with a servant! Oh would I like to have been a fly on the wall to hear that conversation!

"Recently, General Burnside attempted to take Fredericksburg again, but his plans were thwarted, this time by weather. Pouring rain sank our artillery deep into the mud. The Rebs, visible across the river, touted our men with signs that read "Stuck in the Mud" while shouting invitations for our boys to "come on over." We, however, weren't called upon as part of the invading troops, these stories reported to us by the men returning from what they're referring to as Burnside's Mud March.

"As you know, the Irish are a big part of our brigade. They fought at Fredericksburg with more courage than any men I've ever seen. But they not only fight hard, they celebrate just as hard and we've heard many a tale of how they plan to celebrate the upcoming St. Patrick's Day here in camp. I dare say I want to be in attendance to witness the revelry that occurs, with the greenery they intend to decorate our dreary lives and the whisky that will flow. There will be horse races, sack races (between us bored men), pig chases, and mule races. The day should prove enjoyable and I plan to partake in whatever I can to ease the constant tedium of camp.

"Write me, nephew. I look forward to a letter from you. Give warm regards to your father and mother.

"As always I remain,"

Uncle Tom

The days in camp dragged with the usual picket duty and boredom. By early April of 1863, for the first time in Tom's remembrance since the war started, the men were all healthy, had clean uniforms, and were properly equipped.

"Now I know why we've been so well provisioned lately," Tom groused to Galwey.

"The President coming *is* a reason for the troops to look good." Galwey answered. "If *we* look good, the officers look good, and if the officers look good, the boys back east look good. Hence, Mr. President looks good." Galwey waved his hands in front of him. "Even my nails are clean!"

Tom snorted. "We are a fine-looking lot, for now. The President will surely agree when he arrives tomorrow."

"I've been told we'll assemble about a mile and a half from camp. It's the only place large enough to contain everyone. They're expecting over 50,000 men to be there."

"Over 50,000?" Tom whistled. "The Rebs are only just across the river. Are they crazy? Is *he* crazy?

Galwey shrugged his shoulders. "They do what they do, but from the scuttlebutt between officers, nobody's very worried *or* excited about his visit."

"Not after losing so many men at Fredericksburg, and Antietam before that," Tom snarled. He sucked in a deep breath, the fresh memory of the afternoon he spent holed up behind the wall of that grocery store outside Fredericksburg, and losing Arnold and Jacob at Antietam, assaulting him like a fresh wound. He shivered. "Hundreds, no thousands, of men were ordered over and over again to keep going forward, only to be chewed up like meat going through a grinder. The men grumble that Secretary Stanton is responsible for so many losses, but who gives him orders? And here we are, still across the river from Fredericksburg, waiting. Maybe the Rebs will enjoy reviewing the President, too? He'll surely be close enough for them to see him, as well! And maybe take a few pot shots?"

Galwey frowned. "He may well be close enough, but I suspect with 50,000 men at the ready, I don't think any sane gray back is going to come across the river to attack."

Tom nodded. "I presume not. Lincoln will be safer here with all these men surrounding him than he will be on his way back to Washington City."

"That he will."

***

"There he is!" Collins wagged his finger at the figures coming into view of the crowd the next day.

President Lincoln, in his usual dark suit coat with his signature stove-pipe hat, looked lanky, pale, and unnatural on his horse at the front of the parade. His long body bounced with the rhythm of the animal, his sharp elbows jutting out from his side, flopping up and down, while his long legs looked bony and stiff in the stirrups.

The President rode past, trying to look relaxed, but failing miserably beside the flamboyant, handsome General Hooker who sat his horse with the flare that commanded his respect.

There was no cheering, no great outpouring of excitement or affection as there would have been early in the war. Too many men had been sacrificed in a war the North wasn't winning. This man and his cabinet were the ones giving the orders that sent them to be butchered, and the men well knew it.

Days later, anxious to be alone, Tom hurried to his hut to read the letter he'd received at mail call that morning from Gerald. Since Fredericksburg, Collins and Baker had attached themselves to Tom like sap on a tree. Maybe they figured he'd survived the war thus far and was lucky to be around, and they wanted some of that luck. Perhaps they looked to him like the father they missed, or maybe, they'd finally just accepted him as one of the men whose companionship they enjoyed and trusted. Tom didn't know which explanation was correct. He was happy for their company and glad for the companionship, just not every minute of every day.

He hurried inside the ramshackle hut, closed the slatted door behind him, dropped onto his cot, and tore open the envelope. He frowned at the shaky penmanship then realized Gerald had written it himself. Tom snorted gently and smiled. Learning to write left-handed would to be no easy task and, from the length of the letter, it must have taken Gerald hours, if not days, to write.

My Dearest Uncle,

"*We were relieved to receive your letter after the devastating news at Fredericksburg. What a horrible loss for our cause, and our troops. But I was glad to learn most of our company survived, and with such distinction!*

"*I shall try to answer all your questions, as you must be chomping on the bit like one of your stallions for news from home.*

"*First and foremost, I am well. I have begun working with other men in similar positions as I, having lost a leg or arm and that are having difficulty accepting that loss. I find myself seeking out any man I can, hoping to help ease his suffering, as you did me.*

"YES! Glynis and I are to be married! Yes, uncle, married! She is a strong, yet loving, task master and has brought me back from the brink of my own destruction to accept that I am no less a man with only one arm. Surprisingly, to my own thinking, I am better now than I was before because of her. She has taught me humility, how to care for people other than myself, and real love.

"Mother was NOT happy to learn of our affections and our planned nuptials. She yelled and stomped around for an hour at the travesty of it. She shouted how it would embarrass HER amongst hers and father's friends, that I should lower myself and our family standards to marry a servant. And of all things, an Irish one! All I could do was try not to laugh at her hysteria so as not to injure her tender feelings further. I am too happy to allow her childish tirades to change my love for dear Glynis.

"Father, on the other hand, surprised the hell out of me and was happy at my announcement. Yes, happy, Tom, that I'd found someone kind and caring and willing to do whatever was necessary to help me, so unlike his own wife I imagine. He hugged me heartily. I even noticed a tear or two slip from his eyes before he swiped them away.

"Mother has stomped around for weeks now, unwilling to accept mine and Glynis's declaration of love, yet unwilling to do anything harsh that might alienate me from her in the future.

"I have purchased a small farm not far from mother and father outside Cleveland. With ten acres of land, Glynis and I will have enough space to raise a few cattle, some horses, and perhaps some chickens and hogs. Although she brings no dowry, I, of course, have plenty of holdings to keep us quite comfortable.

"Unfortunately, I must close this letter with sad news. Father received a missive from your mother in which she informed us that Anne is a widow. Robert was killed at Sharpsburg, Tom, and Anne is nearly inconsolable. Your mother and Mary try to raise her spirits, but she spends the day mumbling, barely caring for the children she is so heartbroken. Henry, however, is still with the Fourteenth, as of your mother's letter. He is now a sergeant, like you, and Mary frets over his safety every day since learning of her brother-in-law's death. Your mother does the best she can, but with her advancing age and trying to help Anne with her grief and caring for the children, she sounded very weary.

"I think of you daily and pray for your safety always. Until we meet again, I remain,"

Gerald

Tom's hands stilled. The letter fell to the floor. Sweat beaded on his forehead. His mouth went dry and his heart thudded.

His brother-in-law Robert was dead, killed at Sharpsburg. He tried to catch his breath, but it got harder and harder.

Sharpsburg. What the Union called—Antietam.

Tom almost cried out in anguish. *Could his bullet have been the one that ended Robert's life?*

Chapter Thirty-Four

"What's going on, Sarge?" Collins asked Tom.

Tom shook his head. He had no idea. On April 30th they'd finally been mobilized and crossed the Rappahannock River again. On the first of May they'd stopped south of what Tom heard called the Chancellor House, but later that same night they were recalled to bivouac nearer to Chancellorsville.

"We're waiting for orders again." Tom finally answered. He took a sip of his coffee, made a face and spit it out. He tossed the rest away, the brew as thick as sludge after sitting all day while they'd built entrenchments in preparation for a fight nobody expected would come.

"Might as well put some *fresh* coffee and bacon on while we wait." Baker squatted beside the fire next to Tom.

"Might as well." Tom went to grab his sack with the bacon when the early evening exploded in gunfire from the woods ahead of camp.

Supper forgotten, they grabbed their weapons and waited for orders. Lieutenant Mills, replacing Galwey on leave again, came into camp a half hour later.

"We're to stay where we are for now, boys," Mills said, gunfire still popping in front of them.

"What's going on?" Tom asked.

"General Howard's Eleventh Corps was attacked and has collapsed." Mills pointed to where gunfire, shelling, and burning woods lit the coming night sky. "The Rebs managed to flank him and he was forced to retreat—right into French's advancing division!"

Baker whistled and Collins shook his head. "So, we're to just sit here and wait, Lieutenant? Shouldn't we be going to help?" Baker seemed anxious to join the fight.

"Those are our orders, boys. We wait until told otherwise."

Many of the men, including Collins and Baker, grumbled and tossed down their weapons, but Tom was relieved. He'd seen enough battle to last a lifetime and wasn't ready to rush into another one. They could be held in reserve from now till this war was over as far as he was concerned and he'd be happy.

The battle continued in the distance until well after dark. Exploding shells caught the woods on fire in a ghoulish display of fireworks and destruction the men could only watch from afar.

The next morning the fighting calmed and the Eighth moved to the northeast of Chancellorsville, and to Tom's relief, saw no action. They moved again later that day and engaged the enemy from a distance, but with no injuries.

They crossed the Rappahannock, yet again, and returned to the camps they'd vacated only days before, with just two men lost and thirteen wounded.

On their way back to re-inhabit their hut, Collins and Baker jogged up on either side of Tom.

"What are you two loons grinning at?" Tom thought they looked drunk on scotch again.

They giggled like little boys and came to a halt, the other men grumbling as they skirted their way around them to keep from bumping into them. Tom stopped, too.

"Sergeant Pops, we, ah, we just wanted you to know how, how happy we are to have made it through this battle by your side." Baker cocked his head.

Tom's neck jerked backward and he frowned. "You make it sound like you survived *because* of me."

Baker scuffed his foot. "Well, we kinda do think that. You're, well, you're an old man and you been fighting this war since the beginning, but you haven't gotten so much as a scratch."

Tom tried to interrupt, but Baker continued in a rush.

"Me and, ah, Collins think of you as our lucky rabbit's foot."

Tom stared, open-mouthed before he said, "I'm not a rabbit's foot and I'm certainly not lucky." He frowned and shook his head. *The Eighth was the Hibernian Company—the Irish! And they sure as hell hadn't been lucky since more than half of them were already buried on the battlefield! And if* he *was lucky—he wouldn't be here! He'd be somewhere raising a herd of horses, racing whenever the whim struck him, enjoying his life. No, he wasn't anybody's lucky rabbit's foot, especially not his own.*

"Well, no matter what you think, we're sticking with you, Sergeant Pops." Baker's head went up and down with finality.

Collins nodded beside him, the two smiling like the youngsters they were.

Tom's brows lifted. He snorted and shrugged his shoulders. He slapped one arm around Collins' shoulders and the other around Baker's and the three started forward. "Fine boys, who am I to question the wisdom of youth?"

***

"How do you do it?" Tom asked Galwey, just returned from his furlough, the two sitting companionably outside Tom's hut.

Galwey shook his head. "I do somehow seem to be on leave during the worst of it, don't I?"

"Indeed, you do." Tom leaned toward the lieutenant. "So, did you see Gerald? How is he? And my brother, did you see him, as well?" Tom was anxious for news from the only thing he could consider home right now. When he'd learned Galwey was granted a furlough to go to Cleveland for fifteen days, he hastily wrote his nephew and brother, gave the letters to Galwey to deliver, and waited anxiously for the lieutenant to return with their responses.

"Yes, I saw Gerald. He's well."

"Happy?"

"Deliriously so, much to the displeasure of his mother," Galwey said warily. "He couldn't stop talking about his bride-to-be. Your brother seemed happy about the upcoming marriage, but your sister-in-law, she just clamped her mouth shut and turned red every time someone spoke of the young couple.

The two busted out laughing at the same time. "I gather you've figured out his mother is none too happy about her son's choice for a wife?"

"Indeed, I have." Galwey grinned and shook his head. "She might as well have been chewing soap chips for the faces she kept making during my visit when she thought no one was looking." He paused a moment then continued. "She did, however, become more involved in the conversation when I spoke of you. She asked many questions about your health and welfare. If I didn't know her for a married woman, and your sister-in-law, I'd wonder if there weren't something between you two. Even at my tender age it was quite obvious." Galwey's left brow rose in question.

Tom sighed. "If you only knew. To spare you the details, she has, shall we say, an unexplained, and unrequited I might add, interest in me. Let's leave it at that."

Galwey shrugged and continued his story as though he'd never asked. "I have these for you." He pulled out three letters, one from Gerald, one from Ralph and, surprisingly, one from Glynis. He pointed to her letter and said, "She gave it to me when no one else was around."

"She's the biggest reason Gerald hasn't allowed the loss of his arm to throw him into despair. I imagine he told you of his work with other men with similar injuries?"

"He did, and he was very proud of it. And I can say I commend him, am proud to say I served with him, and count him for a friend."

Tom smiled wide. "Indeed, I am, too. He's become a fine young man."

"Oh, by the way, Gerald plans to wait until you return home to have the wedding."

Happiness rushed through Tom. He'd feared missing Gerald's wedding and the thought they'd wait for him made him even more proud of his nephew than he'd been only moments ago. "Thank you for letting me know."

"I'm happy to be the bearer of good news for a change, Sarge."

"We've talked about my family. Now tell me what *you* did on leave, Thomas."

"I had a grand time." His eyes flashed with mischief. "After reviving my mother, who fell into a faint upon my unannounced arrival, I went to the theater and saw a very amusing play called *Seven Sisters*. I ate lots of wonderful food and visited old friends, many of whom don't hold with the war and who were quick to let me know their sentiments."

"What did you say to them?"

"I asked them if they were so dissatisfied with our part in the war why they hadn't joined the Confederate Army! That quieted them quickly enough!" Thomas slapped his knee and hooted with laughter like the young man he was.

He suddenly became solemn. "News of a horrible battle was reported in the newspaper while I was there and I fretted terribly on the fate of my fellows in the Eighth. An article the next day said that the battle had raged for several days at Chancellorsville, but it wasn't as bad as it had been reported originally. The fact there had been an engagement at all surprised me, since all was quiet with no hint of a fight coming when I left at the end of April."

"Well, you're back just in time. I've heard rumors we'll move camp in a couple days to a ridge about a mile north of here where it'll be cooler for the warming weather."

Galwey nodded. "I've heard the same. It sounds to me like we're going to be around here for a while."

"Being here for a *long time* is fine with me," Tom said, hopeful not to see battle again for as long as he could.

Baker and Collins ran up to Galwey and Tom, their faces flushed with excitement.

"Did you hear the news?" Collins asked.

"What news?" Tom and Galwey asked at the same time.

The two looked at each other then back at Tom and Galwey. "Stonewall Jackson's dead!" Baker shouted.

"What?" Tom jumped to his feet and Galwey sat, his mouth agape, staring at the two messengers.

"Stonewall Jackson is dead." Collins repeated slowly, as if to a couple of dimwits.

Tom's eyes pinched, but he ignored the slight. "What happened?"

"When?" Galwey asked.

Baker snorted. "His own men shot him, that's what happened."

Tom's brows furrowed. "What do you mean, his own men shot him? Why would they do something stupid like that?"

Collins chuckled and cocked his head. "Because they're stupid Rebs. It was at Chancellorsville. He'd been out reconnoitering. When he went back into camp I guess those dumb gray back guards thought he was the enemy and shot him. His left arm was shattered and had to be amputated the next day."

Baker cheerfully picked up the story. "He got pneumonia and died two days ago."

Tom's body chilled, despite the warmth in the air. *Stonewall Jackson had lost his arm just like Gerald, only Gerald had been strong enough to survive. Oh, how lucky his nephew was!*

The four men stood outside the hut, Collins and Baker making jokes about how stupid the rebels were that they'd shot their best general, while Galwey and Tom mulled just how much the loss of that general might well change the war going forward. They'd spent months chasing the ghostly Jackson—and now he *was* a ghost.

Not getting the expected joyous response about Jackson's demise from Galwey and Tom, Collins and Baker wandered off to tell their news to anyone who would listen.

Anxious to be alone, Tom excused himself from Galwey, went into his hut, and ripped open Glynis' letter, his curiosity getting the better of him.

Dear Mr. Tom,

"I kin imagine the look on yer face right now, wondering why yer getting a letter from me. I wanted tae thank ye for helping Gerald. Yer so much more than his uncle, Mr. Tom. Yer his best friend. Thanks to you he's helping other men like him. Ye saved his life. I thank ye for that every day. And ye stood by him when he was suffering. I thank the Good Lord my Gerald had ye to lean on in his time of need.

"God Bless ye, Mr. Tom. I pray ye're delivered safe fer the wedding!"

Glynis

Tom sat for long minutes with the letter in his hand, grinning, feeling a tiny bit responsible for his nephew's, and

Glynis's, happiness. He knew how different the world would be for Gerald, and more so for Glynis, if he hadn't been able to drag his nephew off the battlefield that day at Antietam.

He reread the letter again then put it back in the envelope and tore open Ralph's.

My Dear Brother,

"How happy we were to learn you were safe after the horrible news of the defeat at Chancellorsville! One accounting of the battle had the army crossing the river just before the bridges washed away by rising water leaving all those who had crossed to be annihilated. Another report said a huge Confederate cavalry regiment waited to the north to pounce on any Union boys who made it through town. It was sobering and frightening to know you were there amongst those men. Of course, the next day a truer accounting came forth that a battle had, indeed, been fought, so we still worried greatly for your safety.

"I'm sure you've heard the news that Gerald and Glynis are to be married. The news caught me by surprise, but interestingly enough, made me very happy. Although Glynis is not of our class, she has made a huge impact on my son. She forced him to meet his inadequacies head on, made him accept himself for who he is now, not who he used to be. And in the doing, she made us, well me at least, accept who his is now, as well.

He is a proud man, brother, who now helps other men to accept their infirmities as he has and to become better men for it. I couldn't be more proud of him, although I sometimes keep that pride hidden from his mother.

"As you can surely guess, Margaret is not happy about her son's choice for a wife. She stomps around the house, mumbling to herself until someone catches her, then she puts on her fake smile and pretends all is well.

"My wife is a willful woman, Tom. I'm sure you've seen such in your short re-acquaintance with her. I'm also aware of her improprieties. After so many years of marriage, what is a man to do? I turn a blind eye and accept what I cannot change. I was

crazy in love when I met her and couldn't marry her quickly enough. I was foolish to believe I could change her wild ways and would feel the same way about her for the rest of my life. How wrong a man can be!"

Gripping the letter, Tom laid his hands on his lap. *Had Ralph just told him he knew Margaret had pursued him? And that he held no ill will toward Tom for it? And had he just gotten another glimpse into what his life might have been like if he'd married the wild, willful Abby?*

Tom shook his head and sighed, trying to clear his mind of what he'd just read before he lifted the letter and continued to read.

"Gerald and Glynis have both agreed, and I as well, that the wedding won't be held until you return. Of course, we hope that will be soon, but they're both of the same mind. You must be here for the nuptials.

"I pray every day for your safety, Tom. It's ironic, isn't it, that we've only found one another again because of this damnable war. Had it not come to our doorsteps you would still be breeding horses in Clarksville and we would be here, perhaps to visit once every ten years.

"We received a post from mother. She is doing better than she was in the last letter we received. Anne is regaining strength and accepting she is now a widow. Other ladies in Clarksville who have lost their men have formed a sort of club to help one another learn to accept their fates. It has helped Anne much. Mary fares well, also. Henry is still with the Fourteenth Tennessee and, as of this writing, safe.

"I'll close now as I've gotten quite windy. Be safe, dear brother.

"Always I remain, your loving brother,"

Ralph

Tom gently folded the letter and slid it back into the envelope. How right his brother was in that if it hadn't been for this war, they would have remained virtual strangers, in different worlds, not realizing the affection they held for one another—and Tom for his nephew.

Gerald's letter, in his easily recognizable scratchy handwriting, held much the same news, his love for Glynis, plans for the wedding, and his work with others with injuries from the war, not all of which were physical. He was proud, happy, and better than ever.

And so was Tom for having been a small part of it.

Chapter Thirty-Five

"Will it *ever* stop raining?" Collins' whiny question reminded Tom of Gerald's incessant complaining. But right now there was plenty to complain about. They'd been marching for five days, since June the fourteenth, first in the heat and now in relentless, pouring rain.

"I don't know, Collins. I didn't realize it was my job to control the weather," Tom snapped.

Collins glared at Tom then stalked away. He pulled his gum blanket over his head and plopped down in the mud next to Baker, who had already given up the fight against the pelting rain. It had been pouring for two days and setting up a tent was impossible in the slimy, slippery mud. Staying dry was even more impossible, so the men hunkered down wherever they could and did whatever they could to keep from drowning in their sleep.

Tom was sorry he snapped at Collins, but he was exhausted, wanted just one cup of coffee that he couldn't have, and was tired of being soaked to the bone! He grabbed his own gum blanket, pulled it over his head and stalked to an open stretch of mud where he plopped down, crossed his arms over his chest, hunched over and tried to sleep as water soaked his britches, boots, and body.

By noon the next day the rain finally stopped and they moved out again. Passing the old Manassas battlefield, a sense of reverence and awe fell over the men.

Baker jabbed Tom with his elbow then pointed. "Will you look at that?"

Tom had already spotted the shallow graves whose occupants' skeletal fingers, legs, and toes were exposed for all to see after two years of rain had washed away the soil that once covered them. White parched fingers pointed like ghostly specters toward the sky, grim reminders of the two battles fought here. Boots protruded from the ground with many a bony toe poking out of disintegrating leather, while grinning skulls brought a quivering hush to the men who passed.

Tom stared at the graves. *Were these men's lives, any men's lives, worth the price of this war?*

In the days that followed B Company dodged cannon fire and watched a family flee their home to avoid being caught in the middle of a skirmish. Tom was exhausted and felt as though he was walking in his sleep.

Galwey pulled Tom out of line from their seemingly endless march. "Hold up, sergeant." He pointed. "Do you see that?"

Tom peered ahead and watched smoke spiral up into the trees where Galwey had pointed. "What do you think it is? What do you want to do?"

"Let's split up and find out. You take half the men and go to the right and I'll take the rest and go left. Don't let any of those hotheads go charging in until we know what, or who, it is and how many there are. Understood?"

"Yes, sir." Tom turned to the men gathered behind him and put his finger over his lips for silence. He picked out twelve and waved them to his side while Galwey gathered the rest.

"Don't do anything until I do," Galwey ordered. "If there are too many, we'll back away and no one will be the wiser. If we can take them, we will."

"Yes, Lieutenant."

Tom took his men to the right of where the smoke curled into the trees. Galwey went left.

From their vantage point, Tom could see a small Confederate cavalry troop of six or eight men enjoying coffee and relaxing between several farm houses on the opposite side of the road that ran between them.

At the first crack of rifle fire, Tom led his men out of the trees toward the small camp.

When they reached the camp only moments later, the Confederates already had their hands in the air, Galwey and his men relieving them of their weapons.

Tom relaxed as the prisoners were rounded up until the sound of approaching horses a few minutes later drew everyone's attention. All guns turned toward the road, but were dropped when General Hancock and his aide rode up. The general reined his mount to a halt, his aide doing the same as they studied the situation. A grin flashed across the general's face. "Lieutenant!"

Galwey stepped forward and saluted crisply. "Sir!"

"You ordered this?"

"Yes, sir!"

The general grinned. "Well done, Lieutenant. Well done. Take those prisoners to headquarters to be put under guard."

"Yes, sir!"

In a flurry, General Hancock whirled his horse around and raced away, his aide following behind him.

Tom stepped up and laid his hand on Galwey's shoulder. "Well done, lieutenant, well done."

Galwey smiled like a cat with feathers sticking out of its mouth.

"Let's get these boys to headquarters like the general ordered!" the young lieutenant shouted. He waved his hand and whirled in a circle so everyone heard him.

Men scrambled to gather their prisoners.

"Tom, you, Collins, Baker, and Wright follow with their mounts," Galwey ordered.

"Yes, sir!" Tom shouted, happy for a chance to handle the horses.

Collins, Baker, and Wright were obviously with the infantry and not the cavalry for a reason. Hesitantly they grabbed the reins and dragged their reluctant charges behind them, hurrying away with the rest of the company as fast as the animals would go.

Tom took as much time as he could before leaving the abandoned camp. He wanted to give the rest of the company plenty of time to get well ahead of him. Slowly he checked the saddles of the two sadly thin, yet the best of the eight, horses he'd chosen. Jittery with the unfamiliar man working around her, Tom whispered soft words into the bay mare's ears then rubbed her neck, back, and hind quarters until her ears relaxed and she settled down. The horse jumped and pranced with uncertainty when Tom tightened the cinch, but calmed with more soft words and more rubbing. Tom checked the second horse's tack, a red roan, using the same calming process, until they were both ready to go.

He took a deep breath, put his foot into the stirrup, and pulled himself over. The mare jumped, turned in circles, and pranced under him.

"Shhh, shhh, shhh, it's all right, girl. It's all right." He leaned over her long, thin neck and stroked gently as he whispered into her ear. "It's all right girl, it's all right."

She threw her head up and down, danced, and snorted. It took only a few quick jerks on the reins before she realized someone was on her back that knew what he was doing and she stood quiet, her ears twitching. Tom settled into the saddle and almost groaned out loud with the familiarity and joy of it.

The mare calm, he walked her to the tree where the roan stood, untied the reins from the branch, and wrapped them around the saddle horn. Tom clucked the bay into a walk and the roan followed. He kept the mare reined in, going as slow as he could to give the rest of the company as much time as he could to get as far ahead as possible. Finally, leery of being caught alone, he gave the horse her head and they flew down the road, the roan keeping pace behind her.

How he missed this! Missed Satan's Pride and Gray Ghost and the rest of his beautiful horses! Missed being on their backs with the wind and sun on his face! Oh, what he wouldn't give to be in the glorious cavalry instead of marching and fighting on the blistered feet of the infantry!

He gloried in the few minutes he was in the saddle until all too soon he came upon his company and quickly reined in, slowing both animals.

Even in their sad condition the horses weren't winded. He chuckled under his breath. *Oh, how he wished he could give them a proper run—all the way to Cleveland perhaps!*

***

Tom had never seen so many Chuck-Luck games being played at one time in his life! As far as he could see on the open field men squatted, the sound of dice shaking in tin cans causing a cacophony of noise before they were rolled onto gum blankets where the numbers 1 through 6 were painted, trying to match the number shouted to win. Tom mostly watched Collins, Baker, and the rest of B Company enjoy a day without cannon exploding or being shot at, but a few times he took up the dice and enjoyed a toss or two.

When he wasn't rolling dice Tom relaxed in the shade of a big tree on the fringes of the big, open field, away from the others, enjoying the quiet and solitude. They'd been marching for days, following new prey, so he enjoyed this one day of peace, quiet, and relaxation while he could.

The following afternoon Collins strode up beside Tom.

"My feet are so sore I'd be happy to cut them off for the relief it would bring," Collins complained, reminding Tom again of his absent nephew. "I thought yesterday's rest would help, but they're twice as hurtful today!"

"My blisters have blisters," Baker growled, stepping herky-jerky beside Collins. "Except for yesterday, we've marched for days over ground as rough as any we've seen, guarded a wagon train that moved as slow as the mules that pulled them then had to run to catch up when they *did* move. Then we marched some more," he continued, his voice sing song, dependent upon the level of his annoyance. "We've plowed through mud and baked in the sun chasing Stuart's Cavalry, our new prey, and without so much as a glimpse. It's almost July and we're *still* marching to wherever it is we're going." Baker yelped and stumbled when he stepped on a sharp rock.

Tom helped the boy get his balance, deciding whether to tell him and Collins what Galwey had confided in him. There *was* a destination and they were almost there. They were headed for a little town in Pennsylvania called—Gettysburg.

Chapter Thirty-Six

"Wake up, boys." Tom stood over Collins and Baker, the two stretched out beside each other on the ground along the road. The rest of the company was already awake and preparing to march.

Collins opened one eye then the other before he frowned and rolled over. Baker didn't move.

"Come on you two. We're moving out."

"We're always moving out," Collins snarled. "Just five more minutes Sarge. Please…."

Tom shook his head. Collins sounded like a ten year old begging for more time before he had to get up to go to school. But this wasn't school and Collins, Baker and the rest of the men were not ten year olds.

Tom kicked their backs with the toe of his boot. "Get up! Now!"

"All right, all right." Collins jumped to his feet and Baker dragged himself up moaning and groaning, but within minutes the two had gathered their gear and were ready to march.

"What's the word, Sarge?" Collins asked, his rude awakening forgotten.

"The advance guard has spotted the Rebs." Tom kept walking without looking at either man, the two marching on either side of him, as usual.

"Do you think we'll fight today?" Baker swallowed hard and Tom couldn't tell whether it was because he was afraid they would fight, or wouldn't.

Tom shook his head. "Don't know. Don't want to know until we get where we're going and we're thrown into it."

Collins nodded agreement. It seemed the boys' fervor for fighting was lessening as the war progressed and they saw, and survived, more battles.

They marched until after nine that morning before halting, the faint sound of artillery in the distance. Uncertain how long they would be there, no coffee was boiled and only hardtack was broken out. It was after noon before they started again, the boom of cannon growing louder and louder as they drew closer to the front.

"Halt the men, Sergeant," Galwey told Tom that afternoon.

Tom gathered the men and an order from General George Meade was read to them:[3]

GENERAL ORDERS,
No. 67
          HEADQUARTERS ARMY OF THE POTOMAC
                                      June 28, 1863

By direction of the President of the United States, I hereby assume command of the Army of the Potomac.

As a soldier, in obeying this order—an order totally unexpected and unsolicited—I have no promises or pledges to make.

This country looks to this army to relieve it from devastation and disgrace of a hostile invasion. Whatever fatigues and sacrifices we may be called upon to undergo, let us have in view constantly the magnitude of the interests involved, and let each man determine to do his duty, leaving to an all-controlling Providence the decision of the contest.

It is with just diffidence that I relieve in the command of this army an eminent and accomplished soldier, whose name must ever appear conspicuous in the history of its achievements; but I rely upon the hearty support of my companions in arms to assist me in the discharge of the duties of the important trust which has been confided in me.

                                              GEO. G. MEADE,
                                    Major-General, Commanding

Another general replaced. This time General Hooker had fallen. So many commanders had been relieved Tom had lost track. Maybe Meade would lead them to the victory they so desperately needed.

---

[3] From THE VALIANT HOURS, by Thomas Francis Galwey.

He could, at least, hope.

***

Reports trickled in throughout the remainder of the day of heavy fighting at the little town called Gettysburg, but none of the reports gave any idea who was winning.

Waiting around for orders, nervous and anxious, camp erupted with shouting and yelling as men from the Eleventh Corps, Germans as far as Tom could tell from their speech, flooded camp from the battlefield.

He stopped a man limping past, his thigh bloody, the rag tied around it growing redder with each step. "What's happened?"

"Ve fight like lions," the soldier said with pride before his face turned hard. "But ve fight too many. Too many more than us. Da cannon shred us like cheese. It vas horrible, to be sure."

The man waved impatiently and limped away to catch up with the rest of his company. Collins and Baker stepped up beside Tom. "What'd he say?" Baker asked.

Tom rolled his lips and they disappeared between his fully re-grown mustache and beard. He shook his head and sighed. "Basically, they were outnumbered, both by men and artillery. I guess it wasn't our big guns we've heard all morning tearing up the ground boys," he growled.

Tom was antsy and anxious when the order came to move out later that night. As usual, Collins and Baker fell in beside him, his own personal guard and second skin. For his protection, or theirs, he didn't know and it didn't matter. They watched out for each other and he was comforted by it.

When they arrived at the rear of the front, the noise of battle had quieted. In the darkness the creak of rolling artillery, men searching for lost fellows or water for coffee, greeted B Company when they stopped. But settling down for the night wasn't to be. They'd only just gotten comfortable when they were ordered to gather their gear and move out, yet again, and it was hours before they finally stopped for the night.

Sleep didn't come easily to Tom, regardless he was beyond exhausted. They stood on the precipice of a huge battle as far as he could tell. Thousands and thousands of men were already gathered on both sides. Many had already fought today, yet more came.

"Geez, Sarge, it's still dark," Collins whined, rising from his bedroll later that night. "It's black as pitch. Must be the middle of the night."

"It might as well be. It's four o'clock."

"Four o'clock! Hell, we only just bedded down a few hours ago. The roosters aren't even awake yet. What's going on?" Collins needn't have asked as artillery exploded from the front.

Collins scratched his head. "A guy can't even get a good night's sleep before they send him off to fight," he snarled.

"We've been allowed a few minutes to get coffee and wash, so I suggest you get to it and get it done before you're caught with your pants down in that stream over there." Tom pointed, "And without your coffee! It's almost boiled, so I suggest you hurry up!"

"All right, all right, Sarge. I'm goin' I'm goin'." Collins shook the still slumbering Baker awake who jumped to his feet, wild eyed.

"Come on, Baker. We only got a few minutes to get around so get going."

Baker wiped his eyes, ran his fingers through his mop of dark, unruly hair, and followed Collins to the stream where others were already taking advantage of the few minutes given to wash.

Tom had already been to the stream and was just waiting for the coffee to boil.

Ten minutes later they were marching. At six o'clock they reached the turnpike that ran from Baltimore to Gettysburg.

Artillery thundered up ahead and small arms fire popped between explosions. Walking through a cemetery Tom eyed the headstones and fear again crept up his spine.

Onward they marched, a feeling of foreboding descending Tom like a shroud.

Chapter Thirty-Seven

Daylight broke with a breathtaking view, both beautiful and ominous.

"*The company has formed behind a grove, a quaint little cemetery to our right. We can see to our left and our right for miles,*" Tom wrote to Gerald.

All around camp the men utilized what time they had to write what could, very possibly, be a last letter to a loved one.

Tom continued as the day and its uncertainty stretched before him. "*Mountains are to the west and a valley about two miles wide is at our feet. A low ridge bounds the pretty valley, a frightening sight behind it—the men we will certainly face minutes or hours from now. In the middle of the valley to our right is the town of Gettysburg and behind it on the ridge we see the seminary, a yellow hospital flag flying above it as though it were any other day in this quaint town. Farther to the right on the same ridge is Gettysburg College,*[4] *both the college and seminary held by the Confederates.*

"*This letter is written before we go into battle so may hastily stop without closing if given the order to march. Baker and Collins, my new body guards, scratch letters beside me, along with the majority of men in our company. If today is to be our last, we want it to be with words left for our loved ones, as we are of the same mind that this will be a huge fight.*

"*I watch Reb skirmishers on the slope coming from the seminary ridge advancing toward our men who await them in the middle of the valley. From our vantage point, we see everything clearly. Our boys greet them with warm fire, which is returned by the Rebs. What a devastating sight, watching these brave men march toward the enemy and seeing them fall as artillery smoke rises above them. In minutes the pretty valley is already soaked in blood. What will it look like by nightfall?*"

---

[4] Description from THE VALIANT HOURS, by Thomas Francis Galwey, pg. 101.

Tom groaned and rested his head on his chest. *He was so tired he could sleep right here with his knees curled up in front of him.* The pencil nub dropped out of his hand and the paper floated to the ground. Within seconds he was asleep to be jostled awake by Baker, a big grin on his face a few minutes later.

"Catching a few winks there, Sergeant Pops?"

Tom swallowed, scrubbed a hand over his face and frowned. "I guess I'm more tired than I thought."

"We all are, Sarge," Baker growled. "You're not the only one napping between barrages." He threw a hand out and Tom noticed how many men were asleep in very much the same position he'd been. Knees drawn up, chin on their chest, or arms wrapped around their knees and head resting on them.

Baker poked him and handed him his letter and pencil. "Don't worry, Sarge. Your secret is safe with me." He thrust his hand behind him. "Hell, Collins is taking advantage of every second he can get."

Tom grinned back, thankful for the companionship of the two young men who had befriended him since his return from Cleveland.

Baker plopped down not far away, his weapon close at hand, and went to sleep.

Tom scanned the men around him. Good men, young men, some frightened for what the day would bring, others anxious for the glory it might bring. Many scribbled letters, as he did, while others prayed and some slept, despite the never ending artillery explosions ahead of them. His stomach flipped and flopped, every emotion under the sun assaulting him. Hoping to calm down, he continued his letter.

"Hours have passed. The fighting in the valley has intensified, but we continue to wait and watch, which I am grateful for, but I'm sure that gratitude won't last long. We will be called at some point to do our share of the fighting."

Tom wiped his brow as the sun grew hotter. Men continued their scribbling around him, putting down their last thoughts, shoving crumpled letters into their haversacks or shirts for loved ones in case they didn't survive the day. He scanned the young, anxious faces and wondered just how many that would be.

Exhausted still, he let his head drop to his chest again and closed his eyes. Despite the shelling and sounds of battle raging in his ears and head, he drifted off again.

Someone was chasing him. His lungs were on fire and his legs were ready to give out. He couldn't go much farther. *Who was chasing him? He had to know.* He chanced a look over his shoulder.

Robert! It was Robert!

Tom stopped and whirled around. He dropped his rifle and threw his arms wide. "Robert, it's me! Tom!"

Smiling wide, his brother-in-law ran straight toward him. Closer and closer he came until the bayonet he carried at his side slid into Tom's belly like a knife into fat on a ham.

Tom grabbed his stomach his eyes wide with surprise. Blood oozed through his splayed fingers and across his uniform. He laid a bloody hand on Robert's shoulder, expecting regret in his eyes at the realization he'd just killed his wife's brother. Instead Robert smiled wider.

"That, my dear *brother*, is for Sharpsburg!"

Tom woke, trembling. Had the temperature dropped to freezing while he slept? He swallowed and tried to regain his senses. Around him men continued to scratch their last words onto paper. Artillery exploded and gunfire popped in all directions. Slowly, heat seeped back into his shaking body and he stopped shivering.

Minutes later, breathing normally, he put pencil back to paper.

"The day continues and still we wait. It is almost noon and the sweat beads on my forehead and rolls down my face. The artillery is hard at work at the foot of what they call Round Top Hill, its white smoke billowing high into the sky. The battle is desperate all around us and still we wait.

"Exhaustion wears me down. We march at night and during the day with little sleep in between, but you know how that is. How I miss that soft bed in Cleveland....

"It's time to go. Pray for me," he scribbled almost illegibly. He shoved the letter inside his shirt, grabbed his rifle, and with the others, ran toward probable death.

***

The late afternoon sun beat down on the men as they marched past their own artillery toward enemy skirmishers hidden in a cornfield across the Emmitsburg Pike. The Reb fire from the cornfield beyond had kept the Union troops from advancing and B Company was ordered to dislodge them.

Their colors guiding them into the field, B Company charged.

"Stay close, boys," Tom shouted to Collins and Baker on either side of him, the three at double-time.

"Don't you worry, Sarge, we're right beside you!" Collins grinned and nodded nervously, almost tripping as they ran into the cornfield.

Guns popped in front of them. B Company surged as one into the cornfield and the firing stopped.

"They're running!" Baker shouted. He ran full out, but checked himself when he realized Tom was falling behind.

Tom waved his arm. "Go boys, go!"

But Baker and Collins dropped back and wouldn't leave his side, charging ahead shoulder to shoulder, elbow to elbow.

"We've got 'em on the run now!" Baker shouted. "They can't scurry away fast enough."

The retreating Rebs jumped a fence and ran toward the cover of several farm houses in the distance.

Galwey shouted from behind, "Halt the advance! Stop the advance!"

Breathing heavily, Tom was more than happy for the order. He stopped where he stood, put the stock of his rifle on the ground and leaned on it, trying to catch his breath. And he wasn't the only one. Collins, Baker and most of the others did the same all around him.

The charge halted, the men were allowed to rest. They plopped down where they stood and tried to catch any sleep they could, as much as any man might lying on ground only recently vacated by fleeing gray backs with artillery shells streaking overhead, exploding in front of them, and bullets popping all around.

"What time is it?" Collins asked, again reminding Tom of Gerald, either complaining or asking questions he expected Tom to know the answers to.

Tom grinned and shook his head. "Been dark for a little while, so the best I can guess is that it's around nine o'clock."

"It's been mostly quiet for near to an hour. Do you think the fighting is over for the day?" Collins asked. Baker, on the other side of Tom, gently snoring.

"I'm not sure. Seems we should all be able to get some…"

Cannon exploded from the darkness, lighting the sky like a display of fireworks. Baker sat up with a jerk, nearly skewed by a bullet as Tom yanked him back down.

Using the bright explosions, Tom was able to see they were smack in the middle of an artillery battle. Shells passed overhead from their own guns and it was all the men could do to keep from retreating back to the grove they'd left earlier that day, until the shelling changed direction and landed behind them.

"What's going on, Sarge?" Collins' voice was like that of a frightened little boy.

Tom swallowed. He had no idea. "Looks like the Rebs are behind us now, too." He watched the night explode to their rear and it was all he could to keep from retreating—*but to where?* There seemed to be Rebs ahead of them *and* behind them. Or at least that's what the men manning the artillery thought, since explosion after explosion rocked the earth to their rear.

"What do we do?" Baker asked, fearful.

"We stay right here. If we move anywhere, we'll be right in the line of fire, both cannon *and* rifle. Take your pick. We've been here for hours. A few more minutes won't make a difference."

"But…" Collins started to say but Tom stopped him.

"We'll get orders if we're to move. Just stay close to the ground so those Johnny Rebs across the way can't see your shadow, like we can see theirs in the artillery glow, and get shot."

"We're going to get blown to bits if we stay here!" Collins was beginning to panic, as were some of the other men.

Galwey slid in among the men. "Our artillery boys know exactly where we are and where the Rebs are. We're in fine shape so everybody stay where you are and don't do anything stupid!"

There was grumbling amongst the men, brought on by fear and the urge to run, but they settled in on their backs or bellies and watched the light show overhead.

It wasn't until near midnight that it finally quieted again, except for some fighting near the cemetery to their right.

"How's a man supposed to sleep with all that going on?" Baker asked nobody.

"Are we *supposed* to sleep? I'm so tired I could sleep standing up," Collins complained.

Tom didn't say it, but he certainly agreed.

Galwey slithered up beside Tom, Baker and Collins. "Get ready. We're to relieve the men on the fence line ahead."

Tom breathed deep and let it out again. The fence line? A fence that had been pulled down by the company ahead of them, the logs piled one atop the other to offer meager protection from the hot enemy fire in front of them. *It may be quiet now, but if those Rebs see movement it won't stay quiet for long!*

"Yes, sir."

Galwey slipped away to pass the word and soon everyone was slithering on their bellies like snakes toward the fence.

Happy to be relieved, the men they were replacing retreated as quickly and safely as they could and B Company took up residence behind the low-lying logs.

On their bellies, trying to keep sleep at bay, the men watched and waited.

Collins grabbed Tom's arm. "Did you hear that?"

"It's a saber rattling on someone's hip. Be still. Let's see who it is and what they want before we do anything," Tom said.

The man came out of the darkness as though walking to a picnic. "Where is General Ramseur's Brigade?" he asked into the darkness.

Sergeant Fairchild pointed. "That way!" sending him down the ranks to be captured, Tom presumed, since everyone behind the fence knew General Ramseur was a Johnny Reb.

A rifle cocked, the sound like a gunshot in the otherwise quiet darkness. The man realized his error, whirled and fled, and the night opened in another rain of bullets. Minutes later, the men on both sides weary and unwilling to waste ammunition shooting at what they couldn't see, all became quiet again.

Relieved at four o'clock that morning, the men were allowed to sleep until six before ordered back to the fence to relieve K Company.

Back at the fence with daylight upon them, they saw the prior day's death work. The dead lay so thick they had to be shoved out of the way to find a patch of ground to lay down on to gain even minimal protection behind the fence.

It was seven o'clock that morning when heavy fire issued from inside a large barn to the left of where B Company was positioned. From the barn sharpshooters had been taking pot shots at the Union artillery and, occasionally, at B Company, keeping them on edge.

Trying to stay watchful, Tom rolled to his back when a cheer issued from their troops behind them. He watched intently as a battalion, its colors waving ahead of it, charged the barn.

"I guess somebody got tired of those Reb sharpshooters taking pot shots at them," Baker said from Tom's right.

Collins snorted from Tom's left. "Guess they're gonna feel the torch now. We'll see how sharp those shooters are then!" Collins snorted again at his joke and Baker laughed with him.

The battalion charged in, torches lit, and within minutes the building was an inferno. A hundred, possibly two hundred, Confederates ran from the flaming barn in confusion.

"Let's get 'em boys!" Galwey shouted. He stood up, waved his arms toward the retreating Rebs, and led the unordered charge.

Tom, Baker, and Collins shakily got to their feet and ran with the rest of the company after the retreating confederates. Down the ridge and up a slope they chased the fleeing Rebs until they ran smack into enemy batteries. Shells flew anew, exploding too close for comfort.

Emboldened by the artillery protection, the fleeing gray backs turned and fired.

"Retreat!" Galwey shouted. "Retreat!"

B Company fell back to the fence, firing as they went, and regained their previous position.

"That was fun!" Baker grinned beside Tom, his chest heaving from their run.

"Can we do it again?" Collins shouted from his other side.

Tom, on his belly between the two, could only wonder at the exuberance—and ignorance—of youth.

Fun my...!

Chapter Thirty-Eight

The firing was continuous, his exhaustion almost overwhelming. Somehow Tom managed to stay awake, and alive, throughout the day. They learned quickly that the Rebs were zeroed in on them now and to slightly raise their heads above the log fence presented a target too good for the enemy to resist. Man after man in their exhausted states of mind, rose to their knees or lifted a head too high and became fodder for a Confederate bullet.

Later that morning Tom studied a lone tree in the middle of the field between the fence and the Rebs. Several Confederate sharpshooters had taken up position there, taking shots whenever a target presented itself.

"I don't know how much longer I can hold out." Flat on his stomach beside Tom, Collins rested his right cheek on the ground and closed his eyes.

"As long as we have to," Tom said.

"Don't fire, Yanks!" someone shouted from behind the tree. "Don't fire!"

All the Yankee guns were immediately trained on the Reb sharpshooter who brazenly stepped out from behind the protection of the tree, his hands raised, his rifle slung across his back.

"What the...?" Tom watched the man uncork his canteen, and walk to a wounded man on his back under the blazing July sun. A *Yankee*. The sharpshooter knelt down beside the man, lifted his head, and gave him a drink from the canteen.

Both sides of the skirmish lines were on their knees, watching now. A cheer went up from the Yankee ranks and someone shouted, "Bully for you, Johnny!"

Yanks and Rebs alike got to their feet, watching this act of kindness between a Confederate sharpshooter and a wounded enemy. The injured man drank as much as he could before the Reb replaced the stopper in his canteen, stood up, and walked back behind the tree easy as you please.

Safely behind cover again he shouted, "Down Yanks, we're going to fire!"

They were on their bellies in a heartbeat.

The skirmish lines erupted. Bullets flew and cannon exploded as though the kindness between enemies had never happened.

The day progressed, their thirst in the hot July sun overshadowing their hunger, most of their food supplies already gone. So exhausted, some men even managed to sleep along the skirmish line as bullets whizzed overhead and shells exploded nearby.

Tom sighed with relief when, about noon, they were relieved and fell back to the ditch along the Emmitsburg Pike. Once out of the line of fire they found what little they could to eat, relaxed, talked, and boiled coffee when water *or* coffee could be found, while shells, solid shot, canister, and bullets screamed unceasingly overhead.

***

It was near to one o'clock as far as Tom could tell when the Confederate artillery began a fresh bombardment. Tom watched the guns pummel Cemetery Ridge and the Union forces mustered behind a low, stone wall there.

For long minutes Tom recoiled with each belch of the enemy artillery—while he and the rest of the men waited for the Union guns to respond. After what seemed like forever, although it had only been fifteen minutes, the Federal guns finally answered from a grove nearby. What he knew to be eighty Federal cannon exploded in unison, adding to the cacophony of noise in the usually quiet countryside. Dirt and rocks flew like projectiles thrown up from the bowels of the earth, mingling with the solid shot and detonating hollow cannon shells that sent flying musket balls and shrapnel through any unfortunate man in its path. Thankfully, B Company was still hunkered down in the ditch along the Emmitsburg Turnpike and out of the line of fire—for now.

Time stretched on and, as far as Tom could tell it was almost three o'clock when the artillery barrages on both sides quieted. He looked out over the field in front of him, littered with the dead and dying, took a deep breath, and knew what would come next—a full Rebel infantry charge.

"Get ready, boys," he told Collins, Baker, and the rest of his men, all gripping their rifles and ready.

The Rebs charged from the tree line at Seminary Ridge—their Rebel yell preceding them—and headed straight toward the Eighth and B Company.

Tom waited, his rifle at the ready, as the enemy advanced, screaming like wild Indians.

"Fire!" resounded down the line.

The sound of guns exploding in unison was deafening and line after line of Confederates fell, their screams of pain echoing the scream of rifles. Their lines broke. Men who didn't fall dropped their weapons, threw their hands up and surrendered—or ran from the battlefield.

Prisoners were taken and rushed away, rifles reloaded, and the enemy sighted again as another charge headed straight toward the Eighth.

Sweat beaded on Tom's brow and rolled down his face. He used his already wet sleeve to wipe it away, while keeping the next line of charging Confederates in sight. Beside him his two friends stared wild-eyed and ready.

"Fire!" came the order again.

Again their guns discharged, dropping more Rebels in their tracks. More men screamed, surrendered, ran, and died.

Tom's blood was up as men fell around him. He fired and reloaded, fired and reloaded, surviving this battle the only thing driving him.

Time felt as thick as the humid afternoon air blanketing the countryside as surge after surge of yelling Rebels raced up the hill, only to be shredded by rifle fire and bursting cannon.

Tom blinked, stopped firing, and shook his head in disbelief. A lone Confederate officer on horseback urged his men up the hill toward certain death. The men of the Eighth cheered and waved their own colors in response to the man's courage and fortitude.

The honorary flag waving didn't last long and quickly Tom and the Eighth continued their assault on the men running toward them. They fell by the dozens from the onslaught of guns and cannon. Rushing toward the threat of imminent death, Tom watched cartridge boxes and haversacks thrown away as the Rebs turned and ran. Those that didn't run, or couldn't run, fell to their knees in surrender.

More Rebel yells reverberated through the air when another swell of Confederates ran into the wide open field to Tom's right and up the gentle slope—straight into more Federal fire.

Union artillery shredded the Confederates as they climbed a split-rail fence. Those who managed to breach the fence ran into the open field and up the hill toward the waiting Yankees. The Rebel yell became a shriek of pain as more men were hit with the solid shot and hollow shells from the cannon that sent hundreds of men to their deaths in a red cloud of smoke and left nothing of the man that had just stood there.

Tom swung toward the newest threat, moving as they moved. He fired and reloaded the black powder and mini-ball of his Enfield, now adept at the task and getting off two or three shots a minute, each minute like a mere second as the battle raged around him.

To his disbelief, and horror, the Confederates continued up the hill, regardless that hundreds had already been mowed down like a scythe cutting grass. He'd seen the Fourteenth Tennessee Volunteers' flag shot down and picked up so many times, he'd lost track. *Could any of the men from the Fourteenth still be alive? His brother-in-law, Henry? Other men from Clarksville? The place he'd called home most of his life.* A sick feeling washed over him as he sighted and fired at a man coming up the hill. *Could the man he'd just shot be someone he knew? Henry?*

Tom pushed the unwanted thoughts from his head. He was a soldier doing his duty and that duty was to hold this position. He reloaded and fired. Again and again until the wave of men running toward him became less and less. The battle was waning. The artillery had stopped and rifle fire was sporadic, but there was still intermittent fighting here and there.

The Rebel lines had been devastated, but a few still made their way toward the stone wall below Cemetery Ridge. Tom had moved with the fight and found himself alone and in the open between where the Eighth was taking prisoners and the wall giving the Union troops cover. He scanned the area. *Where were Collins and Baker?*

Afraid to get caught alone in the open, he ran toward the wall. His Yankee brothers cheered him on until he scrambled over the wall and plopped down behind it.

Breathing hard, glad to be alive, he poked his head up. A Rebel with long gray hair and long beard, a man who looked like any of the other hundreds of Rebs, was coming toward the wall and right into Tom's line of fire. But there was something familiar about this particular Reb, staying Tom's hand from loading and firing. Instead he watched the man whirl in a circle and dive to his right when he spotted a Union soldier aiming his rifle at his head. The bullet whizzed past. The Reb lifted his rifle and shot the Federal in the shoulder, who fell to the ground screaming.

Unable to fire, Tom watched the Confederate push to his feet and duck just in time to keep from being clubbed by the stock of a Yankee rifle. He turned and swung his own rifle by the barrel and caught the Federal in the side of the head. The man crumpled to the ground.

The Reb fought like a mad man. He whirled, went down on one knee, and reloaded. He stood up and was looking in front of him when a bayonet was thrust into his thigh from behind. He dropped to his knees, screaming, before he whirled and shoved his own bayonet into the belly of his attacker—a boy as young as Collins or Baker!

Tom couldn't watch any more. *Union men were dying at the hands of this crazed rebel! It didn't matter who he was, it was time to stop him!* Tom had been so intent on watching he hadn't reloaded. With an empty rifle he started toward the unknown, yet familiar, man his bayonet ready.

Tom worked his way through the dead and dying knowing the battle was nearly won, but this Reb was still killing and it was his turn to die. The moans of the men around him spurred him on to kill this Confederate still dealing death in this already lost battle.

He stood over the man, on his back on the ground, his eyes closed. *Was he already dead? Or playing possum like they said back in Clarksville?* Tom raised his bayonet, ready to drive it into the man's chest, but again something stayed his hand. *Something* tugged at him, told him not to do it.

The Reb's eyes opened—and Tom knew.

Chapter Thirty-Nine

"Tom?" The injured man croaked like a toad.

Tom swallowed. "Sam?"

The man smiled, revealing a familiar face. "It's me, Tom. Sam Whitmore."

Tom gulped in air and started to shake. He knew his eyes were bugging out of his head he was so surprised to find his old friend Sam here. He'd had no idea Sam joined the Fourteenth Tennessee. The last he knew his friend was in Missouri! He swallowed again and dropped the bayonet to his side, unable to move before looking in both directions, assessing the situation.

Sam looked, too, and seemed relieved to notice the same thing Tom did. The battle was nearly over and most of the men were moving toward the other end of the wall.

Tom dropped to his knees beside Sam. "I've got to get you out of here. You stay here and you're dead, or a prisoner."

Without thinking further than saving his friend's life, Tom slung his rifle across his back, got up, and grabbed the back of Sam's uniform coat, his plan to drag him into a cropping of trees nearby.

Looking around, Tom pulled Sam toward what he hoped was safety, praying he wouldn't be stopped by someone asking what the hell he was doing dragging an injured Reb off the field of battle! He shoved through some bushes and pulled Sam in behind him, Sam grunting with pain, Tom grunting with exertion. He laid his friend on the cool ground and crouched beside him.

"This is the only place I can see to hide you, Sam." Tom was dripping with sweat. "I'll wrap that leg before I go, but other than that I've done all I can." *That's an understatement*, Tom thought. If he got caught doing what he was doing, there'd be hell to pay for both of them.

He pulled a scarf from his pocket and tore the pants leg away from the wound. Sam winced, but gritted his teeth, staying quiet to keep from giving either of them away. Tom wrapped the neckerchief around Sam's leg, Sam nearly biting off his tongue to keep quiet when Tom tightened it to stop the blood from flowing.

Tom leaned closer and looked at his friend for what might well be the last time. Sadness washed over him, but he had to get back or both of them might be discovered.

"Sorry, Sam, it's the best I can do. I have to get back before I'm missed. I hope to see you again someday," were his last words before he shoved back through the bushes to find his men.

It wasn't until the adrenaline quit racing that Tom realized he'd been shot. Blood oozed from a bullet hole in the flesh above his left hip. Nothing serious in comparison to everything else he'd seen, but it still needed to be looked at. He tore off part of his shirt and tied it around his waist to stop the bleeding. He scanned the countryside as he limped back to his company. Complete carnage was the only way he could describe what he saw. Men were strewn everywhere, both dead and dying. Yankee and Confederate alike. The cannon and rifles had done their jobs today. *Oh, that this might be the last horrible battle in this everlasting war!* Tom wanted to scream. *Regardless who won!*

The fates of Collins and Baker suddenly ripped up Tom's spine and he had to find out what had become of his two young friends.

Wandering through the ranks, he asked anyone who could point if they'd seen Collins or Baker. Finally, after thirty minutes of being directed here and there, he found them.

They lay side by side, their eyes closed. Blood stained their uniforms from their shoulders to their feet. "You poor boys," he whispered, looking down on them. "I pray you didn't suffer."

"Don't get all twisted, Sarge," Collins croaked, his eyes still closed. "We're beat up, but not dead, leastwise, not yet."

Tom dropped to his knees beside his Collins. "You're alive! Both of you?" he asked, Baker not heard from on the other side of Collins.

"Me, too, Sergeant Pops. We were fine until we got separated from you. Then this happened." Baker's eyes popped open and he grinned, his white teeth like a beacon through the blood smeared on his face. He sat up with a groan. "Just proves you're our good luck charm. Without you around we got shot!"

They were both covered in so much blood Tom couldn't believe they were alive. "Where you boys hit?"

Collins finally opened his eyes. "Caught one in my calf. I imagine I'll have a limp, if I don't lose the leg, and won't do much dancing either way." He paused then grinned. "There are worse things. Ladies love a wounded soldier. Might work to my advantage," he finished with a sparkle in his eyes.

"And you?" Tom looked at Baker.

"My foot."

"Your foot? You're bloodied from head to toe and the only injury you have is your foot?"

Baker grimaced and cocked his head. "All this," he waved at the blood covering his and Collins's uniforms, "is someone else's. Between charges we dragged many a man off the field. Ours *and* theirs." He swallowed. "There were so many, Sarge. So many." He looked away a moment before he continued. "We couldn't just leave them out there with no water under the hot sun no matter which side they were on. Those that didn't, or couldn't, run we took as prisoners, many of them soaked in blood. We just did what we could."

"You still didn't tell me how you got shot in the foot!"

"Oh, I guess I didn't. Well, it was like this. I was helping some Johnny Reb off the field. He passed out and his rifle discharged right into my foot. Blew the hell out of it, Sarge. I have no doubt they'll have to take it off." He tried to lift the heavily bandaged appendage, groaned and put it gently back on the ground.

"I'm sorry, son."

Baker shrugged and forced a lopsided smile. "It's like Collins said, the women dote on poor, wounded soldier boys like us. We'll be all right. Don't fret about us. It could be worse. We're alive, right?"

Collins, leaning now on his elbows, nodded agreement beside Baker. "The ladies will be drawn to us like moths to a fire, Sarge. Don't you worry 'bout us."

"And we won't see battle again. At least I won't. Don't know about Collins. Long as he keeps that leg he might get sent back, but they sure can't have a soldier hobbling around on one foot on the battlefield!" Baker stated matter-of-factly.

Collins became solemn. "What will you do without us, Sarge?"

Tom shook his head, knowing he'd sorely miss these two young men who had become a big part of his hold on his sanity since Gerald's departure. "The question is, what will *you two* do without your good luck charm?"

"We'll manage, Sarge. You got us through plenty before you shook us and we got shot!" Baker smiled wide and extended his hand. Tom shook it warmly. Collins leaned forward and did the same.

Minutes later Tom and the rest of the company that could still walk, marched away, their prisoners in tow behind them.

Coming abreast of their own cannon still positioned at the Emmittsburg Pike, the artillerymen who had watched them throughout the day's battle cheered the ragged company and their prisoners as they walked by.

"You boys did good!"

"Way to put those Rebs down, boys!"

"You showed them Johnny Rebs who was boss out there boys!" was shouted over and again.

The battlefield now quiet, B Company crossed the Baltimore Pike and headed down into a hollow where they were allowed to regroup and rest.

Tom found a tree and slid down its trunk, his side burning. The bleeding had stopped, but he needed to have it tended. It suddenly struck him he hadn't seen Lieutenant Galwey. Fear rose in his throat like a rock.

"Sergeant Mills!"

A limping Mills came at Tom's call, his arm in a sling. "What can I do for you Sergeant Hansen?"

"Lieutenant Galwey. Is he…?"

Mills smiled. "Our young lieutenant is fine. He's been injured, several times, but he's very much alive. He's over there." Mills pointed to a nearby farmhouse then limped away, still grinning and shaking his head.

Tom pushed to his feet, his hip burning like fire, but he had to see Galwey. Slowly, he walked to the house Mills had pointed to. The only sounds that greeted him when he went inside were the groans and prayers of the wounded and dying and the tearing of cloth for bandages. In his quick assessment, he was surprised to notice confederate wounded among those being tended.

He spotted Galwey. "Lieutenant?"

Galwey turned with a huge grin on his face. "Sergeant! You're alive. I'm so glad."

"And I'm glad to see you, too." Tom looked around, his heart pounding. "So many injured..."

"And dead," Galwey interrupted, his voice gruff. "What of your friends Collins and Baker?"

Tom smiled. "They survived. Baker will most likely lose a foot and Collins will have a limp if he keeps his leg, but they're alive."

Galwey became solemn. "Sergeant Fairchild, *if* he survives, will certainly have the same. I saw him and Sergeant Kelly in a ditch after the battle, both with severe leg injuries." He shook his head and closed his eyes. "So many men lost, Sarge. So many wounded." He cleared his throat and tried to be brave, but looked like the frightened, sixteen year old boy he was.

Galwey's eyes went wide when he noticed the blood staining Tom's side. "You're hurt."

"Just a scratch." Tom weaved on his feet, but waved the injury away as inconsequential.

"You need tending." Galwey signaled two men. "Take Sergeant Hansen to a bed and get him patched up."

"I don't need tending, sir," Tom protested as everything began to blur and spin around him. Amid his protests, he slumped to the floor and into darkness.

***

Tom woke with a start, his heart hammering, his head spinning. He looked around, but everything was fuzzy. He had no idea where he was or how long he'd been there.

"Where am I?" He sat up, wild-eyed and ready to flee.

Hands on his shoulders kept him from jumping to his feet. He cried out in pain at the movement and realization hit him where he was.

"Calm down, sergeant. You're fine. You're safe and have had a nice nap, but now we need your bed."

Tom looked at the doctor then down and rapped his knuckles on his *bed*. A door set across two chairs.

The man shrugged and helped Tom to his feet, his head spinning a moment before he gained his balance and senses. He touched his side and felt the bandage, remembering nothing of being tended. "Thanks, doc."

"I wish everyone was as easy to fix up as you were, sergeant. We lost too many yesterday."

"Yesterday?"

"It's after midnight so, technically, it is tomorrow. You'll be fine, just try and stay as immobile as you can. I know that'll be difficult, but do your best." The doctor waved over two men standing nearby holding an unconscious man between them, his bandaged head lolling to the side.

"Put him there." The doctor pointed to Tom's recently vacated "bed" and the injured man was quickly laid there. "Oh, and change the bandage as often as you can."

The doctor leaned over his new patient, but before he started to work he smiled at Tom one last time, a smile of complete and utter fatigue, but full of determination to save the life of the man in front of him.

Tom shook his head, the dedication of the surgeons coming to shattering clarity to him. They had to be as exhausted as the men, perhaps more so, the few there were working often times until they dropped. He suddenly had a new respect for those who started out in white tending the wounded, who ended up in blood-soaked red, working until they collapsed beside their patients.

"Thank you," Tom said again before the surgeon dismissed him with a slight wave and his full attention on his new patient.

His side throbbing and burning at the same time, still exhausted and unable to locate his company in the dark, Tom found a soft spot not occupied by the dead, wounded, or even the living on the fringes of town. He slid to the ground, curled up in a ball on his right side, and went to sleep.

The next morning he set out to find his company and was, again, smacked in the face with the devastation of the previous day.

He found his company, and the dead, too. The men from B Company who hadn't survived the battle were laid out in rows. Holding his side, Tom walked along the rows to make sure Collins and Baker hadn't wound up among them. He recognized privates Wilson, Brown, and McGuire but, thankfully, didn't see either of his young friends. His stomach bucked at the sight, but there was nothing but bile in his belly. He spit it out wishing it were as easy to get rid of the overwhelming despair that rode his shoulders.

Satisfied his friends had survived the night he scrounged some food and a cup of coffee and did what he could to help bury those who had been identified. Unable to lift, carry, or shovel dirt with his injury, he spent the day scratching names into wooden headstones with his pocketknife to identify those that would rest under them. The men not identified were laid out in long rows to be buried in mass graves later.

Sweating under the glaring sun, Tom stopped his work and looked out over the freshly dug ground around him. His eyes pinched and he swiped at a bead of sweat rolling down his face. He shook his head at the extensive loss of life and destruction brought down upon this small town.

Gazing across what had been a field of battle yesterday, he wondered how many men had been lost on the other side, as well. Men who lived as these men had lived, loving their families, raising crops and children, going to church on Sunday, and going to war because they believed in the cause or because it was the thing to do?

Another wave of despair washed over him like a bucket of cold water thrown on his head. *Would this war, a war that was supposed to last only a few weeks, ever end?*

Chapter Forty

Gliding through the dark water, the lights of Washington City blinked and beckoned in the distance. Tom sucked in a deep breath of the warm June air, trying to reconcile the fact that, for him, the war was over. After more than three long years he, and what was left of the Eighth Ohio and his own B Company, would muster out.

Beside him, Galwey watched the shoreline slide past as the steamboat made its way toward the city.

"I can't believe it's over for us, Sarge. I never thought it would end, or that I would *see* it end." Galwey sighed wistfully.

Tom nodded agreement. He watched the lieutenant and marveled at how one so young had become so revered by his men—and survived so much. He snorted gently and smiled. Perhaps Galwey was *his* good luck charm. After Gettysburg, the two had become close, as though Galwey had replaced Collins and Baker as Tom's guardian. He was always close by, dragging Tom along when orders were passed and making sure the older man was in a safe proximity of whatever was happening around them. Yes, Tom decided with a definitive nod and grin. Young Galwey was *his* lucky rabbit's foot.

"It's a far cry from what we've seen this past year, isn't it Sarge?" Galwey's question pulled Tom from his musing.

Tom shook his head and recalled how they'd marched for weeks after Gettysburg, following the retreating Rebs through Maryland and back to Virginia. Their shoes had fallen apart around their feet and they'd gone hungry more than not, their supplies mostly depleted even before the fight at Gettysburg. They'd marched and skirmished and marched some more until finally, at the beginning of August, they'd gone into camp at Elk Run for two weeks where they'd rested and been refitted with fresh uniforms, shoes, and ammunition.

"Except for New York, this past year has been Hell," Tom said before he added, "As far as I'm concerned, this whole *war* has been hell."

"That it has." Galwey smiled. "New York was certainly more fun than anywhere else we've been during this damnable war, except when I was on leave and back home in Cleveland, of course."

"It *was* fun, even though it wasn't supposed to be," Tom qualified. "Had we arrived sooner we would have been right in the middle of those draft riots and I'm sure *that* was no fun for our boys who had to deal with it. It was our good luck to get there *after* the riots were quieted and all that was left to do was enjoy the city."

"And we enjoyed it, didn't we Sarge?" There was a sparkle in Galwey's eyes and Tom knew he was remembering the two of them going off more than once to get drunk, sing and wander the streets of the big, wild city looking for more drink and food to fill their bellies, and eventually a soft bed to sleep it all off.

Galwey became solemn. "Then it was back to the war and Spotsylvania." Galwey shivered as though caught by a cold wind, but Tom knew it was from the memories that assaulted any man that recalled that horrific battle.

Tom closed his eyes and saw everything as clearly as if he stood on the field of battle right now. Smoke billowed from the guns and cannon as they rained death upon any man caught in their path. He smelled the blood and the death as easily as he smelled the interior of the train he rode in. He felt the stubbornness, ferocity, and courage of every man he fought with, much as Galwey had described it in his journal and shared with Tom.

Someone nudged his shoulder and Tom's eyes flew open. There was a moment of anxious uncertainty before he recalled where he was and who he was with.

"I was…" he stammered.

"I know where you were," Galwey interrupted before Tom could explain. "I've been back there too many times to count. And to Cold Harbor, and every other battle and skirmish we've fought before and after."

"But it's over now, for us anyway," Tom said. "Who would have thought when we all stood shoulder to shoulder three years ago to re-enlist at Camp Dennison that it would turn out this way."

"I was just a kid."

Tom snorted. "And you've aged *so* much these last three years." He knew young Galwey was barely eighteen, if so.

Galwey's face reddened, but he didn't apologize for his age, or lack of, and Tom grudgingly admitted he'd been an exceptionally good soldier and leader, despite his age.

"And now we're only days from home, Sarge."

Tom looked around the train at the others in their company, many of whom he barely knew. He'd stayed so close first to Gerald, then Baker and Collins for so long, he hadn't gotten to know many of the new recruits that had come to them after so many devastating battles, few of whom had survived. Those that had survived looked as anxious as he was to say farewell to this war.

But the war isn't *over!* He reminded himself. Men were still fighting. More battles would be fought and more men would die.

But that was no longer Tom's concern. He'd given the Union cause more than three years of his life. He'd almost lost his nephew and seen many good men, generals and enlisted men alike from both sides of the fight, left behind on the fields of battle. He wanted no more of it. All he wanted was to go home, wherever that might be.

***

The hack pulled away and Tom stood at the foot of the steps to Ralph's opulent home. The irony of the date of his return struck him and he broke into a cold sweat. It was one year ago to the day, July 3, 1864, from when he and his company had joined the bloodbath at Gettysburg. Where so many men had lost their lives, arms, legs, and even feet, he thought with a grimace, thinking of Baker and Collins, whose lives would never be the same. He snorted and shook his head. *His* life wasn't and would never be the same again. He was plagued with nightmares, *if* he slept. A loud noise could return him to the field of battle in the blink of an eye. A shout might throw him back, the words becoming orders given at Antietam or Fredericksburg or any of the other battles he'd somehow managed to live through. The smell of bacon often sent him to a cook fire with Collins and Baker, or Arnold, Jacob, Lawrence, and Gerald. And even a whispered name, like Spotsylvania, was all it took for him to relive the terrors of those years. The faces and broken bodies of the men left behind would flash into his mind's eye as easily as a breath, along with the explosions of artillery and the smells of spent powder, fear, sweat, and death, as real as if he stood on that field in that moment.

But he was better off than most. He was whole where many were not, having left a piece of themselves on the battlefield. Certainly he was scarred in his mind, if not a few places on his body, as were so many, but he was strong and would overcome it. He had to. For him there was no other choice. He was a survivor, had survived, and would survive whatever came next.

Tom sucked in a deep breath and placed his right foot on the first step. His heart thundered and bucked as excitement seeped into him. This was home, for now, at least until the war ended. *Then what? Go back to Clarksville and find Champion Farms burned to the ground? Someone else living in the home he'd worked so hard to gain? And what about his sisters and mother? Would they welcome him home? Or would they call him traitor, his having fought for the cause that killed Robert?* He shook his head. He couldn't worry about any of that. For this moment he had to get on with his life, whatever that life might be, until he could find out if his *real* home and *real* life still existed, and he couldn't do that until the war was over. *And who knew how long that would take?*

The door swung open and Ralph stood in its frame his eyes wide. "I knew I heard a hack! You're here! Sweet Jesus, you're alive and you're here!" Tom's brother ran down the steps and grabbed him in a wrenching hug. A more than welcome hug as Tom squeezed his brother back, tears gathering in his eyes. For him the war was over and there was no sweeter nectar than this homecoming.

Ralph pulled away, turned and shouted into the house. "Gerald! Margaret! Come see who's here!"

The pounding of heavy feet echoed in the foyer before Gerald charged out the door, stopped long enough to see who it was, and bounded down the steps toward Tom.

"You're home! You're truly home!" he shouted, his father barely getting out of the way before Gerald grabbed his uncle in a fierce hug. He squeezed Tom so tight with his one arm Tom coughed. He squeezed his nephew back with as much zeal as he got, the two parting only to smile at one another before they hugged each other again, slapping backs and grinning like two buffoons.

Margaret hurried from inside the house, her face wide with delight, Glynis behind her. The two waited on the porch for the men to finish their greetings before Margaret called out, "Thank the Lord, you've come home!"

She lifted her arms. Tom untangled himself from his nephew and went to her. She wrapped herself around him, and he allowed her warmth to surround him like a warm blanket.

"Welcome home, soldier," she whispered in his ear.

Tom pulled away, looking for some sign of mischief, but saw only a sparkle of happiness in her eyes. *Perhaps this time will be different.*

***

Candles flickered in the chandeliers overhead. Partygoers floated around the dance floor or stood in clusters talking softly.

"It's a long way from the places we've been and seen, eh Uncle Tom?" Gerald's hand was wrapped around a cup that held a lightly tinged liquid, his suit and shirt stiff on his body and around his neck, the right sleeve of his suit coat tucked up and pinned.

Tom nodded. "Indeed." He thought of the places he'd seen, beautiful places where horrible things had happened, and he was more than glad to be away from it forever.

"I heard you last night."

Tom turned back to his nephew.

"The dreams, no," Gerald quickly corrected, "the nightmares got hold of you again, didn't they? You were thrashing around most of the night. And when you weren't you were pacing so you wouldn't go back to sleep and have more."

"And you know this because you were awake from the nightmares you were having, too, perhaps?" Tom challenged.

"Perhaps." Gerald frowned and shrugged.

Tom ran his tongue over his teeth and smoothed his hand over his freshly shaved face. "They got hold and wouldn't let go," he confessed. "It was like a flash of every battle I've fought ran one right after another through my head. Sometimes you're with me, sometimes Galwey or Collins or Baker, even Jacob or Arnold or Lawrence. Sometimes I was alone, searching for someone, but I don't know who, and I never found them. Or I was being chased by faceless soldiers and I see the carnage all over again. I woke up with sweat pouring off my body and breathing so hard it was like I really *had* been chased."

Gerald frowned and nodded. "I know the feeling well." He set the cup down on a side table and led his uncle out of the crowded, noisy room. Once outside Gerald closed the doors behind them and said, "Given time the nightmares will subside, but you must make peace and learn to live with them. And you find something that gives you a reason *to* beat them. Otherwise, you'll go mad." He pointed through the window.

Tom spied Glynis speaking with one of the young ladies in attendance at the festivities in Tom's honor.

"She's what saved me, Uncle Tom. She's tougher than most men. She forced me to do things I refused to do otherwise until I could do them as well as anyone with one hand—or two. She's my rock and I'm damned lucky to have her."

Tom grinned and saw the love in his nephew's eyes and face. "Yes, you are. Most women would have told you to go to hell when you first came home with your foul moods and games, but she stuck with you and got you in line." Tom slapped Gerald on the back. "Like a soldier."

Gerald laughed out loud. "It must be her Irish blood."

Tom was thrown back for a moment to Fredericksburg, watching the Irish Brigade rush toward certain death, before Gerald's voice brought him back.

"She's a fighter, Uncle Tom, and when she took up the fight with me she had only one goal. To win." His left eyebrow lifted. "I don't know if she won or not, since I was the prize, but I'm damned happy she didn't give up on me."

"I'm glad she didn't, too."

Gerald grew solemn. "Since I've been back I've heard terrible stories about some of the boys who survived Fredericksburg and Antietam. They were so broken they lost their minds, Uncle Tom. Some are in asylums, others just wander from place to place, begging food and shelter, and others who couldn't take it anymore just ended it with a rope or gun." He sighed and swallowed. "We saw Hell, Uncle Tom, but we're the lucky ones."

"Don't think I don't realize that every time my eyes open to see another day, despite the fact I hurt and have bad dreams. But I do wake up when so many of our boys never will."

The French doors were suddenly wrenched open and Ralph charged through them. He took one look at his son's and brother's faces and said, "I see you boys are talking about things that should be left alone, at least for tonight. This party is in your honor, Tom. At least make a small effort to enjoy it." He raised his arms for Gerald and Tom to go back into the house. "You should at least be present for the toast, in your honor, which we will do as soon as you go back inside."

"Yes, brother."

"Yes, father."

Gerald and Tom dutifully followed Ralph inside, all the while Tom wishing only for the solitude of his room. He'd been back over a week, the whole city celebrating the return of the rest of its boys since then, and he'd had enough. He'd been hailed a hero by the president of Cleveland's City Council and even by Ohio's Governor Brough. He wasn't a hero. He was a man who'd somehow managed to survive a prolonged war that seemed to go on with no end in sight.

Tomorrow he, Galwey, and those of the Eighth who'd made it home, would be officially mustered out. He'd no longer be a soldier.

Tonight he just wanted to go somewhere quiet, begin making peace with the ghosts of his past, and get on with what was left of his life.

Chapter Forty-One

The last chords of The Battle Hymn of the Republic floated over a quiet and solemn crowd. Many in that crowd had lost sons, husbands, fathers, brothers, and lovers, but were here to honor the service of those men. They were also here to celebrate and honor the men who had fought with the Eighth Ohio Volunteer Infantry—and survived—those men being mustered out on this July 13, 1864.

Young Galwey stood beside Tom, waiting for the words that would make them civilians again, able to go about their lives like normal human beings without fear of being shot at or blown up on any given day. One hundred and sixty-eight men stood in rows, elbow to elbow, each lost in their own memories of where they'd been, what they'd seen, and their comrades that had fallen; the sick, the wounded and the dead that weren't here today numbering more than those that were.

"From Fredericksburg and Antietam to Gettysburg, and from Spotsylvania to Cold Harbor, these men have proven their bravery and perseverance over and over again. They've served with distinction earning the nickname "The Gibralter Brigade" for their unwavering fighting spirit at the Battle of Antietam." The speaker's voice boomed over the crowd, drawing light clapping and head nodding.

Tom felt the men on both sides of him tighten in reaction to the mention of so many horrific battles and the memories they brought. He took a deep breath to quell the familiar remembrances threatening to invade his mind, lest he react poorly.

"Today we are here to release these brave heroes from their duty to the Eighth Ohio Volunteer Infantry, and thank them for their service to this great republic." The orator waited only a moment before the crowd erupted with cheers and whistles. Several of the men stepped out of line, fists balled, eyes wild and ready to fight, who had to be restrained and calmed by their fellows, but within minutes all was calm again and the mustering out began.

An hour later, Tom was a civilian again. He could do what he wanted when he wanted, without fear of being shot at or blown to pieces. But he would live in someone else's home with nothing to strive toward or accomplish.

At least not until this damnable war was over for once and for *all*.

***

Tom stood beside his nephew at the front of the Congregational Church of Cleveland. Reverend Ingersoll stood in front of them, Bible open, reading the words that would bind Gerald and Glynis in wedlock.

"Do you, Gerald Hansen, take Glynis Brock, as your lawfully wedded wife? To have and to hold from this day forward...."

The words bumped around in Tom's head like soap bubbles, floating and popping. He heard the words, but his mind rejected what they represented. Abby. After all this time the thought of her was still like a bullet to his heart or a knife slicing it in two. After all these years and knowing the type of person she truly was, she should have been nothing more than a slight blip in his memory. But she wasn't. He'd given his heart to her. His whole heart and she'd crushed it to dust in her hands.

"I now pronounce you husband and wife. You may kiss the bride."

Gerald and Glynis leaned into one another and kissed, long and passionately, until someone in the crowd cleared their throat and another shouted, "Save some for the wedding night!"

They stepped back, Gerald grinning like a conquering soldier and Glynis red-faced.

The preacher slapped his Bible shut with a resounding pop and shouted, "I give you Mr. and Mrs. Hansen!" Thunderous applause and stomping feet erupted inside the packed church.

Tom jumped. Artillery was suddenly buzzing overhead. He ducked and looked around. So many faces he didn't recognize. *Where was he? Who were these people and what were they doing here? What was* he *doing here? And where was his rifle?*

He was whirling in circles, searching frantically for it, when a hand landed heavily on his shoulder. He turned, his hands fisted and ready to fight for his life.

"Tom! It's all right, Tom. You're safe. We're at the church, at Gerald's wedding. Everything is all right." Ralph's voice penetrated Tom's befuddled mind and he slowly relaxed, embarrassed. Until he noticed so many other men in the congregation being soothed by loved ones, as wild-eyed as he must be, including Gerald by Glynis.

Ralph rushed to the front of the church, raised his hands in the air and shouted, "The reception will begin at our home in thirty minutes. You all know where that is. Don't be late!"

People shuffled out of the pews, some still quieting husbands, sons, and brothers.

Still calming down himself, Tom studied the disbursing crowd. He was among many who had given much. His back and shoulders straightened and he stood a little taller. He was no longer embarrassed by his outburst, only proud to be amongst such honorable company.

***

He was cornered and he knew it. There was nowhere to go except right through her to get out of the stall where he was saddling Lord Buckingham.

"Margaret, please, I don't want…"

She laid two fingers across Tom's lips and leaned closer. Her blue eyes pierced him to his soul. *He had to stay strong against her. He wasn't going to play this game again. He didn't have it in him! Too much had happened.*

"Tom," she whispered in a throaty voice.

"No! Please Margaret. Leave me alone."

"I will."

Tom's eyes popped open. "You will?"

She dropped her hand and sighed. "Yes, Tom, I will leave you alone. And," she bit her lower lip as though trying to decide what to say next. "I, I want to apologize."

"Apologize?" Tom's eyebrows rose.

She sucked in a deep breath. "Yes. I want to apologize for my inexcusable behavior when you've been here before. I, I don't know why I pursued you." She looked deep into his eyes. "Please forgive me."

Tom shook his head in disbelief. He licked his lips and nodded. "Of course, Margaret." He took a deep breath, uncertain whether to believe her. "And it won't happen again?"

"Oh no! Not ever again."

"Why the change in attitude?" Tom couldn't help asking.

She lowered her eyes and bit her lip again. "Well, if you must know, Gerald and Ralph found out about what happened. And Gerald was very unkind when he confronted me about it—even less kind than my husband."

Tom cocked his head, remembering his and Gerald's conversation that night in his room. "He was pretty harsh when he confronted me about our *indiscretion*, too." He thought a moment. "And Ralph alluded that he knew about it in a letter to me while I was still at the front."

"I'm so sorry, Tom, I never meant…I…never."

Tom raised his right hand, palm toward her. "It's forgotten, Margaret. We'll never speak of it again."

"Truly?"

He nodded. "It's something I certainly don't care to remember and it looks like you'd prefer to forget, as well."

"Oh, yes. Yes, I would. We'll never speak of it again." She looked away then added, "Thank you, Tom," before she whirled on her heel and hurried from the barn leaving Tom stunned yet happy. *Maybe the rest of my stay here, however long that will be, won't be so bad now.*

He finished saddling Lord Buckingham, anxious for a quiet ride. Gerald and Glynis were honeymooning in New York and Ralph, although the owner of this fine stable, didn't enjoy his horses much anymore, so Tom was able to pick whichever mount he wanted and enjoy a ride without interference. It was just what he needed—to be on the back of a horse and alone.

Chapter Forty-Two

The train rumbled through the countryside, reminding Tom of many a train ride he'd made with the Eighth. Chasing Garnett's Cavalry, going from one place to another and getting nowhere, it seemed.

Tom had spent the last year enjoying the life his brother had carved out. While waiting for the war to end he'd mostly succeeded at making peace with the ghosts in his head. On occasion a noise or smell thrust him back to the front, but for the most part he was able to cope with the memories that assaulted him throughout the day. The nightmares still caused many a sleepless night, but he'd learned to live with less sleep and, with the accessibility of Ralph's horses, he'd rechanneled his energies into that pleasurable pursuit. He spent an exorbitant amount of time with them, even gave Ralph advice on breeding, which reignited his brother's passion for his horses. Tom felt needed again and the knowledge he had about breeding flowed back to him like a long lost friend.

Tom laid his head back against the seat, remembering the article on the surrender at Appomattox Courthouse he'd read in the *Cleveland Morning Leader*:

The Terms of Surrender – 12 April 1865

"It might have been expected that the extreme liberality of the terms which General Grant laid down for the surrender of Lee's army would raise some objection among the people of the North, who have suffered so long and so gravely from the treason which that army has upheld. The fact that those terms guarantee amnesty not only to the rebel rank and file, who, ignorant and deluded, might very easily be forgiven the opposition to the Union into which others had drawn them, but also the military leaders, including such men as Lee, Longstreet, and other rebel Generals, 'who have sinned against light and knowledge,' might have been expected to provoke dissatisfaction

among ardent lovers of the Union. But it is a noteworthy fact that this feeling was nowhere manifested...."

The war was over. Truly over, and Tom was going home.

He'd communicated with his mother numerous times while in Cleveland. Henry was alive, minus the lower part of his left leg, but alive. His mother, of course, had no dispute over which side Tom had chosen to fight, her allegiances still very much tied to her Boston roots. However, he'd been concerned with his sisters's reception, since both had lived their entire lives in Clarksville and both their husbands had fought, and one had died, for the Confederacy.

The train stopped in the Clarksville station and Tom took a deep breath. He was excited to be home and frightened at what he would find. He jumped to his feet and grabbed his bag of belongings. Sitting here pondering wouldn't get him the answers he sought.

Stopping at the top of the steps he searched the platform for his mother and sisters. His heart skipped a beat when he spotted them, huddled together across the way. As soon as his mother saw him she hurried toward the train. He descended the steps and they met with tears, hugs and kisses.

"Tom!" his mother cried, slathering his cheeks with kisses before she pulled back to look at him and pushed his hair away from his face like she used to when he was a boy. "You've come home." Her voice was a whisper of wonder.

Tom lifted her off her feet and swung her in a circle. "Yes, I'm home, Mother. And for good."

She cried and hugged him harder until he set her feet back on the floor. She waved Mary forward, but his sister held herself in check, unsure, until Henry, unseen by Tom before now, thumped his way between them. The two men eyed each other, aware that a year ago had they been this close it would have been across battle lines.

They stared in heavy silence, the noise on the platform unheard, until Tom stepped toward his brother-in-law. "Where?" He pointed to Henry's missing leg.

"Cold Harbor." His voice was flat with knowing that Tom had been there, also.

Tom rolled his lips and closed his eyes. He sighed. Again he wondered if one of his bullets had been the one that slammed into Henry and cost him his leg, as he feared another might have taken Robert's life at Antietam.

The crutches bumped closer and Henry stood almost nose to nose with Tom. Their eyes locked, searched, waited, and hoped. Tears formed in Henry's eyes, did the same in Tom's, and both men blinked repeatedly to keep them from falling.

Henry looked away and Tom was certain he would walk away from him, but his brother-in-law turned back, and in his face there was determination.

"I, I'm glad you made it, Tom." Henry leaned heavily on his left crutch and lifted his right hand.

Tom grabbed it and shook it. "I'm glad you made it, too. It was a bad time, one I wish I could forget, but it won't seem to go away."

Henry smiled sadly. "I know the feeling. I go back every night."

Tom nodded quickly and grinned. "Me, too."

Henry's brown eyes sparkled with hope. "We're brothers by marriage, Tom, and even though we fought on different sides of it, the war is over. Can we forget it and forge ahead?"

Tom had never heard sweeter words said. "Of course! Yes! Of course! That's what I want, too!" He pumped Henry's hand so hard, Henry wobbled on his crutches. Tom steadied him before he lost his balance and the two men laughed, the joy of it rushing through Tom like a big swallow of whiskey.

The moment passed and they stared at each other again. One who'd worn blue and one who'd worn gray stood face to face, ready to let the past go and move toward a new future.

Henry stepped aside and Mary went into Tom's arms. "Welcome home, big brother. We've missed you."

"I've missed you all, too." He hugged his youngest sister hard, and at the same time searched for Anne. He found her standing a few feet away, her hands balled tight in front of her.

Mary kissed his cheek and stepped away and Anne and Tom stared at each other from across the short distance. He walked toward her and she stiffened, but didn't flee as he suspected she might.

He stopped two feet from her and waited for some sign that she would accept, or reject, him. Her chin went up and her lips curled in indecision. Silent tears streamed from the corners of her eyes. *He'd been at Sharpsburg, where Robert was killed. Did she hold him responsible? Could she forgive him? Would she?*

"Hello, Anne. I..." He opened his arms in uncertainty and to welcome her into them, should she come.

She hurried to him and Tom held onto her like a lifeline. "I'm so sorry, I'm so sorry," he said again and again, as though he were certainly the one responsible for Robert's death.

Anne pulled back and laid a finger across his lips. "Shush." She filled her lungs with air and swallowed. "Robert was a soldier, and you were a solider, who happened to be on opposite sides of the war. Thousands of bullets flew at Sharpsburg and the chances that it was one of yours that killed Robert are astronomical. I choose to believe it was *not* your bullet and, therefore, his death is *not your fault*. You're my brother and I love you dearly. I loved my husband, too, and I thank the Lord at least one of you survived. Welcome home, Tom."

Tom tightened his arms around his sister and hugged her fiercely. Now he knew, whether Champion Farms still existed or not, the war was truly over and he was home.

***

Tom's anxiety at what he'd find was stuck in his throat like a ball of clay. He reined in the horse he'd borrowed from what little remained of his mother's stable and sat there, afraid to go around the last bend that would reveal whether Champion Farms stood or not.

He looked at his surroundings, the way as familiar as it was four years ago, but different, more grown up. The trees were taller, the bushes thicker, and the road more worn.

The chill air of the early May morning felt good on his skin, made him feel alive, and he suddenly couldn't wait to find out what he needed to know.

He laid his heels into the old mare and she trotted around the curve as quickly as she could go toward what had been the culmination of Tom's dreams in, what seemed like another lifetime. Tom yelped when the house came into view. He wanted to jump out of the saddle, certain he could get there faster than the lumbering horse could.

"Thank you, God!" he shouted. He jumped from the saddle before the mare stopped, dropped the reins on the ground, and ran up the steps. At the front doors, he stopped and slowly pushed down the handle. The door opened with a loud creak and he went inside, his heart racing. It smelled abandoned and dusty, but there was still furniture in the study and library, although some of his books were missing. He couldn't believe anything was left at all, and when he ran up the stairs to his room and found a note lying on the neatly made bed in the master suite he thought he'd surely stepped into a dream. He grabbed the note and read:

Dear Mr. Hansen,

Your home was chosen as my headquarters after the final occupation of Clarksville for the accommodations available for our horses, as well as comfortable lodging for our officers.

Upon learning that the owner was fighting for the Union cause with the Eighth Ohio, I made certain it remained in good order for your return.

I give it back over to you with the sincere hope you return to claim it.

Col. S.D. Bruce, Commanding

Tom sat on the bed, the letter in his hand, shaking his head. *How could this be? Surely he was dreaming! Champion Farms had survived! And in tact!* He was rereading the letter for the third time when he heard the front door open downstairs. He froze and listened.

Feet stomped inside and he heard whispering. He looked for a weapon, but couldn't find anything in the sparse room. He'd given up his Enfield long ago with the hope he'd never have to carry a weapon again and was completely unarmed.

He stood up and tip-toed to the top of the stairs. Gripping the rail he looked down into the foyer and couldn't believe what he saw.

"Bull? Is that you? And Nathaniel?"

"Yes, Mister Tom, it's us!" Bull's smile was wide and bright against his dark skin.

"Me, too, Mister Tom!" Nathaniel shouted from beside Bull. An' they's others wid us, too."

Tom shook his head in disbelief for the second time in so many minutes. He'd feared the worst on his return and was finding the best, instead. Champion Farms was whole and his people had found their way back. He ran down the stairs and embraced his two former workers. "I can't believe it. I can't believe you came back!" he shouted.

"Lots of us is here, Mister Tom. They's out in they houses. We come back an' found the house empty an'…"

"Messy," Nathaniel finished for Bull. "So we come in an' cleaned it up some."

Tom stepped back and eyed the two men. These men, these good, fine men, and others who had worked for him, had come back and even taken the time to clean his home in the hope he'd return, too.

Bull had lost a lot of his bulk in the last four years, but he looked healthy. Nathaniel, always thin and frail, looked much the same.

"Where did you go? What did you do?"

"We went north like you tole us, Mister Tom," Bull said. "We went through Kentucky an' into Ohia until we got to Cincinnata. We set up camp there wid other slaves an' waited. It was a long wait, Mister Tom, but when the war got over, we come back here an' hoped."

"For what?" Tom cocked his head in uncertainty.

"That Champion Farms was still here, Mr. Tom. An' that you'd come home." Nathaniel answered. He paused a moment and Tom saw tears in the old man's eyes. "Champion Farms is our home, Mister Tom."

They'd gone north as he'd told them, uncertain what they would find, but went because he'd told them to. They'd trusted him that much. And now they were back.

"How many?"

"They's about ten of us livin' in the quarters. We prayed you'd come back, Mister Tom, an' you did."

Tom felt another rush of emotion and cleared his throat. With everything that had happened today he wanted to pinch himself. *He* had *to be dreaming and just didn't know it.*

Suddenly an idea hit Tom like a bullet slamming into his chest. He clapped his hands with excitement. "Tell everyone to come here tonight at six."

"Sah? I mean Mister Tom?" Nathaniel asked, confused.

"Just tell them to come. I want to thank every one of you that came back." He paused a moment for effect then shouted. "We're going to have a party!"

Bull looked at Nathaniel and Nathaniel at Bull. "A party, Mister Tom? How can you have a party? You jest got back an' ain't got nothin' to have a party wid."

Tom threw his head back and laughed loud and long. "Trust me! I'll find something to celebrate this day. I'm going back to my mother's and see what I can scrounge there. You find what you can here and we'll meet again right here at six for a party!"

Tom pumped both their hands with enthusiasm before he ran out of the house and down the steps. Mounting the horse he turned her down the drive toward Clarksville and sent her off as fast as she would go, as excited as he'd been in years.

This was one party he planned to enjoy!

Chapter Forty-Three

Tom returned to Champion Farms later that afternoon as promised, his mother, sisters, and Henry in the wagon with him, carrying as much food as they could gather and prepare in so little time.

His mother sighed as the wagon rounded the last curve, the old mare plodding along. "I do hope we have enough. It *was* short notice, Tom. We've done our best." Her clouded blue eyes sparkled with hope.

"And I thank you for every bit of it, mother." He gave her a quick kiss on the cheek. "This is a celebration I intend to enjoy no matter how much or how little we have. I attended so many parties when I returned to Cleveland in '64 I lost track, but at each one all I could think about were the men left behind and those who perished from disease and injury *after* the battles were over. This is a *real* reason for celebration. The war is over. My house is whole, my people have come home, and I have my family. I have so many things to be thankful for, Mother."

Mary leaned forward from the rear seat and laid her hand on Tom's shoulder. "We've got rice, gravy, four loaves of quick bread that Anne and I baked as fast as we could, deviled eggs, pickled beets, and two roasted chickens."

"Oh I do hope those chickens are done," his mother worried. "The butchering and cooking *was* rather rushed."

Sitting beside him on the front wagon seat, Tom covered her hand with his. "Whatever we have I'm sure is a thousand times better than what many of those that will eat it have tasted in years. It'll be plenty and delicious. A veritable feast!"

The wagon creaked to a halt in front of Champion Farms. Bull immediately took charge of the wagon while Nathaniel assisted the women to the ground. Tom offered assistance to Henry, but he insisted on getting out himself and landed with a solid thud, his balance, *and* a grin. "See, nothing to it."

"This way please." Nathaniel led the way up the steps, as others who had been waiting nearby grabbed pots and towels covering warm bread from the wagon, and went into the house.

"We's been waitin' for ya, Mister Tom." Nathaniel waved his arm around the room. It looked like every table that could be found was set out for the food. Chairs were spread about, a small area left open for dancing. Flowers had been picked and placed throughout the room, brightening it with splashes of color everywhere and filling the parlor with the sweet aroma of spring.

"It's perfect, Nathaniel." Tom clapped him on the back and the man smiled wide at the approval. Tom felt that rush of emotion threatening again at how things were falling into place. The only thing that would make everything perfect was his horses.

Then it hit him. Pride! He *had* to find Satan's Pride. Ralph had sent him home with a small stake against future profits to help him get the farm going again. At the very least, Tom had to try and find Satan's Pride. His heart swelled with the idea and he was suddenly so anxious about it he wished he could leave right now. One trip to State Line and, perhaps, everything would be as it should.

The party was a rousing success. Tom was reintroduced to former workers, their wives, and their children. There were four children, aged five to ten, and one of the women was expecting. Tom felt like his face might shatter from the smile that just wouldn't go away.

There was plenty of food and it was eaten with a degree of pleasure Tom hadn't seen in a long time. The children played, ate and played some more, their parents watching them closely. When they weren't supervising their children they talked with Tom, his family, or each other. After the meal was finished, fiddles were pulled out and there was singing and dancing, adults and children included.

Tom watched his former employees stomping and clapping, dancing, whirling, and smiling like he hadn't seen anyone do with so much enjoyment in a very long time. He decided now was as good a time as any to approach his former foreman and houseman about how they would proceed forward.

Tom stepped up to Bull, laid his hand on his shoulder, and waved for Nathaniel to come over.

When Nathaniel joined them he said, "Bull, Nathaniel, I don't have anything to offer you right now except food in your bellies and a roof over your heads if or until we get Champion Farms running again, if you're of a mind to stay. And there's no certainty we *can* get it running. The most we can do is try. But I can't do any of it without knowing you two will be here to help me. Are you willing to stay until such time as I can give you wages?" Tom waited for them to answer, his chest tight.

"Why, Mr. Tom, you couldn't send me away if'n you tried!" Nathaniel almost shouted. "This is the home I been waitin' to come back to fo' four long years. I'll be here till I die, if'n you let me."

"Of course you'll stay. And anyone else who wants to! I wouldn't dream of sending you away Nathaniel. I don't care how old and feeble you get." Tom grinned. "And when that time comes, I'll take care of you!"

The smile on Nathaniel's face blazed with the respect and loyalty he felt for Tom.

"I'll be here, too, Mr. Tom. As long as you got a place fo' me, me an' my family will be here to help." Bull smiled and nodded, too.

"Until we get going again, I can't give you much, but you'll have food and shelter, I promise that."

"We knows it, Mr. Tom, an' it's enough fo' us to stay. An' we trusts you, else we wouldn't have come back in the first place." Nathaniel snapped his head up and down in finality.

"And when we do get Champion Farms running again, you'll be well paid for your services, past and present, I promise!" Tom added. He put his hand out and shook each of their hands.

Tom suddenly whirled and shouted, "Everyone! Everyone! Gather round, grab a glass, and raise it high. He waited until everyone had done as he asked. He lifted his glass, as did everyone else. "To the future!" he shouted.

"To the future!" echoed throughout the room.

***

Tom's trip to the stable in State Line was far different than the one he'd made four years ago. Then he'd ridden Satan's Pride, the full weight of knowing he would leave there without him riding *his* back. Now he and Bull came in a wagon intending to bring Pride home, *if* Pride was still there and still alive. The horse was, after all, twenty-eight years old he reminded himself more than once during the trip. The thought that Pride could be gone made Tom feel sick and he pushed the thought away again and again. As with Champion Farms, he wouldn't know if Pride was alive until he got to the stable.

The stable was right where he remembered it. Hearing the wagon's approach the same man he'd met four years earlier hurried toward them, his back more bent than Tom recalled.

"What can I do for you?" His eyes widened when he recognized Tom. "I know you."

"You do. You bought that black stallion from me at the start of the war. I'm here to buy him back." Tom's palms were suddenly sweaty, his breathing shallow as he awaited the man's response.

The stable owner swallowed and wet his lips. "I took good care of him, mister, just like I promised I would, but the war came and, well…."

"Where is he?"

The man scrubbed at his face. "He was a fine looking horse, mister, despite his age. A man came through here on his way to join the Kentucky cavalry who needed a horse, and, well, there's no easy way to say it. He took him. I didn't have that horse more than a few weeks before he was snatched away." The man stepped back, ready for Tom to do him bodily harm, as promised, for not taking care of Pride.

Tom closed his eyes, absorbing the fact that Pride was gone. He cleared his throat. "I understand. I've seen too many animals, my own included, requisitioned for the cause, either cause, without compensation or regard for the owner's needs or promises made."

Tom's shoulders slumped. "You might as well turn the wagon around and head home, Bull."

"Wait," the man laid his hand on Tom's arm before Bull could lift the reins to do as requested.

Tom's head snapped around and the men's eyes locked.

"The man that took him lives in State Line. Could be he'll sell him back to you, if the horse survived the war. I know Mr. Barrow did, but I don't know about the horse."

"Where can I find Mr. Barrow?" Tom's heart was thumping now.

The stable owner gave Tom directions and minutes later he and Bull were headed that way, both hoping the good luck that had followed Tom since his return to Clarksville would continue.

The farmhouse was in need of attention, but Tom had seen worse. So many men returning from the war didn't have a care for their surroundings. They were beaten down, both physically and mentally, many missing arms or legs, some with wounds so deep in their souls they would never be the same again. He could only hope that if Satan's Pride was alive this man would part with him. He had some of the money Ralph gave him and right now only Satan's Pride would do to start his new line. His old friend William Giles already had a brood mare in mind and had assured Tom that, although Pride was older, he'd seen many an old stud cover a mare.

The wagon rumbled up the bumpy drive. A man, his right sleeve pinned up at his shoulder, stepped through the door and onto the porch. He watched intently as Bull pulled the wagon to a halt and Tom jumped down.

"Stop right there," the man called out. "What do you want?"

"My name is Tom Hansen. I'm from Clarksville and am interested in a horse you might have."

The man's face twisted with hatred. He looked at Bull, still seated in the wagon, and shouted, "A damned Reb! Get outta here you traitor! I won't have a stinking Reb on my property!"

Tom waved his arms. "Wait! I'm not a Reb!" he yelled. "I fought with the Eighth Ohio Volunteers, B Company."

The man's mouth closed and his eyes lit with surprise. Slowly, he came down the steps, his left hand extended. "Eighth Kentucky Cavalry, Third Battalion. Spent some time in

Clarksville with the Third during the occupation in '63, so I just assumed if you were from there, you were a Reb. No offense."

"None taken."

The two men eyed each other a few moments before Tom said, "I understand you purchased a black stallion in State Line four years ago. I'd like to buy him back if you still have him."

"I bought that horse on my way to Russellville to enlist." His eyes shuttered with reminiscence before he asked, "You came from Clarksville for one horse long past its prime?"

"I did. Pride is special, given to me by my father for my fifteenth birthday."

"Why didn't you just join a cavalry unit at the start of the war and kept the horse?"

"When I finally decided to join up with my nephew in Cleveland, the cavalry ranks were already full, so I wound up with the infantry and had no need for a mount. My farm and all my stock was taken by the Confederacy at the outset of the war, but Pride took off before they could *requisition* him with the rest," he said with derision. "So I brought him over the state line on my way to pick up the train to Cleveland to sell him and, hopefully, keep him out of the hands of the Confederacy like the rest of my horses." Tom waited, expectant, before he added. "It would mean a lot if I could get him back."

The man sighed. "We may have fought for the same cause, but I can't give you the horse."

"He's alive then?" Tom all but shouted.

"He is, but like I already told you. I can't give him to you."

"I don't want you to give him to me. I intend to pay for him. And well. How much will it take?"

The man scratched his head and thought a minute. "He may be up in his years, but he's still a prime piece of horse flesh."

"I'll give you enough to get a young horse that you'll have for the next twenty years! Why keep an old horse when you can replace him with a young one?" Tom waited a heartbeat then said, "He's extremely sentimental to me, Mr. Barrow. As I said, my father gave him to me when I was fifteen, and he died shortly thereafter."

"How much will you give?"

"May I see him?" Anticipation streaked up Tom's back.

The man turned and yelled into the house. "Carl! Carl, bring the horse around!"

Tom waited, impatient, until a boy of about sixteen came from around back leading a black horse.

"Here sir." The boy handed the lead rope to his father who had met him half way, and eyed Tom and Bull with uncertainty.

Tom felt like a hammer hit him in the chest.

"Pride...." issued from his lips. The horse's head lifted and he turned toward Tom. Tom reached for him. "Pride, it's really you."

The horse threw his head up and bolted toward Tom, jerking the rope out of Mr. Barrow's hand. He slid to a stop in front of his former owner, snorted and rubbed his face against Tom's chest.

"It's me, Pride." He nuzzled the horse's face with his own, rubbed his ears, stroked the horse up and down his back and legs, and found him to be sound. "I'm so sorry I left you, but I'm back now and I plan to take you home," he whispered into Pride's pricked ears. Tom looked up to see the man watching intently.

"How much will you take for him?"

Barrow sighed. "He pulls my wagon and gets me back and forth into town. He's pulling the plow for this year's planting, too. He's worth a lot to me."

Tom took a deep breath. Pulling a plow, just what he hadn't wanted for his beloved Pride. But he was going to give Pride back his dignity and the life he deserved.

"I need enough to buy another horse that can pull the plow and get me from here to town. Maybe enough for two horses," Barrow added with a gleam in his eyes.

The man knew how important Pride was to Tom and would try and squeeze as much money as he could get.

"It doesn't matter to me how much he means to you," Barrow continued. "I gotta do what's best for me and my boy." He eyed Pride, still nuzzling his former master.

"How much?" Tom was getting angry, and impatient. Tom had five hundred dollars in his pocket. If the man held out for more than that, well, he'd cross that bridge when he got to it. For now he would offer what was a reasonable amount for any horse that *wasn't* Satan's Pride, prize racer and stud.

The man took a thoughtful breath.

"Pa! You can't sell my horse! You just can't. You gave him to me!"

"Quiet boy. Mr. Hansen is willing to pay a fair price, right Mr. Hansen?" He turned back to Tom.

"I am."

"I'll give you a hundred dollars. That'll easily get you a fine, young horse."

"A hundred and fifty."

"Pa! You can't sell him! You gave him to me!"

"We can get a better horse, Carl. A young horse, maybe even two. Horses we can train that we'll have for years."

"But, Pa…"

"I agree. A hundred and fifty dollars." Tom put his hand out. He wanted to seal the deal before the boy changed his father's mind.

Barrow reached out before his son could argue further. "Sold."

Tom pumped Barrow's hand, his heart pumping equally as hard.

"Pa, how could you? He was mine. You gave him to *me*," the boy cried before he turned and fled.

Sorry for the boy, but anxious to be on his way *with* Satan's Pride, Tom counted out a hundred and fifty dollars and handed it to Mr. Barrow. "Thank you."

"And thank you." Barrow grinned and shoved the money into his pocket.

Bull jumped down from the wagon and stepped beside Tom.

"Hello, Pride." The horse nuzzled his former handler as affectionately as he had Tom.

Tom tied Pride to the back of the wagon and he and Bull jumped back in.

"Let's go home."

"Yes, sir!"

Bull turned the wagon and headed toward Champion Farms. Pride followed like a very large puppy that had been lost and found and Tom knew exactly how he felt.

Chapter Forty-Four

Life was good! So many things had fallen into place since his return to Clarksville it was hard for Tom to grasp it all. His entire family accepted him, including his sisters, regardless he'd fought for the Union against his brothers-in-law. His home stood, although it was worse for wear and needed many repairs after years of being inhabited by people who cared not for its upkeep. His people had returned and Satan's Pride was home. He had enough money to get his stud farm going again and, hopefully, Pride would restart the line. Indeed, life was good.

He had only one more thing to do before he could put the past behind him and go nowhere but forward.

It was time to find out whether Sam had survived the war. Every time he thought about learning the fate of his friend, his throat constricted with the fear he had not. As much as he wanted to know, that fear kept him from finding out the truth.

When Tom left Sam that day in the grove at Gettysburg his chances were fifty-fifty. His friend had already lost a lot of blood, he was weak, and there'd been no one around to help him. But Tom had done all he could. He knew that, but it wasn't enough to assuage the guilt that it hadn't been enough and that Sam might have died right there, alone in the bushes, not found for hours, maybe even days.

Tomorrow he would make inquiries. It was time to find out if his old friend had come home, too.

***

Tom was so excited he could hardly breathe and ran up the steps to Marmoset. His heart pounding, he knocked and waited, shuffling his feet like a five year old he was so excited to see his friend. He'd found out yesterday in his inquiries into Sam's fate that his friend had, indeed, survived the war and had returned to his family home.

Sam's oldest brother, Charles, opened the door and his face went wide with recognition.

Tom put his finger across his lips before Charles could shout his name. "I want to surprise him," Tom whispered before Charles could announce him.

Charles grinned and nodded. "Of course," he whispered back. "Come in, come in." He waved Tom inside.

Tom stepped into the foyer and was surprised when Charles wrapped him in a hug. "I'm so glad you made it through the war, Tom. Sam told us what you did."

Tom pulled away and shook his head. "I did what I could do, which wasn't much."

"You saved my brother's life. I consider that a lot."

Tom stared at the man who, through his and Sam's youth, had plagued them both with taunts and insults. He almost snorted. *My how the war changed men, even those who didn't fight. Charles had finally grown up!*

Charles turned toward the study, but not before Tom saw the grin on the face of his old nemesis. "Follow me."

Tom followed Sam's brother, but came to an abrupt halt when Charles stopped in the middle of the doorway, crossed his arms over his chest, and just stood there. A few moments later, and after some prodding on Sam's part, Charles stepped aside and Tom walked into a very different looking room than it had been a war ago.

Uncertain how he'd be received, Tom held his breath and waited. Sam looked up and spotted his friend. The joy that spread over Sam's face warmed Tom from head to toe. Sam jumped up and hobbled over. "Tom! Oh my God, Tom! You're alive, and you're here!" He put his hands on Tom's upper arms and stared at him.

Tom stared back at his friend, who looked much older and much more worn, but alive.

"Sam, I'm so relieved you made it, too."

"I made it because of you, Tom. If it hadn't been for you...." Sam heaved a thoughtful sigh and shook his head, "If it hadn't been for you I wouldn't be here."

Tom heard the emotion in his friend's quiet statement.

Tom nodded his head and rolled his lips together. "I'm glad I'm the one that found you, Sam. If it had been anyone else I hate to think of what would have happened."

Sam swallowed and nodded agreement. "I've thanked God for you every day, Tom." Sam dropped his hands from Tom's arms and waved his friend inside the parlor. "Come in, sit down, and tell me how you are."

Tom grinned, walked into the room and sat down on one of the few chairs in the sparse room. Charles and Walt, Tom's other brother who welcomed him warmly, excused themselves so Tom and Sam could talk in private like the old friends they were, despite having fought on opposite sides in the war.

"Tom?" Sam said when they were both seated. "I've wondered about this ever since that day you found me on the battlefield. How did you recognize me under all that dirt and grime, long hair an' beard, an' all the years since we'd seen each other?"

Tom smiled, lifted his shoulders, and shook his head. "Don't know, Sam. There was just something familiar about you. It's what stayed my hand from putting my bayonet into your chest. Maybe it was the hand of God, who knows, but I knew I wasn't supposed to kill you."

Sam swallowed and tears formed in his eyes. "Well, whatever it was, I'm damn glad, Tom. Damn glad you listened to what it was tellin' ya."

Tom leaned forward in his chair. "Tell me everything, Sam. About where you've been since Gettysburg, how you wound up there, everything."

Sam's head cocked and he frowned. "Went to Missoura with Ellie after my tobacco crop failed, but you know that," Sam began. "The story gets pretty hard after that, Tom." He took a shuddering breath before he continued. "The war started long before Sumter for me an' mine in Missoura. My father-in-law was murdered by border ruffians before the war ever began, and my boy went a little crazy over it. When the war did start, he ran off an' joined up."

Tom watched Sam battle the ghosts that obviously plagued him, too, and gave his old friend the time he needed to compose himself before he spoke again.

"My boy was killed at Wilson's Creek in '61. I went a bit crazy myself after that an' joined up to take revenge on you Yanks," he said with a sheepish frown. "Fought with Ol' Pap Price at Pea Ridge. When my enlistment was done I went home, but things weren't good along the Kansas/Missoura border. It was worse than ever. Raiders visited our place more than once and..."

Sam stopped speaking and swallowed several times.

Again Tom gave him time to collect himself, knowing whatever Sam said next would not be good.

With a heavy breath Sam said, "The dirty Redlegs killed my Ellie, Tom. Came in, burned my mother-in-law's house, and killed my Ellie."

Tom stopped breathing and started toward his friend, but Sam stopped him with a raised hand. "I'm all right, it's still hard for me to speak of her without, well, you know."

Tom nodded and his heart went out to his friend. He knew how much Sam loved Ellie, even more than he'd once loved Abby.

"I was afraid the Redlegs would come looking for me at my wife's aunt's house where we sought refuge after Ellie's death. I decided the best thing to do was leave. Ellie's aunt held Yankee sympathies, at least before they killed her niece, so I felt she and my daughter and mother-in-law would be safer there alone without bringing the Redlegs looking for me. So I left. I found out my mother was dying with consumption in Clarksville so I came back to say goodbye. Well, once I got here I got all fired up again about the war an' took out with a bunch o' boys headed to join up with the Fourteenth Tennessee."

"I'm real sorry to hear all that, Sam. Ellie was a fine woman, a fine woman." Tom looked around the room, trying to recall the opulence that had been there when Sam and Ellie were married, seeing only a shell of what it had once been.

"She was that an' more, Tom. She was a fine woman, a good wife, an' a wonderful mother to our children." He looked up, tears brimming. "What about you? How did you wind up at Gettysburg, fightin' for the enemy?" Sam asked with a grin.

Tom grinned back. "When the war started I knew I couldn't stay in Clarksville. I didn't have a wife or children, so I was free to do as I pleased. With my family originally coming here from Boston, my only choice was to fight for the Union and its preservation. Clarksville was so divided I didn't want to have to defend my beliefs to everybody who would surely ask about where I stood politically."

"How'd you wind up in an Ohio unit?"

Tom rubbed his clean-shaven chin. "I joined up with my nephew, Gerald. Headed north and took a train to Cleveland, joined up, and was with the Eighth through the end."

Sam laughed out loud. "I headed south to enlist, but you Yanks had all the trains tied up by then. I got to ride the whole way, but on horseback!"

"Oooh that must have been long *and* hard." Tom grimaced and wiggled in his chair for effect.

"It surely was. But it's a trip I'll remember all my life." Sam looked into Tom's eyes. "So where'd you wind up after you enlisted?"

"After training at Camp Dennison near Cincinnati, we wintered at Winchester, Virginia."

Sam hooted and slapped his knee. "Winchester! The Fourteenth wintered there, too."

"Don't I know it!" Tom groaned. "The residents of Winchester didn't like us blue bellies much. And the women were the worst! Why, one morning in church a lady dropped her Bible in the aisle and when one of our boys picked it up and tried to hand it to her, she just looked at him hatefully and walked away. He was left standing there, mouth agape, her Bible still in his hand." He frowned then continued. "The ladies of Winchester took to walking down the middle of the street so as not to accidentally brush against any of us blue bellies."

Sam grinned. "I heard a few of them stories from the boys in the Fourteenth. They wintered there just after your boys left in March of '62, I believe it was. I hear the town was occupied over fifty times between *both* sides!"

Tom frowned and nodded. "That's about right. Seemed it was in control by us one day and you rebs the next. Sometimes it even changed hands twice in the same day!" He shook his head. "I can certainly understand the residents being a little testy."

"A little!" Sam snorted. "Did you hear the story about the woman who found a wounded Yankee sittin' on her porch?"

Tom shook his head no. "But you'll tell me?"

"Story is the cavalryman had an injured foot. Well, this woman come out of her house an' asked him if he could walk. He told her 'no.' The story goes that she asked to see his pistol. Now why that boy give it to her I'll never know, but she took it, put it to his head, an' told him to git." Sam shook his head. "The injured man started to limp away, an' as he did, that woman raised that pistol an' shot him in the back with his own gun."

Tom took a deep breath. "I guess that's why when we were there the boys didn't take much guff from the residents. We knew they'd shoot us in the back as soon as look at us."

Silence fell over the room a few minutes before Sam asked, "What engagements were you in?"

"Well, at Winchester we joined up with the Fourth Ohio and Fourteenth Indiana and became part of the Army of the Potomac."

Sam whistled and cocked his head. He knew what that meant. The Eighth and the Fourteenth had crossed paths on more than one occasion.

"We fought a battle near Winchester against your Stonewall Jackson."

Sadness washed over Sam at the mention of his former commander. He nodded. "Fought under Stonewall at Chancellorsville."

"Chancellorsville! We were there, too."

"Seems like you boys were about everyplace the Fourteenth was. Were you at Fredericksburg?"

Tom nodded.

"I didn't join up with the Fourteenth 'til early '63, so I missed Fredericksburg," Sam said, "but I was with 'em at Chancellorsville. Guess we could'a run into each other there, eh?" Sam picked nervously at a fingernail.

Tom looked away, remembering the two battles.

"An' then Gettysburg." Sam looked deep into his friend's face. "An' I thank God every day you were there."

Tom grinned and blushed. "We'd heard how so many battles became brothers against brothers or sons against fathers, but I never dreamed I'd actually *look* into the face of a friend and have to decide whether or not to kill him."

"Well, again, I thank God you didn't plunge your bayonet into my chest *before* seein' who I was." Sam sucked in a deep breath, stood up and limped his way over to where Tom sat across from him. He took Tom's right hand in his. "I owe you my life, Tom Hansen. Thank you."

Tom licked his lips and smiled. Tears came to his eyes. "And I thank God every day I was there to give it to you."

Chapter Forty-Five

The war was over, but the after effects lingered on. Men returned to Clarksville, disabled, dismembered, and disheartened. Many who fought for the Confederacy had long memories and reminded Tom regularly that they resented the fact he'd fought for the Union and was still whole.

"Dirty Yank," was whispered under many a breath when Tom entered a store or walked the streets of Clarksville. "Probably yeller. Look at him. He don't have a scratch on him," he heard more than once.

Tom ignored them. He pitied them instead, knowing many of their lives had been destroyed. They were broken men, many of whom had nothing to work toward or look forward to, as he did.

Champion Farms was coming back to life. Pride was still able to do his job, as Tom found out with the first mare he brought to him. A stocky bay filly, Pride had stomped around in his yard, snorting and racing up and down the paddock like a two-year old when he caught her scent two stalls away.

"It'll be a good match, boss," Bull had said, standing beside Tom, both watching Satan's Pride's youthful antics. The mare had turned her backside to Satan's Pride and he'd raced the pasture faster, kicking out his heels, nickering, and throwing his head from side to side. He sniffed, snorted, and strutted, and she presented herself and flirted until they were certain she was in heat and Tom put them together in the same yard.

Without hesitation Pride ran her down, rose up on his hind legs and covered her. In less than a minute, the deed was done then again and again in the days they were left together.

Tom was smiling absently as he walked the sidewalks of Clarksville. Bull had confirmed this morning that Isabel, the first mare Pride had covered, was in foal. Since Isabel's arrival, William Giles had sent four more mares, but Isabel's was the first confirmed pregnancy.

Tom was thinking about the mares, Champion Farms, and how far he'd come since the war ended, when he ran smack into someone. The man grunted and dropped the packages he was carrying.

"I'm so sorry, sir. I wasn't watching where I was going." Tom bent over to help the man gather the boxes strewn across the walk.

"Buffoon," the man said under his breath as he knelt to retrieve the scattered packages.

Tom was leaning over, still attempting to assist the man, when he spotted a woman hurrying toward them.

"What have you done with my purchases, Andrew!" she shouted, too far away for Tom to see her face, but easily recognizing her voice.

The man's demeanor changed immediately, as though someone had yanked on an invisible leash. "I've done nothing, sweetheart. This man ran into me!" he whined.

The woman stopped beside the man and tapped her foot angrily. Tom couldn't look up. He knew who he would see and didn't want to. He'd put her out of his mind for so long he didn't know if he could face her.

"I'm so sorry, sir," she apologized to Tom, who as yet hadn't looked up. "Andrew is so clumsy he could run into a lone tree in the middle of an open field." She giggled gently and Tom felt pity slide up his spine.

"Sir?" She asked. "Do I know you?"

Tom took a deep breath, steeled himself, and stood up. Their eyes met.

"Tom?" she whispered. Her hand went to her chest and she swallowed.

"Hello, Abby." His throat was suddenly dry and all the pain and heartache she'd caused him flashed through his mind at once.

"You know this man?" Andrew tried to sound stern, but only managed to sound whiny again.

"I do," Abby sighed.

The words hit Tom like a sword cleaving his heart. The two words she never said to him because of her vanity and materialistic ideals.

Abby stood there, her eyes glittering in the August sunlight, and he saw barely a glimpse of her former self. The years had not been kind to Abby. She was thin, almost bony, her once beautiful facial features now sharp and angled instead of smooth and inviting. Thick powder had been applied to cover the wrinkles that went from the corner of her eyes into her hairline, but were easily seen under close inspection. Her emerald green eyes had clouded with time and her once shimmering, light brown hair was now dull and limp. Her lips were thin and drawn.

"Abby!" Andrew whined behind her.

She whirled on her husband. "What do you want? Can't you see I'm gettin' reacquainted with an old friend?"

"I'm sorry, my dear. I didn't realize he was a friend. I, I..."

She waved her hand impatiently. "Please, just pick up the rest of my packages and wait for me over there. I'll be along shortly."

Andrew eyed Tom a moment before he dutifully picked up the remaining packages then hurried to where Abby had instructed him to wait.

Abby turned back to Tom and pasted on one of her insincere smiles. "I'm sorry for Andrew, Tom. He's rather a nuisance sometimes."

Tom's eyebrows rose. *Is that how she would have spoken of me had we married?* "He seems nice enough."

Abby almost snorted, but caught herself. "He's, well, he's certainly not you, Tom." She laid her hand on Tom's cheek and he felt a rush of emotion he didn't know he could feel about Abby. Revulsion. He stepped back and her hand fell away, her eyes wide with surprise.

"He's your husband, Abby. You should show some respect. I ran into him. He did not run into me." With a snort of his own, Tom realized he was *defending* Abby's husband!

She flashed a tremulous smile. "He's a fool."

Tom shook his head. "How did I ever love you?" he thought, then realizing he'd spoken the words aloud.

Abby's fingers clutched her throat. "How can you say such a thing, Tom? You loved me. You loved me enough to want to marry me!" She leaned forward and tried to touch his cheek again, but Tom stepped back to avoid her a second time.

Her eyes pinched with anger.

There's the real Abby.

Her chin jutted out, as though remembering herself. "What about you, Tom? Is there a Mrs. Hansen?" There was a sparkle of jealousy in her eyes.

"Oh, no. You took care of that. There may never be a Mrs. Hansen, thanks to you."

"Well, I never," she stammered. "How can you say such horrid things to me, Tom Hansen?"

"The truth is sometimes harsh, Abby."

Her eyes blinked in disbelief. "Now Tom, we were good together. If you hadn't been so hard-headed about keepin' slaves, we might have been married all these years."

Tom shivered at the thought. "We might have and I'm thankful you showed your true self before I walked down that aisle like Andrew did."

She drew in a deep breath. "You're bein' downright cruel now, Tom." She paused and cocked her head. "Do you hate me so?"

"I don't hate you Abby. I'm thankful you ended our relationship before we could marry so I didn't end up like Andrew." He threw a glance toward her husband, waiting dutifully for her to come to him.

She lifted her chin again and her lips quivered. She stood a moment, her eyes blinking, her lips moving, before she drew up her back and said, "And I'm thankful I didn't marry a damned Yankee!" Her eyes pinched and her nose flared in anger.

Tom smiled. Her taunt didn't bother him at all. He was proud of the service he'd had in the Union army and no one, least of all Abby Conrad, would change that.

She stared at him a moment longer before she took a deep breath. "Very well, Tom, I won't take up anymore of your time. Good day."

She turned on her heel and walked toward her waiting husband with as much dignity as she could muster.

Tom watched her go. He felt no regret and no sadness at how things had turned out. Instead, he felt rejuvenated and happy. He even felt sorry for Andrew. Glancing after them, he watched Abby berate her husband and the poor man's back slumped a little more as they walked away.

It didn't matter what Andrew did or how well he did it, Tom thought. *It wouldn't be enough. Anything that man did would be wrong. Anything* any *man did would be wrong, as far as Abby was concerned.*

He looked up into the sky. "Thank you, Lord." He swallowed and nodded. "Certainly my life hasn't been easy, but at least I have one, and without an encumbrance like Abby to make me miserable."

He knew now there was not one shred of love left in him for his former fiancé. He wanted to kick up his heels and shout, the weight of his burden falling away like the shedding of another skin. He felt alive, more alive than he had in too many years to remember, and excited for the future.

Perhaps now he would be able to leave the hurt she'd caused him behind and find a woman to love. A good woman who would treat him as a husband should be treated with respect and mutual understanding.

The life beckoning him was like a blank canvas waiting for the painter's next masterpiece. Tom strutted down the sidewalk with a smile on his face, whistling a happy tune, every step lighter than the last.

Someday he might find a woman to love—but not today.

THE END

RESOURCES CONSULTED

The Valiant Hours by Thomas Francis Galwey, Eighth Ohio Volunteer Infantry, The Stackpole Company, Harrisburg, Pennsylvania 1961 – Footnote references 1, 2, 3, 4 are found here.

www.cleveland.com *Remembering Gettysburg: Eighth Ohio Volunteer Infantry…*

www.celebrategettysburg.com/civil-war-journal-5 Civil War Journal – Battle of Gettysburg: Weapons and Tactics

www.wikipedia.org/wiki/Battle_of_Gettysburg: Battle of Gettysburg

www.civilwar.ws/cws_union_soldiers.htm Union Soldiers – Civil War Soldiers

A Brief History of the 8th Regt. OVI by T.M.F. Downes, Copyright 1990 TMF Downes

Bulletin of the Historical and Philosophical Society of Ohio, July 1961, Cincinnati, Vol. 19 No. 3, *CAMP DENNISON, 1861-1865* by Stephen Z. Starr

www.civilwartrust.com

Cleveland Morning Leader (Cleveland, Ohio), 12 April, 1865, *Chronicling America; Historic American Newspapers, Library of Congress*

Major Battles:

First Battle of Bull Run (Referred to as the First Battle of Manassas in the Confederacy): Fought on July 21, 1861 near Manassas, Virginia. This was the first major land battle of the armies in Virginia. On July 16, 1861, the untried Union army under Brig. Gen. Irvin McDowell marched from Washington against the Confederate army, which was drawn up behind Bull Run beyond Centreville. On the 21st, McDowell crossed at Sudley Ford and attacked the Confederate left flank on Matthews Hill. Fighting raged throughout the day as Confederate forces were driven back to Henry Hill. Late in the afternoon, Confederate reinforcements extended and broke the Union right flank. The Federal retreat rapidly deteriorated into a rout. Thomas J. Jackson earned the nom de guerre "Stonewall." By July 22, the shattered Union army reached the safety of Washington.

Romney, (West) Virginia: September 23-25, 1861. (Confederate) Col. Angus McDonald was in command at Romney when it was attacked by Federals on September 23, 1861. McDonald had been advised by General Lee on September 18th that the Federals were withdrawing from Romney. After feigning an attack through Mechanicsburg gap, the Federals launched their main attack from Hanging Rock. On the 24th McDonald gave way before the stronger Federal force, but retook the town the next day as the disorganized enemy (Federals) retreated across the South Branch Bridge toward Keyser. Federal forces consisted of the Fourth and Eighth Ohio and some members of the Ringgold cavalry under Capt. John Keys.

On October 24, 1861 Federals of Ohio and Virginia infantry (with some light artillery) and some Ringgold cavalry attacked through Mechanicsburg Gap; on October 26th the defenders fled. There was a skirmish at Wire bridge as part of this assault.

http://www.historichampshire.org/civilwar/rom-cw.htm

First Battle of Kernstown: Fought March 23, 1862. Relying on faulty intelligence that reported the Union garrison at Winchester numbered only about 3,000, "Stonewall" Jackson marched aggressively north with his 3,400-man division. The 8,500 Federals, commanded by Col. Nathan Kimball, stopped Jackson at Kernstown and then counterattacked turning Jackson's left flank and forcing him to retreat.

Antietam/Sharpsburg: Fought September 17, 1862. The Army of the Potomac, under the command of George McClellan, mounted a series of powerful assaults against Robert E. Lee's forces near Sharpsburg, Maryland, on September 17, 1862. The morning assault and vicious Confederate counterattacks swept back and forth through Miller's Cornfield and the West Woods. Later, towards the center of the battlefield, Union assaults against the Sunken Road pierced the Confederate center after a terrible struggle. Late in the day, the third and final major assault by the Union army pushed over a bullet-strewn stone bridge at Antietam Creek. Just as the Federal forces began to collapse the Confederate right, the timely arrival of A.P. Hill's division from Harpers Ferry helped to drive the Army of the Potomac back once more. The bloodiest single day in American military history ended in a draw, but the Confederate retreat gave Abraham Lincoln the "victory" he desired before issuing the Emancipation Proclamation.

Second Bull Run/Manassas: Fought August 28-30, 1862. In order to draw Pope's army into battle, Jackson ordered an attack on a Federal column that was passing across his front on the Warrenton Turnpike on August 28. The fighting at Brawner Farm lasted several hours and resulted in a stalemate. Pope became convinced that he had trapped Jackson and concentrated the bulk of his army against him. On August 29, Pope launched a series of assaults against Jackson's position along an unfinished railroad grade. The attacks were repulsed with heavy casualties on both sides. At noon, Longstreet arrived on the field from Thoroughfare Gap and took position on Jackson's right flank. On August 30, Pope renewed his attacks, seemingly unaware that

Longstreet was on the field. When massed Confederate artillery devastated a Union assault by Fitz John Porter's command, Longstreet's wing of 28,000 men counterattacked in the largest, simultaneous mass assault of the war. The Union left flank was crushed and the army driven back to Bull Run. Only an effective Union rearguard action prevented a replay of the First Manassas disaster.
http://www.civilwar.org/battlefields/second-manassas.html

Fredericksburg: Fought December 11 – 15, 1862, was one of the largest and deadliest of the Civil War. It featured the first major opposed river crossing in American military history. Union and Confederate troops fought in the streets of Fredericksburg, the Civil War's first urban combat. And with 200,000 combatants, no other Civil War battle featured a larger concentration of soldiers.
http://www.civilwar.org/battlefields/fredericksburg.html?tab=facts

Chancellorsville: Fought April 30, 1863-May 1, 1863. Maj. Gen. Joseph Hooker's well-executed crossing of the Rappahannock fords on April 30, 1863 placed his rejuvenated and reorganized Army of the Potomac on Lee's vulnerable flank. Rather than retreat before this sizable Federal force, Lee opted to attack Hooker while he was still within the thick wilderness. Late on May 1, 1863, Lee and Jackson conceived one of the boldest plans of the war. Jackson, with 30,000 Confederates, would follow a circuitous route to the Union right and from there conduct an attack on that exposed flank. The May 2, 1863 flank attack stunned the Union XI corps and threatened Hooker's position, but the victorious Confederate attack ended with the mortal wounding of Stonewall Jackson. On May 3, 1863, the Confederates resumed their offensive and drove Hooker's larger army back to a new defensive line nearer the fords. Swinging east, Lee then defeated a separate Federal force near Salem Church that had threatened his rear. Lee's victory at Chancellorsville is widely considered to be his greatest of the entire war.
http://www.civilwar.org/battlefields/chancellorsville.html

Gettysburg: Fought July 1-3, 1863 at Gettysburg, Pennsylvania. Turning point of the war toward a Union victory. On the final day, July 3rd, fighting raged at Culp's Hill with the Union regaining its lost ground. After being cut down by a massive artillery bombardment in the afternoon, Lee attacked the Union center on Cemetery Ridge and was repulsed in what is now known as Pickett's Charge. Lee's second invasion of the North had failed, and had resulted in heavy casualties; an estimated 51,000 soldiers were killed, wounded, captured, or listed as missing after Gettysburg.
http://www.civilwar.org/battlefields/gettysburg.html

Afterword

Thomas Francis Galwey, according to the book THE VALIANT HOURS, by Thomas Francis Galwey, was only 15 years old when he enlisted with the Eighth Ohio Volunteer Infantry's Hibernian Guards. He was a mere 5'4" tall. After returning from furlough he was promoted from corporal to second sergeant. Following the Battle at Antietam, he was again promoted, this time to second lieutenant.

Following the Civil War, also known as the *War of the Rebellion*, the *War Between the States*, the *War of Separation/Secession*, the *War for Southern Independence*, and the *War of Northern Aggression*, among others, the men who fought, on both sides, suffered many of the same traumatic issues our veterans deal with today. Although it wasn't called Post Traumatic Stress Disorder until more than a hundred years later, they suffered in many of the same ways our current returning veterans do. They came home with "wounded hearts," many unable to assimilate back into normal society without having mental breaks, what we now call flashbacks. They were broken men, both in mind and body, and many wound up in asylums to live out their lives in the past, reliving the horrors of the war every day. Many tried to begin again, but were unable to do so because of the flashbacks and nightmares that assaulted them daily, and committed suicide. There were those who did readjust and went on to live normal lives, some living well into their eighties and nineties.

War *Is* Hell, no matter when it was fought, and the men (and women) who do make it home return with the same symptoms of reliving it, regardless what it's called.

About the Author

Diane "D.L." Rogers grew up in New Jersey with a natural love of horses and cowboys, spending many delightful hours playing Cowboys and Indians—the Barbie doll (mostly) ignored. Coming from a family mixed with both northern and southern heritage, she found her love of history, and most especially, the Civil War. She and her cousin called themselves "*Yebels,*" being of "mixed" blood, each one having one parent from the North and one from the South.

As a kid Diane loved to read. She read every Nancy Drew and horse book she could get her hands on. That love of reading led her to her writing endeavors of today.

At the present time, Diane lives south of Kansas City, Missouri, with her husband, her horses, and a multitude of cats. She has two wonderful children, Eric and Kristen, and five grandchildren. Diane loves to hear from her readers. Feel free to do so at: www.dlrogers2@peoplepc.com.